The MILL TOWN

A Doherty Mystery

By **Sam Kafrissen**

International Digital Book Publishing Industries

Florida, USA

For Don, Who Remembers

West Warwick
1958

Chapter One

NAPOLEON AND PEACHES

Doherty stepped into the entryway and flipped on the light switch. The dim bulb provided just enough light for him to make his way up to the office on the second floor. He sorted through his keys until he found the right one and let himself in. The outer office smelled musty from the weekend. He passed through into the back room and lifted the window a few inches to let in some air. His space reeked of mildew and old cigarette smoke. He slipped off his jacket and hat and placed them on the antler rack in the corner. Doherty didn't bother turning on the lamp that sat to one side of his desk.

Although the desk was a little beaten around the edges he'd gotten it for a song at the Sally Ann. Doherty was told a banker who shot himself had once owned it. He sat in his swivel chair and tapped out a Camel. He torched it with his Zippo and fingered the insignia on the lighter before he slipped it back into his pocket. It was an embossed symbol of his old outfit. For a few seconds he thought of Monahan and DeNardo, two of his pals who didn't make it home. But today was not a day to think about the war or the guys who bought it at Anzio.

Doherty put his feet up on the desk and breathed in the smoke. The heels of his cordovans scraped that part of the desk where they always came to rest. In time this spot would become his mark and the next guy who bought the desk would want a discount because it was worn down there. He was still pulling on his smoke and staring at the ceiling when he heard the outer office door open. From the soft humming Doherty knew it was his secretary, Agnes Benvenuti. She always hummed absentmindedly under her breath. Doherty didn't mind since Agnes brought a little music into his day.

When he left the cops to go private Doherty had consulted with his former supervisor, Gus Timilty, for advice. Timilty'd been on the force for thirteen years before leaving under a cloud of suspicion. Rumor was that Gus had gotten mixed up with a slimy pimp named Jimmy Ricks who ran some whores out of Providence. Apparently Ricks worked for the wise guys and this caused Gus some grief. Doherty didn't know the details and never bothered to ask his old friend about them. After he left the force Timilty went to work for Johnny Briggs who ran a security agency in South Providence on Broad Street. It wasn't long before the outfit became Briggs and Timilty. Doherty figured Gus had the kind of connections that Briggs couldn't have scratched up in a lifetime. He met with Timilty twice to get some pointers on how to set up shop. Gus' advice to Doherty was to get a secretary to give his operation some 'class', get a Dictaphone and to insist that his clients pay up front.

Doherty was reluctant to hire any help at first, but then a girl named Lucille Montero, who he'd gone to school with, referred him to her younger sister Agnes. At the time Agnes Benvenuti was looking for a part-time job. Doherty met with her and took her on for $25 a week. For that princely sum she came in three days a week to take phone calls and to handle billing and written communications. Timilty's other advice about hiring a secretary was to make sure she wasn't too good-looking otherwise you might end up regularly planking her on your desk. He didn't know if Gus was speaking from personal experience.

Agnes had a smart mouth that her brain didn't match. She looked all right but was definitely not Doherty's type. She wore glasses and usually tied her hair up in a bun or ponytail. She might've had a nice figure underneath the bulky clothes she always wore, though she never raised a peep in Doherty pants. Agnes' husband Louie was a merchant marine who was off on cruises a good part of the year. She didn't bother telling her husband she had a job and Doherty paid her under the table so as not to leave a paper trail. They agreed that she could take time off when Louie was in port. One time Doherty caught Agnes talking on the phone to one of her many girlfriends. He overheard her say that when Louie came home she greeted "the big galoot with open arms and open legs." That wasn't an image Doherty wanted to consider.

Agnes was efficient enough, though she spent too much time either on the phone with her friends or doing her nails. It didn't matter since Doherty and Associates never got much phone action anyway. The *Associates* was another of Timilty's suggestions; he said it would make it sound like Doherty was running a 'real outfit'. As for the Dictaphone, Doherty put the kibosh on that idea when he found out the thing would set him back $29.95. Once he saw the notes that Timilty wrote he knew why his former boss needed a Dictaphone. He couldn't spell worth a damn. One thing Doherty could thank the nuns at St. James for was that they taught him how to spell, even if it was at the end of a metal ruler. Truthfully, that was about the only thing he could thank the penguins for.

It was a relief when his old man got laid off and couldn't make the parochial school payments anymore because Doherty felt more at home getting his education on the public tab. He even tried a year of college on the GI Bill when he first got back from overseas, but learning about accounting and taxes at Bryant didn't feel too real after spending two years killing krauts.

Agnes stuck her head in the door and asked why Doherty was sitting in the dark. He didn't have a good answer so he turned on the desk lamp. It was one of those long neck jobs with a green glass shade that he learned were called a banker's lamps. It too came with the desk of the prior owner who blew his brains out.

"How was your weekend, boss?" Agnes asked.

Doherty shrugged. "Not bad. Went over to see some fights at the Tiogue Vista on Friday night."

"Did you take Dolores?"

"Naw, I went with Benny O'Neill. He had some good seats. Dolores doesn't like the fights."

"Did you see anybody good?"

"Benny wanted to see this Harold Morton from over at Moosup. He told me before the fight that the kid had promise. Got his lights knocked out in the third round by some Negro boy from Jersey. Benny lost a half a C-note. The Morton kid looked like a palooka to me from the get go."

"Any other interesting bouts?" Agnes asked, trying to enunciate her words, not wanting Doherty to think she was just a simple townie girl, which was what she was.

"The two Callahan brothers from Brockton were on the card. They both won their three-rounders. Nothing special, though the older one opened a cut on his opponent's cheek that was so bad every time he hit him it sprayed blood all over the people sitting in the fancy seats. O'Neill got a kick out of that. Said it's why he never bought ringside. I think it's mostly because he's too cheap. I didn't complain though since I was on his pad."

"Did you go to the club afterwards?" Agnes asked. Doherty understood the girl was trying to get her kicks by hearing about his weekend.

"Yeah, we went for a few drinks. Even met a couple of girls from Warwick out looking for a good time. Turns out they were both married and their husbands were down the Cape golfing for the weekend. O'Neill invited them back to his place but they didn't take the bait. I think they just wanted us to keep buying them drinks. I didn't care for either of them. O'Neill was putting a fast move on this one doll so I played along with the other one to humor him. In the end all I got out of it was a slimmer billfold and a hangover."

"Sounds better than my weekend."

Doherty didn't ask Agnes how she'd spent the last three days mostly because he didn't care. He knew if he did she'd launch into some long boring story about her large boring family like she always did.

"What's going on with you and Dolores? " she asked, once it was clear Doherty wasn't going to inquire about her weekend.

"Oh you know, the same old same old. She won't come to my apartment and since she still lives with her folks… well, our dates usually end up with me kissing her goodnight on the doorstep like we're still in high school. She keeps asking me to put a ring on her finger and I keep thinking of a million reason why I don't want to."

"I don't know, boss. You oughta think about settlin' down. She seems like an awfully nice girl." Doherty agreed, knowing that was the problem. At the moment he wasn't looking for a nice girl.

The conversation had run its course so Agnes retreated to the outer office and Doherty resumed his contemplation of the water stains on the ceiling. He could hear Agnes clicking away on the old Remington. He didn't know what she was typing. Maybe a letter of application for a job where her boss would ask her about her weekend.

Doherty was beginning to nod off having decided that the water stain on the ceiling really wasn't a depiction of the Virgin Mary after all. He heard the door to the outer office open and then a woman sniveling as she murmured to Agnes. His secretary soon appeared at his door to tell Doherty that he had a client. He slipped on his jacket and quickly combed his hair with his fingers.

When he stepped into the outer office the overweight woman who lived two floors up in Doherty's apartment building was sitting in a chair across from Agnes's desk. He knew from the loud fights she and her husband had that her name was Peaches. From the tape on their mailbox he also knew that her last name was Perrault. He invited her into his space.

Peaches Perrault was a large woman. Doherty estimated she tipped the scales at about a deuce and a half. She continued whimpering so Doherty handed her his seldom-used handkerchief, deciding he'd discard it afterwards.

"So what can I do for you, Peaches?" he asked, not bothering to hide the fact that he knew who she was.

Between snivels Peaches found some words. "People tell me you know how to find somebody if he's lost."

Doherty nodded waiting for the fat woman to go on. Peaches Perrault wore thick smeared lipstick and had brassy hair that resembled the orange-yellow stick from the old Crayola boxes. She also had three chins. She was wearing a housedress that looked as if it was made by Omar the Tent Maker. Her shoulders and voluminous breasts were covered by a white angora sweater that must have required the slaughter of a half dozen sheep.

"It's my husband, Ferdinand. I ain't seen him since last Wednesday. I called the police but they said he probably just ran away. One cop even said he wouldn'ta blamed 'Napoleon' for skippin' town."

This last comment reminded Doherty that the locals had been to the Perraults' apartment on numerous occasions to break up their domestic spats. Their shouting matches were ear splitting and Peaches had a tendency to throw large objects at her husband when things really heated up. He also remembered that everyone called Ferdinand Perrault "Napoleon" because he stood about five feet four and weighed around one-thirty wringing wet. Doherty tried to imagine the two of them in bed then quickly discarded the thought.

"Did you have one of your fights before he left?"

Peaches looked sheepish if that was possible for a woman of her girth. "You gotta understand, Mr. Doherty. It ain't me, it's my hormones. That's why I'm so stout." Stout was hardly the word Doherty would use to describe someone as obese as Peaches Perrault. He held his tongue given that she was a potential paying customer.

He leaned back in his swivel chair and interlaced his hands behind his head. "Look, Peaches, I can find your husband if that's what you want, assuming he hasn't left the state. But I can't bring him back if he doesn't want to come."

This set Peaches off on another crying jag. Must be the hormones, Doherty thought. He pulled one of his standard forms out of the wooden filing cabinet and slid it in Peaches Perrault's direction.

"If you want to hire me, I'll need you to read and sign this."

She picked it up in her wet hands, looked at it briefly and then handed it back to Doherty. "What's it say? I'm so upset I can't even read."

"It's an employment form. It says you're agreeing to contract me to do this job, that I can't break any laws in doing it and that everything that occurs from this point on is confidential between the client, meaning you, and me."

"What if Ferdinand don't wanna come home?"

"That's between you and him. But you've got to promise me something, Peaches. If I find Ferdinand and tell you where he is, you can't go there and hurt him. If you do then I'll get in trouble. Will you promise me that?"

Peaches nodded her head.

"I charge fifty dollars for the job plus expenses."

"What are expenses, Mr. Doherty?"

"You know, things like gas, food and a flop if I have to stay overnight somewhere."

"I don't have fifty dollars. Not with me anyways. I can get it - unless Ferdinand took our bank book, the sonofabitch."

Doherty stood up behind his desk. "Hey, hey, Peaches, now don't get all angried up. You have to stay calm if you want your husband to come home. How much do you have?"

Peaches pulled a little change purse out of her handbag. From it she extracted a crumbled up twenty and handed it to Doherty. Andrew Jackson had seen better days.

"I'll take this as a deposit, but if and when I find your husband I'm not telling you anything till I get the other thirty plus expenses. You understand?" This time Doherty didn't wait for a nod. Before she left he had Peaches Perrault sign the form and give him a list of "Napoleon's" closest friends. It was a short list.

Ferdinand "Napoleon" Perrault worked at the Warwick Mill, the big one off West Warwick Avenue. The Warwick was the last, fully operating textile mill in town. Word was that it was only a matter of time before it too followed all the others down South where the owners could pay their non-union workers less for more. Where once there'd been mills hammering away all over town, twenty-four hours a day, now there were only two full-time operations left; the Warwick was the largest. It was five blocks long and ran alongside the Pawtuxet River, which had once powered it and where the owners could dump their waste and the other noxious by-products from the cloth dyeing process. Needless to say no one had swum in the Pawtuxet in a long time.

Most of the fathers of the kids Doherty grew up with had gone to work in the mills as soon as they were old enough to leave school. His own pa had been one of them. By the time Doherty came of age a lot of his schoolmates tried to catch on in the mills, but by then the jobs were already disappearing. If they did get a job, they'd never be able to see it through to retirement as their fathers had. The smart ones stayed in school and a few even went on to college, though not many. The others went to the mills or into Providence to work in the costume jewelry factories.

Doherty's was of the first generation of townies who tried to stay in school until they got a diploma. However, many still packed it in as soon as they could get their working papers. Doherty couldn't blame them. Looking back on it now, school hadn't been any better than the army. And it certainly didn't give him the kind of benefits Uncle Sam did. The boys who did stick it out through high school were mostly the ones who played sports. That way they'd have something to tell their grandkids about.

Doherty knew that the Canucks who worked at the Warwick could be found every night of the week drinking away their paychecks at Tetrault's Penalty Box Tavern. Tetrault's was the favorite spot among the men of French-Canadian ancestry because it was the only place where they could watch the hockey games on TV. Although the Rhode Island Reds were the local team, and the Boston Bruins were the nearest pro squad, most of the Canucks in town still rooted for the Montreal Canadians, or the *Habs* as they called them. This gave them some connection to Quebec where their ancestors had come from. As far as Doherty could tell, none of the Canucks he knew had ever been to Quebec. Hell, who was he to talk. None of the Irish folks he knew had ever been to the Emerald Isle either. It was better that way. It allowed them to envision the lands of their ancestry as some magical places that reality would've only tarnished.

Doherty entered Tetrault's with some trepidation. The Canucks didn't take kindly to the micks, who had their own bars. They took even less kindly to guys like Doherty who wore ties and never worked a day of their lives in the mills. Doherty could explain that his old man had put in twenty years at the Royal, but that wouldn't've gotten him the time of day at Tetrault's.

The first thing that hit Doherty when he walked in was the familiar barroom smell of stale beer and piss. It was a common smell in all the taprooms in town regardless of their ethnic clientele. Sometimes it might be topped off with the aroma of peanut shells. Although a baseball game was on the squawk box over the bar all eyes turned in his direction and the level of conversation immediately dropped when Doherty walked down its length.

He scanned the place looking for a familiar face. He didn't see any. He parked on a stool at one end and waited for the bartender to come over. Five minutes passed and the guy never even looked in his direction. He tried to focus on the TV, but the black and white picture was too fuzzy for him to make out any of the players. It was probably a Red Sox game. At this point in the season they were so far out of it hardly anyone paid them much attention. Doherty drummed his fingers on the bar though the tender still ignored him as if he were a leper. Just then a big arm wrapped around his shoulder and Doherty jumped off his stool ready to fight.

"Son of a fuckin' bitch," the voice connected to the arm bellowed. "If it ain't my old friend Hughie Doherty. How the hell are you?" It took Doherty a few seconds to recognize the face attached to the voice. It was Gerald Broyard, a guy Doherty'd gone to St. James with back in the day. Broyard had gained a few pounds and had lost an equal amount of hair since their time with the nuns.

"Gerald," Doherty said, feigning enthusiasm. "You're a sight for sore eyes."

Broyard had been the bully in the schoolyard at St. James. From the smaller kids he would extort lunch money, cap pistols, pea-shooters and even the cigarettes they'd pinched from parents. He was bigger and tougher than all the other kids so his victims were easy pickings. One day Doherty got tired of being jacked up for his milk money so he punched Broyard as hard as he could in the stomach. The bigger boy was stunned more by Doherty's moxie than the punch itself. What ensued was a schoolyard fight of epic proportions that went on for hours, or so it seemed to Doherty at the time. Finally, Sister Mary Margaret broke it up and dragged Broyard and Doherty via the old ear pinch to the mother superior.

They were suspended for three days and given a month's worth of after-school detention clapping erasers and washing chalkboards. For his efforts Doherty suffered a broken nose that never healed correctly, leaving him with a mid-beak twist he would carry for the rest of his life. But he had drawn blood from Broyard's lip and that made it all worthwhile.

And as often happens when two boys engage in such brawls, they became the best of friends afterwards. Although Broyard continued to run his schoolyard extortion racket, he never bothered Doherty again, and even stuck his nose in a few times when some other toughs tried to give him a hard time. They parted company when Doherty left the parochial school midway through junior high to go to public school due to his family's diminished finances. He heard that Broyard made it only as far as the ninth grade before he was expelled for punching a nun in the face. That didn't surprise him. He'd also learned that Broyard did a stretch at Sockanosett, the boys' reform school in Cranston.

"What're you drinkin' you shanty Irishman," Broyard said loud enough to let the other Canucks in Tetrault's know that Doherty was not one of them. It was funny how all the kids, be they Irish, Italian, Portuguese, Jew, Polack or Canuck hung out together when they were young. Then when they got older they married their own kind, went to their own churches and saloons, and were buried in their own cemeteries. So much for the great *melting pot* Doherty had studied about in school.

"Nothing yet; the bartender is acting like I'm invisible."

This made Broyard laugh. "Hey, my friend, in this place you are invisible - 'less you work at the Warwick or play hockey. Jesus, Hughie, do you remember that fight we had back at St. James?"

"How could I forget? Look at my nose. It hasn't been the same since."

Gerald stood up and waved at the bartender. "Hey, Jacques, get your ass over here and give me and mon ami a coupla drinks."

When the disgruntled bartender finally made his way to their end Doherty said, "I'll have a Jameson neat."

Broyard leaned across the bar. His forearms were about as thick as Doherty's thighs. He wouldn't want to have that recess fight with Gerald now.

"Make that two, Jacques, and give us some 'Gansett backs."

Doherty turned toward Broyard. It had been almost twenty years since they'd seen each other. "So what're you up to these days, Gerry? Last I heard you were up in Socko."

"Socko? Fuck Hughie, that was a long time ago, no." Broyard raised his Jameson and he and Doherty clinked glasses. Doherty took a swig while Broyard swallowed his in one gulp. He followed it with a long draw on his beer. While he did Doherty pulled out his Camels and offered one to the big Canuck.

"I been at the Warwick goin' on fifteen years now," Broyard said without much enthusiasm.

"What's happening over there anyway? I keep hearing rumors they're thinking of shutting the whole place down."

"You think they'd fuckin' tell us anythin'. When they closed the first two shifts, they gave the guys two weeks notice. Two fuckin' weeks! Some of them fellas'd been at the mill thirty, forty years. Then just like that they was out on the street." Broyard slugged down the rest of his beer and signaled Jacques for another round.

"Me, I got a job lined up at Packy's Garage up on Quaker Lane soon as the ball drops. I ain't waitin' to get pink slipped like them others suckers. I'm just hopin' to hang on long enough to get my Christmas bonus. After that I'm gone. Ain't no future in the mills no more. What about you, my mick friend? I heard you was on the force?"

"Not anymore. I left the cops a couple of years ago. Too many bag jobs for my taste. I got my own private security business now. I operate out of a little office on Brookside, just off Washington over Harry's Barbershop."

"Private security eh. What the hell does that mean?" Broyard water cooleted his second shot of Jameson and reached for his beer.

"To be honest with you, I guess you could say I'm a private dick."

"You mean like on the radio. A regular Richard Diamond, eh," Broyard laughed loudly.

"I wish it was so glamorous," Doherty said. "Mostly I find missing people – though most people who're missing want to stay missing. I also collect info on guys cheating on their wives so the missus can get a divorce if she wants. And I get the occasional industrial job."

"Whaddya mean *industrial job*?" Broyard asked.

Doherty hesitated. "I spy for companies who think maybe one of their workers is stealing from them or sabotaging a job on account of he's pissed off at his boss."

"So you're like a goon for the company." They looked at each other without smiling for a few seconds then Broyard let out a big laugh. "I was just funnin' with you, Mickey. Have another drink. This one's on you." Broyard waved again for Jacques who was more amenable now that the two men were his best customers.

"Listen, Gerry, do you happen to know a guy named Ferdinand Perrault?"

Broyard smiled, "You mean Napoleon. The little pipsqueak that's married to two-ton Tessie. Course I know him. Everybody knows him. Why you askin'? He in some kinda trouble? Maybe you think he's stealin' bolts of cloth outta the Warwick."

"No, nothing like that. He's disappeared, and his wife hired me to find him."

"Maybe he disappeared in the folds of her fat, " Gerald said, laughing at his own joke.

Doherty said, "They live upstairs in my building and they fight all the time. She says he's missing, though personally I think he just had enough and flew the coop."

"Wouldn't blame him. Wait a minute, I'll be right back."

Doherty looked to the bartender for another round, but with Broyard gone he returned to being invisible. He could hear Broyard at a table behind him talking to a couple of older guys in a form of French that didn't resemble anything Doherty'd learned in high school or heard in Paris during the war. Broyard returned a few minutes later with a small man in tow. He had one of his big arms over the man's shoulder, escorting him against his will.

"This is my friend Guy. Guy this is Hugh Doherty, an old pal of mine from St. James."

"It's Gee, not Guy," the man under Gerald's arm said using the French pronunciation. He was small, wore a flannel shirt with a vest over it and a wool cap. Although he was probably no older than fifty, his nose was already a whiskey road map.

Broyard shook his head. "Fuckin' Frenchies. They been in Rhode Island their whole life but still think they're Quebecers. Just talk to my friend here, OK, Gee."

"You know a man named Ferdinand Perrault, the one they call Napoleon?"

"Ya, ya, I know 'im. Got that fat wife he always fightin' wid. What you want from Napoleon?"

"You work with him at the mill?"

"Ya, same department, same shift. But he ain't been in for tree, maybe four days. He sick or somethin'?"

"No, he's missing and his wife wants me to find him."

The little Canuck leaned in close to Doherty. "Can I be honest wid you, Mr..."

"Doherty."

"I heard around town that Napoleon's been keepin' company wid his wife's sister. She's no fatty like the wife. I hear she ain't bad lookin'."

"Do you know where I can find this sister?"

"She lives up in Woonsocket, but I think maybe you should look down at Oakland Beach for dem."

"Oakland Beach, huh. Thanks, Gee. Can I buy you a drink for your troubles?" The little man accepted Doherty's offer without hesitation.

Doherty was having a hard time clearing his head as he walked home from Tetrault's. He could feel the Jamesons and the 'Gansett chasers sloshing around in his stomach. He hadn't had anything to eat since lunch so there was nothing for the alcohol to grab onto. Putting one foot in front of the other was proving to be more difficult than it should've been. Fortunately it was a cool night so the air helped him stay on his feet and move forward. All he wanted to do was hit the sack, except that he had to make one more stop before he did.

His best hope for finding Napoleon Perrault was to get down to Oakland Beach in the morning and catch the lovebirds before they left for the day. But Doherty would need a photo of Napoleon to flash around and there was only one person he could get that from.

When he got to their apartment building he stopped at his place to slug down an Alka Seltzer. He opened a can of beef stew and put it on the gas at a low heat. Then he reluctantly mounted the stairs to the apartment of the lovely Peaches Perrault. He knocked lightly but no one answered. He knew she was home because he could hear a TV blaring on the other side of the door. He knocked again, louder this time.

"Who is it?" a voice shouted on the other side.

"Doherty."

Peaches Perrault opened the door but kept the lock chain in place and peeked out. "Oh, Mr. Doherty," she said upon seeing him leaning against her door jam. Through the slit Doherty could see that she was wearing just a slip, which left way too much of her exposed.

"Just a minute, Mr. Doherty. Let me put on somethin' decent." He hoped it would cover more than what he'd just seen on display. Peaches came back a minute later and lifted the chain. She was now wearing an enormous pink terry cloth bathrobe that covered enough of her to make conversation possible.

"If it's about the money, I can give you some more. I got some cash in a jar in the kitchen," she said anxiously.

Doherty stepped into the apartment. It smelled of baked beans and cabbage. Peaches shuffled off to the kitchen where Doherty could see her trying to pry some cash out of an old jam jar. However, her hand was too fat to fit through the opening. A TV was playing loudly in the room he was standing in, which served as both a living room and a dining space. The layout of the apartment was much like his own. Whereas he had only a few sticks of furniture, the Perrault place was crowded with mismatched pieces, many of them covered with doilies and cheap knick-knacks.

Peaches returned to the living room and cleared a fake leather chair for Doherty to sit in. He had to admit it was a relief getting off his feet. Still, he didn't want to stay in the Perrault's apartment any longer than necessary.

Peaches retreated to the kitchen ostensibly to have another go at the cash jar. "I was just about to have some coffee. Wouldja like some?" she yelled to Doherty.

His first inclination was to refuse, but he could use a cup of joe to help him sober up and he felt too drunk to put up a pot downstairs. "Yeah, that'd be nice."

"I only got instant. Do you mind Nescafe?"

Doherty hated instant coffee though he accepted it anyway. He told her he'd have it black. She returned with a small tray with two cups, a creamer and sugar bowl and some bills and coins on it. She handed Doherty the money.

"I only got six dollars and some change. I can give you the rest, maybe tomorrow."

Doherty casually pocketed the six ones and the coins without counting them. When Peaches leaned over to hand Doherty his coffee her robe came open enough to reveal that she wasn't wearing a bra. Her gigantic melons hung almost to her waist. She sat down across from him on a red upholstered couch that looked like it might collapse under her weight. He could see that she was still wearing stockings that were rolled into garters below her knees. They looked like sausage casings.

Doherty tried to avert his eyes by looking at the TV. The Danny Thomas Show was on and Danny was in the middle of one of his pratfalls.

"I love that Danny Thomas, don't you?" Peaches said. "He just cracks me up - always making jokes about his big nose. Is he one of them Jews?"

"I don't think so. I think he's Lebanese."

"Letanese? What's that?"

"Lebanese. From Lebanon. It's a country in the Middle East."

Peaches rocked her head back and forth, her many chins waggling as she did. "Never heard of it. Don't you just love his show, Mr. Doherty?"

Doherty shrugged. "I've only seen it a couple of times. I don't watch much TV because I don't own one." Peaches looked at him cross-eyed as if not owning a TV made Doherty some kind of weirdo. He drank some of the mud that was masquerading as coffee.

"Have you found my Ferdinand yet?" she asked. It was disconcerting to Doherty that his client hadn't turned the TV off or even lowered the volume. Conversation was proving to be difficult because of it.

"I got a lead. I'm going to follow up on it tomorrow. But I need a photo of Napo… Ferdinand I can take with me. Do you have a recent one?"

"I think so. Let me go look. " Peaches waddled off to what Doherty assumed was the bedroom. She came back with a little brass frame and proceeded to extract the picture from inside it. She handed the small photo to Doherty. In it the happy couple was posed standing arm and arm in front of a carousel. In the picture the diminutive Napoleon was all but crowded out by his fat wife.

"That's me and Ferdinand at Oakland Beach. My sister took it last summer. Me and her and the husbands went down there to have some of those delicious doughboys."

Doherty wondered how many doughboys Peaches ate. Then he remembered that her weight was caused by her *hormones*. He assumed it was the same sister the wayward husband had run off with. When he looked up from the photo he noticed that Peaches had spread her legs just far enough from being decent. Doherty quickly stuffed the photo in his jacket pocket.

"Thanks for the picture. I've got to be going."

"So soon, Mr. Doherty," Peaches cooed as she spread her legs a little wider and more mounds of flesh revealed themselves. It wasn't a pretty sight.

Doherty stood up, his own legs still a little unsteady from the booze. " 'Fraid so. I want to get an early start in the morning."

"But you haven't finished your coffee," Peaches said as the gap in her robe grew wider.

"Sorry, Peaches. I don't feel so good. I think I'll just head downstairs and hit the hay." With a bit of a struggle Peaches Perrault got to her feet to show Doherty to the door.

"If Ferdinand don't wanna come home, *you* can come up here anytime," Peaches said, no longer even trying to mask her intentions.

"Thanks again for the picture. I'll get back to you as soon as I can," Doherty said as he slipped out the door, relieved to be on the other side. He was already thinking about looking for a new apartment.

The next morning came a little too early for Doherty. He liked to sleep in given that he usually didn't open the office until around ten. After taking care of business in the bathroom he shoveled down two spoonfuls of last night's beef stew and threw the rest of the slop in the garbage. Doherty kept his old Packard in a garage next to Belanger's Market at the end of Crossen Street. Denny Belanger charged him two bucks a month to shelter the old clunker and expected Doherty to buy his groceries at his market. He mostly complied except for once a week when he went up to Lefty's on Main Street so he could play the daily punchboard number at the counter.

He didn't keep his car on the street because he drove it so seldom he was afraid it might get hauled off to a junkyard, or that the neighborhood kids would smash its windows just for fun. Doherty made sure he left the garage doors wide open before he started up the old sedan, not wanting to asphyxiate himself before he got out of the garage. The beast's engine coughed a few times before it finally caught. Plumes of smoke flowed from the exhaust. Doherty pulled the car out, closed the garage doors, and then let the Packard idle for a few minutes, giving it a chance to belch out its bile.

It was a nice fall day so Doherty rolled down the window, sparked up his last Camel and set out for Oakland Beach. He drove down Main, crossed over the little bridge that spanned the Arctic Mill Dam and took a left up the hill. Two vehicles ahead of him was a Rially school bus emitting enough fumes to dwarf anything the old Packard spit out. Doherty had ridden on a Rially bus one summer when he was forced to do a two-week stretch at a YMCA camp out in Buttonwoods. The old man was still working at the Royal back then so he could afford to send his kids to day camp for a couple of weeks. Doherty hated the camp, though later was glad he went. It was there that he learned two important skills: how to swim and how to box. Both came in handy in the army.

Two young patrol boys stuck red flags out at the New London Avenue intersection and all the traffic stopped. Doherty watched as the school kids poured out of the bus and into Christ the King School on the other side of the road. The boys were dressed in their little ties and sport coats while the girls wore the traditional parochial school uniforms of plaid skirts, button up sweaters and knee socks. Doherty felt sorry for them; they were way too young to be put at the mercy of the crusty old nuns. He swore that if he ever had kids they'd never set foot in a Catholic school. After the bus disgorged the school kids it turned left onto New London while he proceeded straight ahead onto Toll Gate Road in the direction of Warwick.

He slowed as he passed the Kent County Hospital on his left. It was here that his old man took his last gasp, his liver ravaged by alcohol and the cancer. He remembered that last night well: Doherty, his sister Margaret and his mother sitting in the waiting room expecting the doctor to come out any moment with the final verdict. Margaret sat in a corner chair bawling the whole time while his mother looked stoically down at her knitting. Doherty knew she was worrying about how she would make ends meet once her husband was gone. All he could think about was how relieved he'd be to have his old man out of their lives. He'd shed no tears for the rat bastard.

A doctor finally came out and asked if they would like to see Peter one last time before. There were no words after the *before*. Doherty and his mother stood, but when he moved toward the door his mother put her hand on his chest and told him to stay where he was.

"I don't want you to remember him this way," was all she said. Margaret didn't move; she stayed in the corner and continued to cry softly. His mother came back a half hour later and said, "He's gone." That was all she had to say about her husband until the wake.

Between the money Doherty was bringing home from Quonset and the job his mother got working the counter at Pasquale's Bakery, they made ends meet and were able to keep the house. Margaret married a guy she'd been dating since high school. He was working for 3-M at the time and when he got transferred to Minnesota she left West Warwick and never looked back. Although he was working for the government at Quonset when the war started, Doherty still got drafted a year later as by then Uncle Sam needed all the cannon fodder he could get. He sent money home to his mother, as did Margaret, so she could continue to live in the house where they were born.

She passed three years after Doherty was discharged. The last time he saw his sister was at their mother's funeral. When he sold the house he sent half the money to Margaret even though she didn't need it as much as he did. The only time he hears from her now is when she sends him a card and a box of candy at Christmastime. He puts the candy out in the waiting room where it quickly disappears. He suspects Agnes eats most of it but he doesn't care enough to ask.

Doherty parked across from a Rexall drug store in Apponaug Center and went in to buy some butts. Apponaug is what passes for a downtown in Warwick, which otherwise is mostly a bedroom community. The stores on the two blocks of cross streets make Apponaug a smaller version of Arctic. The Rexall sat diagonally across the street from Warwick's large town hall. Doherty bought a pack of smokes and a copy of the *Providence Journal*, just in case he had to spend more of the day out at Oakland Beach than he planned.

After passing under the railroad bridge he took the fork onto West Shore Road, which would take him out to Oakland Beach Road and hopefully to Napoleon Perrault. Doherty'd only been to Oakland Beach a few times, mostly because his old man was either too drunk or hung over on Sundays to take his family to the beach; his mother couldn't because she never learned to drive. Besides, they all had that pale Irish skin that only burned and then burned again in the hot sun.

Oakland Beach had been a popular spot in the 1930s for the hard working people of Providence and the neighboring towns who didn't have the dough or the time to get down to South County where the ocean beaches were. Back then Oakland Beach had its attractions: a midway with an arcade and a merry-go-round. Food joints dotted the waterside, with Gus's being the most famous. The hurricane of '38 destroyed most of the attractions. Some were rebuilt and the area made a bit of a comeback until Hurricane Carol in '53 put the final nail in its coffin. By then people looking for a day trip to the seaside could drive down to Narragansett or Point Judith where the beaches abutted the real ocean.

Oakland Beach was on a peninsula that jutted out into Greenwich Bay, an inlet of Narragansett Bay. In late September most of the summer cottages were already boarded up for the winter. There were a few guest bungalows still open and that's where Doherty figured he'd find Napoleon and Peaches' sister holed up. Doherty moored the Packard in front of Gus's and went in for some coffee and a bite. The place was nearly empty. A skinny waitress with a nameplate on her uniform that said *Dottie* came to take his order. She was about forty. Her dyed black hair and heavy make-up were evidence that she was struggling to look younger. It was a battle she was destined to lose.

"What'll it be, hon?" she asked as she snapped her gum. Doherty wondered if Gus approved of gum snapping waitresses.

"I'll have a coffee, black, and a doughboy."

She returned a few minutes later with his coffee and a steaming fried doughboy covered in powdered sugar. Doherty knew enough not to bite into the doughboy right away for fear of scalding the roof of his mouth.

"You got a minute, Dottie?" he asked, taking the liberty to use her first name.

The waitress looked around the place. "Sure, got more than one. As you can see, we're not exactly busy."

"Slow day?"

"Slow time of year. This place is hoppin' all summer, but once Labor Day comes it turns into a morgue. Can't complain, though. Gus'll keep us on as long as we got customers."

Doherty removed the picture of Peaches and Napoleon from his side pocket. He'd decided to forego the suit today and opted instead for a pair of Khakis and his old Quonset baseball jacket.

"Have you seen this guy around?" He handed the picture Peaches had given him to the waitress. She looked at it carefully, even closing one eye as if that would improve her vision.

"I dunno. That's a pretty large woman your guy's with."

"He's kind of small, makes her look bigger. Do you recognize her? Maybe she's easier to remember."

"Wait a minute. Lemme get Flo, She usually works the night shifts." While Dottie was gone Doherty lit a Camel and flipped the *Journal* open to the sports page. It looked like the Braves were going to be in the World Series again this year. "Damn," Doherty thought. All those years they were in Boston and they stunk up the joint. They move to Milwaukee and all of a sudden they're the best team in baseball. They were even champs last year beating the Yankees in the series.

Dottie returned with Flo, who was a dowdy brunet with a pleasant smile. She was younger than Dottie and wore no makeup at all. Doherty showed her the picture of the loving couple in front of the carousel and asked her the same thing he'd asked the other waitress.

"I seen her in here a coupla times. She's a big eater that one."

"Recently?"

"Naw, not since the summer. I remember waitin' on them; there were two couples. I won't forget her, she ate three doughboys. Not often you see a woman do that."

"What about the little guy with her?"

"You know that's the funny thing. All along I thought he was with the other woman. She was more his size." Doherty nodded in agreement. "They were in here for dinner the other night. I think it was Friday."

"Who was?"

She pointed at the photo. "This little guy in the picture and the other woman - the one I thought was his wife."

"Are you sure?"

"Not entirely, but I'm pretty sure it was them two."

Doherty took this all in and then asked, "If someone was staying out here at this time of year where would they stay?"

Flo thought for a moment. "If they had some bucks they'd probably stay at the Warwick Inn. It's one of the onliest places open right now."

"And if they didn't have a lot of money?"

Flo and Dottie looked at each other and said almost simultaneously, "Dunphey's."

"It's down the street on the corner of Owens and Burr," Dottie said. She gave Doherty directions how to get there.

"Would you like a refill, hon?"

"No, just the check. And thanks girls for all your help."

"Are you a cop or somethin'?" Flo asked.

"No, just a friend." Doherty made sure to leave Dottie a big tip. In fact, it was twice the cost of the doughboy and coffee. Something else he could put on Peaches' tab and probably never collect.

Doherty left the Packard parked in front of Gus's and walked back from the water and down Burr to Dunphey's. When he got there it was clear why the girls thought someone short on scratch would choose this place over the Warwick Inn. Peaches wouldn't have to worry about Napoleon emptying out their bank account to pay in this dump.

The spring on the screen door had sprung so it was flapping in the breeze that came off the bay. The front door to Dunphey's was unlocked so Doherty let himself in. There were a few pieces of threadbare furniture in the hall that led the way to the front desk. The place smelled of mothballs. There was no-body in sight so Doherty hit the little bell that was resting on the counter. He immediately heard rustling in a room in the back. A young guy appeared tucking his shirt into his pants as he did. He had long, greasy hair and pale white skin. He wasn't wearing an undershirt and the front of his shirt was unbuttoned two more buttons than it should've been, showing off his boney white chest.

"Can I help you?"

"Maybe." Doherty placed the photo Peaches had given him on the counter. "Have you seen this guy around?"

The desk clerk looked at the photo long enough to tell Doherty that he had.

"I bet she's a ton of fun, if you know what I mean," the guy said. Doherty was in no mood for clowns.

"How about the man in the picture?" he asked as he placed his hand over one side of the photo blotting out Peaches.

"I dunno; depends on who's askin' and why," the guy said as he raised his head and looked Doherty in the eye. It didn't take a genius to figure out what his play was.

"How about a picture of President Lincoln? Do you think that might jog your memory?" Doherty folded a five lengthwise, tented it and placed it on the counter. The pale guy went to cuff it but Doherty squeezed one end.

"Not so fast. How's about first you tell me something I don't already know."

"Room twelve - upstairs in the back. They didn't come down for breakfast. If they're not up there, try the beach." Doherty let the fiver disappear into the clerk's pocket. He would try to expense this to Peaches as well, though he knew he'd be lucky to see the double sawbuck she already owed him.

He knocked on the door at room twelve and waited. There was no response. He put his ear to the door but didn't hear any rustling inside. Experience had taught him that an unexpected knock often led to nervous noise behind a closed door even when the people were trying to pretend they weren't there. He turned the handle. The door was locked. He descended the stairs and head-ed toward the front door.

"Guess they're out at the beach," the desk clerk said with a smug look on his face.

Doherty turned at the door. "They better be if you want to keep that fin. And another thing, you might want to button up your shirt. A chest like that might drive business away."

Doherty walked back to the beach lot and drifted along the seawall. There weren't too many people out on the sand even though it was a fairly mild day. An old guy was walking his dog and a woman was sitting on a beach blanket about fifty yards down. She was wearing a sundress rather than a swimsuit. Doherty hopped over the wall and began to saunter down the beach. He knew he didn't look too casual with his cordovans on. Still, he didn't want to take his shoes and socks off. As he got closer to the woman she looked his way. Her hair was tied up in a print kerchief that was knotted under her chin. Next to her on the blanket was a pair of men's shoes with black socks tucked into them. They were quite small.

"Nice day," Doherty said in a friendly voice.

When the woman looked up at him she had to shade her eyes with her hand as Doherty was standing directly in the sunlight. She didn't say anything; Doherty was able to clock her face enough to believe she could be Peaches Perrault's sister. This one was prettier and from what Doherty could tell at least a hundred pounds lighter.

He turned and looked at the stone jetty that stuck out into the bay. Someone who looked familiar was fishing off the end of the rocks. Doherty headed in that direction. The woman on the blanket didn't move. As Doherty scuttled along the rocks he was not happy to see that his cordovans had picked up some saltwater along the way. Napoleon was casting his line off the end of the jetty. It didn't look like he'd caught anything, or ever would. Doherty didn't think anyone would eat a fish caught in water this close to the mills.

Napoleon looked over his shoulder at him and continued fishing. He was wearing his trousers rolled up enough to reveal pale ankles covered with black hair. He had a tan windbreaker on over a white tee shirt. The breeze off the water was ruffling his dark hair.

When he finally sidled up to Perrault Doherty immediately noticed the disparity in their sizes. He then asked the obvious question. "Catch anything?" The man didn't answer for a while so they just stood side-by-side staring out at the water. Napoleon reeled in his line and cast it out again in a set rhythm.

"She sent you, didn't she?" the little man said.

"She?"

"Yeah, my wife. Peaches. We're the ones who live upstairs from you."

For a moment Doherty was taken aback by Napoleon's premonition. "How do you know that's why I'm here?"

"'Cause I heard talk around town. I know you're the guy who finds lost people for a livin'. And now you found me." He reeled in his line and cast it out once again.

"Do you want to go home? I won't make you if you don't."

Napoleon didn't speak for a minute. Instead he looked longingly back at the woman on the beach. After a while he appeared to wipe something from his eye. Doherty didn't say anything. He just stood there quietly waiting for the wayward husband to respond.

"I guess," he said resignedly. "I don't have a car so you'll have to drive me."

"I can do that." Doherty looked back at the woman sitting on the beach. She was watching them closely. "What about her?"

"She's got her own car. She'll find her way home."

"Does *she* want to go home?"

"Yeah, I think so. We talked this morning. You know, we had to get away just once, that's all. But it ain't gonna work." Doherty didn't know what Napoleon meant by that and it wasn't his business to ask.

Doherty stayed out on the jetty while Napoleon Perrault walked back to the woman sitting on the beach blanket. She stood as he approached and they engaged in a fairly animated conversation. She was an inch or two taller than Perrault, though so were most adults in this world. Doherty walked slowly down the beach near the water's edge, turned toward the lot and mounted the sea wall. He retrieved his car and drove down to Dunphey's where he sat waiting for Napoleon. Ten minutes later the little man came out with his overnight bag and reluctantly got into the car.

They began their trek back to West Warwick and Peaches. Perrault was quiet and morose for most of the trip. Doherty smoked and cast sidelong glances at his passenger hoping he was doing the right thing. At least he could take some comfort in knowing that he'd done what he'd been hired to do and Peaches' husband was returning of his own free will. Doherty took a longer route back to Arctic giving Napoleon a chance to prepare himself for the homecoming. He also didn't want to drive past the Kent County Hospital again.

About twenty minutes into the trip Perrault turned to Doherty and asked, "How did you know where to find me?"

"That's a trade secret," Doherty answered. "But this helped," he added handing Perrault the photograph of him and Peaches in front of the Oakland Beach carousel. "Your wife gave me that for identification purposes. I promised I'd return it so I'll just leave it with you if you don't mind."

"How much did she pay you to find me?" Doherty figured Perrault was trying to calculate what he was worth to his wife.

"I can't tell you that either. She's the client, not you." They were both quiet for a few minutes.

"Listen, Ferdinand," Doherty began.

"You can call me Napoleon; everybody else does so you might as well. Peaches is the only one who still calls me Ferdinand." After some hesitation he added, "It all started with that movie."

"Which one, the one with Marlon Brando?"

Perrault laughed, "Do you think anybody's gonna mistake me for Marlon Brando? No, the other one. The one with Henry Fonda."

"Henry Fonda never played Napoleon."

"I know. Some other guy did. Some short guy. I seen the movie at the Palace and I guess a lot of the boys from the mill did too. It was the one about Napoleon invadin' Russia. I don't think anybody around here knew what Napoleon looked like before that movie came out."

"*War and Peace?*"

"Is that the one that had that Hepburn girl with the skinny neck in it? Not the Hepburn that was in all them movies with Spencer Tracy. The other one, the young one."

"Yeah, that's the movie," Doherty said. "You know, uh, Napoleon, that French Napoleon was quite a guy. I mean he did conquer most of Europe at one time."

Perrault harrumphed, "Yeah, and look at me. I can't even rule my own family. Tell me, Mr. Doherty, was Napoleon really that short – short as me?"

"I don't know. I wasn't there. It was before my time. But I read somewhere that he was pretty short. But I will tell you something: those Japs in the war, they were short too, and they put up one hell of a fight."

Perrault stared ahead as Doherty turned onto Providence Street and headed through Natick up toward Arctic.

"Sometimes I think I only married Peaches to be near Gloria."

"Gloria?"

"The girl down at Oakland Beach. She's Peaches' sister. I had a mean crush on her when I was in high school. But she was datin' this big football guy and well, look at me, what chance did I have with a girl like that?"

"Did she marry him?"

"No, she married some guy she met at the USO during the war. I was down in Mississippi in the army at the time. When I tried to enlist the first time they wouldn't take me cause I was too small. I woulda done anythin' to get into the action. The next time I went in I put lifts in my shoes and gained some weight. By then they wasn't so fussy about who they took. When I came home Gloria was already married to that other guy."

"And you married Peaches?"

"Not at first. Then well, one thing led to another. Peaches wasn't so... she wasn't so heavy when I first met her, but she wasn't a looker like Gloria neither. Turns out Gloria's husband is a piece of shit. He smacks her around a lot. Gets pissed off if some other guy gives her the eye – like it's her fault she's good lookin'."

"Is that why she ran off with you?"

"I guess. She says she appreciates me. Tells me I'm a real gentleman. She's always been nice to me, not like Peaches."

"You sure you don't want to change your mind. I could always tell Peaches you gave me the slip."

"It don't matter now. Gloria's husband'll tell Peaches what we done. Then the shit'll really hit the fan. I'll be lucky if I ever see Gloria again."

"Can I give you some advice, Ferdinand. Next time you decide to go AWOL, don't run off to Oakland Beach. And if you do, don't shack up at Dunphey's. That punk at the desk gave you up for a five spot."

Doherty forked left at the intersection with Washington Street and continued down Main. He'd be delivering his package home in a matter of minutes.

"One other thing. Tell your wife to hire somebody else next time you decide to take a powder."

They pulled around the corner off Main and Doherty parked the car in front of their building. He offered Perrault one last chance to back out. Instead Napoleon slunk out of the car and walked toward the front door. Doherty followed closely behind.

"I can find my way," the condemned man said.

"Sorry, it's part of the deal. I have to deliver you to the door. I want to make sure there's no trouble."

They climbed the stairs in lock step. When they reached the third floor Napoleon Perrault knocked softly at the door of his apartment. Peaches opened it and the two of them just stood eyeing each other for a few seconds. Doherty stepped back into the hall shadows.

"I'm home, Peaches."

"Oh, Ferdinand," she said with tears in her eyes. She then enfolded the little man in her mounds of flesh. They embraced, both sobbing profusely. Doherty quietly slipped down the stairs. He figured they'd be fighting again by the weekend, if not sooner.

Chapter Two

JUDGE MARTIN DeCENZA

When Doherty entered the office, Agnes, as usual, was on the phone with one of her girlfriends. He waved and went into the back room, hung up his baseball jacket and assumed his standard position behind his desk. He inserted his feet in just the right spot and lit up a Camel. The cigarette was dangling from his lip when Agnes appeared at his door.

She leaned on the doorjamb and said, "Lookin' pretty casual today, boss."

"Well, I didn't think it'd be a good idea to go to the beach in a suit. I might've been a little conspicuous."

"So, how did it go? You know, with Peaches and Napoleon?"

"He went home – reluctantly, but without resistance."

"You didn't have to drag him by the neck?"

"Nope. You know that's not my style. And when we got there they both cried like babies."

"I guess Mickey and Sylvia were right: love really is strange," Agnes concluded.

Doherty liked it that Agnes Benvenuti knew about popular music. That plus her typing skills made her a good secretary. She also ate sister Margaret's Christmas candy before it went bad.

"I'll write down my expenses and what else Peaches owes me. Could you type up an invoice on our stationary?"

"Do you want me to mail it?"

"No, save the four cents; I'll slip it into their mail slot when I get home. I'm not counting on seeing the rest of the money she owes us anyway. I guess it'll depend on how happy she is having him back."

Doherty itemized the expenses and dropped the slip on Agnes' desk.

"I'm going down to Harry's for a while. Maybe get a shave while I'm there."

Harry's Barbershop faced Washington Street downstairs and around the corner from Doherty and Associates. It was Doherty's second home. Actually, it was more like his first given the lack of amenities in his apartment. Harry's was a big operation; it had five chairs rather than the usual two or three found in most of the other shops in town. It was by far the most popular hair joint in Arctic. Harry was a little bald guy with black trim around the edges and chestnut colored skin. Doherty didn't like having Harry work on his head or face because all the little guy ever talked about was 'broads' and how much money he won at the track. Since Harry was already married and ran a barbershop in Arctic, Doherty figured most of his talk was a lot of bullcrap.

When he wanted a cut or a shave Doherty waited for either Bill or Vinny. Bill Fiore was the closest thing Doherty had to a friend, though he'd never seen Bill outside of the shop or without his smock on. But he liked spending time with Bill because the barber knew everything about everybody in town. He talked about girls a lot too, though whereas Harry was mostly full of it, Fiore's talk was for real. Bill had long wavy black hair that was swept back and held in place with just the right amount of hair oil to give it a sheen. He also wore a pencil-line mustache that made him look like the movie character Boston Blackie. A black and white ink caricature of Bill's head in profile hung on the column by his chair. Entwined in Bill's wavy hair were a number of naked women in provocative poses. Whoever drew the sketch knew Bill Fiore pretty well.

The barber gave Doherty the high sign when he came in and told him he'd be about ten minutes. He was working an electric razor over the head of a squirmy young kid. Vinny, who had a hangdog look like Andy Devine, was doing a shave in the adjacent chair so Doherty was in for a wait either way. He took a seat in one of the chairs across from the large mirror that ran the length of the opposite wall. An attractive blond woman was in the chair next to him. She was reading *Argosy*, a popular men's magazine. Doherty stole a glance her way and saw that she was perusing an article about a guy who killed a Kodiak bear with a Bowie knife.

"Do you mind if I smoke?" he asked before he struck up a Camel.

"No, as long as you don't blow smoke in my face," she said in a way that may have meant more, or less.

"Would you like one?" he asked holding out the pack.

"No, thank you. I don't smoke." Doherty watched Bill work on the head of the kid in his chair. He was giving him one of those flattop haircuts that were all the rage these days among young boys.

"Do you come here often?"

That got a smile from the blond who looked up from the Kodiak bear story.

"No. Only when one of my boys needs a haircut - or I need a shave." Doherty smiled and she smiled back.

"My name is Hugh Doherty," he said holding out his hand for a shake. Most men didn't shake hands with women, but Doherty had gotten into the habit because of his work.

The woman took his hand. Her shake was soft and light. "Mildred St. Jean. My friends call me Millie. Please to meet you, Mr. Doherty."

Doherty didn't know what to say next so he went back to smoking and watching Bill, who was now applying butcher's wax to the kid's head to make the hair stand up. Doherty knew this was the last part of the cut.

"By the way, that story you're reading about the guy killing a Kodiak bear with a Bowie knife, it's totally false. It'd be impossible to kill a bear that size with just a knife."

"And how would you know that, Mr. Doherty?"

"I read the story last week; there's no way somebody could kill a bear like that with a Bowie knife. Maybe a small bear, like a cub, but not a full-grown Kodiak. You'd have to plug one of those three or four times with a hunting rifle to bring it down."

"You know that for sure, or are you just saying so because you never killed a Kodiak bear with a Bowie knife?"

"How do you know I haven't?"

"Because if you had then the article would be about you and not this man Rex Strong."

"Maybe I'm modest. Maybe I've killed my share of Kodiak bears, but I don't like to brag about it because I don't want the Kodiak bear population to get all mad at me."

"I don't think you have to worry about that. I haven't seen too many Kodiak bears around West Warwick lately."

"You can't be too careful. I hear they spotted one out in Crompton just last week."

Bill lifted the sheet from the boy's front and the kid bounded out of the chair. When Mildred reached for her purse Doherty was disappointed to see a wedding band on her left hand. Since she had a son he didn't know what he expected. She paid Bill the $1.50 for her son's haircut and tipped him another fifty cents. Bill was his usual gentlemanly self as he thanked her.

"Brendan, this is Mr. Doherty," she said to her son. Doherty reached out his hand even though the boy was already dragging his mother toward the door.

"Sorry. I promised we'd stop at Grant's to buy him some toy soldiers."

Doherty and Bill both watched as Mildred St. Jean and her son Brendan exited the shop. Then Doherty plunked himself down in the barber's chair.

"What'll it be, Baby Huey?"

"Just a quick shave, Beetle Billy." Bill spun the chair around so that they were facing the mirror. The counter in front of them had an array of tonics, shave lotions, gels, pomades, hair oils and canisters holding hot towels, razors and shaving cream. It always reminded Doherty of the setup of liquor bottles behind a bar.

"Nice little twist."

"Huh?"

"The blond. The one you were just talking to while I was cutting junior's hair."

"Who, Millie?"

"Ah, so we're on a first name basis already?"

C'mon Bill, we were just making conversation. Besides she's married."

"Married, yeah, but in name only."

"What's that suppose to mean? Did her husband run out on her?"

"If only. He's Gerard St. Jean. Did you know him?" Doherty shook his head.

"He's younger than us. Poor bastard got brained in Korea. He's up at Howard now in the vegetable ward. Will be for the rest of his life."

Howard was a large institutional complex just over the town line in Cranston. It sat on a vast flat plain bordered on one side by an active farm. It was originally started in a less enlightened age as a hospital for the criminally insane and other people with mental issues. Now it served a variety of cases including a lot of guys who came home from the wars with shell shock, or combat fatigue, as they liked to call it now. It also treated people like Gerard St. Jean who'd suffered serious head injuries, either in combat, a car accident or some other circumstance.

The more dangerous cases were kept in the buildings on the backside along Pontiac Avenue. Doherty remembered riding by there as a kid sitting in the backseat of his father's sedan. The inmates were kept in cages that allowed them to be outside for part of the day. Some of them had their shirts off and they were frightening looking. Doherty didn't want to stare at them but he couldn't help it. It was like when they passed a bad accident on the highway – he didn't want to look but he couldn't turn away either.

Further north along Pontiac was the state prison, the Adult Correctional Institution, or ACI as everyone called it. Beyond the prison was the boys' re-form school at Sockanosett, where Doherty's father always said he'd drop him off if he misbehaved. It was made up of a series of stone cottages with bars on the windows. On the other side of Reservoir Avenue from Howard was the girls' reform school at Oaklawn. It had the same look as Sockanosett. They must have been put up by the same construction company. That's where his father threatened to dump Margaret if she misbehaved, though Doherty couldn't recall his sister ever misbehaving.

"Why doesn't this Millie get a divorce? I'm sure she'd have legal grounds."

"Because she's Catholic. No divorce as long as her husband's still alive, and that could be a very long time. Besides, ever since it happened she's been living with her in-laws. The way I hear it Gerard's mother goes down to St. Anthony's every day to light a candle and pray for a miracle."

"How do you know all this?"

"Hey, Hughie, this is a barber shop. It's where all the town's news is ex-changed. Forget the *Times*; this is where you come if you want the real stories." Bill placed a hot towel over Doherty face. "Why don't you ask her out? She's a nice girl – and good looking too."

"You just got through telling me she's married, with a husband up at Howard," Doherty muttered from underneath the towel. "Now you want me to ask her out. Why don't you ask her out? You're the Don Juan around here."

Bill tipped Doherty's chair back, removed the towel and began to prep him for the shave. "I thought about it, but she's not my type. She's a good girl, and I don't like good girls. I was married to one once and it didn't work out. For me, it's a night here, a night there, maybe a few days out on Block Island. That's all of a woman I can take. When I go home I want to be by myself. But you, you're different."

"Different how?" Bill had covered Doherty face with some warm shaving cream and began to sharpen a straight razor on the leather strop that hung from the chair.

"I'm just saying, that maybe you should ask her out and if you do, maybe she'll say yes. She works up at Francine's on the corner of Main. You could catch her there."

"You mean that little dress shop next to Smith's."

"Yeah, that's the place. It's not a *dress shop*, it's a women's clothing store. You drop in on her there you won't have to deal with the in-laws. But I think you should wear the suit when you do. The baseball jacket just doesn't do it."

"I don't know. Maybe I'll think about it."

After his shave at Harry's, Doherty walked up to the Arctic News to pick up the afternoon *Bulletin*. Like most days when the weather permitted, Willy Legere was sitting in his chair outside on the sidewalk. Willy had graduated from the high school a year after Doherty and enlisted in the navy when the Japs bombed Pearl Harbor. In early '43 his destroyer was hit by Japanese aircraft and went down in the Pacific with all hands on board. Willy was working an artillery gun at the time and one of the shells blew up near him, causing him to lose his eyesight. Most of the crew drowned or were eaten by sharks before a rescue tanker picked up the survivors. Willy was lucky, sort of. At least he survived. For his pain and suffering he got a monthly disability check from the government and a job selling pencils on the street corner.

"Hey Willy, how's it hanging?" Doherty said approaching the blind vet.

"Been to Harry's, huh, Mr. D?"

"How'd you know?"

"I can smell the after shave lotion. You know when you lose somethin' like your eyesight, all your other senses get better. I can hear and smell things I woulda never noticed before." Doherty wanted to say that he guessed that meant there was a silver lining in Willy's dark cloud after all then thought better of it.

"Who you rootin' for in the Series, Mr. D? Looks like it's gonna be the Braves and the Yanks again."

"Well it sure as hell isn't going to be the Red Sox."

"Phew. Forget them. They got Williams and Jensen, and this Malzone kid looks pretty good, but their pitchin' stinks. I still like to think of the Braves as our team even though they're out there in the Milwaukee now."

"I don't. They were so bad for so long. Then they got all these good young players like Matthews, Burdette and that Negro outfielder Aaron right after they moved to Wisconsin. It's enough to make me want to root for the Yankees."

"Hey, don't be so bitter. They still got Spahnie. I mean we almost had an all-Boston series in '48."

"I know, I know, Willy. Don't remind me; 'Spahn and Sain and pray for rain.' If only old man McCarthy had started Parnell or Kinder in the playoff instead of Danny Galehouse, the Sox would've won the whole thing. Forty-eight was their year. Williams'll never see the Series again, mark my words. Not with the bums they got now."

"Would you like some pencils, Mr. D?"

"Sure, Willy, sure. Give me a large package. Sharpening them'll keep my secretary busy for a whole afternoon." Doherty slipped a dollar into Willy's cup. The blind vet also sold plastic American flags like the one pinned to his plaid mackinaw. "You take care, Willy."

"You too, Mr. D."

Doherty wondered how long into the fall Willy Legere would stay in his chair outside of the Arctic News before the cold drove him away. Then how would he supplement his paltry disability checks?

After leaving the News with the afternoon paper and a take-out coffee, Doherty walked the five blocks home to his apartment. Before going in he placed Peaches Perrault's bill in her mailbox. That night he ate a can of spaghetti and meat sauce, read the paper and then went back to the John Steinbeck book he'd been reading about the pirate Henry Morgan. After a few chapters he fell asleep in his chair. Later he made his way to the bedroom, stripped down to his skivvies and dropped in for the night. Before finally dozing off he caught himself thinking about Millie St. Jean.

In the morning Doherty walked to work despite the stormy weather. Although men's hats were rapidly going out of style, he still wore a fedora, especially today because it kept the rain off his head. He was pretty well soaked by the time he got to the office. He could've taken the Packard out of the garage and driven in, but he preferred walking as long as the temperature permitted. As a kid he was prone to carsickness, so even now when he rode if he wasn't driving he at least had to sit in the passenger seat. Mostly, though, he liked to walk. It gave him a chance to think about things. This morning his thoughts kept circling back to Millie St. Jean.

Today was one of Agnes' days off so he left the package of pencils on her desk with a note for her to sharpen them when she got a chance. Doherty whiled away the morning by smoking cigarettes and reading the *Providence Journal*. As usual, at noon he walked up to the Arctic News for a bite. Because of the rain, Willy Legere was not at his post. He thought Willy still lived with his mother but he wasn't sure. The little lunch counter downstairs at the News was Doherty's favorite spot for the mid-day meal. It was patronized mostly by women out on shopping trips and salespeople from some of the neighboring stores. There was hardly anyone there today, thanks to the weather. Doherty wondered if Millie St. Jean ever ate at the little downstairs counter.

He had a baloney and cheese sandwich and covered it with two cups of black coffee. He smoked a Camel and read the rest of the paper after his dish was cleared. When it was time to go he left a quarter on the counter. On his way out he chatted for a few minutes with Eleanor, the elderly woman who ran the register. Doherty was disappointed Willy wasn't around. He needed some sports talk to calm his nerves.

It was almost one when he walked through the glass door at Francine's. A little bell tinkled as he crossed the threshold. Doherty's eyes quickly covered the place. He hadn't been in a women's clothing store since he was a kid out shopping with his mother. He immediately felt out of place. Two women looking at aprons gave him a suspicious glance. Doherty stood near the door not knowing where to turn or look. Millie St. Jean spotted him and came to his rescue.

"Why Mr. Doherty. This is ..." she hesitated for a few beats, "a pleasant surprise. Are you looking for something in a house dress?" A smile turned up at the corners of her mouth.

Doherty shuffled his feet. "No, I was kind of thinking about maybe some lingerie." Two could play the smart aleck game. Just then a small, balding man appeared seemingly out of nowhere. Actually he had come from behind a coat rack that was taller than he was.

"Is there a problem here, Millie?" he asked while keeping his eyes on Doherty.

Millie smiled, shifting her gaze between the two men. "Not really, Mr. Mendelson. Mr. Doherty here just came in to peruse the women's underwear." The little man now looked concerned. Millie reached out and patted her boss' arm. "I'm just kidding. Mr. Doherty is a friend of mine." Mendelson relaxed. They all smiled at each other.

"Okay, Millie. But don't be too long. There's a woman in the back looking at dresses – the expensive ones. And she's going to need a female opinion. I think the one she's trying on is a wee bit too tight." Mendelson then quickly retraced his steps.

Millie turned her attention back to Doherty. "So you were asking about lingerie."

"I was only kidding. Can't say I know all that much about women's under-garments," Doherty said, though he'd been with more than a few women with and without their underwear when he was in the service. "I really wanted to talk to you."

"How did you know I worked here?"

"At the barbershop the other day, Bill told me."

Millie smiled. "Ah, Bill Fiore, the town gossip. Not much gets past that man from what I hear."

Doherty didn't want to get into talking about Bill behind his back so he kept quiet.

"I guess barbershops are kind of like beauty parlors, in a more masculine sort of way."

"Except at the barbershop you can learn how to kill a Kodiak bear with a Bowie knife. I bet you can't pick up useful information like that at a beauty parlor," Doherty said.

"No, though you can find recipes on how to bake a Boston cream pie without it falling apart. Look I hate to break away from this amusing conversation but I do have to get back to work."

"Would you like to go out sometime? Maybe to the pictures?"

"The pictures?"

"You know, the movies. We could go to the Palace. There's a Frank Sinatra, Dean Martin movie playing this week."

Millie laughed. "Oh the movies. When you said pictures I was wondering if you were inviting me up to see your etchings."

This time Doherty chuckled. "Sorry, but I don't have any etchings. And I can't invite you *up* either because I live on the first floor."

"Are you asking me out on a date, Mr. Doherty?"

"Please, you can call me Hugh."

"I don't know. I think I prefer Doherty instead." They looked at each other for a few seconds. Doherty wasn't sure what came next. Aside from Dolores Bradley he hadn't been on a date with a woman in quite some time.

"This movie, is it a musical? You said Frank Sinatra and Dean Martin are in it."

Doherty shook his head. "No, it's a drama. I hear it's sort of like *From Here to Eternity*. There's no singing in it as far as I know. It's supposed to be pretty good. How about Friday night?"

"How about it?" Millie then smiled and reached out and patted Doherty on the arm. "Sorry, I was just teasing. You seem so harmless when you're nervous." Out of the corner of her eye Millie St. Jean saw Mr. Mendelson heading their way.

"Friday'll be fine. Pick me up here at six; that's when I get off work. And please wear this suit. I like a man in a suit and you look so handsome in it."

Doherty spent the rest of the day sitting in his office watching raindrops chase each other down the windowpane. He was trying to carefully plan his evening out with Millie St. Jean. The fact that she liked him in a suit pleased him. Not too many men wore suits on a regular basis anymore. You mostly saw them only at church or on special occasions. Doherty had two that he rotated every other day. He decided to get this one pressed for Friday.

By four the rain had slowed to a light drizzle so Doherty went for a long walk that would eventually take him home. The streets were still quiet, as most of the day shift mill workers hadn't gotten off yet. By six the bars and taverns that lined Main and Washington would be thronged with noisy drinkers. By seven things would get rowdy and a few fights would break out. At least two police cars cruised the main drag every night until the bars closed. By ten things would quiet down again as the workers made their way home, their wallets a few bills thinner. After that the fights would be confined to the households.

Doherty walked down to the bottom of Main and then circled around behind the police station and headed back along the river. Today it ran green and smelled of the dyes and other industrial wastes the mills poured into it. Doherty imagined there once was a time when people swam in the Pawtuxet – maybe back when the whole area belonged to the Narragansett Indians. As far as he knew, the mills had been in West Warwick since before it was even West Warwick, back when his ancestors first arrived from Ireland.

When Doherty got to his apartment building he noticed there was something in his mailbox. He fished out a small manila envelope, like the kind his pay at Quonset used to come in. Inside were three tens, a couple of ones and some loose change along with a note that read, "Paid in Full," signed by Ferdinand Perrault. Doherty wasn't sure if it was exactly what Peaches owed him though he was pleased and surprised to collect anything from the Perraults. He also found it funny that Napoleon Perrault was paying to find himself.

Feeling flush for the first time in weeks Doherty walked down to Belanger's and bought a thick steak, a potato and some green beans. Nothing out of a can tonight. He ate hardy and accompanied it all with a couple bottles of 'Gansett. He listened to the radio for a while, mostly big band music, and then took up Steinbeck's *Cup of Gold* again. By ten Doherty was all in so he decided to call it a night. He figured after expenses he was about thirty dollars ahead from the Perrault case. That would keep the office open for a couple of more months.

In the morning Doherty folded up his suit to take to the cleaners on his way to work. After stopping at the Centreville Bank to deposit some money, he dropped in at the Donut Kettle for a coffee, a glazed donut and a glance at the *Journal*. It looked like the Sox would finish at about .500 - good enough for third place but still thirteen games behind the Yankees. So what else is new? When he finally strolled into the office it was nearly eleven. Agnes was at her desk nervously chewing on one of the pencils Doherty'd bought from Willy Legere. She looked up quickly when he closed the door and pointed with the pencil toward the backroom.

"You got some company."

Doherty looked at his office door, which stood slightly ajar. "You let somebody into my office when I wasn't here?"

"I tried to stop them, but these are not the kind of people you say *no* to."

"People?"

"Yeah, two men. Big men. Official looking." Agnes went back to gnawing on the new pencil apparently feeling that she had violated her boss' trust.

Doherty slid into his office that immediately seemed small with three large bodies in it. He looked at the two men closely. One was a guy he knew from around town named Angel Tuohy. His real name wasn't Angel, but Doherty'd never heard him called anything but. The other guy didn't look familiar. Like his counterpart, he was big and was wearing a tie and jacket, though not as neatly as Tuohy. Agnes must've thought they were cops.

Doherty casually slipped out of his trench coat and hat and hung them on his antler rack. He walked behind his desk and sat in his chair.

"Gentlemen, can I help you with something?"

Tuohy stepped forward and stuck out his hand. "Angel Tuohy. I think we may've met before, Mr. Doherty. This here is Rene Desjardins." The other man didn't move away from the wall or proffer a hand in Doherty's direction.

"The Judge wants to see you." No further explanation was necessary.

The Judge was Martin DeCenza, who everyone knew ran the Democratic Party machine in West Warwick and, for all practical purposes, in Kent County. When Doherty was a kid he and his mother would walk by the party's headquarters, which was located in an office on the second floor of the Plaza Hotel on Brookside, just off Arctic center. The Plaza was no longer a real hotel, it just called itself one. It was a fleabag boarding house, inhabited mostly by single men who worked in the mills and drunks, or those who were both.

When his mother talked about the DeCenza machine the young Doherty used to think there was a big machine inside, like the power looms in the mills, cranking out politics, whatever they were. His uncle Patrick would always greet Doherty by calling him 'a dirty politician.' It was years before he fully understood what Patrick meant. He'd tried his best over the past few years to keep his distance from the local pols and their flunkies like Angel Tuohy and Rene Desjardins. Not being able to before that was why he left the police force.

"When?"

"Tomorrow night, seven o'clock at headquarters," Tuohy said. "And don't be late. The Judge is a busy man and he likes it when people are on time."

Tuohy didn't bother to tell Doherty where the headquarters were because he assumed that Doherty, like everyone else in town, knew where the machine conducted its business.

"Can I ask what this is about?"

"You can ask but I can't tell you. That's between you and the Judge. We were only sent to deliver the message." With that Tuohy and his large companion exited Doherty and Associates.

At five minutes to seven Doherty climbed the dimly lit stairway to the office above the Plaza. It was almost dark out and from the street Doherty could see that the second floor was lit up like a Christmas tree. He was not surprised. With a statewide election only a month away the DeCenza machine would be in high gear. When Doherty was a cop one of his assignments each Election Day was to stand guard at the polls. On several occasions he saw men and women he knew entering a polling place that was not their own. He soon learned that the machine had hired these out-of-work people to cast what were called *graveyard votes*.

The way it worked was that the machine would scour the obituaries in the *Pawtuxet Valley Times* from the previous two years looking for voters who'd died during that time, yet were still on the voting rolls. Then they'd give their people *walking around money* and send them out to vote in a dead person's stead. Because West Warwick was such a small town everyone knew who was alive and who was dead. Still, the poll watchers themselves played along, mostly because they were also on the payroll of the machine. In the end, the people DeCenza wanted elected always got elected and no one was ever the wiser for it. Even as late as the 1950s political patronage was still the name of the game in this mill town.

At the top of the stairs the words Democratic Town Committee were stenciled on the upper third of the frosted glass door. Doherty knocked and the door was swung open by Rene Desjardins. Doherty was looking directly into the hostile gaze of the big Canuck. Desjardins was tall, broad shouldered and had a prominent black moustache. Put him in a mackinaw and some snow shoes and he could've been the villain in a Sgt. Preston episode on TV.

Doherty nodded and was ushered into a big room that was intended to be a function room back when the Plaza was a real hotel. It was full of desks that ran in two lines up each side of the room. Many of them had green bankers lamps on them like the one Doherty had in his office. Mostly men, and a few women, sat at them pouring over large sheets of paper, which he assumed were voter rolls. A few workers looked up and gave him a once over, then quickly went back to their business.

The walls were covered with campaign posters. The most prominent ones touted Dennis J. Roberts, who was running for reelection as governor. A few smaller ones were for Theodore Francis Green, who was the state's elder statesman and U.S. Senator. Green was instrumental in establishing the prominence of the Democratic Party in Rhode Island and has served in the Senate since Roosevelt was president. The posters were from four years ago. Green would not have to stand for reelection until 1960. The newspapers said he'd probably retire by then as he would soon turn 92.

The other posters promoted John E. Fogerty, this district's U.S. Rep, and Aime J. Forand, the one from the other half of the state. There were also posters for Democrats running for lesser state offices, few of whom Doherty'd ever heard of. At the end of the large room sat a small glassed in office where three men were engaged in a heated conversation. One of them he recognized as Judge Martin DeCenza. Doherty wisely hung back until the other two men left the office. Then Angel Tuohy came to escort him in to see the Judge.

DeCenza was in shirtsleeves and his tie was pulled down a notch to let his neck breathe. He was a small man in his fifties, with reddish hair turning to gray and reading glasses perched on the end of his nose. He was energetic while exuding a distinct air of command. When Doherty approached DeCenza looked up from the volume of papers on his desk and greeted him warmly.

"Hugh Michael Doherty, it's a pleasure to finally meet you," DeCenza said. Though his hand was small when they shook, he had the firm grip of a career politician.

"Mr. DeCenza," Doherty said taking the man's hand. "Or would you rather I called you Judge."

"Please, call me Judge. Everyone else in town does. Here, have a seat," he said pointing to a chair on the other side of his desk. He instructed Tuohy to close the office door.

"So, Mr. Doherty, I understand you were quite the war hero."

"I don't know about that. I got a few medals, but then again everybody who was at Anzio got medals, even the dead guys."

"Yes, Hugh, but not everyone got a Silver Star." DeCenza had taken the liberty to use Doherty's first name and Doherty wasn't about to take it back. "The town was mighty proud of you."

"I guess I was one of the lucky ones. Lucky to come home alive."

"I think I knew your father, Peter Doherty; worked at the Royal Mill if I'm not mistaken. A fine man. Twas a shame he had to leave us at such a young age."

Doherty looked the Judge straight in the eye and said, "My father was a drunken bum who killed himself with booze."

DeCenza nodded his head. "Well that may be. Still, he died at a young age." Doherty wanted to say 'none too soon' but held his tongue. He wondered who DeCenza had sent out to vote in his father's place the year his old man died.

"You look like you're pretty busy up here," Doherty said taking in the full operation of the room.

"Well, it is an election year. Are you a political man, Mr. Doherty?"

Doherty considered the question. "I know that Eisenhower's the president."

The Judge shook his head and chuckled. "I suppose as a veteran you voted for him?"

"Have you ever been in the service, Judge?"

"No, not really. I was already in my forties when the war broke out. The various jobs I held here in West Warwick during the war were considered essential services on the home front."

"I didn't vote for Eisenhower because enlisted men don't like officers - and they particularly don't like generals. I voted for Stevenson, both times. Didn't do much good but what the heck."

"You didn't vote for Ike even though he's considered the great war hero? After all, he did get elected president primarily because of his leadership during the war."

Doherty leaned forward, "With all due respect, Judge, I don't remember anybody shooting at Eisenhower, do you? I saw a lot of war heroes fighting and dying in Italy, and Eisenhower wasn't one of them."

"I was hoping that perhaps you voted for Stevenson because you're a Democrat."

"Way I figure it, I'll leave all that Democrat and Republican stuff to guys like you."

"Listen Hugh, would you like a drink?"

"Sure, whiskey would be fine – neat please." The Judge signaled for Tuohy to bring each of them a tumbler poured from a fancy bottle of Crown Royal. When Doherty took a swallow it went down a little easier than the Jameson he was used to. The Judge took his with ice and water.

Once they were settled in with their drinks the Judge asked, "Do you mind if I tell you a little bit of history and about what goes on here?" He didn't wait for Doherty to answer. "This town wasn't incorporated until 1913, which makes us the newest town in the state. And do you know why that's' so?"

Doherty shook his head, "No, not entirely."

"Well, you see back then a number of men who lived in and around Arctic, men with backgrounds like ours, didn't like the fact that the fancy pants mill owners and businessmen over at Governor Francis Farms and places like that in Warwick were sucking so much money out of our part of the town and giving us nothing but low paying jobs in return. The Republican Party, which served their interests, controlled all the levers of power in this county. After years of frustration, men like my father petitioned the state legislature to have this part of Warwick separated from the main township. But as with everything it all came down to money and politics. You see Warwick has always been a Republican stronghold, controlled by what are called *rural interests*. The commercial center of the town, and the whole county for all practical purposes, was here in Arctic. And because of the mill workers, this part of

Warwick was always solidly Democratic. The Republicans didn't like that and they felt threatened as our population grew. So they rigged things to make sure they controlled all the county offices. But in 1912 the Democrats took over the state legislature and that's when West Warwick's petition to become a separate town was granted."

"And now all the people who live in town and work in the mills vote the way you tell them to."

Judge DeCenza slammed his hand down on the desk and all eyes in the big room turned in his direction. "Do you think those Yankees over in Warwick ever gave a damn about the working man. If it wasn't for the Democratic Party, the mills and factories would still be without unions and the people who work in them would not be making a decent wage."

"Yeah, but now all the mills are closing. Moving down South for the cheap labor."

"Aye, so it tis. And there's only so much we can do about that. The mill owners can get those hillbillies and Negroes down there to work for less than our men and women, and without unions. There's no way we New Englanders can compete with that anymore. But by God, as long as the mills are here, I'm going to make sure the workers get a fair shake."

"I appreciate your efforts, Judge. And I'll be sure to continue to vote Democrat if that's what you want. But what exactly does all this have to do with why you asked me up here?"

The Judge had calmed down and everyone else in the outer room had gone back to their ledgers. Doherty didn't want to look back over his shoulder, afraid he might see the hostile glare of Rene Desjardins burning a hole in his back.

"Did you follow the gubernatorial election in '56?" the Judge asked.

"Not really. I probably voted for the Democrat, whoever that was."

"It was Dennis J. Roberts, and he won. This is what happened, Hugh: our candidate, Roberts, was the incumbent, but he had a real challenge on his hands from an Italian fellow from Providence named Christopher Del Sesto. When the ballots were first counted Del Sesto was declared the winner by a little over 400 votes. But his margin of victory was based on his lead in the absentee ballots. Those are ballots cast by voters who are going to be out of state, say like servicemen, or shut-ins who can't get to the polls on Election

Day. Most of those people cast their ballots by mail before the election. But Roberts wasn't going to go down without a fight. He and the state Democratic Committee filed a suit that challenged the legality all 5000 plus absentee ballots. Their claim was based on the premise that those votes had all been cast *before* Election Day. They took their case all the way to the state Supreme Court."

"And what was your position on these disputed votes?"

"Well, because I'm a member of the state committee I had to go along with the suit. Personally, though, I thought Del Sesto had won fair and square. But Denny kept the fight going practically till Christmas. The papers dubbed it 'The Long Count'."

"Kind of like the second Dempsey-Tunney fight?"

"Yes, but not exactly. You see the court was already wired for the Democrats. Denny's brother sits on the bench, though in this case he obviously had to recuse himself. Some of others, however, like Chief Justice Flynn and Frank Condon had been elected to the court back in the 1930s under what you might say were *dubious circumstances*."

"And so Roberts won?"

"Yes, I'm afraid so. The court threw out all 5000 of the absentee ballots and Denny won by 700 votes."

"What does that mean for this year's election?"

"Well, we have the classic rematch, like Dempsey and Tunney. Only this time Roberts will probably lose. He seriously wounded himself with his behavior two years ago. The election is just over a month away and all our polling shows that Del Sesto has a marginal lead at this point. My concern now is that we hold the rest of the slate together and not let Roberts drag everyone else down with him. Without a presidential contest on the ballot, the turnout will be much lighter than in '56. That always means fewer Democratic voters."

Doherty thought to suggest that DeCenza could turn out more of graveyard votes but held his tongue. "Once again, can I ask what all this have to do with me?"

"It's my understanding that you have a unique talent for finding people who are lost or missing. Like the recent disappearance of the fat woman's husband."

This caught Doherty off guard. "How did you know about that?"

"My dear boy, it's my business to know what goes on in this town. If I'm considering hiring someone like you to find a lost person I need to know what his track record is."

"Who's lost that you want me to find?"

"The Kent County Republican Committee Chairman. A man named Spencer Wainwright."

"I'd think you'd be happy having a Republican missing. One less vote against your guys."

"I appreciate your levity, Mr. Doherty. However, it does not serve our party's interests for the county chairman of the opposition party to be missing this close to an election."

"Why not?"

"It comes down to simple mathematics. Providence County is the most populous county in the state and is a strong Democratic enclave. South County and the East Bay still belong to the Republicans. Therefore as Kent County goes, so goes the state. If Mr. Wainwright continues to stay among the missing, it won't be long before that Republican mouthpiece, the *Journal-Bulletin*, begins to suggest that foul play is involved - foul play possibly perpetrated by the opposition party. They will characterize Wainwright's absence as an attempt by our party to sabotage this county's Republican organization on the eve of what is looking more and more like a very close election. It is therefore in our best interests to find Mr. Wainwright and convince him to reassume his role as chairman."

"Can I ask one question before I accept this job?' DeCenza nodded. "Has there been foul play?"

The Judge considered the question carefully. "If there has, it has not been by anyone in our organization. That's all I know for sure at this stage. The upshot is that I'd like to hire you to find Mr. Wainwright and return him to his previous status. That is if you're not too busy." Doherty was convinced DeCenza already had full knowledge of his rather empty calendar.

"Okay I accept. My rate is $50 plus expenses."

DeCenza smiled at his new employee. He reached into his desk and pulled out a thick envelope, which he handed to Doherty. "There are two-hundred dollars in this envelope. If, or when, you find Spencer Wainwright and return him in one piece to his place of business, you'll get another two hundred."

Doherty softly whistled through his teeth.

"One other thing, Mr. Doherty. I don't want you to keep any written records of this transaction. Our arrangement must be strictly off the books. The fewer people who know about this the better. Now, Mr. Tuohy will help you get started." Judge DeCenza stood and extended his hand, "Goodnight, Mr. Doherty. I look forward to hearing from you. And don't forget to vote on November 4th."

Angel Tuohy walked Doherty to the headquarters' exit. As he opened the door Doherty quietly asked Angel if he would step down to the street with him for a few minutes. Tuohy looked over his shoulder before following Doherty down the stairs. Once out in the night air Doherty lit a cigarette. He offered one to Tuohy. Instead the big guy took out his own pack, though he did accept a light from Doherty's Zippo.

"Angel, can we talk honestly here?" Tuohy did not answer. "You know what this is about, right?" The big man offered a slight nod. "Why don't they just go to the cops if this bird's lost?"

Tuohy nervously looked up at the lighted windows on the second floor. "Our information is that this isn't the first time Wainwright has disappeared. The Republican people did go to the Warwick police, but they wrote it off as him just taking another powder. You know how that goes."

"No I don't. Could you give me a little more dope on this Wainwright."

Tuohy chewed on his bottom lip and looked up at the second story window again. "We been told that Wainwright is a skirt chaser. Got a girl in every port so to speak, even though he's married."

"If you know so much why didn't the Judge send you out to find him?"

Tuohy pulled on his smoke. "He doesn't want any of his people getting within ten feet of this. He wanted to hire you because you're totally outside the organization."

"Any idea where I should start?"

"Yeah, a couple. Wainwright's a partner in a real estate operation over in Warwick at Hoxie Four Corners called Cooper and Wainwright. You might want to drop in there to see if you can shake something out of his business associates. He's also got a summer place down at Great Island. You know in South County."

"Yeah, I know where Great Island is. What about the wife?"

"I'd stay away from her if I was you. They say she's a handful and the less people who know you're nosing around the better off we'll all be. And whatever you do, make sure this doesn't boomerang back onto the Judge. That would cause a lot of trouble for everybody."

Doherty thanked Angel and left him pulling on his cigarette.

Chapter Three

SPENCER WAINWRIGHT

In the morning Doherty got out a map to check for the best route to Hoxie Four Corners over in Warwick. One of the drawbacks of walking everywhere is that every time he ventured outside of the town limits it was an expedition. The Four Corners were on the other side of the Hillsgrove Airport, the state's only commercial, non-military airfield. It was a rather small operation since traveling by air was still something of a luxury for most Rhode Islanders. When they went anywhere out of state people here still chose to use their cars or ride the old New York, New Haven and Hartford Railroad.

Doherty drove up the Post Road along the west side of the airport and then turned right onto Airport Road. This was the most direct route to the Four Corners. Although he'd seen plenty of aircraft going in and out of the air station at Quonset, the hubbub around a commercial airport still fascinated him. He slowed down as he passed by the big hangars that housed commercial airplanes that were far bigger than anything he'd seen at military airfields. He couldn't imagine what it would be like to fly in a plane of that size. Further along the road were the smaller hangars that housed mail, small freight delivery planes and private aircraft.

Just after turning right onto Warwick Avenue Doherty spotted the office of Cooper and Wainwright Real Estate in a small building that fronted right on the avenue. He drove down another block and parked the Packard beside a boarded up store. He didn't want anyone inside Cooper and Wainwright to eyeball his junk heap. It might give them the wrong impression of his financial situation.

The office had a large picture window that looked out onto Warwick Ave. Two cars were parked out front. One was a little two-toned Nash Metropolitan painted green and white; the other a non-descript Dodge sedan. The office was neat, clean and generally colorless in all other respects. It also appeared to be empty, so once inside Doherty coughed to make his presence known. A young woman came out from a back office. She looked surprised to see Doherty standing by the door next to a potted plant. He figured they didn't do too much walk-in business here. The girl was pretty well put together and carried herself like she knew it. She was youngish and had curly black hair that sat up on her head in a beehive. She also had a sizable rack to go with it. Her skirt was just tight enough that her chassis would catch the trailing eyes of most observant men. She wore stockings that were slightly on the dark side of flesh tone. Doherty caught himself thinking about the garter belt that held them up.

"May I help you?" she asked in a voice that was pleasing like warm milk.

"Yes," Doherty said. "I'm in the market for a new home."

She smiled in a way that he might've taken as a come-on if she were in a different line of work. "Well you're in the right place. My name is Annette Patrullo. I'm an agent here," she added as if she was trying to convince herself.

She didn't offer a handshake though Doherty wouldn't have minded holding her digits for a few seconds. With her dark hair, large breasts and the name Annette, she reminded him of an older version of the girl from the Mouseketeers.

"Hugh Doherty," he said introducing himself.

"Please, Mr. Doherty, have a seat." She pointed to a chair as she squeezed herself behind a desk. Her tight skirt made it difficult for her to get into a comfortable sitting position. He wanted to ask if she was alone in the office then thought it might send the wrong signal.

"Let me get some preliminary information." Annette Patrullo had a little trouble with the word *preliminary*, but given her sweet voice Doherty didn't mind. She asked him the usual questions: name, address, telephone number, etc. When she asked if he was married Doherty said that he was and his wife's name was Mildred. He noticed that the Patrullo girl was not wearing a wedding band herself.

"Do you mind if I ask you about your employment?"

"No, not at all. I'm self-employed. I run a security business over in West Warwick. It's called Doherty and Associates."

"Security," she repeated not entirely certain what that meant. Doherty wasn't about to help her.

"And what would you estimate your yearly income to be?"

"Depends on the year. For this past year I'd say it's been about six thousand, give-or-take." If Doherty made half that he'd had a good year.

"And does your wife work?"

"No, not right now. She's expecting, in the spring."

Annette smiled again. "Well, congratulations. So what exactly are you and your wife looking for, Mr. Doherty?"

"We were thinking of maybe a small Cape, nothing too fancy. With perhaps a yard and a short walk to school when the little one is ready." Doherty realized he might be laying it on too thick and decided he should dial it back a little.

"What do you think your price range is?"

"I don't know. We were thinking maybe something around twelve thousand. You know, in that ballpark."

Annette nodded and wrote down some figures on Doherty's application. "I think we might have some cute little cottages for you in that price range. Will you be getting a bank mortgage? Most loan agents these days expect buyers to put down at least twenty percent."

"I know that, but you see I'm a veteran. I think I qualify for one of those government loans. You know, the kind we can get through the GI Bill."

"Yes indeed, as a veteran you would qualify. Most vets can get a low interest FHA loan with as little as 5% down."

"FHA?"

"Federal Housing Authority. They give out loans to servicemen, veterans, and people who work for the federal government. It's a pretty sweet deal for someone in your position." She smiled again and it was not displeasing.

"Look, Miss Patrullo, before we go any further can you tell me if Mr. Wainwright is around?"

This question set the girl back a bit. "Why no, he's not. I'm afraid he's currently out of town. But I'm sure I can answer any questions you might have."

"I'm sure you can, and you already have. But, you see, my boss told me I should speak directly to Mr. Wainwright. That he might be able to give me a special deal on a house that might ordinarily be a little above my price range."

Annette Patrullo was now feeling a little uncertain about her new client. "Your boss? I thought you told me you were self-employed. I believe you said you were in…" she shuffled her notes for a minute. "You said you were in the *security business.*"

"I am. He's not really my boss, more like my primary client at the moment. Anyway, Judge DeCenza told me I should speak directly to Mr. Wainwright and he would fix me up with a good deal."

"Are you by any chance referring to Judge Martin DeCenza from over in West Warwick?" she asked nervously.

"Why yes. Do you know him?"

"Only by reputation," she said. This Patrullo girl was catching on quickly. She knew something was fishy. "Look, Mr. Doherty, why don't I put together a few listings and sometime next week you and your wife can come by and I'll take you out to look at some properties." Doherty knew a bum's rush when he was getting one and this was a first class edition.

"Sure, that'd be fine," he said as he stood up. "Please tell Mr. Wainwright that I'm sorry I missed him and that Judge DeCenza sends his regards."

Doherty left the real estate office and circled around to the other side of the street. He positioned himself in the shadows between two buildings where he had a clear view through the front window of Cooper and Wainwright. Annette Patrullo hit the phone almost as soon as Doherty left. Ten minutes later she came out and hopped into the little green and white Metropolitan and sped off. Doherty got back to his Packard in time to put a discreet tail on her. He hoped she wasn't smart enough to think he'd follow her. Nevertheless, he hung back a few car lengths just in case.

She looped back around the airport and headed south down the Post Road, which doubled as Route One. Her toy car was easy to keep within eyeshot given that the little thing didn't have enough horsepower to go over fifty. Somewhere south of East Greenwich, down near Quonset, Doherty figured out where she was headed and it wasn't home. He would've continued to tail her but needed to get back to town to prepare for his date with Millie St. Jean. Besides Doherty wasn't sure the old Packard could make it all the way to South

County and back without breaking down. He'd have to leave his business with Wainwright and Miss Patrullo for the weekend. Give them both a chance to stew over the fact that Martin DeCenza was on Wainwright's case.

Doherty picked up his freshly pressed suit and got back to his place in time for a shower and a shave. He splashed on an extra palm of aftershave to sweeten the pot. He thought about driving the Packard into town, but it was a warm night so he hit the pavement instead. He was early enough that he had to dawdle across the street from Francine's until he saw Millie emerge from the shop. He then watched Mendelson lock up and walk away before he crossed to the other side of Washington. Millie had her hair done so that her blond waves turned up just where they reached her neck. She was wearing a lightweight, pink cloth coat over a gray pleated skirt and a blue button up sweater. A white round collared blouse peaked out at the neck. She had on black shoes with low heels. When Doherty drew close enough she smiled and took one of his lapels in her hand and fingered the wool of his suit.

"Nice threads, Doherty."

"It's the same one I had on the other day. I got it pressed for you," he added shyly.

"Well I appreciate that. So few men wear suits nowadays. I miss that."

"Does that mean you're the old fashioned type?"

"In some things, yes. But not in everything."

They began walking down Washington toward the Palace Theatre. Doherty took the outside, closest to the street as he'd been taught to do when escorting a woman. "What's something you're thoroughly modern about?" he asked.

Millie thought for a minute. "Well…" she began but hesitated.

"C'mon, name one thing, just one?"

Millie looked at Doherty, her face turning red. "You won't laugh, will you?"

Doherty smiled. It felt easy being with Millie St. Jean. Easy and fun in a way it'd never been with Dolores Bradley.

"Depends on what it is," he smiled.

"I like Elvis Presley. I think he's cute. No more than cute, I think he's sexy. There, now I've said it."

"Elvis Presley. The guy with the greasy hair and the sideburns?"

Millie giggled. "And don't forget the hip bumps."

Doherty shook his head, "Why Millie St. Jean, you are a surprising woman."

They walked on without saying a word for the next block. Then Doherty turned toward her and said, "Sexy?"

"Why does that offend you, Doherty? A woman using a word like *sexy*?" "

"No, it doesn't offend me. Should it?"

"Some men might be. Let's get something straight between us right away. I'm twenty-seven years old, which means I wasn't born yesterday. I have two boys, one nine and one seven, and I can assure you they weren't delivered by a stork. I may not've had the kind of …er…experience soldiers like you had, but that doesn't mean I can't think Elvis Presley is sexy."

That pretty much ended conversation between them until they got to the theater. The double feature started with a movie called *Cry Terror!* starring James Mason. It would be followed by the Frank Sinatra/Dean Martin picture *Some Came Running*. At the concession counter Doherty sprung for a box of popcorn, a box of Dots, a Coca Cola for himself and lemonade for Millie. He was feeling flush thanks to the money the Judge had given him.

The first movie was already running by the time they took their seats. They whispered a few things to each other about the film as they watched it though otherwise they mostly focused on the screen. Doherty thought several times about taking Millie's hand then decided it was too soon. During the intermission Doherty excused himself and returned to the concession counter to buy a package of M&Ms and another Coke while Millie watched the previews and the cartoons.

The Sinatra movie was about a soldier coming back to his hometown three years after the war ended. Once there he got into a lot of trouble, to the embarrassment of his respectable brother and his brother's bitchy wife. He also got mixed up with two women, a floozy he met on the bus at the beginning of the story and later a smart society girl he apparently knew before he went into the army. Sinatra played the soldier named Dave, an aspiring writer. The society girl praised his work even though she thought it showed that he was an angry and troubled vet. Dean Martin played Sintra's friend, a likable gambler named Sam, who never took off his big Stetson hat. Doherty tried to distance himself from the story by concentrating on Sinatra as an actor. He decided he liked him better as a singer.

Although the movie came out thirteen years after the fighting stopped, there were parts of it that hit Doherty close to home. He wondered what Millie might be feeling given what had happened to her husband in Korea. When it was over Doherty decided it wasn't such a good choice of picture to see on their first date.

They stood outside on the sidewalk not saying anything as the rest of the crowd flowed around them. For once Doherty was at a loss for words.

"Would you like to get a coffee or something?" he asked.

"How about some ice cream. It's such a nice night and we won't be able to get ice cream much longer."

Doherty agreed, "Ice cream it is. We can go to the Candy Kitchen right up the street." Millie smiled and that was where they headed.

The Candy Kitchen was owned by the Perakises, a Greek family who had run it for as long as Doherty could remember. One of the sons who had worked there as a kid, was now Doherty's doctor. He had an office down Main Street just past Doherty's apartment building.

Millie ordered an ice cream sundae with vanilla ice cream, chocolate sauce, whipped cream, nuts and a cherry on top while Doherty got a sugar cone of pistachio. She was a good eater. Doherty hoped she didn't end up like Peaches Perrault. Halfway through her sundae Millie asked Doherty to help her finish it.

"Somebody's eyes were bigger than her stomach."

Millie patted her belly. "Thank God for that. When you picked me up at Francine's I hadn't had a thing to eat since lunch. Popcorn and Dots don't add up to a very healthy meal." Doherty reached across the table and began to shovel some of Millie's sundae onto his cone.

"So, what did you think of the movie, Doherty?"

"Which one?"

"Either."

"I sort of preferred the first one. I like James Mason. I think he's a really good actor."

"What else has he been in?"

"He played Rommel in *The Desert Fox*. Not that he looked anything like Rommel. When I was in the service we saw a lot of newsreels and propaganda films with Rommel in them; he didn't look like James Mason."

"Who was Rommel? I didn't see that movie."

"He was Hitler's chief general in North Africa, and would've been in Italy too, but he got wounded and was sent back to Germany. That happened before we were dropped into Sicily so we never had to go up against him. A good thing too because he was one tough customer."

"What happened to him after that?"

"They say he was mixed up in the generals' plot to kill Hitler. First they said he died of a heart attack. Later it came out that he was forced to commit suicide. Anyway, Mason did a good job playing him in the movie even if he didn't look like him."

"What else has he been in that I might've seen?"

"His most famous role was in *A Star is Born*."

Millie smiled, "Oh, right. He played Judy Garland's husband - the one whose career is fading just as she is becoming a star. I remember now. Boy, Doherty, you sure know a lot about movies."

Doherty didn't look directly at Millie when he said, "I guess I've seen quite a few of them. I don't have much else to do at night since I don't own a TV."

"Maybe you should get married. Then you could have a whole tribe of kids to keep you busy." The suggestion of marriage, given Millie's situation, turned things a little sour.

Sensing this Millie asked, "What did you think of the other movie? Was the business about Dave coming home from the army and doing all that drinking – did that seem real to you?"

Doherty shook his head. "I can't say. For me it now seems like such a long time ago. I wasn't a frustrated writer like him either. When I got home I went right back to work at Quonset. I needed to help my mother make the payments on our house. I didn't have much time to think about the war and stuff."

"But you became a policeman, so you must have been looking for something. You know, something more exciting and more challenging than working at Quonset."

"My Uncle Patrick knew I was bored working down there and he had this friend, Gus Timilty, who was a sergeant on the force at the time. Gus spoke to a few people and next thing I knew I was in a uniform again."

"That's all there was to it?"

"I did have to take the exam, but any knucklehead could've passed it. As long as you could read."

"Which I can assure you many men in this town can't."

"Yeah, I know. Those are the guys who left school early and went into the mills; guys like my father. That wasn't for me. Besides, there's no future in the mills anymore."

Millie spooned her ice cream around but ate little of it. Doherty continued to pick at her sundae. "Why didn't you stay with the police?"

"It wasn't what I thought it was going to be. You know, after the war I wanted to get away from all that military stuff. That's why I left Quonset. I thought with the cops I could do some real good but it didn't turn out that way."

"How did it turn out?"

"The cops were corrupt like everybody else in this town. Most of them were on the take looking for their share of the dough. Maybe underneath people are all like Sinatra's brother was in the movie. Trying to make enough money to put on a good front. Not caring about who they hurt along the way."

"I almost cried at the end when Ginnie got shot. At first I thought she was just some dumb Dora, chasing after Sinatra who acted like he was so much better than her. But in the end she turned out to be the best one of them all, didn't she?"

Doherty nodded his head. "I guess she did. Maybe that's why she had to die and the rest of them got to live."

Millie thought about this for a while and then said, "Was it like that in the war? Did only the good die while the others got to live?" This question struck Doherty as one she might've been asking herself ever since her husband was wounded.

"No, it's not like that at all," Doherty answered. "It's a total crap shoot. Soldiers die because the bullet or the shell hits them and not the guy next to them. Period. There's no rhyme or reason to it. It just happens. I mean the whole thing is crazy. They drop you into some country thousands of miles from home and you're supposed to kill these other guys you never even seen before. And the other guys, the enemy, most of them're a long way from home too. So you kill them before they kill you. Then when you see their bodies up close they look just like guys in your outfit or guys you knew back home. In a different world you might've even been friends. It's a totally crazy situation."

"But don't you feel now that it was all worthwhile. I mean we couldn't just let the other side win, not after seeing the pictures of those camps. I mean they were so, so evil."

"Their leaders were, sure. Yeah, we had to do what we did. But when it was over a lot of good men, and women, were dead – and for what? So we could come home and get right back in the rat race?"

"But at least you won. We didn't even win in Korea. And poor Gerard…"

Doherty had been afraid Millie's husband would eventually find his way into their conversation. And now he was there in front of them just like her uneaten sundae.

"He was only a boy, Doherty. Barely out of his teens. He felt guilty that he missed the big war. Gerard saw the men and the older boys marching in those parades down Main Street with the brass bands. He was envious and wanted some of that glory for himself. So when the call went out for Korea he enlisted. Leaving me with one boy in a crib and another in my belly. And now he's in a bed up at Howard just wasting away." Doherty wanted to reach out and take Millie's hand like he'd wanted to in the theater but he didn't.

"Do you see him much?"

"I go up there once every week. Mr. Mendelson is so nice – he let's me off early on Tuesdays so I can visit with Gerard. But it's not like he knows I'm there. I talk to him and I read to him, but it's all for me and I know it. I guess it's so I won't feel guilty."

"What about your boys? Do they ever go with you?"

Millie looked sad. "I took them at first. I wanted them to know they had a father who was a real person not just somebody in pictures propped up on the mantel. I didn't want the other kids at school to tease them about not having a father. But they don't want to go anymore. There's nothing for them to do there. My mother-in-law says I should take them anyway, but I can't bring myself to do that. It's not like she goes much herself. I guess it's easier for her to remember Gerard as he was rather than see him as he is now."

"I'm sorry, Millie. I really am."

"Sorry? Sorry for what," she said harshly. "Sorry that you came home alive and can go to the movies and eat ice cream, and…" Millie then began to sob quietly into her napkin. "I think we should go, Doherty. I don't want to make a scene."

They stepped out into the night. Doherty offered to get his car and drive Millie home. She said she'd rather take the bus so he decided to walk her to the stop.

"You know, Millie. I don't even know where you live."

Her tears had now subsided. "I live down in Clyde with my in-laws, and the boys, of course." As they drew closer to the bus stop Millie took Doherty's arm.

"I'd like to do this again, Millie, if you wouldn't mind."

She looked at him with a surprised expression. "Are you sure - after what just happened?"

"I'm very sure. I was kind of hoping you might find me sexy like Elvis Presley."

Millie laughed. "I doubt that, but it's worth a try." They stood at the bus stop and this time Doherty took her hand without hesitation. When the bus came into view she hugged Doherty and kissed him softly on the cheek.

"I guess I'll see you around Francine's, Millie."

"I'll look for you in the lingerie department."

Early Saturday evening Doherty cautiously entered Tetrault's Penalty Box Tavern in hopes of finding Gerald Broyard reasonably sober. The day shift mill workers got off an hour early on Saturday so they began drinking earlier as well. The place was dimly lit as usual and there was no game on the boob tube tonight. Doherty wasn't even going to try for a drink, though he was smart enough to wear his baseball jacket this time rather than a suit. He walked the length of the bar and didn't see Broyard. Not being one of Tetrault's regulars, as before, he attracted a few hostile glances. Then he spotted the little man, Guy, sitting at a table with three other men knocking back shots of some brown colored whiskey.

Doherty walked over. "Hello, Gee, remember me?"

The little man looked up through bleary eyes that were giving him trouble in the focus department. "I'm the one who went looking for your friend Napoleon. He was down at Oakland Beach like you said." Guy narrowed his eyes to slits to improve his vision.

"Ya, ya, I remember you. So he was down there with that girl, eh?"

"That's where I found him. Thanks for the tip. Can I buy you gents a round?" Doherty asked. The four old timers did not refuse. The bartender took the order. Doherty got a Jameson for himself and sat down at their table without being asked.

"It's a good ting you found Napoleon. They was goin' to can him at the mill. They don't like us takin' time off, even when we're sick," Guy said. Doherty recalled the many times his old man had almost gotten fired because he was too hung over to make his shift at the Royal.

"Did he go back to the fat wife?" Guy asked.

"Yeah, he did, and so far I haven't heard any pots or pans being thrown around their apartment." The drunken men at the table thought that was funny. No doubt they were familiar with thrown cookware or being hit with rolling pins wielded by their wives. Doherty fronted the men another round and then asked if they'd seen Gerald Broyard.

"He'll be in soon," Guy said. "He don't like to come in too early on Saturday. He likes it better later on when the fightin' starts. That Gerry, he's a tough man, no."

Doherty pointed to his nose and told them how Broyard had given him its twist back in the schoolyard. They all thought that was good one and offered Doherty a toast to his crooked nose. They were into their third round on Doherty's tab when Gerald Broyard strode through the door. He gave the tavern the once over and immediately spotted Doherty drinking with the four old men. He pulled a chair over, turned it backwards and sat down with his big legs splayed out. Broyard was wearing a light blue bowling shirt with his name on the sleeve.

He slapped Doherty on the back. "Hey, Hughie, whaddya doin' here on a Saturday night? Doncha know this place can be dangerous for somebody who ain't a Canuck."

"Dangerous for everybody after you come 'round, Broyard," said Guy.

"Oh, I see what's goin' on here. I bet my friend Doherty's been standin' you old coots some rounds." Broyard then signaled to the bartender to bring him one too and to put it on Doherty's tab.

"I need your help, Gerald."

"So this ain't a social call after all. What're these old timers into you for? About three bucks so far?"

"I need a car."

"Eh, don't we all. What would you like, one of them new Chevrolet Impalas, or maybe a Cadillac Eldorado?"

"I already have an old Packard, but it's not reliable and I've got to drive some distances this week. You said something about knowing people up at Packy's Garage last time I was in here."

Broyard looked around the bar and then back at the four old timers at the table. They were too far into their cups to pay much attention to what Doherty was saying.

"Why don't we walk over there for a few minutes," Broyard said as he eased Doherty up from his chair.

When they were a discreet distance from the four drunks Broyard leaned in close and said, "I don't want nobody to know about me leavin' the mill. Soon as they find out you got other plans they shitcan you."

"I understand. But I still need a car; nothing fancy, just one I can count on to get me down to South County and back without crapping out."

Gerald smiled. "I ain't even gonna ask you what's in South County. When do you need this car by?"

"Tomorrow."

"Jeez, Hughie, tomorrow is Sunday. That might not be so easy."

Doherty pulled out a ten spot and slipped it into Broyard's hand. "Maybe this'll help move things along?"

Broyard looked at the bill and said. "Wait here. I'll be right back. I gotta make a phone call." Doherty leaned against the bar and waited. He didn't want to return to the old drunks and get hit up for another round. Tetrault's was filling up and the noise level was getting noticeably higher. Doherty wanted to be out of there before the unscheduled boxing matches began.

Gerald returned a few minutes later. "Be at Packy's at ten tomorrow mornin'. Do you know where it is?"

"I can find it."

"Ask for Armand – tell him you're the guy I sent. He'll have a good car to rent for however long you need it. You'll have to pay, but that don't seem to be a problem for you right now."

"Thanks Gerry. I won't forget this."

Yeah, yeah. Just don't say nothin' about me leavin' the mill – not even to Armand or anybody else at Packy's." Doherty took this last remark to mean that Broyard's plan to leave the Warwick and hook on at the garage might be nothing more than a pipe dream.

The first thing Doherty saw when he turned up Quaker Lane the next day was the DeCenza Brothers Dairy. It was the biggest operation of its kind in town and was owned by some relatives of the Judge. All of the little cardboard milk cartons given to kids in the town schools came from DeCenza Bros. As a result every student in West Warwick, be they public or parochial, had been on at least one field trip to the dairy. Doherty remembered being dragged through the plant by the nuns on three separate occasions.

The Packard lumbered its way up the steep hill on Quaker Lane to the top where it merged with the Bald Hill Road. He was told that Packy's Garage would be on his right just past the hilltop. He didn't see it until he'd passed it by because it was part of an Esso station. He made a u-turn and pulled back into the station. When the Packard crossed over the hose that ran out to the pumps he could hear a loud dinging sound. The place looked deserted, closed for the day, as were most gas stations in West Warwick on Sunday.

Doherty parked by the pumps and went to peer inside. The windows were crusted with grease so it was difficult to make out anything. Nothing stirred. He walked around to the side where the garage was located. Rusted car parts leaned up against the outside walls and old tires were strewn about. Cars were neatly parked to the side of the garage – many in various stages of disrepair. A few lacked fenders and bumpers while others were complete smash jobs, no doubt waiting for some insurance rep to declare them totals. Further around to the back of the garage were half a dozen cars that appeared to be fully intact.

The big bay door to the garage was fastened with a large bolt lock that was fitted through a ring cemented into the pavement. A faded sign hung askew over the bay door announcing that this was indeed Packy's Garage. Next to it was an office door. Doherty turned the knob but it too was firmly secured. He checked his watch. It was almost ten after and there was still no sign of life anywhere on the premises.

Just as Doherty was walking back to his Packard a red and white two-tone '57 Chevy in mint condition pulled in on the other side of the pumps. It had the kind of muffler that made the car rumble even when the engine was idling. A young, skinny guy with long black hair greased back on the sides emerged from the Bel Air. He was in his mid-twenties and wore a white shirt buttoned up to the neck and a faded black sport coat that was frayed around the cuffs. He was a good-looking boy in a greasy sort of way.

"Armand?"

"Yeah. Sorry I'm late. I had to take my mother to Mass. You Doherty?" Doherty nodded his head. Armand walked over, ignored Doherty's outstretched hand and peered inside the Packard.

"Thing's a beast. Looks like an upside down bathtub," was all he said. Armand pulled a cigarette out from behind his ear and lit it. It had a stain on it from his hair oil.

"Let's go inside where we can talk. We're not suppose to be open on Sunday."

Doherty followed Armand around to the office door by the garage bay and inside. The room was cluttered with paper everywhere. Its walls were festooned with color pictures of beautiful, long sleek cars with large chromed fins. There were also pictures of what Doherty assumed were souped up hot rods. On the wall behind the desk was a grease smudged Michelin Tire calendar. A girl in a skimpy bathing suit with her breasts hanging out was draped across what look like a Ford Fairlane convertible. Doherty gave it a good once over and then turned his attention back to Armand.

One side of the office was glass and looked out into the garage. There were at least eight cars in there in various stages of repair. Toward the back were a couple of customized cars from the thirties and forties with big, chromed engines from more recent models. The place smelled of paint combined with a burning odor.

"What's that burning smell?" Doherty asked.

"That's lead. It's what we use to fill up the cracks and dents. We put it in with a weldin' torch."

"Isn't that a fire hazard with all this paint around?" Armand ignored Doherty's question.

The young guy sat down behind the crowded desk and took out a pencil. His cigarette was now dangling from the corner of his mouth. He wrote some notes on a pad that Doherty couldn't read.

"What kinda car are you lookin' for?"

"One that runs better than mine. I need to do some chasing around the state over the next few days and I can't rely on my Packard. Most days I can't get it to go over forty-five."

Armand looked at Doherty and shook his head in disgust. "I can sell you somethin' newer. Somethin' better than that shit box you got out there." Doherty didn't mind the Packard being described this way since it was how he often referred to it himself.

"I can't afford to buy a new car right now; besides I usually walk wherever I go." Armand looked at him as if to say a real man in 1958 did not walk anywhere. "How about you rent me something?"

"I can set you up with a nice '55 Chevy, very reliable. Ten dollars a day plus gas, three hundred mile limit. It's not cherry but it'll be a lot nicer than the car you're drivin' now." The insults were coming fast and furious, but Doherty needed a car on the cheap so he kept his mouth shut.

"How about five a day, two hundred miles and I'll bring it back topped off?" Armand considered the offer as he took his smoke down to the filter.

"$7.50 per with no mileage limit – and you bring it back with a full tank."

"Deal," Doherty said and shook hands with Armand.

"Pull your Packard way around back. I don't want that tuna can to be where anybody'll see it. I'll get the Chevy for you."

Once Doherty had stowed his car as far away from the main road as he could, he walked back to the front where Armand was leaning against a blue and white 1955 Chevy Bel Air sedan. It had a little rust around the rocker panels and the upholstery inside was split in a few places though it might as well have been a Lincoln Continental as far as Doherty was concerned.

"How much do you want up-front?"

"Gimme twenty-five and we'll settle up for the rest when you bring it back. Be careful with the gas pedal; this here vehicle has a lot more pick-up than your... Packard." Doherty knew Armand wanted to say 'shit box' again but now that real money was about to change hands decided to be more polite. Doherty peeled off two tens and a five and handed them to the young guy who slipped them into his back pocket.

"Do I need to sign anything?"

Armand shook his head. "Naw, not really. I'll know where to find you if the car don't come back. The registration is in the glove compartment and I'm thinkin' you already got a license." He handed Doherty the keys and indicated which was for the ignition and which for the trunk.

"Happy motorin'," Armand said as he fished out another cig.

Doherty headed south down the Post Road. He passed through the heart of East Greenwich and by the turn-off to Goddard Park. That was where his department at Quonset used to hold its Fourth of July picnics every year. They consisted of softball games, burnt hot dogs and all day drunks.

Doherty didn't know exactly where Great Island was though he thought it was somewhere in the Pt. Judith-Galilee area, at the southernmost tip of the West Bay. When he was on the force there was a guy named Klinoff who always bragged about having a house on Great Island. Apparently it was a private island and in order to get a place there you had to be approved by the island's association. Klinoff said that his wife's brother had fixed it up for them. Doherty could never understand how a beat cop like Klinoff could afford a summer place down in South County until he learned that the guy was taking pay-offs to provide protection for a certain high stakes card game. Klinoff also hooked up cops and mill workers with loan sharks who would carry them when their checks ran out before their bills did. It was a sweet racket and Klinoff wasn't the only cop on the take. Guys like him were a dime a dozen and another reason Doherty left the force.

The Chevy provided a swell ride; it was smooth and speedy, two traits the Packard never had. He passed by Quonset and Davisville. The big sign with the Seabee mascot on it stood outside the gates. It was a large bee with a Tommy gun in his front feelers and tools in the back ones. The feisty looking bee wore a navy cap on its head. The sign was flanked by two mothballed aircraft that had flown out of the Naval Air Station here during the war. Naval aircraft was still built and repaired at Quonset, which was what Doherty had done after being discharged from the service. He could've stayed on there and been set for life – that is if he didn't die of boredom first.

Davisville was where the Navy construction battalions, or CBs as they were called, trained before they were sent overseas. Most of this base was closed down after the last troops came home in '46. It was reactivated in '50 with the outbreak of the war in Korea. Doherty'd read in the papers recently that it was now being used for something called "Operation Deepfreeze," which was the government's effort to explore and set up bases in Antarctica before the Russians did. The Cold War had given both operations new life. President Eisenhower had even flown out of Quonset a couple of weeks before after a three-week golf vacation over in Newport.

A little further along he passed by the new drive-in movie theater, the latest thing in movie watching for families - and for teens, who used them as a place to make-out and cop some feels. Around Silver Lake Doherty dropped off the main road and headed east toward Narragansett. He hadn't been by the ocean in quite a while so he wanted to make sure it was still there. Cruising in the Chevy made him feel like king of the road. Narragansett was the largest beach town in that part of the state. Nobody he knew ever called it Narragansett though; it was either "Gansett", like the beer, or more often just "the pier." In the summer people would say they were going "down the pier."

Doherty cruised slowly along the road by the sea wall. It was an unusually warm day for that time of year so a lot of people were out on the stroll. Teenage girls sat on the wall in their short shorts waving at guys who trolled by in their hot cars revving their engines as they did. Even in the Chevy Doherty wasn't one of them. He passed by the Towers whose arch extended over the road. It was the pier's most famous landmark. Doherty lit a Camel and rested his arm on the edge of the open window. He could smell the sea air and it made him think of Millie St. Jean. He thought about keeping the Chevy for a while and maybe taking her on a day trip down here.

He rolled along the shore road toward Scarborough, South County's most popular beach. When Doherty was at Quonset after the war, he and some of the other guys would come down to Scarborough on Sunday afternoons during the summer. They were young and healthy and all full of piss and vinegar, glad to have come out of the war in one piece. Most of them weren't married yet so lying on the beach checking out the dollies was pure freedom back then. Doherty was a good swimmer so he'd often go out into the waves and try to body surf. Sometimes the teenage lifeguards would blow their whistles and signal him to come in closer to the beach and he'd ignore them. Later in the afternoon he and some of the other guys would stroll down the beach to Olivo's, which had shaded picnic tables right out on the sand where you could drink beer and eat clam cakes. Doherty always had to be careful not to spend too much time in the sun on account of his white Irish skin.

They'd sit at a table and make suggestive remarks to the girls who walked by in their tight fitting bathing suits. Sometimes a few would join them for drinks and cakes. Doherty suspected some of them were underage, which was why they were so accommodating. No one at Olivo's seemed to mind. If they got lucky with one of the girls, they would stay down into the evening drinking more beer, eating chowder and stuffed quahogs and trying to stretch the day out as long as they could. Come Monday morning they'd be back on the line at Quonset, hung over and sunburned. Doherty spent a few of those Sunday nights making out on the beach or by the sea wall with some cute little filly whose name he couldn't even remember the next morning.

He was so busy musing about those days that he missed the turn off for Galilee and ended up at Pt. Judith. He parked the car and walked out onto the pier. The boats for Block Island left from this landing. It was still warm and being here reminded him of the time he came down one summer to watch them bring in the catches from the annual Tuna Tournament. That year the guy who won hauled in an 800 pound blue fin. It was the biggest fish Doherty'd ever seen and he couldn't imagine what a man had to do to boat something like that. A fish of that size could fill a lot of those little cans.

Back at Galilee Doherty stopped in at George's Restaurant for a bowl of chowder and a half dozen clam cakes. This was the kind of fresh seafood you couldn't get up in West Warwick, even on Fridays. He asked the cook behind the counter how to get to Great Island and got directions that took him around through Jerusalem and across a narrow causeway bridge and onto the island. At the entrance to Great Island there was a sign that said something about it being a private community, etc. but Doherty paid it no mind. He didn't see many telephone wires crossing to the island so his hunch was correct that trying to look up Wainwright's number in a local phone book would've been a waste of time.

Great Island was by no means the playground of Rhode Island's wealthy. That was over in Newport across the bay or further west along the seaside in the stretch from Matunuck to Watch Hill. Great Island was for those middle class folks who had just enough extra money to buy a little summer bungalow close to the ocean. Still, it was definitely a step up from Oakland Beach. The island stuck out into what was called Pt. Judith Pond. The pond was really a backwash from Rhode Island Sound and ultimately the Atlantic. Since it was already fall, many of the homes were unoccupied despite the Indian summer weather. Most of the houses Doherty saw as he cruised around the island were small, one-story jobs made out of wood or cinder blocks. They would never rival the summer cottages at Newport.

The streets had such nautical names as Abalone, Tidewater, Conch and Scallop Shell. Doherty followed East Shore Road up that side of the island and then crossed over to Harbor and onto Marine Drive. Marine turned out to be the only fully paved road; all the others were mostly packed down dirt.

There were hardly any cars around and none of the houses had driveways. The cars that he did see were either parked on the grass in front of the houses or on small patches of crushed shells beside them. The grass was mostly brown this late in the season. Great Island didn't strike him as the kind of place where people spent a lot of time tending to their lawns. Several of the houses had small boats with tarps secured over the top of them parked on trailers in their yards. The island must've been a hub of activity in the summer, though Doherty kind of liked the sense of abandonment it gave off at this time of year.

He figured Wainwright had enough scratch to afford a house with a water view. It might not be any bigger than those of his neighbors, yet it would bring the water into play. For that reason Doherty didn't bother with the roads that crossed through the center of the island and stuck mostly to those that ran along the edges. He took a spin around a loop called Franks Neck Road, which afforded the most expansive views; there was no one home at any of the little cottages there. The next turn out toward the water went up a short hill, an incline really, and that's where he spotted Annette Patrullo's unmistakable Green and White Metropolitan. It was sitting on a crushed shell patch next to a red and black Buick Riviera that looked big enough to eat the Metro.

Doherty left the Chevy far enough away to insure that the sound of his car wouldn't reach Wainwright's house. Aside from the two vehicles in front of a modest wood frame bungalow, the only other sign of life on Oyster Road were the seagulls flapping overhead. There was no bell so Doherty knocked on the front door. There was no response. He tried again with the same result. He shuffled around the side careful not to make any noise in doing so. At the back of the house was a small stone patio that opened up to a panoramic view of the marsh and the summer cottages across the water. Two lounge chairs were pointed in that direction. Annette Patrullo was splayed out in one and a guy Doherty assumed was Wainwright in the other. A small cocktail table sat between them with two glasses of clear liquid on it. A lime was hooked over the rim of each.

Doherty walked out into plain sight. The woman spotted him before Wainwright did. She gasped and quickly nudged him. He immediately rose from his chaise and headed in Doherty's direction. As he did Doherty quickly sized up the real estate man. They were about the same height though Wainwright was a good ten years older and twenty pounds lighter than Doherty. He had brownish hair parted on one side and combed over into an Ivy League cut. There was some graying at the temples. Wainwright wore sunglasses, a blue knit shirt, green pants with tiny whales on them and brown boat shoes without socks. He was the very picture of a hail-fellow, well met. Miss Patrullo stood behind Wainwright using him as a shield between her and Doherty. She had on tight white shorts and a black top from which her breasts protruded like the front of a '56 Cadillac. Her black hair was tied up into a nest on the top of her head.

"This is private property," was the first thing Wainwright said. "You have no business being here." It was a challenge Doherty chose to ignore, like the sign that told him Great Island was a private community.

"He's the man I told you about, Spencer. The one who came to the office on Friday." Doherty couldn't figure out whether her nervousness was the result of genuine fear or because she'd unintentionally led Doherty to her missing boyfriend.

"What is it that you want here?" Wainwright asked, hands now firmly on his hips.

"I was hired to find you and now I have."

"I don't understand."

Doherty took out his wallet and flashed Wainwright his PI license. "I'm a private investigator. A client hired me to find you. I'm just doing my job."

Wainwright seemed confused. He looked back at the girl and then at Doherty. "I ought to call the police. You're trespassing on my property. This is a private island."

"You can call the police if you want, but then you're going to have to explain Miss Patrullo here, and that might affect your position as a member in good standing with the Great Island Association. Look, I'm not here to bring you any harm, Mr. Wainwright. But I think it'd be a good idea if we had a little chat. One that doesn't include your friend here."

"OK, but first you have to tell me who your client is," Wainwright said, though his challenge had lost most of its vigor.

Doherty shook his head. " 'Fraid I can't do that. In my business I have to guarantee my clients confidentiality unless they want their identity to be known." They had reached an impasse.

Annette chimed in, "I bet it's that Judge DeCenza from West Warwick. That was the name he used the other day at the office."

"Judge Martin DeCenza?" Wainwright asked with a puzzled expression on his face. Doherty remained silent.

Wainwright turned to the girl, "Honey why don't you go into the house and make Mr. Doherty a drink – and take your time about it." He turned back to Doherty. "Gin and tonic all right?"

"Sure. That'll be fine."

Annette wiggled her way through the screen porch into the house. Doherty admired the view as she did. Wainwright then walked him out toward the edge of the marsh.

"What do you... I mean, what does your client, want from me?" Wainwright not only dressed like an ivy leaguer but he spoke like one too. Doherty took him for either Harvard or Brown.

"My client believes it would be in everyone's best interest if you were to return to your role as Republican County Chairman, to your real estate business, and to your wife; though he really doesn't care all that much about the last one."

"Mr. Doherty, can I be frank with you?" Doherty didn't say anything, so Wainwright went on. "Are you married?"

"No."

"Ever been?"

"No."

"Well I am, as I'm sure you well know. But I'm caught in a loveless marriage. Have been for quite some time now." Wainwright looked wistfully out at the marsh as he spoke.

"Why don't you get a divorce? Lots of people do nowadays."

"Do you know how difficult it is to get a divorce in this state? Practically the only grounds for divorce are adultery or physical abuse. And I can assure you I do not beat my wife."

Doherty was having a hard time mustering up much sympathy for Spencer Wainwright's plight. "Looks like you wouldn't have any trouble working up a case of adultery. You could just fix it so your wife finds out about you and that little twist inside. You do that and it'd be in the hands of lawyers in no time."

"I couldn't do that to Annette."

"Give me a break, Mr. Wainwright. And whatever you say next, please don't let it be because you're in love with her. She's young enough to be your daughter."

Wainwright tried to look offended but it didn't go over too well. "Why is it so god awful important that I return to my real life?"

"Look, it didn't take much for me to find you and her down here. If your wife has a mind to, she will as well. My client's interest is simple. He needs you to get back to Warwick and your duties as party's chairman until after the election. Then if you and Miss Patrullo want to fly off to Acapulco he doesn't really give a damn."

Annette Patrullo came through the screen door balancing three glasses in her hands. She put them on the glass top table.

"Annette, honey. Could you bring our drinks over here? And then wait for me there." Annette sashayed over to the two men with their drinks. She handed Wainwright his first and made it a point of giving Doherty her meanest look as she handed him his. He was gravely offended. The gin tasted like hair tonic to Doherty, but it went perfectly with the day and Spencer Wainwright's outfit.

"Why does your client care so much that I be back at my post with the committee? I'd think it would better serve his purposes if I were absent until after the election."

"Not really. After what happened two years ago he feels it'd be best for both parties if this election was run on the up and up. According to the papers your guy Del Sesto is the odds on choice to be the next governor anyway, which would make up for what Roberts did in '56. You staying missing might mess things up in Kent County where I'm told the swing vote is. If it looks like my client or his people are somehow responsible for your disappearance, which your friends at the *Journal-Bulletin* would no doubt imply, it wouldn't be good for his party."

Wainwright was now lost in deep thought. "If I go back, will you keep Annette out of this?"

"Annette? Annette who?"

"What shall I tell my wife?"

"I don't know or care. Tell her you had an emergency call because the police thought somebody'd broken into your summerhouse. Tell her you been down here the whole time where there're no phones and no way to get in touch with her. Tell her whatever you have to."

"You know I can't afford to divorce her right now – and it's not only because of the legal issues."

"What else then. Is she sick or something?"

"No, it's the money. All our funds are tied up in this big project I'm working on. If she were to sue me for divorce at this time it would be catastrophic for my real estate business and for me personally. I can't do it. Not now anyway."

"I understand," Doherty said, though he really didn't. "Then if I was you, I'd keep that little package over there under wraps for the time being. You may need her later on."

The two men walked back to where Annette Patrullo was sitting in the lounge chair. She was now wearing dark sunglasses. Doherty finished his drink and shook hands with his host.

"Let's get one thing straight, Mr. Wainwright, and I'm saying this with Miss Patrullo as a witness. I never forced you into doing anything you didn't want to do, isn't that right?"

Wainwright nodded in agreement.

"Just so we all understand each other, there's no blackmail or coercion involved here, right?" Wainwright uttered a yes.

With that Doherty drove off the island leaving Wainwright and his young squeeze in their little love nest.

Chapter Four

TONY GRAZIANO

Two days later Doherty and Bill Fiore were sitting in the shoeshine chairs at the back of Harry's shooting the breeze. Doherty'd already given Bill a bare bones version of his venture down to South County to retrieve the Republican County Chairman. He left out the parts that might have compromised his client or Wainwright. Bill was between cuts and Doherty was getting his cordovans buffed up when Angel Tuohy lumbered through the front door.

Angel walked directly toward them. The barber and Tuohy obviously knew each other as they exchanged greetings. Then without prompting Fiore left the two of them alone. Angel assumed Bill's former seat and asked the shoeshine boy for a 'spit shine'.

"Your secretary told me I could find you down here."

"It's where I come when business is slow, which is most of the time. I see you didn't bring Bluto along with you this time."

Angel began to speak but Doherty interrupted, "Don't tell me, the Judge wants to see me?"

"Indeed he does."

"When?"

"How about now? Looks like you've already had your hooves brassed up."

Doherty shook his head and chuckled. "Doesn't he ever have any judging to do?"

"He's not really a judge any more."

"He's not?"

"No, he's the town solicitor. Has been since the end of the war."

"The town solicitor? What does that mean?"

Angel said out of the corner of his mouth, "It means he runs things. We call him *Judge* as a kinda honorary thing since he was one once. He likes it like that."

Doherty tipped the shoeshine boy and rose to keep an appointment with Judge DeCenza. Tuohy hung back.

"I don't get an escort this time?"

Tuohy shook his head. "Naw. After this shine I gotta go see a man about a horse. I'm thinkin' you can find your way to the office by yourself."

Things weren't as busy at Democratic headquarters as they'd been previously when Doherty went up to see the Judge. Though there were fewer workers in the big room today, DeCenza was moving from desk to desk to see what people were doing. When Doherty entered the Judge greeted him warmly and led him into his private office. As usual, DeCenza was impeccably dressed in a dark suit with a club tie. The remnants of his once red hair were neatly combed across his head to cover his balding pate. Since it was barely one in the afternoon the Judge didn't offer Doherty a drink this time.

"Hugh Doherty, I can't thank you enough for the work you did this weekend. My people tell me that our friend Spencer Wainwright is back at his office and back at party headquarters. Apparently, there was some suspicion about a break-in at his summer place. Turns out he was down at Great Island the whole time securing his property."

Doherty took out a cigarette and sat down across from the Judge.

"Yeah, I heard the same story. Poor fella. I suppose that's what happens when you own too many houses. Looks like once he got things, um, *secured* at the beach house, he was ready to return to his regular life. Any word on whether he went home to the wife?"

"I believe he has, though I'm told there is trouble in that part of paradise."

"Happens in the best of marriages. It's what keeps me in business."

While Doherty smoked the Judge unlocked a drawer in his desk with a small key and extracted a thick manila envelope. He slid it across the desk in Doherty's direction just like he did the first time they met.

"This is the balance of what we agreed upon, plus expenses."

"Expenses?"

"Yes, it's my understanding that you had to rent a car for your sojourn down south - from Packy's Garage I believe. There's an extra hundred in there for the inconvenience. This will allow you to keep the car for a while if you wish. Maybe take that nice Millie St. Jean out for a fine dinner somewhere."

Doherty shook his head in sheer admiration. "I've got to hand it to you, Judge. It would be pretty hard getting a fastball by you."

DeCenza smiled, amused by Doherty metaphor. "Mr. Doherty, knowing what goes on in this town is my business, just like finding lost people is yours. Since this endeavor ended so successfully, would you be interested in doing some more work for me in the future?"

Doherty gave this proposition for a few seconds of serious thought, not entirely sure what he'd be getting himself into. Yet he couldn't argue with the pay out. "I might, as long as it doesn't have anything to do with politics."

"Ah, Mr. Doherty. Don't tell me you're one of those high minded men who thinks politics is a dirty business?" Doherty didn't bother to answer.

DeCenza continued, "You know what Bismarck said about politics? He said, 'Politics is the art of the possible.' That's what I deal in, the art of the possible."

"I think somebody else once said, 'politics makes for strange bedfellows'," Doherty replied.

"Yes, that's true. So perhaps, Hugh, we are not so different after all. I do understand your aversion to working in the political arena. However, I have a potential job for you that may be more up your alley. An acquaintance of mine, a fellow who runs a small costume jewelry foundry in Providence, has been losing money despite what appear to be highly profitable sales. He has concluded that someone inside his company may be embezzling from him. I was thinking of you when I told him I knew a man who could unravel this mystery for him."

The Judge then pulled a gold Cross pen out from inside his suit pocket and wrote a name, address and phone number on his note pad. He tore it off and gave it to Doherty.

"Contact him if you're interested. It has nothing to do with politics and you won't owe me a single thing for the referral." Doherty looked at the note and stuffed it into his pocket. He then rose and shook hands with the Judge. As he turned for the door, DeCenza called after him.

"Oh, Mr. Doherty, you forgot something," he said with a sly smile, holding out the manila envelope. Doherty laughed at his own blunder, and kept laughing all the way down to the street.

Back at his office Doherty phoned the foundry owner, Tony Graziano, at his place in Providence and they agreed to meet later that afternoon. Before heading off to the big city Doherty stopped in at Francine's to ask Millie out for that weekend. She agreed, though once again insisted that it be Friday night rather than Saturday which Doherty would've preferred. He told her he'd pick her up when she got off work, only this time in his car.

The jewelry foundry was located in the Olneyville section of Providence, south of downtown and not far from the Italian section of Federal Hill where Rhode Island's most notorious crime family had its headquarters. The manufacturing and wholesaling of costume jewelry was the state's largest industry now that the textile mills were rapidly closing. Graziano's Foundry was a small operation compared to the big plants in Providence and Pawtucket like Coro and Trifari. As it turned out some of Graziano's clients were these very companies for whom he did some high-end custom molding.

Graziano was a heavyset, gregarious Italian fellow in about his mid-forties. He wore a broad smile on his face when he told Doherty how he'd started out on the shop floor at Coro and worked his way up to a supervisory position. Once he'd accumulated enough cash Graziano said he took his expertise and industry know-how and opened his own specialty business. From their very first handshake Doherty could tell that the owner had done serious manual labor at some point in his life.

After a preliminary discussion about his concerns, Graziano introduced Doherty to his bookkeeper, Louise Saccocia. She was a friendly and attractive girl who'd been recommended to Graziano by his wife because Louise was one of the few girls she'd grown up with who went on to school beyond high school. She'd spent two years at Bryant Business College after graduating from Bay View, the high class Catholic girls school in Warwick. Louise Saccocia took Doherty through the books and tried to explain on a level he could understand the discrepancy in the bottom line. He'd been down this road before with other clients so he had a rudimentary idea of how the money was disappearing.

Back in his office Graziano told Doherty that he suspected one of his crack salesmen of being the culprit. Apparently, the man had been in a few months before asking for a raise in his commission rate. On the advice of the book-keeper, Graziano put the salesman off until his quarterly collectibles came in. After that the salesman, a fellow named Frank Thompson, had acted standoff-ish and even refused to attend the company picnic that Graziano hosted at the end of each summer. Since then company money was disappearing though Thompson's sales remained high. Graziano suspected Thompson was either making side deals on inventory without recording them or getting kickbacks on discounted sales. He also thought Thompson was preparing to jump to another outfit.

Doherty and Tony Graziano decided the tactic they would employ would be for Doherty to introduce himself to Thompson as a wholesaler recom-mended by his boss. In their discussions Doherty would offer Thompson a variety of sweetheart deals to entice the salesman into showing his hand. To get things rolling Graziano set up an appointment between the two for break-fast the next morning at a coffee shop on Federal Hill. Doherty spent the rest of that afternoon huddled with Graziano trying to absorb as much as he could about the technical aspects of his business.

In the morning Doherty parked outside of a place called DeFranchesci's at the Olneyville end of Atwells Avenue. He was early so he sat in a booth and ordered a Danish and an Italian coffee. The guy he took to be Thompson came in fifteen minutes later. He certainly didn't look like a crook. He wore a rumpled raincoat and horn-rimmed glasses. Though he was wearing a sport jacket and tie, his wrinkled shirt and poorly knotted tie did little to indicate Thompson was a hotshot salesman.

They spoke briefly about their respective career paths; all the while Doherty laid out one believable lie after another. Meanwhile Thompson kept readjusting his ill-fitting glasses that kept slipping down his nose.

Finally it was time for Doherty to set the trap. "So, Frank, are you happy at Graziano's?"

Thompson took off his glasses and wiped them on a napkin. "I like Tony. He's a good man, and a real craftsman at what he does."

"But?"

Thompson hesitated at first. "Part of the problem is my wife. She wants to have another baby and doesn't think I make enough money. She blames Tony for that. She refuses to go to any company events anymore so I don't go either because I don't want to be the only guy there without his wife. She's always telling me I should try to hook on with one of the big outfits in the city. I know I could make more money with them, but half the time the sales directors at those firms don't even know the names of their salesmen. With Tony, I'm like family, even though I'm not Italian. But you know how Italians are: once a friend, always a friend - until you're not."

Doherty didn't know what this last remark meant but he let it slide. "You said your wife is part of the problem; what's the other part?"

Thompson demurred long enough to order another cup of coffee. Doherty waited for an answer. He had baited the trap though Thompson's next comment came at him out of left field.

"It's that Louise, the bookkeeper. I got a feeling Tony's been screwing her on the side."

"I don't know Louise." Doherty said, choosing to play dumb.

"She's the company's bookkeeper. She's pretty good looking, and Tony's wife Linda – well she's put on more than a few pounds over the years. Don't get me wrong, Tony's a good guy and a good businessman, but he doesn't know how to keep books. The first two years I was with him he was always in trouble with the state tax people. He wasn't stealing or anything, he just couldn't keep his records straight. It was Linda who talked him into hiring her friend Louise. Said she was a whiz when it came to bookkeeping."

"Why does this bother you?"

"At first I didn't think anything of it. After a while though, I couldn't help noticing the way Tony looked at her. I knew it was only a matter of time before his little head got the better of his big head. I tried to tell him that maybe she wasn't on the up and up, but whenever I did he'd get pissed off at *me*. Accused me of saying what I did because I wanted more money and Louise was telling him not to give it to me."

"Sure I'd like to make more money, all the salesmen would. My sales are up nearly 15% over last year, but he tells me he can't pay me any more right now. He says Louise doesn't think he should offer any raises until the end of the quarter. The quarterlies don't mean anything since they already know at the end of every month how much business each salesman's bringing in. But now Tony'll only listen to his bookkeeper. He hears the word *quarterlies* and all he can think about are the quarterly taxes he failed to pay back when he was doing the books himself."

Thompson shook his head. "Look, I'm sorry, Mr. Doherty. I shouldn't be going on like this. You've come up here to do business with me and all I'm doing is telling you my troubles."

"Hey, don't worry about it. I like Mr. Graziano and his operation. I'd like to do some business with you people, but you're not giving me anything here, Frank."

"What do you mean, 'not giving you anything'?"

Doherty sipped his coffee, trying to remain cagey. "You know, like maybe a little personal discount would be nice. A you-scratch-my-back, I'll-scratch-yours kind of arrangement. Something between us that Graziano wouldn't have to know about"

Thompson looked confused. "I can give you our numbers. If there's going to be any further discounts, I'd have to run them by Tony. I'm not authorized to offer you more than that."

"Hey, it's no skin off my nose," Doherty said. "I just thought maybe you and me could do a little something on the side. You know what I mean."

Thompson stood up and grabbed the check. "No, I don't know what you mean. Maybe that's how people on your end operate but I don't. You want some kind of special deal, you'll have to talk to Mr. Graziano about that; I'm just a salesman."

Thompson paid the check at the counter and stormed out.

By Friday Doherty had figured out that Graziano was getting fleeced not by Thompson or any of his other salesmen. It was the bookkeeper who was distracting him by letting her boss play hide the salami with her. Tony was devastated when Doherty delivered the bad news. Graziano confronted Louise and as it turned out not only was she cooking his books to her benefit, she also had a boyfriend helping her who'd already done some time on a bunko rap. Letting Tony occasionally mount her on his desk was a side play to divert his attention from their embezzling scheme. The poor bastard was practically in tears when he wrote out a check for the $250 he'd promised to pay Doherty for getting to the bottom of why his company was losing money.

Chapter Five

MILLIE ST. JEAN

Doherty pulled the Chevy up in front of Francine's at six sharp. He smoked a butt while he waited for Millie. When she didn't show by six ten, he went into the shop. Millie was standing inside the door with her coat on. Mr. Mendelson was with her. They both looked uncomfortable. Doherty uttered a hello to each of them.

"Sorry I'm a little late. Mr. Mendelson would like to talk to you before we go," Millie explained.

Doherty looked at the little man. He was no bigger than Napoleon Perrault and the few wispy hairs he had growing around the sides of his head were sticking out at odd angles. Doherty was fully prepared for Millie's boss to give him the 'you better treat this girl with respect' speech.

"Millie tells me you were in the war, Mr. Doherty. Is that true?" Mendelson asked.

"Yeah, I was, mostly in Italy – and later on in Germany for a while."

Mendelson seemed at a loss for words. "You know my brother Frank used to own this store and my wife and I ran the curtain shop next door. When we first started out we were the only Jews that owned businesses here in Arctic. It wasn't easy back then as you can imagine."

Doherty could indeed imagine what the Mendelsons must have gone through. When he was at St. James' the nuns used to tell their students on Good Friday that the Jews killed their Lord. Like most parochial school kids

Doherty bought it as fact until he got to high school and learned that Jesus was a Jew himself.

"Have you ever had any Jewish friends, Mr. Doherty?"

"I used to play ball around the neighborhood with a kid named Joey Rosenberg. Joey had the best baseball card collection I ever saw. His father owned the Richfield down Main at the big intersection."

Mendelson smiled and said. "Arnie Rosenberg. I knew him well. A big man. They say he used to be a professional wrestler."

"He was. Joey showed me pictures of him in the ring. He told me his father played a bad guy and his wrestling name was 'Abie the Jew'. Joey said his father once wrestled Gorgeous George. I remember one time Joey and me were pitching cards against the wall at the station and this guy came in and got into an argument with Joey's father. He called Mr. Rosenberg a 'Jew bastard'. Joey's father picked the guy up off the ground by his jacket and threw him across the hood of his car. I'd never seen anything like that before except in movies. They moved away when Joey was about twelve. I don't know what happened to them after that."

"Well you'll be happy to learn that Arnie now owns a big, full service garage down in East Greenwich, right on the South County Trail," Mendelson said, still smiling. "I hear he's doing really well. For some reason it's called 'Ike's'. Must've been the name of the previous owner."

"I always wondered what happened to Joey."

Millie coughed, as a way of letting the men know that she was still there.

Mendelson continued, "Things have changed here in West Warwick since the war. There are a lot of us with stores in town now. We Jews are more accepted than we were before. I'd like to think it's because of what brave boys like you did over in Europe that changed people's minds. How you defeated the Nazis."

"I was only doing what I had to do, same as the next guy."

"You've seen the films of the camps, haven't you Mr. Doherty?"

"Yeah, I've seen them. Ike made sure we all saw them before we were discharged. He wanted us to know what we'd been fighting against. I don't know what you Jews did to get people so pissed off at you, but as far as I'm concerned you're now paid in full. Personally I don't allow any of that anti-Jew talk in my presence anymore. Not after what I saw over there."

"I appreciate that, Mr. Doherty. You know, I'm very fond of Millie here and I hope you will treat her with the kind of respect she deserves." Doherty'd been waiting for this.

"I'll definitely do that. I can tell Millie's a good girl and I promise you I will treat her as one."

Mendelson reached out and took Doherty hand in a firm two-handed clasp. Doherty was surprised at the strength of the little man's grip. "My people owe soldiers like you a great deal. It's because of you that we were saved from extinction."

Millie talked about everything except what Mendelson had said as they drove over toward Warwick. She made some comments about how nice the Chevy was and how happy she was to be getting out of town. Doherty was quiet the whole way. He was still sweating when they pulled into the parking lot of the Maryland Chicken Coop on the Bald Hill Road.

They were seated right away and when the waitress asked if they'd like a cocktail, Doherty ordered a Jameson straight up. Millie ordered an ice tea. Doherty lit up a smoke and Millie noticed that his hands were shaking.

"Are you all right, Doherty?" He didn't answer right away. "Was it something Mr. Mendelson said, you know, about the war?"

"I don't like to talk about it, Millie. I don't even like to think about it if I can help it."

"You'll have to excuse Mr. Mendelson. He can get very emotional sometimes. He told me some of his relatives were killed in one of those camps. Is it true that the Germans gassed people like they say?" Thankfully the drinks arrived and Doherty took a strong belt of his.

"Yeah, they gassed them all right, and worse. Can we talk about something else? I don't want all this talk about the war to ruin our night out."

Millie smiled and touched Doherty's forearm. "Sure, I understand. But could you do me a favor in return. Would you please not smoke while we eat? It spoils my appetite."

Doherty smiled back and stubbed out his cigarette. The waitress reappeared to take their order. Doherty ordered fried chicken. It came with mashed potatoes, gravy and green beans. He also asked for a bottle of 'Gansett. Millie chose the fish and chips and more ice tea.

"You don't like chicken? It's the specialty here. It's why they call it the Chicken Coop."

"In case you haven't noticed, Doherty, it is Friday."

He laughed. "Oh, right. Catholics are only supposed to eat fish on Friday. I forgot about that."

"Does that mean you're not a practicing Catholic anymore?"

"To be honest with you, Millie, I haven't been to Mass since my mother died. I think the war beat all the religion out of me."

"But I've heard it said that there're no atheists in foxholes."

"I think that's a lot of baloney. Guys pray to God all right when somebody's shooting at them, but that's only because they're hoping to survive. After what I saw and did over there, it's hard for me to believe God would allow things like that to happen. I mean where was God when all those innocent people were being gassed?"

"But some of them survived. Maybe that was all part of God's plan. That they live to tell us about the terrible things men can do so that we'll act better in the future."

Doherty reached across the table and took the girl's hand. "I like you, Millie. You're a good person and I respect the fact that you still have religion. I like to think I'm a good guy too, but I don't have that kind of faith anymore, and I don't think I ever will again. You'll have to take me the way I am. And if you can't, I'll understand."

Their meals arrived and nothing more was said about God or religion or the war. They ate voraciously and after splitting some strawberry shortcake for desert agreed they were stuffed. Doherty paid the check and left a generous tip to impress Millie.

"It's a good thing I didn't take you to the Jolly Chef," he said as they were walking to the car.

"Why's that?"

"Their specialty is steak and steak sandwiches. Not a proper Friday meal."

"The fish and chips were very good. Friday's about the only time you can get fresh fish around here."

When they got into the car, Millie asked him if they could go for a ride.

"Doherty, why do you think they call that place The Maryland Chicken Coop? Is Maryland famous for its chickens?" Millie asked once they were out on the Bald Hill Road.

"Beats me. I always thought Rhode Island was famous for its chickens. You know, the Rhode Island reds." They drove out toward Tiogue. He thought it'd be a nice night to take a spin around the lake. Millie slunk down in her seat and breathed in the night air.

"Millie, why Friday night? Why did you insist that we go out tonight and not tomorrow, especially since you knew you could only eat fish?" Millie sighed heavily but didn't answer; he didn't press the issue.

At the lake he parked the car and they went for a walk along the shore. Millie took Doherty's arm as she had the night they'd gone to the movies.

"My in-laws think I'm out with my girlfriends. We always go out on Fridays, sometimes to bingo, or to the movies. My mother-in-law calls it my *girls night out*.. They watch the boys and put them to bed so I can have a night off."

"Does that mean they don't know you're out on a date with me?"

"Yes, and they don't need to know either," she said firmly.

When they got back to the car, Doherty asked Millie if she'd like him to take her home.

"Not yet. Why don't we go to your place?"

"My place?"

"Yes, your place. You have a home don't you?"

"Yeah, but it's kind of a mess. You know how bachelors are."

"No, I don't know how bachelors are. But I want you to take me to your place – unless you don't want to."

Doherty drove back to Arctic, turned down Main and parked on Crossen outside of his building. He looked around to make sure there wasn't anyone on the street before he came around to open her door. He then quickly swept Millie into his first floor digs. She stood at the edge of the living room with her coat still on. Doherty quickly pulled down the shades before switching on the lights. Then he did his best to make the place presentable.

Millie looked around. "You weren't kidding when you said your bachelor pad was a mess, were you?"

"Can't say I didn't warn you. Would you like something to eat or drink?"

Millie slipped out of her coat and tossed it across Doherty's easy chair.

"I'm sorry. I should've taken your coat. I don't get much company here. Truth is, I hardly ever get any company."

"Do you have any liquor?"

"Excuse me?"

"I asked if you had any liquor. You know, alcohol."

"I thought you didn't drink."

"Wrong again. I drink. I just don't like to drink in public. I don't find it very ladylike."

"I have a bottle of Jameson; it's Irish whisky."

"I know what Jameson is, Doherty. That would be fine, with water and ice please."

Doherty went into the kitchen and cleaned out two drinking glasses. He returned with them half filled – his neat and hers with water and ice. Millie was checking out his bookshelf.

"You have quite a few books here, Doherty. I didn't take you for a reader."

"What did you take me for?"

Millie shrugged. "I don't know." She sipped her drink. He could tell by the face she made that Millie wasn't used to hard liquor. "What are you reading now?"

"A book called *On the Beach*. It's about the world at the end of an atomic war. Most of it takes place in Australia. That's where the last survivors are, waiting for the radiation from the fall-out to kill them."

"Sounds awfully gruesome."

"It is, but it's kind of interesting too. It's about how people act when they know the end of civilization is near."

"Could you put the radio on?"

"Sure." Doherty switched on his RCA and spun the dial. Some up-tempo rock and roll came on.

"Not that. Something softer please."

"But I thought you liked Elvis and those hep cats?"

Millie smiled. "There's a time and a place for everything."

Doherty moved the dial and found a station that played mellower sounds. Millie sat on the sofa and sipped her drink. Doherty sat down beside her. Dean Martin came on singing "You Belong to Me."

"I'd like to go there sometime, to see the pyramids along the Nile," she said wistfully.

"Me too, I'd even like to see the marketplace in old Algiers and I don't even know where Algiers is." They had a good laugh over that.

"The truth is, Doherty, I feel like I've never been anywhere. I've hardly ever been out of Rhode Island. There's a whole world out there to see and I'm stuck here. At least you've been to Europe."

"Yeah, unfortunately there was a war going on at the time. Made it kind of hard to be a tourist."

"But you went to Paris, didn't you?"

"I went to Paris on leave. The city was nice but the people there were sad, and hungry."

Millie sighed. "I got pregnant when I was seventeen. Gerard was the only boy I'd ever been with. His parents didn't know it when we got married because I wasn't showing yet. I hardly even knew him – and now I never will."

"Did you love him?"

"I don't know. What does a girl know about love when she's that young? I just wanted to get out of my house and Gerard gave me a chance to do that. He was a sweet boy, and now he's gone. Gone for good. Still here, but gone." Millie said sadly.

She then leaned over and kissed Doherty on the mouth. It was a strong kiss, not a friendly peck. He could taste the whiskey on her breath. When he kissed her back he felt something stir inside him. She stood and he stood besides her, thinking she was about to dash out the door. She reached up and put her arms around his neck and drew him to her. They kissed again and their bodies pressed against each other.

"Can we go into the other room?" she asked. Doherty hesitated, not recalling whether he'd made his bed that morning. They went into the bedroom; the bed was partially made so it didn't look uninviting. Doherty switched on the bedside lamp and fluffed up the pillows. Millie then switched it off. They undressed furtively in the dark. She left her slip on. Then they kissed lying on the top of the covers.

"Do you have any safes?" she whispered in his ear. Doherty had bought a box from the PX at Quonset, ones he once hoped to use with Dolores Bradley. Though he knew if Dolores ever slept with him she would've preferred to run the risk of getting herself pregnant and forcing Doherty to marry her.

They made love, eagerly at first and then slowly and with more feeling. Doherty hadn't been to bed with a woman he felt something for in a long time. He was nervous, scared and excited, all at the same time. When they were finished Doherty reached for his cigarettes.

"Please don't," Millie said.

"Why not?"

"It's what they always do in books and in the movies afterwards. I don't want to be your movie."

Doherty hugged Millie as tightly as he could, then they made love again in a way that left him feeling something he'd never felt before. When they were through Millie pulled her slip down and sat on the edge of the bed. He could see her shoulders shaking and knew she was crying.

He wrapped his arms around her from behind and said softly. "Millie, I'm sorry. I shouldn't have. Please don't cry. I'm so sorry."

She turned toward him with tears running down her cheeks. "It's not you. Don't be sorry. It's just. It's just that I'm still too young for my life to be over. For this," she said waving her arm to take in the bedroom. "Not to be able to do this anymore. Oh, Hugh, please," then Millie rested her head on Doherty's shoulder and cried her eyes out.

Doherty didn't know what to say, so he just held Millie St. Jean until her pain passed. She got up and put on her panties. He sat silently in the dark and watched her pull on her stockings and hitch them to her garter belt. She then gathered up the rest of her clothes and retreated to the bathroom. While she was gone Doherty dressed himself. He could hear the water running, and wondered if Millie was trying to wash him out of her hair like the song in *South Pacific*.

When Millie came out she asked Doherty if he'd take her home. They didn't speak on the ride down to Clyde. After Doherty made the last turn as Millie instructed she told him to drop her off a few houses away from her in-laws. She did not want them to see the Chevy or him. She kissed him on the cheek before she slid out of the car. He watched her quickly scurry up the front steps of a neat, white house, three doors down. Once she was safely inside and the porch light was extinguished, he lit a Camel and sat in the car smoking until it burned down to his knuckles.

Doherty was uneasy for the rest of the weekend, not knowing what to make of how his date with Millie ended. He went into the office late Saturday morning and wrote a report on his work at Graziano's Foundry up in Olneyville. Agnes would be in on Monday and she'd type it up so that it would be neat and official looking for their files. He'd also cash the $250 check into his business account when the Centreville Bank opened after the weekend.

Doherty walked up to the Arctic News for lunch but there was a line for seats at the counter so he decided to come back later. When he got outside Willy Legere was just setting up his chair for the day. Doherty stopped for a smoke and a chat. Anything to keep his mind off Millie St. Jean and the previous night.

"Hey, Willy, how's the boy?"

"Oh, Mr. Doherty, I didn't hear you come up the street."

"I didn't. I was inside the News hoping to get a bite, but it's too crowded down there."

"You know how it is on Saturdays. All the housewives are in town doin' their shoppin'. Usually makes it a pretty good day for me though. So whaddya think of the Series so far."

"To tell you the truth, Willy, I haven't been following it. I was up in Providence on a job all week."

"Then you missed it, Mr. D. The Braves are up two games to none. They won both games out in Milwaukee. Spahn went ten to win the first and the Braves shellacked Turley in the second. He dint even get outta the first inning. Looks like it's gonna be a repeat of last year."

"I tell you what, Willy. I'll bet you five bucks against two packs of pencils that the Yanks still pull it out."

"Ah, go on. No way they can win it now. They don't have no pitchin' left. Me bettin' against your five would be like takin' candy from a baby."

Doherty found Willy's enthusiasm for the old Boston team endearing. "OK, Willy. I tell you what. I'll put my fin up against two packs of pencils, and you throw in one of those little American flags too. That's only fair, since you already got me two games to zip."

Willy stuck his hand out into the air in front of him. Doherty stepped around and shook it. "You're on, Mr. D.," the blind vet said.

Doherty walked down toward Main. He passed by Francine's and was going to stop in to see Millie, then decided against it. It was Saturday and the little shop would be packed with women. He continued on to St. Onge's Men's Store where he hoped to buy a couple of ties. He wanted to check out some new dress shoes too because his cordovans hadn't recovered from the saltwater they picked up on his trek down to Oakland Beach. Unfortunately, the shoe department was overrun with school kids and their mothers looking at the Buster Brown's.

The big stand-up poster at the entrance to the shoe department showed Buster Brown in his famous Dutch boy red hat and suit with the big blue ribbon around his neck. Next to him was his boxer dog Tige. The banner read: "That's my dog Tige, he lives in a shoe. I'm Buster Brown. Look for me in there too." Buster Brown shoes all had the same image of the boy and his dog embedded on the inner sole.

Doherty strolled over to the tie racks and picked out a dark blue print one and a brown striped one. Though his buddy Ed Nunan was working the counter, he was too busy today to chew the fat. Doherty peeled off a couple of singles to pay for the ties and Ed put them and the sales slip into the pneumatic tube system that the store had recently installed. The money would be sent to some central location where it would be deposited and then the change would be sent back with a receipt via the same tube. The system was a big hit with customers when it was first put in. Doherty thought it was just a gimmick used to attract the curious. It had increased St. Onge's business, though salesmen like Ed thought it was installed because the store's management didn't trust the help.

On his way back to the office, against his better judgment, Doherty did stop in at Francine's. It was very crowded and as soon as Mendelson saw him he made a beeline in his direction. Doherty greeted the little man in a friendly fashion. Millie's boss simply said that there were too many customers and she could not see him now. Doherty would have understood given the amount of traffic in the store, but there was something about the way Mendelson said it that made Doherty think the message had more to it than that she was busy.

Feeling confused Doherty went back to the office to smoke and listen to the ball game. He might've gone down to the barbershop to chat with Bill Fiore except that Harry's would be busy like every place else in town. Saturday was when all the mill workers got their hair cut and even worse, brought their kids in. Meanwhile at Yankee Stadium, the New Yorkers shut out the Braves

4-0 in game three. Don Larsen, who'd pitched a perfect game in the Series two years ago, was strong all afternoon and Hank Bauer drove in the Yankee runs with a single and a home run. Doherty was sure Willy Legere wouldn't sleep well tonight, worried about his beloved Braves. Doherty wondered if the blind man could still see things in his dreams.

It was drizzling Sunday morning when Doherty woke up. He trudged across the street to Lambert's Drug Store to get a pack of smokes and the Sunday *Journal-Bulletin*. Lambert's was one of the few operations open in West Warwick on Sunday morning. It was ostensibly a drug store and soda fountain, though the shady characters who blew in and out of Lambert's backroom all day indicated that the place doubled as a bookie joint. Still, Bill Lambert, a large, hearty fellow who always wore suspenders to hold up his pants, was nice to the neighborhood kids who came in to buy comic books, penny candy and the occasional cabinet. Sometimes, if one of the youngsters came up short on coin, Lambert would give him candy on the house.

Back in his apartment Doherty rustled up some bacon and eggs and threw down three cups of coffee, all the while scanning the Sunday news. Most of the sports pages were taken up with stories about the World Series, while the news pages were all about the upcoming state election. The only other story to garnered any significant print was the one about the government's investigations into the quiz show scandals that were unfolding in Washington.

Since Doherty didn't have a TV, he hadn't gotten caught up in the hoopla around the popular TV quiz shows that gave away thousands of dollars in prize money to seemingly ordinary Americans with photographic memories. He was aware, however, from seeing their faces on magazine covers, that some of the contestants had captured the imagination of the public. Now, apparently, the whole thing was beginning to unravel like a cheap suit. Several of the losing contestants had come forward to explain that a few of these widely watched shows were rigged right from the get-go. Doherty thought this was some kind of just dessert for people who believed that what was on TV was on the up and up.

After lunch Doherty tuned into the fourth game of the Series. He half listened as the Braves venerable ace Warren Spahn tossed a masterful two hit shutout to give the former Boston team a decisive 3-1 lead in games. The Yanks young leftfielder, a guy named Siebern, lost two balls in the sun, which provided the Braves with all the runs they needed. Even Mel Allen, the Yankee announcer, who was the ultimate hometown shill, expressed some grudging admiration for Spahn's performance. Spahn had been the Braves top pitcher even when they were in Boston. In fact he opened a Hayes Bickford diner named after himself not far from old Braves Field right before the team up and moved to Milwaukee. Doherty suspected it was just a Hayes Bickford again now that the lefty had taken his considerable talents to the Midwest.

When the rain let up Doherty went for a long walk, trying as best he could not to think about Millie and how much he'd enjoyed being with her Friday night. When he got back he took up *On the Beach* again and read until he got to the part where the stiff, unemotional scientist organizes a dangerous auto race in which several drivers are killed. The guy, who was named Osborne, figured that with the world coming to an end why not hit the track as fast as a man-made machine would take him. After all, the entire book was about how modern machinery annihilated human civilization. Through the process of elimination, Osborne ends up winning the very last Australian Grand Prix.

On Monday Doherty arrived at the office earlier than usual. He hadn't slept well so he welcomed the first light of dawn. Agnes strolled in at ten as she did most days when she was on duty. Doherty gave her a brief verbal rundown of what he'd discovered up in Olneyville the previous week. She didn't feel the least bit sorry for Tony Graziano and Doherty didn't try to convince her she should. Maybe infidelity was just a guy thing. He gave her his notes and asked her to type up a report for their files and a receipt to send to Graziano for the $250.

About a half hour later Agnes knocked on Doherty's door to tell him that there was a man to see him. She might have said a *client* though he wasn't sure. Doherty told her to send him in.

The guy was of medium height and had the wide blocky shoulders of a mill worker. He had a good fifteen years on Doherty, but still fashioned one of those close-cropped military cuts that had fallen out of style after the war. He did not have a friendly look on his face. Doherty stood up though he didn't move from behind his desk.

"Good morning. Can I help you?"

"You Doherty, or *associates*?"

"I'm Doherty. What can I do for you?"

"You can stay the hell away from my daughter-in-law, that's what you can do," the guy said, taking a few menacing steps forward. He was tough looking yet soft with age; one good gut punch would easily bend him in half if it came to that. Doherty continued standing with the desk between them. He widened his stance in case he had to make a quick move.

"So, I take it you're not here on business, Mr. …?"

"St. Jean. Gilbert St. Jean. I heard you been runnin' around with my daughter-in-law Millie, and I'm here to tell you to stop it as of right now."

"Do you mind if I ask where you got this information?"

Gilbert St. Jean bit down hard on his lower lip. "Let's just say a little birdie told me."

Doherty rolled this information around his brain for a few seconds. He then strode around the desk and placed himself a few feet in front of his new adversary. He had a couple of inches and a good ten pounds on the older man.

"Let's get something straight between us right off the bat, Mr. St. Jean. Millie and I aren't running around anywhere. Maybe we went on a couple of dates, and the way I see it, that's really none of your business."

St. Jean went to take a step forward then thought better of it as Doherty balled up his fists.

"It is as long as she and her kids are livin' under my roof!"

"So what do you want to do, keep her locked up till she turns into an old lady? Millie's a young girl. Doesn't she deserve to have a life?"

"She's a married woman. Married to my son and …"

"Your son is up at Howard with a smashed up brain. Does that mean Millie has to play nun for the rest of her life?"

This time St. Jean did take that step forward. "Why you sonofabitch!"

Doherty reached out and gently placed his hand of the man's chest. "I wouldn't if I were you. It won't end up nice."

St. Jean backed up and looked around the office. He was embarrassed and didn't know what to say or do next.

"Why don't you have a seat, Gilbert, so we can talk about this like grown men, not like kids out in the schoolyard."

St. Jean slumped into a chair looking defeated. "It not me, it's my wife. If she finds out about you and Millie it'll kill her. Marie thinks our boy's gonna make some kinda miraculous recovery. Everyday she goes down to St. Anthony's to light a candle for him. She won't listen to anythin' the doctors say. She's convinced he's just gonna wake up one day."

"And you, what do you think?"

Gilbert St. Jean lowered his head and shook it. Through a strained voice he said, "I know he's not comin' back – not now, not ever. But I'm his father; he's the only boy I got."

Doherty pulled out his cigarettes and offered one to St. Jean. He took it and Doherty lit them both.

"Look, Gilbert, I'm not a bad guy, and I have a lot of respect for Millie. She's in a tough spot. The law might give her a divorce, but you and I know the church never will. Besides she lives with you and your wife and she appreciates all you've done for her and your grandkids. I don't want to do anything to mess that up. But, you see, I like Millie, and I know the more I see her, the more I'm going to like her."

Millie's father-in-law was at a loss. Finally he said, "The easiest thing would be for you to break it off. But sooner or later there'll be some other guy. And maybe that guy won't be so considerate. Maybe he'll be the kinda guy that uses women. Don't get me wrong, I know Millie's got a good head on her shoulders, but she's awful lonesome. There're a lotta guys in this town who'd take advantage of that."

"So where do we go from here?"

St. Jean shook his head. "I dunno. But whatever you two do, my wife can't find out about it. I don't even wanna think about what would happen if Marie found out Millie was seein' some guy. Best thing would be if you and Millie saw each other on the QT for now."

Doherty had been leaning against his desk. He now stood and offered St. Jean his hand. "I appreciate that, Gilbert. And I promise I will treat your daughter-in-law with the utmost respect. But that's all I can promise you."

St. Jean stood and took Doherty's hand. "Yeah, okay."

Doherty breezed through the outer office telling Agnes that he'd be back in a while. Within minutes he was at Democratic headquarters. The door at the top of the stairs was locked so Doherty pounded on it. He heard people moving around inside so he continued to hit the door. It opened a crack and

Rene Desjardins peered out at him over his mustache. Doherty tried to push his way in despite Desjardins' attempt to block his entrance.

"Sorry, Mr. Private Eye, but the boss is busy right now."

"I don't give a shit what he's doing. I want to see the Judge, and I want to see him now!"

Doherty tried to push by the bigger man again. This time Desjardins stepped outside and slammed Doherty up against the wall of the little hallway at the top of the stairs. Doherty lowered his stance and hit the Judge's flunky with a solid left hook to his midsection. The big Canuck folded over, the wind knocked out of him. When he did Doherty hit him flush on the jaw with his right fist. Desjardins tumbled past Doherty and fell down the staircase. Suddenly there was a commotion in the big room and a rush of people to the door. The Judge stood safely in the rear with Angel Tuohy beside him.

"What the hell is going on here, Doherty?" the Judge shouted above the heads of his staff people. Doherty stood his ground though his shirttail was now hanging out of his pants and his tie was askew. He eased his way through the others toward Judge DeCenza. When he got close, Tuohy pulled his jacket back far enough for Doherty to see that he was packing a revolver in a shoulder holster.

"Looks like your boy Rene accidentally fell down the stairs, Judge."

"What is the meaning of this unwarranted intrusion? We're having a private meeting here and you barge in like some kind of street corner thug. I won't have that here. Not at party headquarters."

The others were murmuring now. DeCenza turned his attention toward them.

"Why don't you all go back to work while Mr. Doherty and I go into my office to have a civil conversation. That is if Mr. Doherty is capable of civility."

The Judge escorted Doherty into his back office. This time Tuohy accompanied them and stayed close by.

DeCenza sat down behind his desk. His face was still beet red.

"Angel, tell Lillian to see to Rene, will you please." Tuohy stuck his head out and called out some instructions to a woman who was flitting around the big room like a bumblebee. Tuohy, however, was not about to leave the Judge alone with Doherty – not after what happened at the stairs.

"What exactly is the problem that caused you to burst in here like gangbusters?"

Doherty tried to calm himself. "I just had a visit from Gilbert St. Jean."

The Judge shook his head. "Gilbert St. Jean? Doesn't ring a bell."

"Don't play dumb with me, Judge. Nothing goes on in this town without you knowing about it. And there isn't a person in West Warwick of voting age that you don't know."

"Oh, that Gilbert St. Jean," the Judge said coyly. "I believe he's the father-in-law of your friend Millie St. Jean, is he not?"

"I'm not as stupid as you might think, Judge. I know it was you or one of your flunkies who told him that I was seeing his daughter-in-law; the same daughter-in-law that's suppose to be pining away for her brain dead husband."

"Ah, yes, the young man that's institutionalized up at Howard." The Judge leaned back in his chair. The blood had drained from his face and he'd returned to being the calm, commanding presence he usually was. "A very sad story, for that to happen to such a healthy young man," he said shaking his head in sympathy. "Though I suppose you saw a lot of that in the war, didn't you, Mr. Doherty?"

Doherty didn't answer. He was trying to dope out what the Judge's intentions were.

"Yet now I hear that you're squiring his young wife around. Do you think that's the decent thing to do under the circumstances? With all the fish in the sea and you choose to hook one that's already married. I wonder what the Monsignor would think of that? It certainly would be most embarrassing if young Mrs. St. Jean were denied communion at St. Anthony's this Sunday, in front of her children and her husband's parents."

"You bastard!" Doherty blurted out. Tuohy instinctively took a step closer to his chair.

"Calm down, Mr. Doherty. First, you rudely push your way into my office and now you wish to bite the very hand that feeds you. Did I not just give you five hundred dollars for one short car trip down to South County? And then, did I not send you up to Providence for a job that netted you what – two hundred fifty dollars for two days work? From my position it looks like I'm your chief benefactor."

"I thought those jobs had no strings attached to them?"

The Judge smiled though it was not a benign grin. "Everything in life has strings attached to it and it's about time you learned that."

"I still don't understand why you had to stick your big fucking nose into my personal life as well."

"Please, Mr. Doherty, you know I don't like the use of that kind of language in this office. After all this is Democratic Party headquarters; this is where the people's business is conducted. That is what I do, conduct the people's business, and I intend to keep on doing it for a good long time. And as for you and your little private detective operation, where you eschew all things political because you don't want to get your hands dirty." Judge DeCenza now leaned forward to emphasize his next point. "All I have to do is say word one and you will never get another client in this state. Do I make myself clear?"

Doherty abruptly stood to leave. "Clear as a bell, Judge. But if I were you, I'd still be careful where I stepped. Even those fifty dollar wing tips you wear step in shit sometimes."

It wasn't until Tuesday morning that Doherty learned that the Yankees had taken game five in the series 5-0. Apparently "Bullet Bob" Turley, one of the Yank's aces, had regained his season long form and shut down the Braves to cut their series lead to 3-2. Still, with a day off for travel, the games would return to Milwaukee where the Yanks had to contend with Spahn again, and if they survived that, with Lou Burdette in a seventh game. Burdette had won three games over the Yankees in the series the previous year and was awarded the fancy sports car they gave to the MVP. Under normal circumstances Doherty might've been more excited about his bet with Willy Legere, but his visit with the Judge had left a bad taste in his mouth. He also knew he'd have to spend the next few weeks constantly looking over his shoulder for Rene Desjardins.

It rained hard that day so Doherty drove the Chevy into town. He'd called Packy's on Friday and rented the car for another week at the same rate. Agnes wasn't in on Tuesday so when the phone rang a little after eleven he had to answer it himself. It was a guy named George Donniger, who ran a custom jewelry design business in Pawtucket. Tony Graziano had referred Doherty to him. In a nutshell he told Doherty that he thought his shop foreman was stealing some of his design ideas and selling them to Ginolfi, one of the big costume jewelry outfits in Providence. He wanted to hire Doherty to see if this were the case. Doherty quoted him his standard fee and agreed to drive up to Pawtucket the next day. Before he hung up, Doherty asked Donniger if a Judge Martin DeCenza or anyone else besides Graziano had given him Doherty's number. The guy seemed perplexed by the question, but said the only person he'd spoken to was Graziano.

After lunch Doherty dropped down to Harry's to share a smoke with Bill and to give the barber an abridged version of what had transpired between him and DeCenza.

"Damn, Huey. You do not want to get on the wrong side of the Judge. That man's got the power to squash you like a bug. Maybe not physically, but professionally anyway," Bill said.

"What's a fella to do, Bill? I can't sit by and let him ruin Millie St. Jean's life. I just can't figure out what his game is."

"If you ask me, it's all about control. He gets you a couple of jobs and you start feelin' like you're on Easy Street. The next thing you know, he's got you by the short hairs. Maybe he's still pissed off 'cause you wouldn't play crooked when you were a cop."

"I don't know. I just got a call from a guy in Pawtucket who wants to hire me for some industrial snooping and all I can think of: Is DeCenza's behind this? How am I going to do my job if that's the first thought that comes into my head every time I get a new client?"

Bill stuffed out his cigarette. "I gotta get back to work. It seems to me you got an even bigger problem, my friend."

"Yeah, what's that?"

"Rene Desjardins. The word around town is that he's one mean son–of–a-bitch. You better keep your eyes peeled for him."

Doherty went back up to the office yet had trouble keeping his head straight. He wanted to see Millie but knew that Tuesday was the day she went up to Howard to see her husband. At six he shut things down and drove home. Once there, he shoveled a can of Chef Boyardee spaghetti and meatballs into a pot and lit the gas under it. When it was ready he gobbled it down with a couple of 'Gansetts while reading the afternoon *Bulletin*. The front-page story about the gubernatorial race indicated that the rematch between Roberts and Del Sesto would turn on the vote in Kent County. Since both candidates were from Providence they'd probably split the city vote, with Roberts carrying most of the Irish and some of the Italians, while Del Sesto would get the support of those Italians who would hold their noses and vote Republican.

The other big news story was how congressional investigators were circling the quiz show scandals like sharks smelling blood in the water. The person they most wanted to fess up was a guy named Charles Van Doren, who won a chunk of change on a show called *Twenty-One*. Doherty remembered seeing Van Doren's puss on the cover of *Life* about a year ago. Back then they were shopping him as America's smartest and most eligible bachelor. Now everyone wanted him to admit to being a cheat and a liar. What a great country.

As Doherty read the paper he could hear that the rain had picked up outside. He thought about flipping on the radio to drown it out then began to appreciate its rhythmic beat. Sometime after seven there was a knock on the door. He must have been dozing because the sound startled him. No one ever came to Doherty's apartment so his first thought was that it was Rene Desjardins looking for some payback. Doherty grabbed the Louisville slugger he still kept in his bedroom from his baseball days at Quonset. When he got to the door instead of asking who was there, he flung it open with some force, hoping to catch the unwanted visitor by surprise. Millie St. Jean was standing in the doorway, dripping wet. They looked at each other for a few seconds and then she burst into his arms. Doherty wrapped her up with his left as his right was still holding the baseball bat.

"God Millie, you look a sight. Come in and dry yourself off." The rain had soaked through Millie's coat so that even her dress was damp. "What're you doing here, anyway?"

"I had to see you. After what my father-in-law said to me, I just had to see you."

"Let's get you out of these wet clothes first. How did you get here?"

"I walked from the center. I didn't have an umbrella and it started to rain awfully hard." Doherty ushered Millie into his bedroom and handed her a robe to put on. It was a little threadbare but better than what she was wearing. Without shame she stripped off her dress in front of him. Doherty turned to leave.

She looked up at him and said, "Please don't go." Millie was standing in her bare feet wearing only her slip and undergarments. Doherty came to her and took her in his arms and they kissed as if they hadn't seen each other in years.

Later when they were lying under the sheets naked, Millie propped herself up on her elbow and looked at Doherty with a teasing smirk. "I have a confession to make," she said. Doherty steeled himself for the worst. "I'm not really a blond."

Doherty laughed. "Yeah I noticed that the drapes didn't match the carpet."

"Where'd you get that lovely expression from?"

"Just another pearl of wisdom I learned while serving Uncle Sam."

"I get my hair dyed at the Magic Mirror every two weeks."

"While we're in the mood for confessions, will you tell me what your father-in-law said?"

Millie reached out with her free hand and took Doherty's head and kissed him deeply. Then she leaned back and said, "He told me he went to your office and tried to get you to stop seeing me. He said he liked you, but that there were people in town who could hurt us both if we continued to do this."

Doherty reached over for his cigarettes and lit one. Millie asked if she could have one too, which threw Doherty for a loop. He was even more surprised that once she was lit she actually inhaled. "So is smoking like drinking for you – something you only do in private?"

"I try not to smoke if I can help it, especially when I'm around the boys. But sometimes I have to when I'm upset. I usually prefer the ones with filters."

"What is it that you're so upset about? Is it because your father-in-law came to see me?"

Millie nodded her head. "That's part of it. But I'm also upset because today when I went to visit with Gerard, all I could think about was you. You and me together like this."

"That doesn't make you a bad person. Maybe by seeing Gerard you realized again what's been missing from your life."

Millie wrapped her arms around Doherty's neck. "Oh, I'm so scared." She hugged him tightly and he hugged her back.

"What are you scared of, Millie?"

"I don't know. Everything. Two weeks ago my life was all set, not happy, but set. I had my job, my kids. I was living with my in-laws, spending my nights watching TV with the family. Then I have a short conversation with a total stranger in a barbershop of all places, and now everything is upside down. What are we going to do, Doherty?"

"We could do some more of this if you'd like, " he said as he stubbed out his cigarette.

"I don't want to bring trouble into your life."

"Nor me into yours. But I don't want to stop seeing you either. We can get through this, Millie, if we stick together. I mean how can something that feels this good be wrong?"

Afterwards Millie got out of bed, no longer ashamed to show herself naked in front of him. Doherty noticed that she was a little wide in the hips, which kind of pleased him. She dressed slowly and casually, no longer needing to hide in the bathroom or turn the light off. Doherty rose too and threw on a pair of khakis and a tee shirt.

"Your father-in-law was worried that his wife might find out about us. I think we should try to keep this from her for now, okay?"

Millie agreed. "I guess that makes you my secret lover, like in the song."

"Unfortunately, not secret enough. There are some people in this town that are trying to use this against me, but I'm not going to let that happen. And I'm not going to let anyone hurt you."

"It's all right, Doherty. I'm a big girl. I've already been hurt about as much as a woman my age can be. I don't care what happens as long as my boys are protected and I can continue to see you. This is the first time in years I've felt like I have got another chance at life, and I'm not going to let it get away."

Doherty drove Millie to her in-laws house in Clyde. As he'd done before he dropped her a few doors down and waited until she was safely inside. He didn't know what story she'd spin for them, yet for the first time since they'd met he felt that he and Millie could handle anything that came their way.

Chapter Six

GEORGE DONNIGER

George Donniger's operation was located near the historic Old Slater Mill by the Seekonk River in Pawtucket. By his own account he ran a small, classy jewelry design business. Most of his clients were either rich nabobs who lived on the East Side of Providence, connected guys from Federal Hill who had money to throw around, or out-of-towners who bought on his rep alone. Donniger explained to Doherty that he had learned his skills while studying jewelry making at RISD.

"I didn't know they had such a program at the School of Design," Doherty said.

Donniger smiled. "I know, it sounds a little femmy, but you got to remember Providence is still one of the jewelry capitals of America. Most of it's costume stuff these days, though I do sell a lot of my designs to the big houses in New York like Tiffany and Cartier.

"I bet those folks are good for a lot of dough."

"Sometimes. But like everything else in the fashion business, one year you're hot and the next year they've moved on to someone new."

"That doesn't tell me what your problem is with your foreman."

Donniger was very tall yet agile for a big man who moved around his office easily. He wore his dark hair longer than was fashionable and his clothes were clearly expensive yet understated. While Doherty waited patiently Donniger dragged out a couple of large books containing photos of his designs.

He flipped open to a page that showed a bracelet and earring set – mostly gold studded with diamonds.

"This is one of my most recent signature designs. It would sell for two, maybe three thousand in New York."

"So?"

"I believe my back stabbing foreman sold this design to Ginolfi so they could make some costume jewelry knockoff with cubic zirconium or maybe even rhinestones instead of diamonds. You know what that's like? That's like painting a mustache on the Mona Lisa." Donniger hesitated a moment and looked quizzically at Doherty.

"I know what the Mona Lisa is," Doherty said. "I saw it at the Louvre in Paris when I was there in '45. Look, I understand your feelings are hurt, Mr. Donniger. First I need to ask if you've patented these designs?"

"Of course, I have," he replied indignantly. "And my patent attorneys, both in Providence *and* in New York, have the papers on all my designs. We're talking about my livelihood here, Mr. Doherty."

"Okay, then I suggest we devise a plan to ensnare your turncoat foreman and the Ginolfi Corporation. But you should keep something else in mind: Ginolfi is a big operation with thousands of dollars at their disposal to fight something like this. They could tie you up in court for a long time. Meanwhile, their cheap knockoffs of your stuff would be out on the street the whole time."

Donniger smiled at Doherty's last comment. "Let me assure you, Mr. Doherty, I am not without resources of my own. This may look like a small operation from the outside, but some of my clients are extremely well-heeled people. If something like this were to go public it could cause Ginolfi a great deal of embarrassment – embarrassment they can ill afford. I have a feeling that just the whiff of a lawsuit will make them back off."

"Well, let's hope so."

George Donniger and Doherty spent the balance of the day devising a strategy to unmask the foreman's betrayal. Once Donniger had briefed Doherty on how the design-to-production process worked, they agreed that Doherty would be introduced to Ginolfi as a broker for Donniger and Co. Since Doherty knew little or nothing about design, they thought it would be best if he approached the costume jewelry outfit merely as a middleman hired by Donniger to sell them several of his latest designs.

Donniger knew the people in Ginolfi's design department would be aware of his reputation and skeptical at first of his desire to sell his original designs to a costume jewelry manufacturer. The cover story would be that Donniger was in financial straits and needed a quick infusion of cash. He explained that it was not uncommon for custom designers to sell some of their work to costume manufacturers to supplement their often-unpredictable cash flow. Doherty would approach Ginolfi with five of Donniger's designs – three the designer didn't really care about and the two he suspected his foreman had already dealt to Ginolfi for a tidy sum.

Once back in West Warwick Doherty stopped at the Clyde Press to have a half dozen business cards printed indicating that he was a jewelry broker. He decided to use his own address and phone number on the cards to minimize the potential for any charges of deception. The extra sawbuck he slipped the printer at Clyde insured that the cards would be ready by the next afternoon.

Later, sitting at his desk Doherty studied the designs Donniger had given him and the descriptive material that came with them. He thought this would provide him with enough expertise for his meeting with Ginolfi's design staff. In the meantime Donniger phoned the big outfit and set up a time for Doherty go up there on Thursday morning. Although he'd quoted Donniger his usual fee, the designer insisted upon paying him three hundred dollars for his efforts and hinted there might be a bonus at the end if Ginolfi came to a quick settlement with his company.

When Doherty got to the office he clued Agnes in on the deal. He let her know that someone might call asking for him as a jewelry broker and that she should just play along. He left out most of the other details. She was puzzled yet agreed to do as she was instructed once Doherty indicated that there might be something in it for her sweeter than his sister's Christmas candies.

On Wednesday the Yankees evened the Series by beating the Braves in ten innings. Despite a valiant effort, Spahn was unable to close out the game and get his third win as his teammate Burdette had done the year before. Turley came in to relieve in the tenth and got the last out with a Braves runner on third. Doherty didn't think Willy Legere would sleep well that night.

Along with Coro and Trifari, Ginolfi was one of the largest costume jewelry operations in Rhode Island, if not in the country. They'd been in business since 1910. An Italian immigrant named Francisco Ginolfi and his uncle began the company. The uncle dropped out of the equation early on and Ginolfi and Ginolfi simply became Ginolfi. Later the family picked up a few partners and for a while it was something called GPK, the initials representing whom the others were. Then it reverted back to GINOLFI, all capitals with a crown over the G. It has remained that way since before the war.

Doherty had to admit he was a little nervous entering the meeting room until he saw who his counterparts were on the other side of the table. One was a guy in his late thirties with a ruddy complexion and an open collared shirt that allowed too much of his dark chest hair to show. The other was younger and wore an ill-fitting suit and thick horn-rimmed glasses. They introduced themselves all around and Doherty doled out his business cards just so the rush job from Clyde Press wouldn't be wasted. The one with the chest hair was named DeSalvo, the other Bertrand.

After some preliminary chitchat about the weather, Doherty pulled out Donniger's design books and began to flip through the pages of one.

DeSalvo reached across the table and put his hand on the book to stop Doherty's search. "Before we get started here, I think Teddy and I would like to ask you why somebody with Donniger's reputation is looking to sell his designs to Ginolfi? Far as we know he's like a top shelf designer and we aren't exactly Tiffany's."

Doherty leaned back in his chair and took in the two design buyers; they were easily not the classiest guys in town. As he and Donniger rehearsed, Doherty took his time letting the two men stew a little.

"Well, it's like this: Mr. Donniger's has a big show coming up in New York right before the Christmas season, and to be honest with you, money is kind of tight right now. He figures if he can sell a few of his lesser designs to you folks, that would help him raise the cash he needs for New York."

DeSalvo and Bertrand consulted with each other and agreed that Doherty's explanation held water. They knew from previous experience it wasn't uncommon for custom designers to take this route on occasion.

Bertrand now spoke. His voice was surprisingly high-pitched. "That sounds reasonable to us. Why don't you show us what Mr. Donniger has to offer?"

Doherty immediately flipped to the page showing a bracelet–necklace combo that Donniger was more than willing to part with. The Ginolfi men gazed hungrily at the design. Bertrand made some notes on a pad. Doherty could tell they were hooked.

DeSalvo looked up smiling. "What else you got for sale?"

Doherty turned to a decorative pin design that Donniger was hoping to pawn off on these sharks. After carefully perusing it they decided they liked that one as well and wrote down the design style and number. Then Doherty turned to the bracelet and earring set that Donniger suspected his foreman had already pedaled to Ginolfi. They were very distinctive with beautiful diamonds placed against gold settings. Bertrand looked closely at the designs, even raising his glasses to get a better view of them. He then flashed a glance at De Salvo that someone not in Doherty's business might've missed.

"I think we'll pass on this one," Bertrand said very precisely.

Doherty continued his presentation though he knew that the two buyers had shown their hand. The fourth piece was a pin and earring set that Donniger himself had characterized as a 'piece of junk.' Again the two buyers nodded their heads and wrote down the particulars. Then Doherty flipped to the highlight of the presentation, a necklace that would have dazzled even a casual observer. It was a piece Donniger told him with the appropriate jewels would sell for ten grand in New York or London. Looking at this photo the Ginolfi boys seemed visibly nervous. Apparently Donniger's foreman had let his greed get the better of him. Instead of pitching Donniger's mid-range designs to Ginolfi, he'd mistakenly gone to the top of the class.

"We're interested in the first two and the fourth design you showed us, not the other two," Bertrand said, this time in a voice that was a little shaky.

Doherty leaned back in his chair again and patiently surveyed the men on the other side of the table. He detected some apparent discomfort. "That's very interesting," he said, choosing not to add anything else.

Finally DeSalvo spoke, "Yeah, why's that?"

"Well, to begin with, the designs you rejected are two of Mr. Donniger's best and most distinctive pieces."

"We could see that, but hey, we're not exactly in the fine jewelry trade here," DeSalvo said. "Ginolfi's is a costume jewelry operation, it doesn't sell that haute design stuff." He pronounced the French word as 'hoot.'

"You didn't give me a chance to get to my next point. We happen to know that Mr. Donniger's foreman already sold you those other two designs a few weeks ago. Designs, I might add, Mr. Donniger has airtight patents on. In other words, if Ginolfi were to manufacture costume knockoffs of those two pieces you could be criminally charged with patent violation and possibly with receiving stolen property. Add to that the scandal Ginolfi would face when Mr. Donniger files a lawsuit against your company."

DeSalvo clenched his fists and placed them on the table. Meanwhile Bertrand was feverishly cleaning his glasses.

"What are you, some kinda cop?" the former asked.

"No, I'm a private investigator hired by Mr. Donniger. My client has no desire to get into a pissing contest with Ginolfi. As far as he's concerned, you're in two different businesses … and he would like it to stay that way. For that reason he is prepared to offer you a deal."

DeSalvo was boiling now, "Look wiseguy we don't have to make any deal." Bertrand reached across and placed a hand over his partner's outstretched arm.

"Calm down, Ralph. Let's hear what Mr. Doherty has to offer."

"My client is prepared to sell you the three designs you chose from the catalogs at a reasonable price in exchange for you formally agreeing, in writing, of course, to name the person who pitched you the other two designs. This agreement would also have to be attested to by a lawyer."

"That's all he wants?" Bertrand asked.

"Not entirely. He also wants you to relinquish any claim you have on the two designs you obtained in a less than legal fashion and an assurance that Ginolfi will never produce any items even remotely resembling them without Mr. Donniger's permission."

"And if we don't agree?" DeSalvo said, again trying to sound tough while holding a pair of deuces.

"Then Mr. Donniger will be forced to have some of his high end clients weigh in on his behalf. They will contact your superiors at this company and I have no doubt that would result in the two of you getting your asses fired. You might even face criminal prosecution as well."

Bertrand and DeSalvo looked at each other and then Bertrand spoke, "Have Donniger's lawyer put this agreement in writing and in the meantime we'll stop all production on our versions of these items as soon as this meeting is over. If at all possible, we would prefer that this arrangement remain be-tween the three of us and Mr. Donniger."

Doherty stood up and reached out his hand. "Gentlemen, it's been a pleasure doing business with you. I'll make sure Mr. Donniger takes all the appropriate steps as soon as possible." Both men reluctantly shook Doherty's hand.

Chapter Seven

BERNARD PRESSMAN

Doherty stopped off at the Centreville Bank Friday morning and deposited some of the cash Donniger had slipped him when he reported back from his meeting with the Ginolfi's reps. He knew Donniger would fire his foreman and do all he could to insure the guy never worked again for a jewelry outfit in Rhode Island. In time he would turn the screws on Ginolfi as well.

He picked up a coffee at the Donut Kettle and a copy of the *Journal* on his way back to the office. Just as he'd anticipated, the Yankees beat the Braves 6-2 to close out the Series in Milwaukee. Turley relieved Larsen in the third inning and finished out the game for the second day in a row. For his efforts "Bullet Bob" was given the brand new Corvette as the series MVP. Willy Legere hadn't set up in front of the Arctic News yet so Doherty would have to wait to collect on his bet.

As he was climbing the darkened stairway to his office Doherty heard some stirring at the top. He immediately thought of Rene Desjardins and readied himself for a fight. Instead he discovered an elderly woman cowering at the dark landing. He unlocked the office door and invited her inside where he quickly flipped on the lights.

"Are you Mr. Doherty? " she asked in a soft voice as Doherty cranked open a window to ventilate the airless space.

"Yes, I am. And you are?"

"My name is Eunice Pressman. I asked about you around town. They say you specialize in finding lost people."

"Why don't we go into my office and talk about your situation," he said, escorting the elderly woman into his backroom.

Doherty cracked the window and switched on his desk lamp. Eunice Pressman sat in a chair across from him clutching her purse to her chest. She was small boned with gray hair set in a permanent with a touch of blue rinse to it. It clung closely to her head where pink parts of her skull could be seen through her thinning locks. Her face was a road map of wrinkles. Doherty judged her to be somewhere in her mid to late seventies.

"What can I do for you, Mrs. Pressman?"

"It's my husband, Bernie. Bernard. He's missing." She extracted a tissue from her handbag and dabbed at her nose and eyes.

"How long has your husband been gone?"

"Since Wednesday morning."

"Have you contacted the police?"

"Yes, I did - this time. Usually my son-in-law and I can find Bernie. He hardly ever strays outside of our neighborhood or downtown. However, we've looked everywhere and he was not in any of the usual places. I'm worried because he's been gone for two nights now. I'm afraid something terrible might've happened to him." Her eyes began to water and she wiped them with the now sodden tissue.

"From what you've said I assume your husband has wandered off before?"

The woman reluctantly assented. "He's not right in the head anymore. I've tried to watch over him, though sometimes when I go to work or out shopping, he slips away. Most of the time he just goes for walks around the streets near where we live. Last week we found him wandering down by the river in his pajamas. I don't know what to do. He seems to be getting worse."

"What did the police say?"

"Oh, they were very nice. They had me fill out a missing person's report and all. It's just that they won't go out and look for Bernie like Ronnie and I do."

"Ronnie is your son-in-law?"

"Yes. He's married to my daughter Julie. He's a good boy, but I can't always call him away from his job. He works down at Benny's. Will you help me find my husband, Mr. Doherty?"

"Do you want to hire me officially, Mrs. Pressman?"

"Oh yes, of course."

Doherty pulled out one of his standard forms and handed it to the elderly woman.

"You need to read and sign this. I charge thirty dollars a day plus expenses. I don't anticipate there'll be any expenses since your husband probably hasn't left town."

The woman took a pair of reading glasses out of her bag and read the form carefully and then signed it. "I can write you a check now if you'd like."

"We can settle up later, after I find your husband. Before I get started you'll have to give me a little information about him."

"Well, Bernard was a lawyer. He had a private practice with another man in Providence for over forty years. He had to give up the practice when his partner died and Bernie's memory began to fail him. That's not so good if you're a lawyer you know. It was very sad. He's been retired for three years now and his condition has just gotten worse."

"Do you think he's suffering from dementia?"

"Yes, of course he is. I didn't want to admit it at first. I mean he was always a little forgetful. But when he started going for walks and couldn't find his way home we became very concerned."

"Are there any special places he likes to go or special interests he has?"

"He loves ice cream. Ronnie and I would sometimes find him at the Candy Kitchen or at Central Ice Cream. A few times he went out and got ice cream and didn't have any money to pay for it. It was quite embarrassing. The people in the shops were very nice about it. Ronnie would have to take care of the unpaid bill. And he'd always give them something extra for their trouble."

"Any other interests?"

"Bernie loves football. He watches the college games every Saturday and the Giants games on the TV every Sunday. Bernie played football at Dartmouth when he was a student there. When we were younger we would go to the high school games together all the time. I didn't much care for them but I would humor him because I knew how much he enjoyed watching the boys play. He'd give me a running commentary of everything that was going on on the field. We haven't gone in a few years now. Otherwise his only other interest is watching television. He loves that "I Love Lucy" show; it's his favorite." At this point Mrs. Pressman began to sob more openly. Doherty handed her his handkerchief and waited patiently.

"Look, Mrs. Pressman. I will do my best to find your husband. After I do you'll have to make some decisions about the future. Sounds like you may not be able to take care of him anymore. Have you thought about putting him in a nursing home?"

The woman shook her head and dabbed at her nose with Doherty's handkerchief. "I know, I know. That's what my daughter keeps telling me, but he's my husband. We've been married for fifty-two years. Are you married, Mr. Doherty?"

"No, can't say that I am."

"Then you don't know what it's like. Bernie's been my best friend my whole adult life. It's so hard to see him like this."

"I know Mrs. Pressman, and I'm very sorry. I'll find your husband, but after I do you and your family will have to deal with his condition. You know it's not going to get any better." The client rose as if to leave. She handed back Doherty's wet nose rag.

"One other thing: Do you have a recent picture of your husband?"

The woman rifled through her purse. "Here, this is similar to the one I gave to the police. It's from a few years ago. He looks pretty much the same, except that his hair is a little whiter now. It was taken in front of the building where his law office was about a year before he closed his practice."

"And how can I reach you?"

"My home number is on the contract and I work in the afternoon at Woolworth's three days a week, Monday, Wednesday and Friday. At the cosmetics counter." Doherty rose and showed the woman to the door. By now Agnes was at her desk in the outer office, talking loudly on the phone to one of her girlfriends. Doherty interrupted and introduced Mrs. Pressman to his secretary.

When he returned to his office Agnes popped her head in.

"What was that all about, boss?"

"Missing husband."

"Phew, at that age? What he'd do, run off with some gal he met at the senior center?"

"Nothing so glamorous. Sounds like the old guy's got dementia. Wanders off and can't find his way back home. Pretty sad situation. They've been married fifty-two years and she's trying to take care of him yet can't seem to manage it anymore."

Agnes shook her head, even though old age was still a far off concept to her. "How'd things go up in Pawtucket?"

"Great. I closed the case much to the satisfaction of the client. A good payday with possibly more to come. I'll give you the report to type up later. In the meantime here's the deposit slip for the money I put in the bank this morning. Looks like we'll be in the chips for a while. That means you'll get paid this week."

"I told you boss, you don't have to worry 'bout me. I got confidence in Doherty and Associates."

"Let's just take it one week at a time. Right now I'm going to see if I can scare up something on the old guy who's lost. Man the fort while I'm out."

Doherty's first stop was the Sweet Shop. He flashed Pressman's picture, but no one on the counter had seen him there in weeks. He next stopped at the Candy Kitchen where he chatted with Pete Perakis about the weather and the World Series. When he showed Perakis Pressman's picture he told Doherty that the old man had been in last week, eaten a hot fudge sundae and afterwards admitted he didn't have any money to pay for it. Pete said Pressman looked disheveled; he'd been in several times before and there'd never been any trouble. Later that day, Perakis said, Pressman's son-in-law came by to settle the old man's tab. The kid slipped Perakis two extra bucks for the inconvenience. The son-in-law also suggested that Pete and his help not serve the old man in the future unless he paid up front. Perakis was apologetic. Doherty brushed it aside, telling him he understood the situation.

He passed by the Arctic News where there was still no sign of Willy. He then stopped in at Smith Drugs further up Washington. It was famous for its soda fountain, which served the best cabinets in town. No one there had seen Pressman in weeks though he was well known at the counter. He next tried Chagnon's without success and then Central Ice Cream. Central was the last place Pressman stiffed on the bill only to be bailed out later by his son-in-law. Otherwise no one'd seen the missing man for a few days.

Doherty sauntered down Main stopping at every store along the way where he knew someone who worked. Most people recognized Pressman yet hadn't seen him lately. Doherty wondered if he would've been better off cruising for the old man in the Chevy.

When he got near Francine's he decided to stop in to say hello to Millie. It was Friday and he realized he hadn't spoken to her in a week. Fortunately when he stuck his head in Mendelson was nowhere to be seen. Millie spotted him right away and quickly scurried over.

"Hey stranger, where've you been?"

"I'm sorry, Millie. I was up in Pawtucket on a case all week. I should've stopped by earlier."

"Shut up, you big lug," she said, playfully punching Doherty in the chest. "Can I see you tonight?"

"Girls night out again?"

She pressed her finger to her lips. "Shh, somebody might hear."

"You want me to pick you up?"

"Why don't I come by your place? I'll be there around seven. I thought I'd bring some food and make you a home cooked meal for a change. In the meantime you can spruce up your bachelor pad."

"That's sounds nice. I'll see you at seven then. Call me at the office if you need anything."

"I think I'll be all right." Millie leaned up and pecked him on the cheek. "See you later, Doherty."

He was practically walking on air by the time he approached Willy Legere at the News. "I hear ya, Mr. Doherty. Come to collect your pound of flesh?"

"Why Willy, did you really read *The Merchant of Venice* in high school?"

"Had to, Mr. D. We all did. They even made us memorize the mercy speech. That Shakespeare was a pretty smart guy wasn't he? Though I gotta admit I dint understand what he was sayin' half the time."

"Ah, but it's the other half that counted."

"Here's your two packs of pencils and your flag," he said handing Doherty his rewards. "Do you believe those damn Yankees? The Braves got 'em three games to one with the last two at home and they still lose the Series."

"Could've been worse, Willy."

"Oh yeah, how's that, Mr. D?"

"They could still be the Boston Braves. Then how would you feel?" When someone else came by to purchase a pencil, Doherty slipped a five spot into Willy's cup.

He grabbed a sandwich and a coffee downstairs at the News and then headed back to the office. Near St. John's Church he passed by a pair of crone-like old nuns shuffling along in their full habits. They were both clinging to long strands of black rosary beads with silver crosses dangling from them. They gave Doherty a disapproving look as they passed by and he returned the favor.

Agnes was out on her lunch break so Doherty spent the time writing up the Donniger report on a pad with one of Willy's number two pencils. When Agnes came back he handed her the summary and asked her to type it up in duplicate. He told her he was going to drop down to Harry's to see if Bill Fiore knew anything about the lost husband of his new client.

The barber was busy with a shave so Doherty climbed onto one of the shoeshine chairs to get his cordovans buffed up. When Bill was finished he plopped into the neighboring chair and lit up a Winston. He had a troubled look on his face and was unresponsive when Doherty tried to engage him in some talk about the World Series.

"We got a problem here, Huey," he said in a grave voice.

"Yeah, what's that Beetle?"

"It's Harry. He told me he doesn't want you hangin' around here no more. Says you can only be in here if you're gettin' a cut, a shave or a shoeshine."

"C'mon Bill. What the hell's that all about? Where's that little prick? I'll give him a piece of my mind."

"Calm down, Huey. It ain't Harry, though he is a little prick. It's the landlord; he told Harry he don't want people just hangin' around the shop any more."

"What about Jukebox? He practically lives here," Doherty said referring to the retarded man who was at Harry's almost every day.

"Well, technically Jukebox works for Harry. He sometimes sweeps up hair from the floor and Harry gives him a buck now and then."

"I still don't follow. What the hell's going on?"

"Turns out Harry's landlord is a cousin of Martin DeCenza, and DeCenza has a hair across his ass about you. I told you to be careful with him. You've gotten on his bad side and there's no tellin' what you'll have to do to get off it."

"Sonofabitch!"

"You got that right. But for now I'm warnin' you, you can't be hangin' 'round here any more. I gotta look out for my job too you know."

Doherty patted Bill on the shoulder. "No problem, buddy. I know it wasn't you. I just have to ask you one thing before I go." He pulled out Pressman's picture. "Ever see this old guy wandering around town." Bill looked at the picture carefully.

"I may've seen him once or twice, but I'll tell you who would know - Jukebox. He walks all over Arctic. I don't think that boy ever sleeps." Bill then called Jukebox over to the shoeshine stand. Jukebox, which was what everyone called him, got his name because he liked to hang by the radio at Harry's and knew the lyrics to all of the songs it played.

Harry preferred singers like Sinatra, Rosemary Clooney, Patti Page, Ella, and stuff like that. And Jukebox sang along with all of their songs. He was probably in his thirties now but had the mind of an eight year old. He always wore a ratty woolen topcoat even in the summer. In the cold weather he added a faded red knit cap to his wardrobe. No one'd ever seen Jukebox take his coat off. Doherty wasn't sure where Jukebox lived though everybody in town treated him kindly. The guys at Harry's had more or less adopted him, and even Harry, who was a prick to most people, allowed Jukebox to hang around and sweep up the shop.

Jukebox approached the shoeshine area softly singing "Fly Me to the Moon." Doherty shook hands with him and Jukebox giggled. He wasn't a bad looking kid even when he twisted his mouth into a crude shape when he talked. He showed Jukebox the picture of Bernard Pressman and asked him if he'd ever seen the old gent around.

"See him everywhere. Sometimes he still have his pajamas on. I tell him he catch cold doesn't put a coat on." Jukebox went back to his song. *"Let me play among the stars."*

"Have you seen him lately?" Jukebox looked like he was thinking as he continued to sing.

"Saw him yesterday," Jukebox said.

"Where?"

Jukebox thought again. "Up at the ball field watchin' the football team practice. He looked cold. Dint have no jacket on. I tried to tell him to put a coat on but he ran away. He gonna catch a bad cold walkin' around like that."

"The football field is a long way from here. Did you walk up there?"

"Jukebox walks everywhere. I walk all over town. Once I start singin' there ain't no place I can't walk to." Doherty handed Jukebox two bucks and thanked him. He paid the shoeshine boy and bid goodbye to Bill.

"I'll be in for a shave on Monday. Keep the chair warm for me. And Bill, one more thing."

"What's that?"

"Tell Harry to go jump in a lake."

"'Fraid I'll have to pass on that, Huey."

He checked back into the office and told Agnes he'd be gone for the rest of the day and wouldn't see her till Monday. She was busy working on the Donniger report and just gave him a wave as he left. He walked home, got the Chevy out of Belanger's garage and drove down Main toward the football field. He passed by the Royal Mill where his father had worked until his liver gave out. The field was tucked on a plot of land back behind the junior high, about a half mile away from the high school itself. The baseball field, where Doherty'd spent many of his happiest hours as a teen, was adjacent to the football one.

Football was the most popular sport at the high school. Many of his friends played it and had their noses broken and teeth knocked out in the process. It was the biggest sport in town and on Saturday afternoons and Thanksgiving Day it seemed as if all of West Warwick turned out for the Wizards' games. The team was state champs on a number of occasions, often defeating far bigger schools from the cities to the north. It was the one thing the town could be proud of.

The tough sons of tough mill workers played football for all it was worth. For many of them glory on the high school gridiron would be the highlight of their lives; after that they followed their fathers into the mills. For the few who were really good or smart, there was the promise of a college scholarship. For the others, their last Thanksgiving Day game would be the end of the line.

Doherty'd never liked football; baseball was always his game. He preferred the easy rhythm of that warm weather sport. It was still the national pastime and to him there was no sweeter sound than a wooden bat hitting a baseball.

Back when he played Doherty was a ropey hitter who lashed singles over the infielders' heads and doubles into the outfield gaps. He was fast then, often turning one-baggers into doubles and two-baggers into triples. He played the outfield, had a rifle for an arm and could cover a lot of ground. He excelled in high school and even went to one of those open tryouts for the big leagues. A few feelers came his way, but he went to work at Quonset instead after his old man took sick and lost his job at the mill. Doherty played for the team at the Point and was better than most of the other guys in that league. When the war came, all his dreams about making it to the big leagues evaporated in Italy. Thanks to a piece of German shrapnel his right knee was never the same. His once lightning speed was gone for good.

The football team was wrapping up its practice as the sun began to fade for the day. While the players exited the field Doherty walked over to where some of the coaches were standing around shooting the bull. One of the younger ones looked familiar. Doherty approached him and said, "Don't I know you?"

"Yeah, you know me. I'm Jimmy Alves, and you're Hugh Doherty. God, I haven't seen you in a pig's age." Alves was an athletic looking guy, now in his thirties. He still gave off the impression he could tote the pigskin pretty good.

"Jimmy Alves? Weren't you a year behind me in school?"

"Two to be exact. You were a hell of a baseball player if I remember correctly."

"And from what I hear you turned out to be a terrific football player."

"I was good but not as good as my older brother Stevie. He got a scholarship to Boston College; made third team All-American. Me, I played a couple of years at URI, but was never a star."

"You coach here at the high school now?"

"Yeah, and teach phys ed. too. I mostly coach the defense. We got a real good team this year."

"So I read in the *Times*. You guys have game tomorrow?"

"One o'clock. St. Raphael's of Pawtucket. Right here. Are you still with the cops?"

"No, I'm out on my own now. Got an investigation agency right in the middle of Arctic. That's kind of why I'm here." Doherty pulled out the picture of Pressman and asked Jimmy Alves if he'd seen the old guy around.

"Wait a minute." He turned and yelled toward the other coaches, "Hey, Nick, come over here for a minute," A large dark skinned guy trotted in their direction. His nose looked like it had been broken in three different places.

"Nick Collardo, meet Hugh Doherty. Hugh was a big baseball star here back in the day." The big guy just grunted.

"This old man look familiar to you, Nick?"

Collardo studied the picture then said, "Ain't that the white haired guy comes by to watch practice sometimes. I think I seen him here yesterday. I remember he was over there by the fence arguin' with that crazy guy, what's his name?"

"Jukebox," Doherty chimed in. "The one that's always wearing a woolen topcoat."

"Yeah, that's right. The both of them were here yesterday. I see that crazy guy walkin' all over town. Is he who you're lookin' for?"

"No," Doherty said. "I'm looking' for the old guy with the white hair. Have you seen him today?"

The two coaches shook their heads. "Not today, yesterday for sure," Collardo said.

"Well, thanks for your help, and good luck tomorrow."

"Good to see you, Doherty. You still play any ball?" Alves asked as he was backing away.

"Naw, I jammed up my knee in the war. Afraid my ball playing days are behind me."

Doherty drove home in time to take a shower, shave and "spruce up" his apartment as Millie had suggested. He made sure he had clean dishes, clean sheets, a fresh bottle of booze and a few safes left in his night table. He put some lower watt bulbs in the living room lamps to create a more romantic atmosphere. He was swaying to some music on the radio and thinking about Millie when she knocked at his door. He checked his watch. She was early.

Doherty smiled as he swung the door open. Only it wasn't Millie St. Jean on his threshold, it was Rene Desjardins and another guy.

"Expectin' someone else, Doherty?" Desjardins said, his mouth smirking under his bushy mustache. Doherty was sorry he'd dressed in his best sports clothes, which he now suspected were going to get messed up. He tried to push the door closed but Desjardins already had his foot inside the jam. It didn't take much for the two men to barrel their way in.

"If you guys don't get out of here, I'm going to call the cops."

"By the time they get here, we'll be finished with you, smart guy," Rene said.

Doherty backed slowly toward the bedroom door. Desjardins grabbed him by the scruff of the neck and Doherty heard his shirt rip. The Canuck tried to butt Doherty's nose with his forehead, but Doherty leaned to the side and the big guy's head hit him on his collarbone instead. Now angry, Desjardins cuffed Doherty on the side of the head with his right fist causing him to momentarily see stars. The other guy slipped behind him putting Doherty at a loss for a counterattack. Desjardins slammed him up against the wall, and when Doherty bounced off it Rene hit him hard in the ribs. Doherty ducked under his next punch and hit the big man in the midsection. But Desjardins was ready for him this time and didn't absorb the full impact of Doherty's punch.

Desjardins' smaller companion came around to his side and kicked Doherty hard just below his left kneecap. Again Desjardins tried to smash Doherty against the wall, but Doherty spun sideways through the doorway to his bedroom and fell to his knees. As he did he reached behind the door and grabbed his Louisville slugger. The two men didn't see this because Doherty's arm was blocked by the partially closed door.

When the big man pushed into the room Doherty swung the bat as hard as he could against Desjardin's hipbone. Rene let out a wail. Then Doherty cracked him behind his left knee and he went down with a thud. Doherty jumped to his feet just as the second man came into the room. With one short swing Doherty hit him behind the head and knocked him to the floor.

Doherty could feel himself becoming more and more enraged. He couldn't stop thinking that Millie might've been here when these two goons arrived. He stood astraddle Desjardins and when the big Canuck tried to get to his feet Doherty let him have it in the ribs. Desjardins rolled to his back and Doherty finished him off with a solid smash to the groin. Desjardins emitted an ungodly scream and curled up into a fetal position with his hands between his legs. Doherty turned back to the little man who was still trying to clear his head. Doherty switched the bat to his left hand, walked over and punched the man in the face twice. The second punch drew a significant amount of blood from his nose.

By now several of Doherty's fellow tenants had gathered at his door to see what the commotion was all about. Among them were Ferdinand and Peaches Perrault.

Doherty turned to the Perraults and yelled, "Napoleon, call the police, right now!" Perrault scurried away and Doherty went back to check on his assailants. Desjardins was still writhing on the floor holding his balls and moaning in agony. The little man was sitting up and trying unsuccessfully to stanch the flow of blood from his nose and mouth. Doherty looked around to survey the damage. A lamp was broken and a chair upended. All things considered, the breakage was pretty minimal.

Millie St. Jean arrived at almost the same time as the police. Doherty asked Peaches Perrault to take Millie up to her apartment until they left. One of the cops, a guy named Sean Gallagher, had been on the force when Doherty was. He took notes and filled out the report on the breaking and entering and assault and battery while his partner cuffed Desjardins and his companion and marched them out to the squad car. As they passed through Doherty noticed that the big Canuck was having a lot of trouble walking. The smaller man was given a compress to absorb the bleeding from his nose. Doherty hoped Desjardins' little friend would bleed all over the police cruiser on their way to the station. If he did the cops would give him a good beating of their own in return. Before he left Gallagher told Doherty he'd have to come down to the station the next day to fill out a full report.

Once the police were gone, things quieted down and Peaches and Millie returned to his apartment. Peaches tried to linger, curious about what had occurred until Doherty firmly suggested that she should go back upstairs. Napoleon was nowhere to be seen. Without comment Millie went into the bathroom and began rifling through Doherty's medicine chest to see what he had that could ease his pain. She sat him down on the toilet and used some rubbing alcohol, which stung, and Mercurochrome on the cut above his left eye where Rene had landed his first punch. The rest of his pains were in his back and side, the result of his assailant throwing him up against the wall and hitting him in the ribs.

As Millie ministered to Doherty's wounds she tried to pry some information out of him as to why he'd been so viciously assaulted. Doherty was evasive, not wanting her to know that his current beef with Rene Desjardins stemmed from his anger over Judge DeCenza's meddling in Millie's life. He told her it had to do with a grievance Desjardins had from a previous case involving a woman the big man had mishandled. Millie continued to prod him for more details. He told her that his client's right to confidentiality prevented him from telling her more. He didn't know if she bought it, though she didn't pursue any further questioning.

Millie got Doherty to swallow a couple of aspirin and suggested that they might want to call it a night. He told her he felt fine, which he didn't, and convinced Millie to stay at least to make him dinner.

"Darn," Millie said. "I forgot the groceries upstairs in the Perraults' apartment."

"You better get them before Peaches gobbles everything up."

Millie smiled for the first time. "She is kind of a big woman, isn't she?"

"It's her *hormones*."

"What?"

"Never mind. It's a private joke."

Millie retrieved the groceries from the Perraults and whipped up a pork chop for Doherty and a piece of fish for herself. She accompanied them with mash potatoes and creamed spinach, one of Doherty's favorites. He washed his meal down with a couple of 'Gansetts, while Millie satisfied herself with some tea. After they'd eaten Doherty admitted that he didn't feel so good and maybe he should take Millie home. There would be no love making tonight. If she was disappointed Millie was too good of a sport to say so. She offered to take the bus, but Doherty told her it was late and the busses ran erratically on this part of Main at night.

They kissed in a friendly manner when Doherty stopped the usual three doors away from her in-laws. He would've liked more even though his neck hurt so badly that he could barely turn his head to the side. Once back home he knocked off a couple of shots of Jameson and a few more aspirins before hitting the hay.

Doherty didn't look any better for wear in the morning. The blood from the cut above his eyebrow had clotted and the bruising and discoloration around the eye looked worse than it felt. Most of the real damage was in his back and ribs where it couldn't be seen, only felt. He put on a pair of Khakis, a gray sweatshirt and his fedora in hopes that his hat would cover the cut. But the hatband pressed against the bandage so Doherty tossed it in favor of a black knit toque. Looking at himself in the mirror, the image that came back was of a beat up longshoreman – kind of like Brando's character at the end of *On the Waterfront*. His Quonset baseball jacket completed the outfit. He was too stiff to walk so he drove down to the police station to file his report and to find out what happened to Desjardins and his busted up friend.

Doherty hadn't been in the little police house since he'd left the force. Plans were for the old shack to be torn down within the year and replaced by a new, modern building that would house the town offices as well as the police and fire stations. The town fathers had floated an expensive bond issue for the new construction. Its cost had upset a lot people in town in light of how many workers were being laid off from the mills. Nevertheless, the town fathers, men like Judge DeCenza, would have their way regardless of what the average shmo thought.

Inside the station the paint was peeling and the plaster was cracked in a number of places. Like most folks in town, Doherty wouldn't be sorry to see the old building demolished, though for him it was mostly a case of the bad memories it held. Gallagher wasn't on shift so Doherty was interviewed by a guy named Murphy who wore a suit instead of a uniform. Murphy kept asking Doherty about the nature of his quarrel with Desjardins. Doherty was as evasive with the cops as he'd been with Millie. He reiterated that it was the result of a previous case in which he'd intervened on behalf of a woman who was being threatened by Desjardins that Doherty helped run away. When the cop asked why no police report was filed, Doherty simply said, "You know how women are." That seemed to satisfy Murphy. He then asked Doherty if he wanted to press charges against the two assailants. He rolled the idea around and then decided yes, he did. He knew this would stick the knife a little deeper into DeCenza.

Murphy said, "I'm glad you are. It turns out the little guy, name of Louis Charboneau, is in the country illegally. Comes from some Podunk town in Quebec; lives in a flop here and has no visible means of support."

"What does that add up to?" Doherty asked.

"Means we're gonna kick his ass back across the border and let the Mounted Police in Quebec take care of him. Somethin' tells me he's already got a record up there."

"What about Desjardins?"

Murphy waggled his head. "You can press charges if you want, and you probably should. But I have to warn you, he's on Judge DeCenza's payroll, and you know what that means around here."

"I'll press anyway. Let the bastard worry about his court date; it's least I can do."

Murphy shuffled some papers around his desk. "One other thing, the Judge's man Tuohy, that big Irish fella, was in here this mornin' payin' Desjardins' bail."

"I'm not surprised. I know Tuohy, and I know the kind of yank the Judge has in this town. It's one of the reasons I left the force."

From the expression on his face it was obvious that Murphy did not take kindly to this last comment.

"I'll tell you one other thing right now, Murphy. If that big Canuck comes after me again, the next time I'll put him down for good."

"Can't say I'd blame you. But do us a favor, at least make it look like self-defense. We don't want any static from the chief when DeCenza finds a reason to get hisself involved."

Doherty bought a pair of hot dogs at the New York System and washed them down with a Coke and another handful of aspirin. He didn't feel so bad when he was on his feet; it was the transition from sitting to standing that caused him the most pain. After lunch he drove out to the high school football field and parked the Chevy a few blocks away so as to avoid the traffic when he left. He pulled the toque down low on his forehead, paid his fifty cents and went into the spectator area. The game was midway through the second quarter and the locals already had a 20-7 lead over the boys from St. Ralph's. Doherty found high school football pretty boring. Since most high school kids couldn't really throw a pass with much accuracy or catch one, they ran the ball ninety percent of the time.

Doherty picked up some glances from people in the crowd, mostly because few grown men wore knit toques anymore. Still, it was better than having his ugly cut staring them in the face. As he mounted the bleachers he caught sight of Millie, her father-in-law and her two boys sitting about halfway up. She didn't see him but Gilbert St. Jean did. He squinted at Doherty, making sure it was really him, and then shot him an angry look. Doherty ignored St. Jean and kept climbing up the stands. Fortunately Millie never took her eyes off the field.

At the top row sitting by himself was a white haired man wearing only a thin windbreaker, a jacket unsuitable for the cool, fall weather. The only other people sitting up there were two teenage couples busily making out, oblivious to the game and the old man down the row. Doherty sat down beside Bernard Pressman and introduced himself.

Pressman hesitated as if he were searching for his own name.

"You're Bernie Pressman, aren't you?" The old man looked confused at the reminder so Doherty decided to change the subject. "How's the game going?"

Pressman turned his gaze back to the action on the field. "Very good," he said. "The Browns are murdering the 49ers. That colored boy, Jim Brown, he's a terrific runner."

"The Browns?"

"Why of course, the Cleveland Browns. They're the ones in the white uniforms." Doherty looked at the players on the field. The West Warwick gridders wore uniforms very similar to those of the professional team from Cleveland hence, Pressman's confusion. "Personally, I prefer the Giants; they're my team, but they're not playing today – so we'll just have to watch the Browns."

Doherty didn't respond and the two men watched the game in peace. He stole a glance at the teenage couples nearby. They were kissing so hungrily that the areas around their mouths were red where they'd been rubbed raw.

"Are you a football fan, Mr. ...?"

"Doherty. Not really. I prefer baseball. That was always my game."

"Not me," Pressman said. "Baseball is for pantywaists. I played football in college, you know."

"At Dartmouth, wasn't it?"

"Why yes, it was at Dartmouth," Pressman said, his eyes suddenly glossing over as if he were back in New Hampshire fifty years ago. "How did you know I played at Dartmouth?" he asked after a few awkward seconds.

"Your wife told me."

"My wife. You know my wife?"

"Yeah. That's why I'm here. Mrs. Pressman sent me to find you. You haven't been home in three days and she's been worried about you."

"Are you from the police?" Pressman didn't wait for an answer. "You're from Howard, aren't you? They're going to put me in the nut house. My wife Julie and that boy Ronnie she's always nuzzling with. She wants to get me out of the way so she can marry him. She thinks she's got me fooled, but I see the way he's always touching her behind my back. I'm not blind you know. They're going to put me in Howard to get me out of the way." Pressman was getting agitated and Doherty wasn't sure what to do next.

"Isn't Julie your daughter? Your wife's name is Eunice and the young man, Ronnie, is your son-in-law."

Bernard Pressman now looked thoroughly confused. At that point the game broke for halftime and Pressman settled into a quiet attitude. He seemed lost in some kind of dream world.

"I'm going to get a hot dog," Doherty said. "Would you like me to get you something?"

Pressman smiled, "Yes a hot dog would be nice, and a cup of coffee too. It's awfully cold out here today."

Doherty went to the concession stand, keeping one eye on the old man the whole time. A cop named Eddie Lussier, who Doherty knew well, was working the gate. After picking up the refreshments Doherty sidled up to Lussier and filled him in on the deal with Pressman.

"What do want me to do?" the cop asked. "Escort the old man out?"

"No, I'll take care of that. You could call into the station and have somebody there contact his wife. Tell her I'm with her husband. That would at least put her mind to rest."

"Will do."

On this trip up the stands Doherty noticed that Millie had spotted him then quickly turned back to her kids. When he returned to the top of the bleachers he gave the old man his coffee and hot dog. Then he took off his Quonset jacket and put it over Pressman's shoulders. Pressman's shaky hands spilled some of his coffee and Doherty mopped it off his chin and the baseball jacket with his handkerchief.

By the end of the third quarter Pressman had fallen asleep and his head was resting on his chest. West Warwick pulled away thirty something to seven and Doherty'd seen enough football for one day. He gently prodded the old gent and asked him if he was ready to go home. At first Pressman looked confused then consented. Doherty guided him to his car. On the way out he gave Lussier the OK sign.

In the car Pressman resumed his nap, his head rolling over onto Doherty's shoulder. When they pulled up in front of his house his wife, daughter and son-in-law quickly came out onto the porch. The place was a big yellow Victorian with white trim. It had nice foliage around it and was very neatly kept. As the son-in-law helped Bernie Pressman out of the car, Doherty carefully removed the baseball jacket so as not to upset the old man. When Pressman was safely inside the daughter came down the steps to thank Doherty. She was short like her mother and had a shrunken face that made her look old before her time.

"He was at the football game?"

"Yeah. It was a hunch I had. Your mother said he liked football and somebody'd seen him up there at the practices a few times. We didn't stay till the end. It wasn't a very close game so he didn't miss much."

"I wish that were so," she said sadly. "I'm afraid daddy misses a lot these days. Do you have parents in town, Mr. Doherty?"

"Used to, but I don't any more. They're both deceased. They died pretty young."

"I think in some ways that's better. I hate seeing my father like this. He had such a brilliant mind when he was younger. Now he can't even remember if I'm his daughter or his wife."

The woman quickly raised her hands to her eyes to stop any tears that might appear. Doherty sensed it was time to leave. The Pressmans' daughter thanked him again for all he'd done. He sat in the car and watched her retreat into the house. He wondered how many more days Bernie Pressman had left in this house where he'd raised his family.

Chapter Eight

ANNETTE PATRULLO

On Monday Doherty set out on foot for the office. Two of the young boys who lived on the other side of his building were tossing a baseball up against the wall of the *Times* office. It was something they did regularly until the manager, Henry Constable, came out and chased them away. Henry was always very agitated so the kids started calling him "Nervous" just for spite. Doherty had witnessed this routine countless times and wondered why the kids' mother never put a stop to their game. It must have been aggravating for the people inside the *Times* building to hear the repeated "thwack, thwack, thwack" of the ball against their office wall.

"No school today fellas?" Doherty asked by way of a greeting.

"Naw, it's a holiday," the one missing his front teeth said. He must have been about seven.

"Really, what holiday is it?"

"Doncha know, Mr. Doherty. It's Columbus Day. He's the guy that discovered America."

"I thought the Indians discovered America."

"Huh?" the other kid, the older one with the freckled face, said.

"Never mind. You should stop that ball game. Your buddy Nervous'll be out any minute now."

"Ain't it a holiday for the newspaper too?"

"I doubt it. I don't think the newspaper office takes a holiday except on Sundays." Doherty continued on his way into town.

He was late to work for a change thanks to the three shots of Jameson he'd taken the night before to ease his back pain. Agnes was already at her desk banging away on the Remington. He hoped she was working on the Donniger report. After throwing his secretary a quick "good morning" Doherty went into his office not wanting to have to give her a long explanation about how he got the cuts on his face. As he chalked down his notes on the Pressman case he couldn't help thinking about how one day your brain could make all the people near and dear to you strangers like the old man's had. Doherty thought he'd rather put a bullet through his temple than end up senile like that. While he was ruminating about brainpower draining away with age, Agnes knocked and stepped inside the door.

"There's a girl out here to see you. She seems awful upset."

"Aren't they all?" Doherty said dryly. "She give a name?"

Agnes shook her head. "No name but she says you know her from a previous case. She's a real looker, boss."

Doherty smiled, straightened his tie and finger combed his hair. "Well, in that case send her in."

Agnes returned with Annette Patrullo in tow. She was about the last person Doherty thought he'd ever see again.

"Thank you Agnes. That'll be all – and can you close the door on your way out." The secretary gave him a cross-eyed look.

As she had when he first met her at the real estate office, Annette Patrullo was wearing a form fitting black skirt and a tight blouse that left little to the imagination. Her dark, wavy hair was teased up into a beehive that sat vertically on the top of her head, adding a good three inches to her height. If a girl could cash in on her body alone this one was worth a million bucks. Then again, girls did cash in with their bods all the time. Annette certainly had with Spencer Wainwright.

"A pleasure to see you, Miss Patrullo. This is … a bit of a surprise. Is Wainwright missing again?"

"As a matter of fact, he is," she said as she took the chair across from his desk. "What happened to your face?"

"I walked into a door."

"Looks like it packed a pretty good punch."

"Maybe your boy Wainwright went home to his wife," Doherty said changing the subject.

Annette hesitated, apparently not sure yet how much she wanted to share with Doherty until she became his client. "I thought that at first. I told Mr. Cooper I was concerned about Spencer's absence so he went by the house. According to him the missus hasn't seen her husband in two days."

Doherty leaned back in his chair and took out his cigs. He offered Annette Patrullo one but she took a pass. When she crossed her legs Doherty got a good look at her shapely gams. It helped him understand why a guy like Wainwright would consider throwing his old life away for a girl twenty years his junior.

"Maybe he's got another girl on the side. Rumor has it you weren't the first senorita he stepped outside his marriage with."

Annette gave Doherty a tired look. "I'm here to hire you to find Mr. Wainwright. You did it once before for somebody else, so you can do it for me. I don't care what you find - even if he is shacked up with some other girl."

"You want my advice, Miss Patrullo, save your money. Guys like Wainwright have roaming eyes. One week it's you, the next it's some other little twist."

"I don't really want your advice, Mr. Doherty. I want your services. And let's get something straight between us, I may be young but I'm not stupid. I been around the block a few times myself and I don't think Spencer's disappearance has to do with another girl. I got a feeling something bad has happened to him. And before you ask, the answer is yes, I've already been down to the Great Island house. He's not there and hasn't been since that day you convinced him to go back home."

"And you know this how?"

Annette shook her head and readjusted some of her hive. "I have a key to the beach house. I went through the place. I remembered how we left it. If he'd been there with another woman I would've smelled it."

Doherty was too polite to ask what she would have smelled. Instead he pulled out one of his standard forms and handed it to her. She moved her lips as she read it, and lovely red lips they were. She signed the form and gave Doherty fifty bucks in cash.

"Why do you think something other than him running off with another girl is what's happened to Wainwright?"

Annette considered her answer very carefully. "Because something at work's had Spencer all in a tizzy. He was upset about some big project he's been working on. It was a deal he'd pumped a lot of his own money into. Apparently things weren't going right, though I don't know what the problem was."

"Can you find out?"

Annette hesitated again. "I can look through his files. Spencer was very conscientious about his record keeping. I'd know where to look; Cooper wouldn't have a clue."

"Then for now why don't you see what you can find in the files and I'll work the personal angle. I'll talk with his wife and with Cooper, and anybody else who pops up."

"Whatever you do, Mr. Doherty, you can't use my name, especially not with Spencer's wife."

"No problem there. You're my client now, so you have full confidentiality – unless, of course, we discover a crime has been committed. In any case, we'll keep in touch with each other. Should I call you at this number?" he asked as he scanned the signed agreement.

"There or at Cooper and Wainwright."

"And one other thing, Miss Patrullo. If Spencer shows up or you find out he's been playing house with some other girl, let me know right away. No matter how much it hurts."

She gave Doherty the same seen-it-all look as before. "All right. I have to say ever since I got involved with Spencer I've always secretly expected the worst."

"Let's hope that's not the case."

The Wainwright home was in a fairly new development high on a hill off the Post Road between Warwick and East Greenwich. It afforded its residents a pretty nice view of Apponaug Cove and Greenwich Bay. The project was so new that some of the lots around the houses hadn't even been landscaped yet. On other lots heavy equipment stood idly waiting for new building permits. Apparently houses were built here mostly on spec.

The Wainwright abode had a nice lawn that looked like it'd been rolled out with strips of sod. The house was one of those midsize, split level jobs that were all the rage. A breezeway connected it to a large, two-car garage. Spencer

Wainwright's Roadmaster was nowhere to be seen. One of the garage doors was open and the chrome fins on the ass end of a light green Oldsmobile 88 stuck out.

Doherty parked his Chevy on the other half of the drive. One more big payday like the Donniger case and he could make Packy's a fair offer to buy the car. He got out slowly and took a long look around. There was no sign of life anywhere. If there were kids in this budding young neighborhood most of them would be back at school today after celebrating the holiday for the Italian explorer's *discovery* of America. Doherty pressed the doorbell button and for the next ten seconds could hear chimes going off throughout the house. From somewhere deep inside a muffled voice shouted, "Just a minute."

A woman appeared on the other side of the screen door. Doherty's first thought was that it was late enough into the season that someone should've already replaced the screen with the glass storm. He introduced himself and held up his wallet for the woman to see his investigator's license. She looked at him skeptically and didn't say anything for an awkward moment.

"Could you please pass your card through the screen door?" she asked finally. Doherty hesitated then fished the card out from behind its plastic window and slipped it through the crack in the door the woman had allowed before she relocked it. She looked at it carefully while Doherty shifted his weight from foot to foot. Then she opened the door and invited him in.

There was a short hallway that dropped down a few steps at its end to a room that Doherty took to be a den. To the right off the hallway was a living room that wasn't quite large enough for the Red Sox to take infield practice in though big enough for a game of pepper. The furniture in this room was covered in plastic and looked as if no human buttocks had ever creased it.

Doherty followed Mrs. Wainwright into a good-sized kitchen that was a few steps up and adjacent to the sitting room.

"I suppose you're here about Spencer," she said without prompting. "Did Ben ask you to come by?"

"Ben?"

"Ben Cooper, my husband's partner. He was here on Saturday wondering if Spencer was at home this past weekend. You see my husband likes to go down to our beach house most weekends. I prefer to stay up here once the season is over."

She was speaking quickly and rather nervously. This gave Doherty a chance to get a good snapshot of Mrs. Wainwright. She had shoulder length dark hair swept into a flip perm at the bottom. A few strands of gray nibbled at the edges. She was on the other side of forty, but still well preserved save for the crow's feet that were beginning to creep out from the corners of her eyes. She was tall, carried herself well and her overall looks could best be described as *splendid*.

"Apparently your husband is missing," Doherty said avoiding the question of who hired him.

"Would you like some lemonade, Mr. Doherty? I just made a fresh pitcher."

"Excuse me?"

"Lemonade. You know, lemon juice, sugar, water. I'd offer you something stronger but technically it's still morning."

She came over to the counter where Doherty was standing and placed a tall, thin glass filled with ice cubes and lemonade in front of him. A fresh lemon slice hung over the lip. It reminded Doherty of the gin and tonic with the lime slice Annette had served him at Wainwright's beach house. Must be a family tradition. The wife was wearing the kind of housedress you see in magazine ads that no woman ever did real housework in.

"Has anyone thought to look for Spencer down at the house on Great Island?"

Doherty weighed his response. "Yes, they have. He's not there and apparently hasn't been for some time."

"How do you know that? Did *you* go down there to check?"

"Not personally, but one of my associates did," he lied.

She shot him a knowing smile. "So, Doherty and Associates has associates. You could've fooled me. I took you for a one-man band. How's the lemonade? Not too tart is it."

"No, it's fine. I like it a little tart."

"I'll bet you do," she said as her hand swept back a strand of hair that was not in her face to begin with.

"Do you have any idea where your husband might be, Mrs. Wainwright?"

"Please call me Helen," she said reaching again for the non-existent stray lock. "How well do you know my husband, Mr. Doherty?"

"Not very well at all. I was just hired onto this case yesterday so maybe you can fill me in a little, Helen."

The woman smiled when Doherty used her first name. "My husband is what you might call a serial philanderer. He tends to like them young and stupid, or at least younger and stupider than he is. Sometimes his dalliances last only for a few days or a week. Though once it went on for almost six months," she said with a sigh. "I'm sure he says things to them like 'My wife doesn't understand me,' or 'I'm thinking of getting a divorce.' But in the end he always comes crawling back home with his tail between his legs.

"Why don't you divorce him?"

Helen Wainwright let out one of those fake "ha, ha," laughs. "Look around you, Mr. Doherty. How do you think I got all this? Say what you will about Spencer, but he's been a good provider for me and the children – financially anyway. We have a son at Williams and a daughter in her junior year at Bay View. Money may not grow on trees but my husband knows how to shake it off them. If it was up to Ben Cooper, we'd all be in sackcloth. Ben has the name but Spencer brings in the money."

"And for that you're willing to sacrifice your pride?"

Suddenly Helen Wainwright turned cross. "Don't you get all high and mighty with me, Mr. Private Eye. How do you make your living? Sneaking into motels, taking pictures of men or women having affairs with someone they're not married to. Or do you spend your time sitting in cars on stakeouts while BO takes up residence inside your cheap suit?"

"Actually most of my business is finding lost people like your husband," he said trying his best to remain calm.

She threw out that fake laugh again. "I'll bet you dollars to donuts that Spencer isn't *lost*. If he were I'd have contacted the police. He's probably shacked up with some new slut. I wouldn't be surprised if it was that greasy twat he hired as a secretary. I see the way Spencer's eyes follow her when she shakes her ass around the office."

Their conversation had clearly taken a downward turn and Doherty wanted to wrap things up before they went any lower. "Besides Miss Patrullo, is there anyone else you can think of that might know where your husband is?"

Helen Wainwright looked down into her lemonade. She probably wished there was a shot of gin in it right about now. "I don't know. He could have a new playmate of the month. I try not to think about what Spencer is up to when he's not here."

"What about political or business associates?"

"Politics. Now that's a laugh. Spencer only agreed to serve as county chairman because he thought it would be good for business. And it has been. Otherwise what he knows about politics you could fit inside a thimble."

"What about business associates? Can you think of any enemies he might've made through his business?"

"Frankly, Spencer's business ventures have always bored me. I'm only interested in the comforts they bring us. On that score you'll have to talk with Ben Cooper. He'd know more about who the company is doing business with than I." At this point Helen Wainwright took a gander at her expensive looking watch. "I hate to cut this charming conversation short, Mr. Doherty, but it's getting late and I have a luncheon engagement at the club."

Doherty finished his lemonade and wrote his phone number on his note pad and handed it to Mrs. Wainwright. "If you hear anything, please call me. Also, be sure to call if the wandering minstrel comes home to his castle."

She showed Doherty to the door. "By the way, you never told me who hired you to find my husband."

"Sorry, " Doherty said. "That's confidential."

Wainwright's partner, Ben Cooper, agreed to meet with Doherty on Friday morning at the office near Hoxie Four Corners. As he'd done earlier, Doherty took the route that allowed him to drive by the airport at Hillsgrove so he could watch the planes taking off and landing. Sky travel still fascinated him, even though it was becoming more and more common, especially for people of means.

Annette Patrullo and another, older woman were at their desks when Doherty entered Cooper and Wainwright Real Estate. Annette eyed him and smiled. She didn't say anything, just pointed at the other woman. Doherty approached that woman and told her he had an appointment with Mr. Cooper. She introduced herself as Margaret Whitmore and showed him to Cooper's office.

Ben Cooper was hunched over his desk carefully looking at a development chart through glasses perched on the end of his nose. He was considerably older than Wainwright and had the flaccid body of a man who did little exercise short of hitting a golf ball. His light brown hair had plenty of gray mixed in and was combed over the top of his head in a failed attempt to hide his creeping baldness. When they shook hands Cooper's was small and soft as Doherty expected it would be. He removed his glasses and offered Doherty a seat next to his desk.

"I've been hired to find Spencer Wainwright."

"Yes, yes, I know," Cooper said impatiently. "His wife has called me three times, each time accusing me of hiring you. I believe on the last call she referred to you as 'that dreadful man'."

"I met with Mrs. Wainwright day before yesterday. She wasn't very helpful."

"Oh you can't blame Helen. She tries to project a hard-boiled exterior, especially where Spencer's absences are concerned. But this time I think she's a bit worried herself. Your visit might've had something to do with that."

Doherty rolled his shoulders, trying to project his own air of not caring. "Maybe she's worried her sugar daddy absconded on her this time."

"You shouldn't be too hard on her given what Spencer has put her through."

"I'm starting to get the impression that Spencer Wainwright is not a very popular guy."

Cooper smiled knowingly. "Quite the contrary, Mr. Doherty. Spencer is very well liked by just about everyone. He's what you would call a hail-fellow throughout the county. His problem is not his popularity, it's that he's an inveterate skirt chaser. I suppose he can't help himself given his good looks and easy charm. I, on the other hand, have never had that problem. I believe most people find me rather old fashioned and stodgy."

"Probably safer that way," Doherty said.

"Oh, I don't know. Sometimes I sort of envy Spencer and his peccadilloes. Like with that Miss Patrullo out there. She's quite the little honey, isn't she?"

"I thought you were old and stodgy, Mr. Cooper?"

"Don't get me wrong. I may no longer eat, but I can still read the menu. I do have eyes after all. It's one of the reasons I didn't oppose Spencer when he chose to hire her as his secretary, and protégé. It's my belief she's the one who hired you to find her missing lover. Am I right?"

Doherty shook his head. "I can't tell you that. My clients have to remain anonymous. It'd be bad for business if I let on who's paying my tab."

"Understandable. I do know one thing, though. It wasn't Judge DeCenza this time."

Doherty was knocked off stride by Cooper's last remark. "How did you know about Judge DeCenza?"

Cooper leaned back and rested his hands over his rather substantial belly. "Let's just say I have my ways. You see sometimes it suits our business for me to play the role of the befuddled older partner, leaving Spencer to act as the young hot shot."

Doherty took out his Camels and asked Cooper if he could smoke. The older man pointed to a sign on his desk that said "No Smoking Please."

"Unfortunately, I have a rather bad case of asthma. Smoke in confined spaces like this only irritates it."

"Fair enough," Doherty said as he replaced the pack of smokes in his inside pocket. "What about Wainwright, any idea where he might be?"

"Normally I would think he's down at his summer house. He spends an inordinate amount of time there, especially in the off-season. Methinks it's often with one of his chippies. But Helen said you told her that one of your *associates* had already checked out that possibility."

Doherty nodded his head.

"There's one small problem with that, Mr. Doherty. According to my inquiries you have no *associates*. So if you didn't go down there yourself, I think I know who did. And when she didn't find him on Great Island she hired you to search for him. But that's neither here nor there, since you can't tell me if she's your client or not. To be honest with you, I don't really care." There was a pregnant pause in the conversation.

Doherty was about to pursue another line of inquiry when Cooper leaned in close and whispered, "However, if I were you, I wouldn't be too quick to believe everything that one tells you." He crooked his head in the direction of the outer office as he spoke.

"I've been told that Mr. Wainwright was working on some big project recently; something that was making him very nervous. What do you know about that?"

Ben Cooper stood and walked to a map on the wall behind his desk. On his feet he didn't stand much more than about five-six and had a decidedly pear shaped physique. The map was of the Warwick, Cranston, West Warwick, Coventry, East Greenwich area and some smaller outlying communities.

"You see the red pins on this map. They represent the houses I have personally sold in the last ten years. As you can see there are quite a few of them. Right now I'm averaging six property sales a month. Times are changing, Mr. Doherty. People are moving away from the manufacturing centers in and around Providence and out to what we now call the suburbs. The GI Bill helped jump start this housing boom, and now with an increase in the standard of living, housing has become more affordable than ever. People are no longer feeling the need to live side by side with their own kind."

"But one thing you don't see on this map are very many red pins in West Warwick. Why? Because West Warwick is a dying mill town. Arctic used to be the commercial center of Kent County, but it won't be for much longer. In time there will be other commercial centers all over the county – some small and others quite large."

"Thanks for the lecture, Mr. Cooper, but what does this have to do with Wainwright being missing?"

"Some people will say that I am not a wealthy man because I lack ambition. But they would be wrong. My ambition lies in providing good, affordable homes for the kind of middle-class people I just spoke of. My income has been steady and quite substantial for a man of modest needs like myself. Throughout my career I have tried to do an honest job for an honest commission."

"I still don't get the point."

"The point is that unlike myself Spencer Wainwright is a very ambitious man. Dare I say, a dangerously ambitious man. To Spencer it has always been about how things appear; hence, the fancy cars, the big house on the hill, the perfect wife, the summer cottage, the country club membership, and of course, the political position. But you know what, Mr. Doherty. It's all hokum. I happen to know that Spencer's houses are mortgaged to the hilt and that he's personally leveraged with a number of banks throughout the state. So, as a private detective one thing you may want to ask yourself: Is Spencer Wainwright in some kind of financial trouble? And the answer would be yes. From my perspective his whole life is nothing but trouble."

"That's all well and good, but you're going to have to give me something more specific to work with."

Cooper sat back heavily in his desk chair. He shook his head from side to side. "Follow his ambitions, Mr. Doherty. Somewhere in Spencer's grandiose plans his vision may have exceeded his grasp. And I don't mean where women are concerned."

When nothing more was said for a few moments Doherty rose to leave. "Thank you for your time, Mr. Cooper. I don't think you've helped me very much."

Cooper didn't bother to get up. "Don't be so sure, young man. I've succeeded in the real estate game all these years by being perceptive about people. Think about what I've told you today."

As Doherty moved through the outer office Annette Patrullo caught his eye and signaled for him to meet her outside. Doherty circled around the back of his Chevy and stood in the shadows on the side of the building. A few minutes later Annette came out and feigned looking for something in her little Metropolitan. When she saw Doherty she took a glance back at the office and quickly skirted around the corner.

Doherty could smell her perfume as she moved in close. She handed him a manila folder. "I found this in the files. The dates on the papers in it are pretty recent. I think it's what Spencer was working on when he disappeared. I don't understand it all 'cause there's a lot of technical stuff in here. I thought maybe you could make heads or tails out of it. What did Cooper have to say?"

"We can't talk now; he'll be suspicious if you're out here too long. Despite what you might think, he keeps a close eye on you. Can you come by my office tomorrow?"

"Saturday's a busy day. I don't usually finish up until five, five-thirty."

"Come to my office after that. I'll wait for you." Annette Patrullo gave Doherty an arresting smile. That made him even more wary of her.

It was near lunchtime when Doherty returned to Arctic. He parked the Chevy outside of his office on Brookside and walked uptown to the News for lunch. Willy Legere was at his post outside.

"Hey Willy, how's the boy?" Doherty said greeting the blind vet.

"I'm OK, I guess," Willy said without enthusiasm.

"Aw, c'mon Willy, you're not still sore at me for winning the bet, are you?"

"Naw, that ain't it, Mr. D."

"Then what is it?"

"I dunno. I always get kinda low when fall comes 'round. You know, I miss the baseball already. And now it's startin' to get cold. Pretty soon I'll have to close up shop out here."

"There's always football. Lots of folks around here follow football. It's on the TV most weekends."

"I hear what you're sayin' but I ain't a big football fan. Them games are only on two days a week and you can't really listen to a football game on the radio. With baseball I can sit out here in the summer, listen to my transistor and chat with people all day long. You know how it is."

Doherty didn't know how it was because he had two good eyes and could still earn his own living. Willy was a disabled vet and would be for the rest of his life. He'd live with his mother until the old lady died and then he'd live in her house alone, supporting himself on the meager checks the government sent him each month. Doherty would miss the regularity of the baseball games on the radio as well, but he'd never miss them like Willy Legere would.

"Tell you what, Willy. You give me your address and when the weather gets too cold for you to be out here, I'll come by and we'll talk baseball all winter. I don't much like football either, so we can talk trades and young prospects and what have you. I'd kind of like that."

Willy looked in Doherty's direction from behind his dark glasses and smiled. "Hey, that would be swell, Mr. D. Let me tell ya somethin', my mother makes the best pies in town. You come over, I'll have her whip up a good one just for you."

Doherty patted him on the shoulder. "I'll plan on it, Willy. And tell your mom I prefer cherry."

"It's a deal."

After his usual ham sandwich and coffee lunch, Doherty made a quick stop at Francine's to see if he and Millie were on for that evening. Millie was busy and acted a little distant. She asked him to come by at six though she didn't inquire about any plans he might've made.

Back at the office Doherty began looking over the files Annette Patrullo had given him. There was a lot of material about several shuttered mills in the West Warwick–Warwick area that were owned by a company named

Sherbrooke Industries. It appeared that this company had bought up some of these properties for a fraction of what they were once worth. They did it by simply paying some of the back taxes. Since most of these buildings were abandoned, and in a few cases in a state of decrepitude, Doherty couldn't figure out why anyone would want them.

The focus of Wainwright's recent interest was on one of the more picturesque old buildings in town, the Bradford Soap Works, which sat right alongside the Pawtuxet River. In the folder was a rough sketch of a plan to turn this particular property into an office and housing complex. Having people live in an old mill building didn't strike Doherty as a very attractive notion, but what did he know about real estate development. As far as he could tell, most people these days preferred to live in single standing homes or in duplexes if they could afford them. From what Ben Cooper had said, the days of living in large apartment buildings was giving way to the movement to the suburbs. Those who lived in Providence or Pawtucket that didn't have the money to get out were the only ones left behind in apartment buildings. Them and single men like Doherty

Aside from Wainwright's, one other signature appeared as a cosigner on the Soap Works documents, that of a Frank Ganetti, Jr. Doherty'd never heard of this person. The other documents in the file were various studies dealing with water conditions, zoning codes, building permits, rental agreements, etc. The scientific stuff in the file was way over Doherty's head though he was able to make some sense out of the other documents. What he concluded was that Spencer Wainwright and this Frank Ganetti, Jr. had purchased the old Soap Works building from Sherbrooke Industries for $30,000 and were planning to convert it into office and rental units. Normally thirty grand for a property that size wouldn't have been much, though it would take a hell of a lot more than that to make the old building habitable.

Doherty'd been so immersed in trying to understand what was in the documents that he'd lost all sense of time. When he checked his watch it was already past five and he still had to shave and shower before meeting Millie. He'd planned a special treat for them; he was going to take her to a classy Italian restaurant in Cranston called Twin Oaks. He was told it was a little hard to find but worth the effort.

He parked outside of Francine's and stood on the sidewalk jiggling the change in his pocket while he waited. He pulled out a smoke and lit it just seconds before Millie came out of the dress shop.

"Hiya, babe. How're you doing?" he said turning on the charm. Millie was not flattered. In fact, she didn't say anything. She just stood in front of him looking at the sidewalk.

"What's the matter, cat got your tongue?"

Millie gave Doherty a harsh look. "I can't go out with you tonight. I don't know if I can ever go out with you again, Hugh." She called him 'Hugh', which was not a good sign.

He pulled hard on his smoke. "Why? What's the matter, Millie? If it's about last Friday, I explained to you about those guys."

"And I believed you. Perhaps I was being naïve."

"I don't follow." Doherty was totally confused.

"A man came to visit my father-in-law. A big Irish fellow, named Toomey or something."

"Tuohy, Angel Tuohy. I know him; he works as an errand boy for Judge DeCenza."

"He told my father-in-law that he shouldn't let me see you anymore. He told Gilbert about what happened at your apartment the other night and that there might be more incidents like it in the future. He said you were in big trouble and it was dangerous for me to be around you. He implied that my seeing you could be dangerous for me and my in-laws as well."

"Jesus Christ!"

"Please, I've asked you before not to take the Lord's name in vain."

"I'm sorry, Millie. I can explain, though it's all kind of complicated."

"You said what happened last Friday was about that man, a woman and some old case. That it had nothing to do with me or us, or … oh, I don't know what or who to believe anymore."

"Look, Millie. I haven't been entirely on the level with you. I don't mean about you and me, but about some other stuff."

"Why don't you tell me all about it as you walk me to the bus."

"The least you can do is let me drive you home."

"No, I'd prefer to take the bus."

As they walked down Washington Doherty decided to tell Millie as much as he could without making her feel responsible for his troubles with Martin DeCenza.

"It goes back some years now to when I was on the police force. You might not know this, but your father-in-law and other men in this town can tell you that Judge DeCenza's machine runs most things here in West Warwick. People vote the way they want them to and in return the party takes care of them in its own way. When I was on the force one of the first things I learned was that the police were always at the Judge's beck and call. And that was only part of it. If somebody was arrested the machine didn't want arrested, then he got released right away. And if there was somebody who wouldn't play ball with them, well that somebody found himself in trouble all the time. Sometimes it was with the cops, sometimes with the tax people or the health department or zoning board if they were in business. And if they owned a taproom there was no end to the number of people they'd have to grease just to stay operating. If they didn't then they'd suffer damages they never bargained for. And of course, the cops would never catch the ones who did it."

"Is that why you left the police force?"

"Yeah, pretty much."

"If things were so bad, why didn't you just leave town?"

Doherty shook his head. "I don't know. I thought if I went into private investigations I'd be totally on my own. I mean I don't have a storefront so I wouldn't have to worry about my windows being broken. And I don't have merchandise so I wouldn't have to worry about theft. Maybe I was the one being naïve, thinking I could stay clear of the Judge and his machine."

"I still don't understand why those men attacked you like they did."

"I'm not sure either. But, you see, a while back, right around the time I met you, the Judge hired me to do a job for him. It was a simple case of finding a guy who'd gone missing. You might've read about it in the papers. His name was Spencer Wainwright, the Republican County Chairman. I was struggling financially at the time, so against my better judgment I took the case. The Judge paid me well, and it came in handy because I needed the money to cover my bills and keep my office open. What I didn't bargain on, Millie, is that once the Judge has his hooks into you, he thinks he owns you. I've refused to be his 'boy' and he doesn't like it."

"And that's why those two men tried to beat you up?"

"Not entirely. I had a run-in with the big one with the mustache once before, and I roughed him up a little bit. He didn't like it and neither did the Judge, who he does muscle work for. I think the other night he came to my place to return the favor."

They were almost to the bus stop. Millie stopped and looked at Doherty. "I still don't understand how this involves my in-laws and me."

"I don't either. All I know is that the Judge has been trying to make my life miserable ever since that job. Just last week he fixed it with Harry so as I can't be in the barbershop anymore unless I'm there on business. I mean Bill Fiore is one of my only friends, and now I can't even hang out with him."

"What about us?"

"The Judge knows we've been seeing each other. Hell, the son of a bitch, excuse my French, knows everything. That's why he approached your father-in-law and got Gilbert to come in to warn me off you. When that didn't work he came back at you, only this time making it sound like you're in trouble along with me. But it's really all about me; it doesn't have anything to do with you," Doherty added trying to convince himself of that as much as Millie.

The bus was rapidly approaching the stop. "I'm not so sure about anything right now, Doherty. I think you and I should take a little recess until some of this blows over. I've got my boys to think about."

"What do you mean by a 'recess'? We're not in school anymore, Millie."

"I don't know, Hugh. I just don't know." Millie reached up and put her hand on Doherty's cheek. She kissed him lightly on the lips, and then stepped through the bus' open door.

Doherty spent the next three hours at Paddy's, an Irish taproom on Main, whose sign simply featured a green shamrock with its name in the middle. It was where the Irish millworkers went to ease their pains by drinking away a good part of their weekly paycheck - a ritual Doherty's father had regularly engaged in when he was working. Doherty knew a few of the younger guys in the place but was in no mood for conversation, particularly a drunken one. He threw back a half dozen doubles of Jameson with 'Gansett chasers. He was so loaded by the time he walked out, he decided to leave the Chevy parked right where it was on Main and staggered home as best he could. He fell asleep fully dressed, though not before leaving most of his binge on the floor by his bed.

Saturday was a day for recovery. Doherty hadn't been on a bender like that since V-J Day and was no wiser for it. He didn't know what to make of last night's conversation with Millie and thought maybe she was right for them to take a break until his business with the Judge got sorted out. He also knew he hadn't seen the last of Rene Desjardins.

A long walk helped him clear his head. It was late afternoon by the time he strolled into the office. He wanted to pick Bill Fiore's brain even though he was banned from Harry's Barbershop except as a customer. He could've used a shave but Saturday was kids day at the shop and having a mob of whiny tots running around wouldn't have done a thing for his hangover.

The office was musty, as Agnes had locked it up tighter than a drum when she left on Friday. Doherty flipped open the windows and took a hit off the coffee he'd picked up at the Donut Kettle. He lit a cigarette to keep the coffee company and then revisited the Wainwright folder. Shortly after six there was soft knock on the door. Doherty figured it was Annette Patrullo, but couldn't be too sure so he asked who it was before opening up. It was indeed the hot little number who'd lit the fire in Spencer Wainwright's pants.

She was wearing a purple blouse made out of some kind of shiny, imitation silk. It was buttoned one button too little for someone trying to sell houses to young families. Her skirt was of maximum tightness and once again Doherty wondered how she could sit down in it and still maintain a demure appearance. Although her hair was teased up as usual, she had lost control of some of it and a few curls sprung loose here and there. Her make-up was also a little worn from a hard day of showing houses.

Doherty offered Annette a chair and a cigarette. She took the former and pulled her own pack for the latter. Winstons, one of those filtered brands. Each sat and smoked for a few minutes. Annette kicked off her black high-heeled shoes.

"Tough day in the housing market?"

"A long day. Lots of showings, but no sales. It's hard without Spencer there. He's the one who usually closes the deals. I'm too new at this game to bring the ponies home."

"I like your racetrack comparison, though it doesn't seem to match up with selling houses."

"We're not just selling houses, Doherty, we're selling dreams," Annette said with the flicker of a smile.

"Right. Dreams with a twenty year mortgage attached."

Annette took a long puff on her smoke. Doherty noticed traces her red lipstick left on the filter. "Nobody said dreams come cheap."

"They do if all they are is dreams."

Annette Patrullo leaned forward and Doherty could see a hint of cleavage at the break in her blouse. He didn't think she showed her boobs off like this for her clients, though maybe she did. Everyone in the ad game says sex sells these days. "What have you found out about Spencer's business?"

"Maybe I should ask you the same question?"

"Maybe you should, but since I'm paying the bills, how's about if you go first."

"What do you know about West Warwick, Miss Patrullo?"

"You can call me Annette in here. And to answer your question, I know it's a grubby little town that's seen better days. There were a lot of mills here once and not too many anymore. My mother used to come into Arctic to shop every now and then. She hardly ever does anymore."

The young woman stubbed out her cigarette and sat back in her chair. She crossed her legs and Doherty made it a point to check out her pegs as she intended. They were encased in nylons though that didn't do anything to diminish their appeal. He tried to divert himself by thinking about Millie St. Jean, but was having trouble conjuring her up at the moment.

It was Doherty's turn. "You can say it. West Warwick is a dying town. Has been for at least a decade now. Pretty soon it'll be a once-was place, not like Warwick or Cranston, which are soon-to-be places. The old mills take up too much space and no new businesses of that size will ever replace them. Even so, it turns out your boy Spencer had this crazy idea that he could turn one of these behemoths into a combination office-apartment complex. Personally I can't see who'd be attracted to such an idea."

"Is that what was in the files I gave you?"

"More or less. One had a sketch of the old Bradford Soap Works turned into a beautiful living and workspace. Apparently he and a partner bought it on the cheap, though it'd still take some serious scratch to turn it into Spencer's dream."

Perhaps it was Doherty's imagination but Annette suddenly seemed a little dewy eyed. "Spencer always thinks big. Who knows, maybe it'll work out the way he's planned. Is it a good location?"

"Actually it's beautiful setting right alongside the river. Nice old building too. It even has a Victorian style tower at its center. Must've been quite the place in its heyday. I was still a kid when most of the operation closed down."

"Well, you know what they say in the real estate business: the three most important features in selling a property are 'location, location, and location'. Spencer might be onto something other people can't see. He likes to think of himself as a visionary."

"What about you? Do you think he's a *visionary*?"

Annette was a little taken aback by the question. "Me. I don't know about that visionary stuff. I'm just a working girl trying to make a living. I worked in stores when I first got out of high school but that didn't do anything for me. This is my first real, professional type job. Spencer promised he'd teach me the ropes."

"And has he?"

"You could say that, though I didn't bargain on some of the extracurricular activities that came along with them. But, hey, a girl's gotta eat, doesn't she?"

Doherty's first impulse was to be judgmental then thought better of it. Annette was his client, and besides, who was he to judge the behavior of others.

"Has it been worth it?"

"To be honest with you, yes it has. Spencer's shown me things and given me things I wouldn't've been able to get on my own. I can see what he's like, and even though he tells me he and his wife are gonna get divorced, I know that's not happening – least not on my account. So for now I'll just go along for the ride and hope I've got enough sense to know when to get off."

"When will that be?"

"I don't know. Probably not till I get my own real estate license. After that, who knows? I might surprise you, Doherty. Turns out I'm pretty good at this house-selling thing. Not as good as Spencer, of course, but most people aren't.

I also know I got a good body, 'cause I see you and other guys always checking me out. And I gotta a brain too. I plan on using both of them to take care of myself."

"No interest in getting married and having kids?"

"Course I do. Every girl does. But it'll have to be the right man and at the right time. Till then I'm looking out for number one." Annette paused and took a good look around Doherty's shabby little room. "I don't see any family pictures here in spite of that tale you tried to pass off on me about the wife and a little one on the way. I suspect you're not married and you already got a few years on me."

"Like you, I haven't met the right person yet."

"Well you better step on it. Not many girls these days wanna have an old man for a husband, especially once the kids come along."

"Do you mind if we change the subject?"

Annette lit another Winston and purposely blew smoke in Doherty's direction. "Whatever you say, Mr. Detective."

"Have you ever heard of a man named Frank Ganetti?"

Annette looked at the ceiling as she tried to recall the name. "I don't think so. Doesn't ring a bell. I'd have to look in our files to be sure. Is he one of Spencer's clients?"

"Not exactly. From what I can gather from these documents," Doherty said patting the files that were sitting on the desk in front of them, "this Ganetti is Wainwright's partner in this mill renovation deal. For all we know he could be a silent one. It seems that he and Wainwright were looking at a number of other abandoned properties in town as well – almost all of them old mills."

"Name still doesn't sound familiar. Maybe you should ask Mr. Cooper about him."

Doherty shook his head. "Cooper didn't appear to have much interest in Wainwright's pie in the sky projects. He struck me as more of a meat and potatoes kind of guy."

"Yeah, if your meat of choice is hamburger. Ben Cooper's idea of a good week is selling a couple of little Capes and making a few hundred bucks in commissions. If it wasn't Cooper's company to begin with, Spencer would've sent him packing a long time ago."

"That may be true, though right now it's Ben Cooper who's sitting comfortably in his little office while your Mr. Wainwright is lost in space. Sometimes it doesn't pay to be too ambitious."

"I'll keep that in mind when I get my own agency. Personally I'd rather eat steak every night than hamburger. So, what're you gonna do next?"

"I guess I'll try to track down this Ganetti character. But I've got to warn you, Annette, your man may very well be shacking up with some bimbo while I'm busy spending your dough."

"You said that before. I didn't like it then. I like it even less now. Just find him, okay. Let me worry about the money," she said as she stood up.

"Yes, Miss Patrullo. That's what I do best. I find the wayward and bring them home." As she was leaving Annette Patrullo dropped her cigarette butt on the floor and stomped it out with her black high heel.

Chapter Nine

GUS TIMILTY

There were no Frank Ganettis listed in the Kent County phone book. A couple of other Ganettis had made the cut but no Franks, Francises or plain Fs. Doherty did locate three Frank Ganetti listings in the Providence book. One was on Smith Street, another on Blackstone Boulevard on the posh East Side, and a third for a Frank Ganetti, Jr. CPA on Weybosett Street, which Doherty thought was somewhere downtown.

On Monday morning he put in a call to his old friend and mentor Gus Timilty. Timilty was Doherty's superior when he first went onto the police force, but he was forced to leave when he got mixed up in some shady business involving prostitutes. He hoped to catch Gus at Briggs and Timilty, the security company he worked for in Providence.

A sweet voice answered the phone. He asked for Gus and was told that Mr. Timilty was busy with a client. Doherty left a call back number. A half hour later the office phone rang and Doherty let it ring until Agnes picked it up and announced "Doherty and Associates." When she transferred the call to Doherty's phone, Timilty's voice came on the line.

"Sounds like you took my advice and went with the cute secretary and the *associates* idea."

"Except the secretary isn't all that cute and people keep asking me who my associates are."

Gus let out a mild chuckle. "That may be true, but I'll bet at least once you've said 'one of my associates is looking into that'."

"You got me there, Gus. How the hell are you?"

"I'm doing great, pally. Couldn't be better. Best thing I ever did was leave the cops. At least now I can earn an honest living."

"Something tells me if you're raking in the dough it isn't entirely honest." Gus barked out a knowing laugh.

"So what can I do you for Mr. Doherty and Associates?"

"I got a few things I need to talk to you about, but I don't feel like doing it over the phone."

"Okay. Why don't you come up to the big city for lunch tomorrow? I'll meet you at Ballard's, say around one. You know where Ballard's is, don't you?"

"Ballard's huh? Yeah, I think I know where it is, though it might be a little steep for my budget."

"Sweat it not, pally. Lunch'll be one me, or should I say on one of my clients. I can write you off as a business expense. You'll be one of the *experts* I needed to consult on something or other. See you at one, then. I've got to run. Have to be over at the courthouse by eleven."

Doherty was not fond of driving into Providence. The traffic was always bad and even though the downtown grid made some sense, once you got around the edges all the streets were one way and always in the wrong direction. Ballard's was located on Pine about a block from the river. Sandwiched between the financial district and the courthouses, it attracted a lot of suits during the lunch hour. Most of those suits were pretty expensive and they all sat with martini glasses in front of them. Doherty chose to wear one of his own, hoping to blend in with his off-the-rack outfit from St. Onge's.

Gus was already at a table across from the bar when Doherty arrived ten minutes late. His old buddy was nursing some brown liquor in a tumbler. The bar area was paneled in dark wood and just about everyone in the place was a guy over thirty with a jacket and tie on.

"Hey Doherty, how the hell are you?" Gus said loudly as he rose and took the younger man's hand. With his other hand he squeezed Doherty's upper arm. The two of them feigned a few punches. "You look pretty good for a guy who's still stuck in West Bumfuck Warwick."

"Small town life agrees with me. Unlike Providence, I never have trouble finding a place to park there. Hell, most of the time I can walk wherever I go."

"Small town, small time is what I always say."

"You ought to know. You spent the best years of your life there."

A waiter came by to drop off some menus. While he was there Doherty ordered a Jameson while Timilty asked for another Dewar's on the rocks.

"So what do you recommend?" Doherty asked perusing the menu while purposely ignoring the prices listed on the right.

"The lobster Newburg is one of their specialties, and the sirloin is pretty good too. I've had both."

"Sounds better than the ham and cheese I usually eat for lunch."

"Hey, pally, you got to learn to expense lunches onto your clients. You'll eat better that way." The drinks arrived and Doherty pulled out a smoke. He offered one to Gus but the older man waved him off.

"I'm trying to cut down. Doctor's orders." Doherty noted that Gus had put on a few pounds and his dark hair now ran wild with gray. Still, dressed in a dark gray pinstriped suit, striped shirt, and club tie, he looked the very model of success. His shirt alone probably cost as much as Doherty's suit.

The waiter came back to take their food order. Doherty opted for the sirloin, rare; Timilty chose the Newburg.

"You said you had some things to discuss with me. So have at it, pally."

"Are you familiar with a guy named Frank Ganetti?"

This name clearly piqued Gus' curiosity. "Senior or junior?"

"Junior as a matter of fact. Why?"

"Well I was hoping you'd say that given that Frank Ganetti, Sr. is presently doing ten to twenty up at the ACI."

"Jesus. Who the hell is he?"

Timilty leaned forward and looked at him intensely. "Don't you read the papers? Frank Ganetti, Sr. was the boss of the Manton Avenue gang. He still may be for all we know."

"And who exactly are the Manton Avenue gang?"

"They're what you might call subcontractors for Rhode Island's number one crime family. I assume you know who they are."

"Course I do. Everybody in Rhode Island knows about the Federal Hill crew. What do you mean by subcontractors?" Timilty finished his Dewar's and whistled the waiter over for another. Doherty decided not to try to keep up with his old friend, especially since he had to drive back to town later.

"What do you know about the mob – or La Cosa Nostra as they like to call themselves?"

"Well, I know they're Italian, Sicilian for the most part. That they operate out of Providence here, and have organizations all over the country."

"And outside of the U.S. as well. One of their biggest operations is in Cuba. It's why so many Americans take their vacations there. They can gamble legally in Havana, screw any putan they can afford, smoke the best cigars in the world and indulge in any other vice they want. Plus, it's one place the feds can't reach. My understanding is that the mob is wired into the Cuban government from top to bottom."

"Around here, from what I can tell, they make most of their money on the other side of the law: you know, things like loan sharking, prostitution, labor rackets, gambling and now maybe even drugs," Doherty said.

"You got that right, pally. These guys got money up the ying yang. Only problem is how do they unload so much funny money. How do they make it clean?"

"I don't follow."

"Look, Doherty, why do you think the mob operates out of Providence instead of up in Boston? Boston's three times the size of this town. You want to know why? Because they don't have to deal with the crazy Irish down here, present company excluded, of course."

"Of course."

"In Rhode Island, you can buy off whoever you need to on the cheap. Up in Beantown the greedy cops and politicians want a bigger slice of the pie. Then there're the Irish mob guys to worry about as well. On top of that if some mob guy is involved in a killing in Massachusetts they might actually do an investigation. Down here they only go through the motions. Besides mob guys usually only kill other mob guys."

"You mean like that Tiger Mansuedo, who was shot, what thirty times, in that Portuguese bar over in East Providence?"

Timilty laughed. "I guess you do read the papers after all."

"And if I remember correctly, four other people in that bar took some slugs that night too. Innocent bystanders."

"Innocent my ass. Nobody in the Lisboa Lounge is an innocent bystander. They might not have a long rap sheet yet, but innocent? I don't think so."

"That still doesn't tell me anything about Frank Ganetti, Jr."

"I was getting to that," Timilty said, but waited because the food had just arrived. When the waiter withdrew he started in again. "Do you know what the Federal Hill guys do for legitimate businesses?"

"Haven't a clue."

"Mostly vending machines and juke boxes. You know why?" Timility didn't wait for a response. "Because they can clean a shitload of money through those machines. It's almost impossible for anyone to keep track of how many coins go into or are taken out of them in a given week. That's assuming that some-body on the law enforcement side even gives a damn."

"Don't tell me they wash all their illegal cash through vending machines." Timilty ate a large spoonful of his Newburg and uttered a moan of satisfaction. "Of course not. They can't really. There's too much of it. Some of it gets sent offshore to the islands like Cuba and the Bahamas where the governments are even more crooked than here in Rhode Island. But the big thing for the mob these days is legitimate investments. They buy up real businesses and with creative bookkeeping they can show more profit than they actually make. All they got to do is keep scrupulous records, and occasionally pay off some bent cop or taxman. Right now rental units are an attractive means for washing money."

"I don't follow. How do they do that?"

"It's pretty simple. They buy a large building or complex with business suites or apartments. Then they officially charge the occupants a certain amount of money for rent, often slightly more than a tenant would be willing or able to pay. When it comes time to collect the rent they give the tenant the extra cash needed to pay the landlord that makes up the difference. In the end they're really paying themselves while it looks like the money is coming out of the tenant's pocket. It's a great scheme as long as they don't get too greedy and the rents they record are reasonable and not ones that nobody'd be able to afford."

"But how much can they make on a scam like that?"

"Depends on how many units they own. People I'm in contact with tell me these guys are buying up office spaces and apartment buildings left and right. Most of the time they use dummy corporations as fronts so nothing can be traced back to them. That's where your guy Frank Ganetti, Jr. comes in. He

grew up being a bagman for the Manton Avenue crew. His specialty is han-
dling money for the big guys. His old man, Frank Senior, was a smart cookie,
though obviously not smart enough to stay out of prison. However, he did
make sure his son would look respectable. Frank Junior went to Brown then
Harvard Business School. He's got all the right diplomas up on his wall and
all the right contacts. And try as they might, nobody in law enforcement can
connect him back to his father's outfit. Except that…" Timiltty paused here.

"Except what?"

"If I was a gambling man, I'd lay six to one odds that what Junior is really
doing is using his Ivy League smarts to find ways to bury a lot of funny money
in legitimate investments. The government's problem is that so far Junior's
been a lot smarter than their people."

"What about the feds, or the IRS?"

"Oh don't think they're not trying. You see Junior has a way of putting the
right face on all of these legitimate investments. His way of operating is to find
some straw man, somebody whose credentials are beyond suspicion, and use
him as a front."

"Somebody exactly like the guy I've been hired to find," Doherty said.
He told Timilty about his on again, off again, on again search for Spencer
Wainwright. Gus knew who Wainwright was from his political role though not
from his real estate business. Doherty filled Gus in on the plans Wainwright
and Ganetti had put together to convert the old Soap Works into office and
apartment space. Timilty was impressed with the scheme.

"I got a hunch something went wrong somewhere along the way," Doherty
said as he showed Timilty the lab reports.

Timilty looked over the documents very carefully. "Sorry, pally. This stuff
is a little out of my league."

"Mine too, that's the problem."

"Not to worry. I got a guy who can decipher all this stuff for you in a matter
of minutes. He works up at Brown in the Bio-Chem Department. Does mostly
research from what I can tell."

"How do you know a guy like that?"

"A couple of years ago I was doing some investigating for this lawyer. It
turned out some chemical company was dumping sludge out its back door
and people in the adjoining neighborhood were all getting sick; I mean ugly

kind of sick: skin rashes, fevers, breathing problems, the whole nine yards. The company, of course, denied any responsibility. Then some kid died and my lawyer got the case. He filed a big lawsuit, and sent me up to talk to this doc at Brown. Guy's one of those Jew eggheads. He gave us exactly what we needed for the suit. Took him less than a week to link the illnesses to the crap the company was dumping. The chemical company paid out thousands of dollars to people in the neighborhood and even agreed to clean up their mess. This doc figured out that the run-off from their plant had leached into the water supply."

"How come I didn't read about this in the papers?"

"Because the terms of the agreement were that everybody involved, and by that I mean all the victims, had to sign a non-disclosure form in order to get their cash."

"Somehow that doesn't seem right."

"Right or not, these poor slobs got more money in one hit than any of them would've made working the next ten years. They could've gone to court and maybe in a decade or so gotten more, but by then the lawyers' bills would've eaten up half the money. Sometimes you just gotta take the pot when the money's on the table. Anyway this doc up at Brown was the lynchpin. Here's his name and phone number," Timilty said as he wrote down the info on the back of one of his embossed business cards. "But I suggest you try to find him at the lab since that's where he spends most of his time. He's strange, but he's smarter than you and me put together."

Doherty and his old boss finished their lunch and talked about inconsequential things for next half hour. As promised Gus picked up the check. When they shook hands outside of Ballard's, Doherty felt indebted to his old friend.

Doherty found Dr. Leonard Shapiro in a research lab on the third floor of the Bio-Chemistry Building, which was just outside the main Brown campus. At first Doherty felt a little intimidated, having never before been inside the hallowed halls of Rhode Island's famous Ivy League college let alone in a science research center. Shapiro looked like the kind of guy who slept in his lab coat. He wore it with the same level of comfort lawyers and bankers wear three-piece suits. When they shook hands Doherty noticed that Shapiro's mitt was very large but soft. He had the hands of a man whose hardest labor each day was adjusting the lens on his microscope.

Shapiro was about a decade older than Doherty, tall but slightly stooped, no doubt the result of spending many hours a day bent over a lab table. He had a large head with dark, thinning hair, and was wearing the kind of wire-rimmed glasses seldom seen outside of ivy-covered walls. A slide rule stuck out of one of the pockets of his lab coat. From the moment he opened his mouth Doherty could tell that he wasn't a local.

"You're not from around here are you?" he said.

"No," Shapiro responded. "I'm from the Cleveland area. Went to Case Western, and then came east to do my doctorate at MIT. What about you? Are you a local man?"

"Born and bred Rhode Islander. West Warwick High School, U.S. Army, WW II."

"Ah, so you were in the war," Shapiro said in a soft voice with a hint of Midwestern twang.

"Infantry. Italy mostly, then Germany some toward the end. How about yourself?"

Shapiro was a little hesitant to respond. "I worked for the War Department. Did research in the field of chemical weapons."

"I thought the Geneva Convention outlawed those?"

Shapiro hesitated again. "It did, but only the use of them. Every country continued to do research into chemical warfare. We were being cautious since we knew from our intelligence that the other side was doing the same. It was our understanding that the Japanese were working on a very intensive germ warfare program in their labs. My superiors were afraid they might use them if it looked like they were going to lose the war. It was common toward the end for many Japanese soldiers and pilots to go on suicide missions. I'm sure you heard about the kamikazes. So we didn't know what to expect. Luckily, they never did use any outlawed chemicals."

"Probably because we dropped our own chemical weapon, the A-Bomb, on them first."

Shapiro shook his head in disagreement. "Technically speaking the atomic bomb was not a chemical weapon. Or at least we didn't think it was at the time."

"What about all that radiation fallout stuff?" He asked thinking about the book *On the Beach* he just finished.

Shapiro carefully considered his answer. "I suppose you could say we didn't know the extent of it until the bombs were finally dropped, though personally I don't accept that. Some of our scientists, men like Oppenheimer and others, warned of just that eventuality. In any case, it's all water under the bridge now. I can assure you chemical weapons research still continues to go on all over the world."

"Even here at Brown?"

Shapiro shook his head. "Not as far as I know. Not in this lab anyway, but you never can tell. Everything is so top secret these days now that we're in competition with the Russians. After all, we can't depend on them playing by the rules since they never have. Therefore, we do what we have to."

Doherty'd taken this part of the conversation about as far as it would go. "Do you mind if we bring things back down to earth. I got some documents here that I can't make heads or tails out of. Gus Timilty said you might be able to help me."

"Yes, Mr. Timilty called me yesterday to ask if I'd assist an old friend of his. I assume you're that friend. Why don't we step into my office?"

Dr. Shapiro led Doherty into a small cubicle in which three of its four walls were lined with filing cabinets. If there was any order to the chaos in the room, Doherty couldn't detect it. Shapiro sat at his desk and offered Doherty a chair facing it. He pulled out a pipe and began to load it with tobacco from a leather pouch. Doherty didn't like pipes mostly because a lot of the candy ass, junior grade officers in the Army had smoked them. He supposed it was what they learned at college, along with how to treat enlisted men like dirt. Doherty took the occasion to light up a Camel.

He handed Dr. Shapiro the files and the scientist perused the chemical analyses very carefully, occasionally dropping an "Uh-huh" or an "I see" as he did. Doherty was almost finished his cigarette when Shapiro finally looked up. The pipe was stuck in the corner of his mouth and the tobacco smell was a little too sweet for Doherty's taste. Still, it was the doc's office so he wasn't in a position to gripe.

Shapiro looked at him and said, "As we like to say out in Ohio, it appears that somebody was trying to sell someone else a 'pig in a poke'."

"Which means what in plain English?"

"As far as I can tell, according to these documents Mr. Wainwright and Mr. Ganetti bought this property, what was it?"

"An old mill. A soap manufacturing plant to be exact that sits flush along the banks of the Pawtuxet River. Nice setting."

"I see. Nice or not, there's no way they'll be able to develop it into the kind of usage they project in these plans."

"Why not?"

"Apparently because the water table in and around the building has been contaminated, probably from chemicals that leached out from the soap works. However, the purchasers did not know this because according to the dates on these documents they purchased the building and the adjacent land before they were given the results of the soil test samples. If I'm reading these reports correctly, it appears that the seller, this Sherbrooke Industries, knew that the plant would be useless for anything other than industrial purposes. Of course, the new owners can always manufacture soap there if they wish."

"But it wouldn't be of any use for housing or office space?"

"Not unless the people living or working there never planned on drinking water or bathing. I'd say it's completely useless for that kind of human activity or habitation."

"So a pig in a poke is?"

"An old, rural expression for a con job. It looks as if Sherbrooke Industries knew all along that the property would be no good for anything other than manufacturing. There's no fraud here unless they also knew beforehand how the purchasers planned to use the property." Doherty wondered if Wainwright and his silent partner had had a reason to keep their plans for the old Soap Works under wraps and purposely didn't let on to the Sherbrooke people that they planned to covert the old soap works into office and living space.

"Does that mean that Sherbrooke Industries committed no crime by selling the local buyers this so-called pig in a whatever?"

"As I said, only if they knew before the sale what the buyers were planning on doing with the space. If that were the case then Sherbrooke Industries would've had a legal obligation to share any soil tests they'd already done themselves with the buyers *before* a purchase and sale agreement was signed. If they did know and didn't tell them, then that might constitute fraud on their part. Or so the buyers' lawyers can claim. I'm sure your friend, Mr. Timilty, can shine more light on the legal issues here than I can."

Doherty rose to thank Dr. Shapiro. As he did the good doctor asked Doherty for the address of his place of business.

"Why do you need my address?"

"To send you a bill, of course. You don't think I do this kind of work for free do you?"

Doherty scratched down the address and phone number of Doherty and Associates on a page in his note pad, tore it out and gave it to Shapiro. He made a mental note to go to the Clyde Press when he got back to town to order up some business cards. Not having them was making his operation look small time.

At first Doherty thought the banging he heard was part of his dream. He often had violent dreams, not necessarily related to the war, though violent nonetheless. When the noise wouldn't go away he slowly opened his eyes. He checked the clock on the night table. It told him it was a little after two a.m. When the banging continued Doherty leaped out of bed wearing only his boxers and a tee shirt. His first thought was it was Rene Desjardins so he slipped on his shoes and then grabbed the Louisville slugger from behind the door. The knocking grew louder.

"Who's there?" Doherty asked anxiously.

"It's Gus goddamnit. Open the door before I wake up the whole neighborhood."

Doherty figured Timilty'd already done that. He unhooked the newly installed chain and flipped the lock. Gus Timilty stood in the doorway looking much more disheveled than he had during their lunch at Ballard's. He was wearing a leather jacket and a flannel shirt partially sticking out of stained tan pants. His hair was mussed like he'd just gotten out of bed.

"What's all the commotion about?" Doherty asked as his former boss pushed by him into the apartment.

"Shut the door and lock it." When he looked back at Doherty he said, "What's with the baseball bat?"

"I had a run-in with a couple of DeCenza's heavies last week. I thought you might be them. The bat's my only reliable weapon."

Gus snorted. "You got anything to drink?"

"There's a bottle of Jameson in the kitchen."

"Good. Pour us two doubles and bring them in here." Doherty did as he was told. When he handed Timilty his glass the big man downed the whiskey in two gulps.

"What the hell is this all about, Gus? It's two o'clock in the damn morning."

Timilty strode into the kitchen where he poured himself another double. When he returned he said, "I got a call from a friend of mine on the city police force, guy named Monahan. Told me they just pulled a body out of the river near Swan Point. Said it belongs to guy named Wainwright, some kind of big deal in the Republican Party."

"Spencer Wainwright?"

"From the description he gave me it sounded like the same guy you been looking for."

"Mary, mother of God. Was he shot or just drowned?"

"According to Monahan the corpse had a slug in his knee and another one in the back of the head."

"Why the shot in the leg?"

"Looks like somebody tortured your guy before he plugged him for good. This doesn't sound like some random killing. My guess is it was a professional job."

"You think it was somebody from the mob?"

"Likely contenders from what you've told me. The hit might've been called in by his partner, Frank Ganetti, Jr."

"Shit."

"Look, Doherty. I'm not going to stand here and tell you how to do your job, but it won't be long before the city cops find out you were looking all over the state for this guy. For all you know they might even like you as a suspect."

"Hell, Gus, I was just working a case."

"Then they'll come after you to get the name of your client. Besides both you and your client could be in danger if the people who nailed this guy you were looking for think you know more than you should. That's why I brought you this," Gus handed Doherty a brown paper bag. Inside was a thirty-eight-snub nose pistol – a five shot.

"It's fully loaded and totally clean. All the numbers have been filed off. In this business you should've had a piece already. I suspected you didn't, which was why I brought you this one. So take it for now till you can get yourself a legal permit and your own gun."

Doherty hefted the pistol in his hand and looked at the hard, cold steel. He hadn't handled a side arm since he'd left the police force. He thought about giving it back to Gus, but if what his old friend said was true, he might need it right away.

"Another thing, pally. If you don't want to deal with the cops till you can get this sorted out, you should make yourself scarce for a few days. You know, hide out somewhere they wouldn't be likely to find you."

"When do you think Wainwright's murder will hit the news?"

"Not till they inform the next of kin, which I assume is the wife. So you might have some time to make your own inquiries before that happens, though not much time."

"Gus, thanks for the heads up."

"You bet. Call me if you need any help. And whatever you do, Doherty, keep your head down. These are the kind of people who take no prisoners."

After Gus left, Doherty checked out of his apartment within fifteen minutes and drove around for as long as he could keep his eyes open. When they started to flutter he drove out to Tiogue Lake and parked. It was too late for the make-out crowd and there were no cops around, so he pulled the Chevy off the road and caught some shuteye. When he awoke he checked his watch – it was a quarter past seven. The mist laid a heavy blanket of gray over the lake. He felt for the thirty-eight that he'd slipped in his belt around at the small of his back. It made sleeping a little uncomfortable.

He drove up Cowesett Avenue and headed east toward the bay. He then turned onto the Post Road and made the now familiar drive out by the airport. Along the way he picked up a black coffee to help him meet the day. It was after eight by the time he got to Hoxie Four Corners. He parked in a lot across from Cooper and Wainwright, drank his coffee and smoked a couple of Camels while he waited.

Just before nine Annette Patrullo pulled up in her green and white Metropolitan. Doherty watched as she went inside and settled comfortably behind her desk. He waited another ten minutes, made a thorough check of the immediate area and then crossed Warwick Avenue and entered the real estate office. Everything seemed like business as usual. There was no frenzy that might have attended the news that one of the senior partners had been shot through the head the previous night.

Annette raised her eyes when Doherty approached her desk.

"Jesus, you look like somebody who slept in his clothes last night," she said.

"To be honest with you, I did. Is Cooper in?"

"Not yet. He doesn't usually come in till later in the morning. Unless he's got an appointment with a client looking at a cute little Cape," she added sarcastically.

"Anyone else here?"

"Margaret's in the back putting some files away." Annette leaned forward and wagged her nose in Doherty's direction. "You don't smell too good neither."

"You and I have to go for a ride – right now. Tell Margaret you're taking me out to look at some houses, and that you'll be back in a couple of hours."

"What's all this drama about, Doherty? If I stay out of the office too long I could miss some important calls."

"Just do as I say. I'll explain in the car. I can't afford for us to have a scene here."

Annette looked at Doherty for a few seconds trying to figure out if it was safe to go with the unkempt detective. She went to the rear of the office to inform Margaret Whitemore that she was going out with a client and would be back around noon. To complete the pretense she took a handful of house files with her. She grabbed her bag and the two of them left the office. Annette headed toward her car until Doherty intercepted her.

"We'll take mine. It's parked across the street."

"Why. Mine too small for you?"

"No. It's just that your car sticks out like a sore thumb."

Annette looked confused yet followed Doherty across Warwick Ave to his Chevy. It was rush hour and the traffic had picked up on the busy road. They had to do some dodging to get across safely – no mean feat for Annette in her tight skirt and heels. A few drivers honked their horns as they went by. Doherty wasn't sure if it was because they were crossing against traffic or because the drivers thought Annette Patrullo was a hot tomato.

When they got in the car Annette asked, "Are you kidnapping me, Doherty?" She asked in a way that sounded like she wouldn't be sorry if he was. He pulled out onto Warwick and headed north.

Doherty lit a Camel. "Do you mind if I smoke?"

Annette slumped down in the passenger seat and her skirt rode up a little higher than it should for a professional real estate agent. "Hey, it's your car, do what you like. Just do me a favor and open your window. Between the cigarette smoke and your body odor it's feels a little close in here."

They drove in silence for about a mile. "I got something to tell you and I didn't want to say back at the office."

"Have you found Spencer?" she asked hopefully.

"Yeah, in a way I have."

"That doesn't sound too good."

"It's not. Apparently the city police pulled a body out of the Providence River last night that fits Spencer's description."

"How could that be? We didn't hear anything about it at the office. There must be some kind of mistake," she said, desperation squeezing its way into her voice.

"It's not official yet. They're trying to locate his wife before they make an announcement. They need her to come in and identify the body."

Annette pulled a pack of Winstons out of her purse and lit one. He could see that her hands were shaking. She threw the spent match out the window. "Cooper told me yesterday that Mrs. Wainwright went down to Great Island to 'see for herself,' whatever the hell that meant. She's probably still down there. How did he die? Did he drown?"

"No, he was shot in the head, at point blank range. Apparently shot in the knee before that. Looks like whoever killed Spencer wanted him to suffer before he finally finished him off."

"Oh, my God. Oh, my God!" Annette was now trembling all over. The girl wrapped her arms around herself. Doherty reached across the seat and laid his hand on her shoulder.

"That may not be the worst of it," Doherty said. "Whoever killed Spencer could be after us as well."

"After us? Jesus, what for?"

Doherty didn't answer for a while, not sure how much he could confide in Annette. "That deal Spencer was working on, the one described in the files you gave me; that deal took a detour down Queer Street before it even got off the ground."

"I don't understand. Is that why Spencer was killed?"

"I'm not sure yet. I'm still trying to piece it all together. But it looks like whoever Wainwright was mixed up with thought he'd taken their money under false pretenses. The mill conversion deal was never going to happen because the water was contaminated."

"I don't follow. Wasn't the mill on the town's water system?"

"Apparently not. The place they'd bought was the old Soap Works. It had always run on its own wells. Somewhere along the line chemicals from the factory had seeped into the water table that the wells were tapped into. So no matter how attractive they made the old building look as potential office and living space, it wasn't practical because they would never have a clean water source."

"How could Spencer be so stupid? I mean he was a top shelf real estate guy. Everybody said so. He knew the game inside out. How could he be fooled by something like that?"

"Well, at first I thought maybe his greed or that of his partner got the better of him. You know how that can happen. However, according to the documents you gave me the water wasn't tested till after the deal was signed."

"But he must've thought of something like the water beforehand," she said, pulling heavily on her cigarette. Only the lipstick encrusted filter was left of Annette's Winston.

"All I can figure is that either he didn't want anyone to know what his plans for the property were, or he bought it from people he trusted, people he trusted without reservations. Maybe the sellers assured Spencer that the mill was on the town's water system when they knew for fact that it wasn't. That could be why Wainwright ran into trouble with his partner."

"You mean that Frank Ganetti guy?"

"Could be. Turns out Frank Ganetti, Jr. is the money brains behind the Manton Avenue Gang, who I've been told are subcontractors of Rhode Island's most famous crime family."

"You're shitting me. Spencer's partner in this deal was a mob guy?"

"So it seems, though apparently young Ganetti has maintained a pretty clean profile. I figure Spencer took a lot of money from him up front for this deal, and when the deal went south…"

"So did Spencer.' Annette said finishing the sentence. She then fumbled in her purse for another cigarette. "I can't help but say this, Doherty, but you're scaring the hell out of me."

"It scares me too, Annette." They drove further along Warwick Ave into Cranston.

"I have a friend who works as a PI in Providence. He was the one who told me about Spencer's death. So far, nothing's gone public, but he warned me that you and I should find safe places to hide out, at least until the cops start their investigation. It won't be long before they link Wainwright to Ganetti even if we try to bury the documents. Is there somewhere I can take you where you'll be safe?"

Annette considered the question for a while. "I don't know. I could go to my sister's but she and I aren't really on speaking terms these days. As for my parents, they would know something was up if I came back home. On top of that I don't want to listen to my mother crowing about how she knew something bad would happen when I got involved with a married man."

Annette was silent in thought for a while. "I got a cousin who lives up in Providence off North Main Street. I could call and see if she'd let me stay at her place for a few days. She's not the kind to ask a lot of questions. I'll tell her I got some man trouble and I need be where he can't find me. Knowing her, she'll fall for that."

Doherty turned up Elmwood and headed toward the city. They stopped along the way so Annette could call her cousin from a pay phone. When she got back in the car she said, "All set. She said she understands how men can be."

Doherty followed the directions she gave him to North Main Street. They drove past the Providence Arena where the Reds played hockey and where Doherty once went with his Uncle Patrick to watch Gorgeous George wrestle. After a few turns they found the cousin's house. Before she got out of the car Annette wrote down the cousin's phone number and gave it to him.

"What are you gonna do now?"

Doherty considered the question. "I'll try to lay low. In the meantime I'll see what I can find out about Sherbrooke Industries, the company that sold the Soap Works to Spencer."

"You be careful, Doherty. Sounds like we could have some dangerous people on our tails."

Chapter Ten

WILLY LEGERE

Doherty made himself scarce for the rest of the day. He phoned Agnes at the office and told her he wouldn't be in for a few days. He encouraged her to take a short vacation herself and promised to make it worth her while moneywise. Never one to look a gift horse in the mouth, Agnes didn't ask any further questions. Before she rang off she informed him that no one had called or been in that day.

Once it got dark Doherty drove down to the Centreville section of town and eventually found the house he'd been searching for. It was a ramshackle job at the end of a dead end street. When he approached the front door he saw that the storm was swaying limply on its hinges. Doherty pressed the doorbell but heard no sound inside. He waited a few moments and then knocked. Without inquiring who was there a stout middle-aged woman opened the door. Her hair was an unattractive mash of gray and black. She was tall but not tall enough to successfully carry the weight that rode around her midsection like a Dunlop tire. Her face spoke of suspicion and fatigue.

"What do you want?" she asked in an annoyed voice, not bothering to preface her question with a greeting.

Though he hadn't shaved or slept more than four hours in the past forty-eight, Doherty put on his best smile. "My name is Hugh Doherty. I'm a friend of your son Willy."

The woman gave him a harsh look and said, "My son is blind. He doesn't have any friends, only people who take pity on him." She stood her ground and didn't move or say anything more. The standoff lasted until Willy Legere came out from an inner room. He was wearing blue work pants, a sleeveless undershirt and only white socks on his feet. He didn't have his sunglasses on and his blank eyes stared awkwardly over Doherty's shoulder.

"Hi there, Willy," Doherty said.

Legere seemed confused. "Mr. Doherty, this is a surprise. What're you doin' here?"

"Sorry to barge in on you like this, Willy, you too Mrs. Legere, but I need to borrow a favor."

The Legeres look hesitant until Willy said, "Sure, Mr. D. Sure, whatever you need." Willy's mother was not so accommodating. Her eyes continued to bore down on the stranger at her doorstep.

Willy turned awkwardly in the direction of his mother. "I told you 'bout Mr. Doherty, ma. He comes by my stand outside the News almost every day to talk baseball. He's one of my best customers," Willy added as if he ran a store instead of selling pencils on the street. Mrs. Legere made an unpleasant guttural sound.

"What do you need, Mr. D.?"

Doherty spoke to Willy without once taking his eyes off his mother. "I need a place to stay for a couple of days. I'll pay you for the help, but nobody can know I'm here." Now Mrs. Legere's suspicious antenna was on full alert.

"What's this all about? Showin' up at this hour, pretendin' to be a friend of my son and askin' to stay here. Don't you have no one else to go to – a relative or somethin'?" she asked.

"That's not fair, ma," Willy broke in. "Mr. Doherty's my friend. He comes by to talk to me everyday. Ain't that right, Mr. D.?"

Before the mother could butt in again, Doherty said," Sure, Willy. We're friends. Fact is you're about the only good friend I got right now."

Willy turned in his mother's direction. "See. Now don't be rude, ma. Invite the man in."

The next thing he knew, Doherty was sitting in the Legeres' living room drinking a beer with Willy and trying to explain to his mother that he was a private eye and had made some enemies because of a case he was working on and that he needed to stay away from his office and apartment for a while until things blew over. He told them they would be in no trouble themselves because nobody would suspect him of being at their house. He purposely neglected to tell them that the people looking for him might be members of the mob.

Not satisfied, yet no longer willing to object to Doherty's presence in her home, Mrs. Legere got up and went into another room. He could hear a squawk box in there playing some comedy show accompanied by canned laughter.

Willy Legere was excited to have a friend sleep over. It was as if he were a kid again with two good eyes and a baseball game to play the next day. Doherty tried to pump up the drama concerning his circumstances without letting Willy know just how dire his predicament was. Around ten Mrs. Legere showed Doherty to a small, spare room on the second floor. It smelled dank and moldy. She threw some sheets and a blanket on the bed and indicated that Doherty could make it up himself. After she left, he dressed the bed, stripped down to his skivvies, and stretched out on it. He needed some time to dope things out. Ten minutes later he heard some feet shuffling down the hall and then a soft knock on the door.

"Can I come in, Mr. D.?"

Doherty opened the door. Willy Legere was standing there in a pair of blue and white striped pajamas and moccasin style slippers. His dead eyes looked beyond his houseguest. Without his ubiquitous baseball cap Willy's lank brown hair hung down in front over his brow.

"What's up Willy?"

The blind vet walked past him into the stale bedroom. "This used to be my room when I was a kid," he said. "It ain't much to look at now, but back then I had pictures of my favorite ballplayers all over these walls. Nowadays I sleep down the hall in my father's old room."

"Where is your old man, Willy?"

"Oh, he's gone. Been gone a long time now."

"Dead?"

"I wish. No he skipped out on me and my brother and ma when I was twelve. Dirty bastard never gave my mother nothin' 'cept a black eye every once in a while."

"A drinker?"

Willy shook his head. "Not really; just a mean son-of-a-bitch. He worked at the Lippit until it closed and then came over here when the mill was still the Waterhouse. When it changed hands he and a bunch of other guys got laid off for good. My father was always at war with the world. You know what I mean, Mr. D.?"

"Yeah, I do, Willy," Doherty said shaking his head. "My old man was a drunk, plain and simple. He probably meant well, but by the time he got home come Friday night half his paycheck had gone down his gullet. I know their lives were hard. It was hard for a lot of men in this town yet some of them still took care of their families and made sure their kids were raised up right. My old man wasn't one of them. You ever hear from your father?"

Willy's eyes got red but he wouldn't allow himself to cry. "He called me when I first come home from the hospital. I got written up in the papers and I guess he saw the articles. I didn't even know he was still in the state. He asked me how I was doin' and all that. Then he wanted to know if the government was goin' to give me a big check to make things right. That made me so mad. I told him I was one of the lucky ones, luckier than the guys who went down with the ship. I told him I never wanted him to call me again. I was gonna say I never wanted to *see* him again, but that wouldn'ta made much sense since I couldn't see him anyways. You know what I mean?"

"Sure kid, I understand."

"So, Mr. D. is there anythin' I can get you till it's safe for you to go home?"

"If you got an extra razor, and maybe a toothbrush, that'd be nice."

Willy headed for the door. "I'll ask ma to see if she can find them things. I'm sure she'll come up with somethin' you can use."

He moved through the doorway without touching the doorjambs. Having grown up in this room Willy knew it in his mind's eye so well he didn't have to use his real ones. Doherty thought it was like when you walk through your own place at night without the lights on. You don't bump into things because you just know where everything is.

Chapter Eleven

FRANK GANETTI, JR.

I n the morning Mrs. Legere made Doherty and Willy ham and eggs. It was the best breakfast Doherty'd had in weeks. Afterwards he shaved and cleaned his teeth with a razor and brush Willie's mother had found in the downstairs bathroom. Doherty drove Willy into town and dropped him off in front of the News. He then cruised by his apartment building. He slouched down in the seat as he did so; there were no suspicious cars parked nearby. He took a cruise by his office and saw that the coast seemed clear there as well. Still he wasn't taking any chances.

He drove back down Main and stopped in at St. Onge's as soon as it opened. He bought a new package of underwear and a white shirt. Under the guise of trying the shirt on for size he ducked into the dressing room and changed into the new duds. Before leaving town he stopped in at the Donut Kettle for another cup of coffee and the morning paper. The *Journal* ran the story about Wainwright's murder under the fold on the front page.

Doherty did not read the whole thing – only up to the part where it said that one of Warwick's most prominent citizens appeared to have been shot at close range and that the Providence police were launching a full investigation. There was no mention of the knee shot.

With the coffee cradled between his legs Doherty headed out Providence Street north toward the city. When he got there he wasn't surprised to see that Frank Ganetti, Jr.'s office on Weybosett Street was in the center of Providence's small financial district. Doherty made one full pass by the downtown building and then parked the Chevy a couple of blocks away. It was past ten so he assumed Frank Ganetti, Jr., CPA would be in his office. The building was old but clean. It had one of those large, open foyers with a mosaic seal imbedded into the floor. It was some kind of compass/sundial design that Doherty couldn't quite figure out. He took the stairs up to the second floor.

Ganetti's office door was wood with a frosted glass upper half that bore Ganetti's name and accounting business stenciled in black in the lower left hand corner. A young woman was sitting at a desk facing the door when Doherty entered. She had short reddish blond hair and was cute in a pixyish sort of way. She wore a blue button up sweater with a lacy collar sticking out at the top. Doherty was surprised. He thought Ganetti'd be the kind of guy to have a secretary more along the lines of Annette Patrullo.

"Can I help you, sir?" she asked in a soft squeaky voice that went along with her looks.

"I'd like to talk to Mr. Ganetti."

She gave him a sympathetic yet disappointed smile. "I'm afraid Mr. Ganetti's not in right now."

"Do you expect him soon?"

The pixie began moving her hands nervously across the top of the desk, squaring off some papers that were already neatly aligned. Either she was lying about Ganetti not being in or was just plain scared.

"I don't know," she said vaguely. "Can I ask the nature of your business?"

"Sure. When he comes in could you tell Mr. Ganetti that I'd like to talk to him about Spencer Wainwright? My name is Doherty and I'm from West Warwick."

The pixie fumbled for a piece of paper; she wrote down Doherty's information and then asked him to spell *Wainwright*. As she scribbled Doherty noticed some dark movement through the space at the bottom of the door to Ganetti's inner office. If Ganetti wasn't in there then someone else was. In either case Doherty's business with the secretary had hit a dead end and he wasn't about to barge into the mobster accountant's office not knowing who or what was on the other side. Instead he politely thanked the girl and hit the stairs.

Rather than head back to town, he decided to take a walk through the Arcade across the street occasionally strolling out to the balcony to keep an eye on Ganetti's building. He wanted to see if anyone interesting exited from it in the next half hour. Doherty was on the second floor of the Arcade when a rather strong hand reached out and gripped his shoulder from behind. It felt like a vise. His first reaction was to knock it away but was glad he didn't when he felt the cold steel up against the back of his head. A gruff voice told him to keep walking. He did as he was told until they reached the men's room at the end of the corridor. Once there, Doherty was roughly pushed through the swinging door.

Inside the washroom he and the guy with the raspy voice were joined by third man. The two backed Doherty up against a wall. The second man, a short, wiry character with heavily pomaded jet-black hair, frisked him, and quickly relieved Doherty of the thirty-eight he'd gotten from Gus Timilty. The other guy, the one with the strong shoulder grip, was big enough to fill a doorway. He wore a topcoat, a fedora and had a face that looked like a bunched up fist. Though he was well into his forties he was the kind of guy Doherty didn't want to mess with, especially given the size of the piece he held in his hand.

"Looky what we got here, Angelo. A thirty-eight with the numbers rubbed off. What're you doin' with a gun like this?" the smaller one asked Doherty, his face no more than a foot away.

Doherty didn't say anything. The big man moved in closer and pushed his cannon into Doherty's forehead. Doherty could smell the mix of garlic and tobacco on Angelo's breath. Or maybe it was the smell of his own fear sweat.

"Da man asked you a question," the big one said waving his gun at Doherty. There was a trace of old world accent in his voice.

"I'm a private investigator," Doherty said as calmly as he could under the circumstances. "I was hired to find a guy named Spencer Wainwright. Before I could find him he was fished out of the Providence River day before yesterday with a big hole in his head. I'd heard he was in business with Frank Ganetti, Jr. so I went to see Mr. Ganetti. I was hoping he'd know why my guy was killed. That's pretty much all I know." The big guy looked at his partner but didn't lower his pistol.

While the little man sized up Doherty the big one moved back and rested his considerable bulk against the bathroom door, blocking the entrance of anyone else wishing to use the facilities.

"What about this here gun?" the smaller guy said dangling the .38 between his thumb and index finger. His teeth were yellowed and fanglike; he reminded Doherty of a weasel. Although he was younger and smaller than the big guy he was no less menacing.

"Two nights ago I'd heard through a friend, another private detective, about Wainwright being killed and dumped into the river. He thought I might need some protection just in case."

The little guy stepped in even closer. Doherty couldn't take his eyes off the dark hairs that protruded from his nose. "In case of what?" he snapped.

Now he had to figure out where to go next, keeping in mind that these might be the very men who killed Wainwright.

"In case somebody thought I knew more about Wainwright's business than I should. Somebody who might want me to, uh, disappear." Now it was out there for them all to chew on. "Who are you guys, anyway?"

"Whaddya think, Bobby?" the big guy asked the younger one.

"I dunno," the smaller one said. Then he turned his attention back to Doherty. "Look, Mr. Private Eye, seems like we all got a problem here. You see we work for Mr. Ganetti, Senior. Frank Junior ain't been seen in two days and his father was worried 'bout him. When you come nosin' round the office this mornin' we thought maybe you was mixed up in him bein' missin'. Capische?"

Doherty looked from one of the muscle guys to the other. The big one had lowered his pistol a few inches. That was a good sign. "Yeah, I capische. I don't mean Mr. Ganetti, *Junior* any harm. All I know is that he was involved in some business deal with the Wainwright guy and … " Doherty didn't know what to say next. He couldn't very well let on that he thought Frank Junior was responsible for Wainwright being murdered.

The little guy spoke instead, interrupting him. "Soon as his father heard that Junior was missin' he sent us to look into things. We don't know nothin' 'bout no Wainwright mook. But now you tell us this guy who was popped was in business with Junior?"

"I thought Frank Senior was in prison."

"That don't mean nothin'. He still calls the shots," the big guy put in.

"Did his father know about Junior's investments? I mean the legal stuff."

"I dunno. That ain't exactly our department. Alls he heard was that Junior was nowhere to be found. You don't know nothin' about that do you?" The young guy asked, menace returning to his voice.

"I don't even know who Frank Junior is. I've never met the man. What I do know is that he was involved in a development deal with Wainwright that went south. It looks like both of them stood to lose a lot of money in the process."

Bobby leaned in close again. "How is it that you know all this?"

"It's my job. I'm a private detective, remember. I investigate things."

"Who hired you to find all dis out?" Big Angelo asked.

"I shouldn't tell you, but it probably doesn't matter now. Some girl Wainwright was screwing hired me to find him when he didn't show up to screw her. After I went looking for him everything else turned up along the way. She doesn't have anything to do with Frank Junior's business or with Wainwright being killed. She was in love with the chump and just wanted me to find him. I thought I'd find him off screwing some other girl, but that's not what happened. Instead he turned up dead."

"Whaddya we do now, Angelo, with this jabroni here?" Bobby asked the big guy. Doherty wondered if the choice was between letting him go or killing him.

There was an unpleasant silence in the washroom. Doherty could hear one of the faucets dripping as the two guidos considered his fate.

Finally Bobby turned back to Doherty. "Look buddy, we got no reason to hurt you. For all we know maybe what you're tellin' us is true. Our job is to find Frank Junior and protect him. My advice is for you to stay the fuck outta this. You found the guy you was suppose to find. Unfortunately he was already dead. I don't know if that means you won't get paid, and personally I don't really give a shit. But if we find you nosin' around in our business or lookin' for Frank Junior again, it could be you that ends up dead. Capische?"

"Yeah, I capische. What about my gun? Can I have it back?"

Bobby snickered. "Well, since it don't have no numbers on it, there's no way you can prove it's really yours. I think the best thing is for me to keep it. 'Sides, don't you know it's a felony in Rhode Island to have an unregistered handgun, 'specially one without numbers on it. You get caught with this little snubby, you could end up in jail."

With that the three men singly departed the Arcade's men's room. Doherty couldn't get back to West Warwick fast enough. It would be a while before he ventured into Providence again.

Shaken, but undaunted, Doherty returned to town, glad for the moment to be rid of Frank Ganetti's boys and the big city. He cruised by his apartment building and pulled over in front of Clyde Press. He picked up his new business cards, paying for them with the last few bills he had in his pocket. Before walking back to his place he stopped at Lefty's to drop a nickel on the daily number punchboard. There was no sign of anyone unusual on Main or Crossen so Doherty decided to return home. He was in desperate need of a shower and a change of clothes.

He left the Chevy in front of the printers and walked into town to his office. There were no strangers lurking about so he mounted the stairs above the barbershop and slipped into Doherty and Associates. Everything was as it had been when he left. Agnes had pulled the plastic cover over the Remington and there were no notes anywhere. He thought of calling her to tell her it was safe to come back to work then decided it might not be after all. He struck up a Camel and lifted the phone. First he put in a call to Gus Timilty; the secretary at Briggs and Timilty told him Gus wasn't in at the moment and she didn't know when he'd be back. Doherty asked for his former boss to give him a call back.

Before making the next call Doherty uncovered the small box of business cards. He'd had a hundred printed because Clyde Press gave him a good price on that number. In large letters they said *Doherty and Associates* in the center. In the left hand bottom corner was the word *Contact*, with a colon after it and the name *Hugh M. Doherty*. In the right hand corner was his office address and phone number. He'd considered putting '*Expertise in Finding Missing Persons*' on the cards then thought better of it given that his most recent cases had expanded his practice beyond that.

He took the number out of his wallet, cradled the phone against his ear and dialed Annette Patrullo's cousin. The phone rang ten times but no one answered. They were either not at home, or afraid to pick up. He felt he should alert Annette as to what went down with Ganetti's goons at the Arcade. While waiting for Gus to call back Doherty again took out the files Annette had given him regarding Wainwright and Ganetti's purchase of the Soap Works property. Despite being warned off the case by Frank Senior's men, he thought his next move was to find out what he could about Sherbrooke Industries.

Just as Doherty was about to take a hike up to the Arctic News for lunch the phone rang. He waited until the third ring before lifting the receiver. He answered as Agnes would, "Doherty and Associates."

"It's me, Gus. What's going on?"

Doherty spent the next five minutes filling his old friend in on his encounter with Angelo and Bobby at the Arcade washroom in Providence. As he spun out the tale he could hear Gus breathing heavily on the other end.

When he was finished Timilty said, "You want my advice: get your ass as far away from those guys as you can. You don't want to be messing with people like that."

"I was thinking the same thing, but…"

"But what?" Gus cut in.

Doherty paused, carefully considering where he was going next. "I can't let it go. I need to find out why Wainwright was killed, and by who."

"I'll tell you why he was killed," Gus said, his voice rising as he did. "He was killed because he pissed away some serious mob money. You've got to understand something, pally. The only thing those guys care about is their dough. They don't like losing it, and they particularly don't like losing it to somebody outside their organization."

"I'm sorry, but something tells me Frank Junior didn't have Wainwright killed. According to the guys I met in Providence, he's missing too."

"It doesn't matter who the hell did it. Whether it was Manton Ave guys or somebody from the big boss' crew. The point is it's no longer your goddamn problem. I don't want to see anything bad happen to you."

"I'd like to take a look at this Sherbrooke Industries. Any idea how I can go about that?"

"You're not listening to me are you? Those guys who jacked you up in the men's room, they mean business. They tell you to keep your nose out of something, then you better keep your nose out of it. Otherwise you're going to end up without a nose - or maybe worse."

"You haven't answered my question, Gus."

"Jesus, Doherty, you are one stubborn sonofabitch."

"Sherbrooke Industries. How do I track that deal?"

The phone was silent on the other end. "Gus, you still there?"

"Yeah, I'm still here. You want to find out about the deal Wainwright and Ganetti made with this Sherbrooke whatever it is. Simple. You go down to town hall and look up real estate transactions in the registry of deeds. It's all public record. You got a date on this?"

"I got a couple of them."

"Look Doherty, you can pursue this and that's fine by me, just don't say I didn't warn you. And if the shit hits the fan I'm not going to be able to give you any cover."

"I was just asking for advice, Gus, not for you to watch my back."

There was another pause on Gus' end. Finally he said, "You're a good guy, Doherty. But as far as this business is concerned, you're acting like a rank amateur."

"Thanks for the help, Gus," Doherty said and hung up.

He walked up to the News and ducked inside for a quick bite. When he emerged Willy Legere had set up shop.

"Hey, Mr. Doherty, where you been? I think my mom's gettin' used to havin' you around."

"That's nice, Willy, real nice. But it looks like I'll be moving back to my place later today. When you get home tell your mom I'll come by to pick up the rest of my stuff tonight."

"Are you sure that's what you should be doin'?" Willy asked in a disappointed voice.

"Yeah I'm sure. There's no reason for me to put you and your mother in any kind of danger. But I do appreciate your hospitality. If there's anything I can do for you folks, you just let me know."

"Ah go on, Mr. D, you done plenty for me already. Just comin' by and givin' me the time a day is enough. You know how much I like talkin' baseball."

"Sure kid, sure. You're a good friend, Willy. Look I've got to run; I'll catch up with you later, okay." With that Doherty dropped his last two bits in Willy's cup.

On his way to town hall Doherty stopped in at the Centreville Bank and took thirty bucks out of the company's account. The hall was located way down Main on Pike Street in what had once been a private mansion built in the 1830s and owned by the Kenyon family. Later it was owned by the Pikes, who conveyed it to the town in 1925 to be used as the town hall. Since then it has doubled as the Registry of Motor Vehicles so there was always a lot of people crowding in to get their license and registration renewals. Doherty hadn't been there since he put the Packard on the road. Today it was relatively quiet.

In a year or so the hall offices were scheduled to be moved to a new public service building in the center of Arctic where they would share space with the cops and firemen. The old building would probably continue to be used as the registry unless it was sold off as a private residence or business. It was a nice old house, but it hardly qualified as a town hall in an age of characterless municipal buildings. The design for the new building had none of the classical look of the post office or Centreville Bank, both built with government money during the Depression. It would have that squared off, highly functional look of modern public buildings.

He knew where the registry was, but had to read the index plates on the wall to the left of the main door to find out where they recorded the deeds. The Tax Collector's and the Assessor's Offices were on the first floor across the way from Motor Vehicles. The Registry of Deeds was on the second. He took the stairs and found the office at the end of a short corridor. It was in a room he thought must've once been someone's bedroom back when the building was a private home. The wooden door had a brass plate on it that identified it as the Registry of Deeds.

Rather than knock Doherty walked right in. There was a long counter with two desks behind it facing each other sideways from the entrance. Two women, each with their hair in buns sat at each desk; one was fat and young, the other older and skinny. After a short while the skinny one noticed Doherty and walked to the counter. She was wearing the kind of eyeglasses that rose up almost into horns at the end and were fastened to a chain that ran loosely around her neck. Her hair was mostly gray and she wore no make-up, not even lipstick.

"Can I help you?" she said in a voice that indicated that she really didn't want to.

"Yeah," Doherty stammered. "Can I look up the records of a real estate transaction here in town?"

"I suppose so. They are public records," she said, still not being particularly helpful. There was an awkward pause. Then she said, "I need to know the date and the address and whether it was a commercial or residential transaction."

"Oh, right. It was in August of this year. I don't know the address, but it was the old Bradford Soap Works sale."

With this last comment the fat woman looked up from what she was doing. Doherty assumed it was because everyone in West Warwick knew the Soap Works and how it had stood vacant for so long. The woman at the counter asked Doherty to fill out a request form that required him to write down his name and address as well as the document he wished to examine. She then disappeared into a back room. While she was gone the fat clerk kept nervously eyeing Doherty. He was dying for a cigarette yet didn't know if they allowed smoking in the town hall.

A few minutes later the skinny clerk returned with a large ledger that she placed on the counter in front of him. "You can't take this book away from the counter though you can look at it for as long as you wish. The deed transfer you were asking about is on page 35." She then returned to her desk. Without much effort Doherty found the record of the transaction where she'd indicated it would be.

Everything seemed to be in order. Strangely Sherbrooke Industries listed its address as a post office box in Sherbrooke, Quebec. He skimmed down to the bottom of the page and saw that the property had been sold for $30,000 to Spencer Wainwright as his bill of sale had also indicated. Below that was the signature of a name that sounded vaguely familiar.

"Excuse me," Doherty said loud enough for the clerks to hear. "Can I ask you something about this deed?" The skinny woman reluctantly returned to the counter. "This signature here, who does it belong to?" She swung the ledger around and pushed her glasses up onto her nose.

"Looks like it says Roland Champlain."

"And who's Roland Champlain?"

She looked back at the other woman and let out a quick laugh. "Are you sure you live here in town, Mr. Doherty?" she asked checking his request card to make sure she had his name right.

"I know the name, I just don't recall from where."

"Mr. Champlain owns the town's largest lumber yard; the one down on Main. He serves on practically every important committee in town."

"So let me get this straight. The Soap Works property was owned and then sold by a company based in Quebec yet the deal was actually transacted by one of West Warwick's leading citizens as the seller of record. Why would it've been done that way?"

"I can't answer that question. We just record the transactions, we don't ask how or why. It could be that in order for a Canadian company to buy and sell property here in Rhode Island it needed a local representative to stand in for them. That's the only thing I can think of. What do you think Cecile?"

The fat woman looked up. She eyed Doherty and the skinny woman nervously. "I don't know," she mumbled and went back to the papers on her desk. Doherty took a few more notes and then thanked the clerk for her help. She didn't bother to respond. She just took the ledger and returned it to the back room.

As Doherty was descending the stairs he heard the clicking of heels behind him. It was the fat clerk Cecile hurrying to catch up to him. There was now a good-sized crowd trying to push their way into the motor vehicles office. He stopped in the doorway of the hall; she quickly pointed outside, apparently not wanting to be seen talking to Doherty with so many other people around. They exited the building separately and walked up Main toward Arctic. Once outside Doherty lit the cigarette he'd been craving. He walked slowly until the fat woman caught up to him a few blocks on.

"Can we walk a little farther up the street?" she asked. "I told Jeanette I was taking my lunch break." Doherty adopted a leisurely pace as the woman was already puffing from the weight she was hauling.

"You got something you want to tell me that you couldn't talk about back in the office?"

"Uh huh."

"What is it?" They passed the old Masonic Temple and she suggested they turn down the side street where they'd less likely be seen.

"It's about that Sherbrooke Industries," she said, having to stop now to catch her breath. Doherty paused with her and calmly smoked his butt.

"What about them?"

"Well, they've been buying a lot of other properties here in town, not just the Soap Works. Other old mills and out buildings from the mills."

Doherty was confused. "Why would they do that? Most of those abandoned mills look pretty useless to me."

"I don't know exactly. I suspect it's because they could buy them cheaply. Sherbrooke Industries bought most of them just by settling some of the back taxes. According to our records, the original owners abandoned them or declared bankruptcy, so the town had to take over the properties. That Sherbrooke company bought them directly from the town and they paid only a fraction of the taxes owed."

"How do you know all this?"

"I didn't at first. Like Jeanette I just recorded the transactions without asking any questions. But I got suspicious when Sherbrooke's name kept popping up. It's not often that a foreign company buys up properties in our town. So I asked my brother-in-law, who's a lawyer, what he thought of these deals."

"And what did he say?"

"He made some inquiries about Sherbrooke Industries. He told me they were a company in name only."

"Meaning what exactly?"

"Well, according to him they're nothing more than a postal box up in Quebec. He thinks they were only created so that some other people could buy up these properties under their name. He referred to them as *fronts*. Do you know what that means?"

"It means someone provides a false front for the real buyers."

"Do you know who that could be?"

"Not off the top of my head, but I got a pretty good idea where to start looking."

"Oh really, where?"

"With Roland Champlain, the lumberman."

"Whatever you do, don't tell anyone I gave you this information. I could lose my job." With that Cecile took her leave and waddled off to grab a quick lunch while Doherty tried to figure out the best way to approach Champlain.

Once back in his office he tried to ring up Annette Patrullo again. This time her cousin answered the phone. She hesitated when Doherty asked to speak to Annette. She eventually gave up the phone once he convinced her he was the guy who'd dropped Annette at her place.

"Where the hell have you been?"

"I went out shopping with my cousin. She had to get some things at Shoppers World. Then we went by the office so I could pick up my car. Enough with the questions already."

"I thought I told you to stay out of sight."

"Hey, I got sick of hanging around the house watching old lady soap operas."

"I got some bad news for you." Doherty then proceeded to recount to Annette his run-in with Ganetti's goons.

"You didn't give them my name, did you?"

"I tried as best I could to keep you out of it, but I did have to tell them my client was some girl Wainwright was making nice with."

"Why did you go and do that?"

"Mostly because the big one was holding a gun to my forehead and I wasn't interested in joining Wainwright in the river. I figured if they thought you were looking for Spencer because he was your lover boy it would throw them off your scent. My impression is that for now they're more interested in finding and protecting Frank Junior."

"So what do I do now, stay cooped up here with my cousin and her whiny kids?"

"Look, Annette, if these guys don't come looking for you, it's only a matter of time before the cops do. They might already see you as a suspect in Spencer's murder."

"Why would I want to shoot my boyfriend?"

"Maybe because you were mad at him or jealous. You could've hired somebody to do it for you. It's called a *crime of passion*. It's how cops think. But it's not just them you have to worry about; sooner or later Ganetti's boys'll figure out who you are and then … "

"What're you suggesting?"

"Well, you could turn yourself into the police and ask for protection."

"No thanks. Any other ideas, bright boy?"

"You could always fill up that Metropolitan of yours and start driving south. The first tank would probably get you as far as New Jersey."

"I don't know anybody in New Jersey," she said anxiously.

"I'm just saying if you want to avoid any trouble, you could take a powder and leave town."

"Jesus, Doherty. What the hell have you gotten me into?"

"Gotten you into! Do I have to remind you it was you that hired me? And that brings up something else, you still haven't paid me the balance of what you owe me for my services."

"What services?"

"For finding Wainwright."

"You didn't find Spencer, the Providence police did."

"Yeah, but it was me who almost got his brains blown out snooping around on your behalf."

"Hey, that's no skin off my nose."

"The least I deserve is some compensation for that – and for not giving you up to those two hoods. I can also try to protect your identity when the Providence cops come around."

"I thought we had a confidentiality agreement?"

"Read the fine print on your contract. There's no binder of confidentiality if a serious crime's been committed, and last I checked, murder qualifies as a serious crime. Since the person I was looking for ended up dead, it won't be long before the police are all over me."

"So what do you want from me?"

"How about a hundred bucks and I'll do everything I can to keep you out of this till you have a chance to find a new place to live – preferably as far from Rhode Island as possible."

Annette didn't answer right away. Doherty waited patiently.

"I'll get back to you, Doherty. But don't call me here again." With that she hung up.

Angry and frustrated Doherty headed toward home, though not before taking a brief side trip to the Champlain Lumber Yard. The operation was only a couple of blocks from Doherty's apartment yet he'd never been in the place. He wasn't exactly the Mr. Fix-it type. The company's two large red buildings stood open on one side sheltering a wide array of lumber. Alongside one was a smaller building, also red, that had a sign on it that said 'Office'. Since it was late in the day the yard was pretty quiet. There were a few workers sitting around smoking cigarette and shooting the bull.

It wasn't hard to find Champlain in the small building. There was no secretary in or outside the office, only a middle-aged man in a plaid flannel shirt sitting behind a desk working an adding machine. Doherty stopped at the doorway and coughed to get the man's attention. The guy held up a finger indicating that he wanted Doherty to wait while he finished adding up a column of numbers. Doherty was still seething from his conversation with Annette. He tried as best he could to be patient. Finally the guy in the plaid shirt waved him into the office.

He stood and introduced himself as Roland Champlain. Doherty reciprocated and handed Champlain one of his newly minted business cards. The yard owner read it carefully. Champlain was of average height and build, had rugged good looks and thick black hair that he combed straight back from his forehead. He smiled at Doherty with piercing brown eyes while he placed his card into the corner of a green desk blotter.

"What can I do for you, Mr. Doherty?" Champlain asked politely. You don't get to be one of the town's leading citizens by being rude Doherty decided, unless you're Martin DeCenza.

"I'm interested in what you know about Sherbrooke Industries."

Champlain blinked, then put his hands on his hips and looked at the floor. No answer was forthcoming. "And who wants to know this?"

"I do."

"According to your card, you're a private investigator. Therefore I assume you're working for someone. I'm only asking who that someone is."

"I'm afraid I can't tell you that. My client chooses to remain anonymous at this time."

Champlain took a few steps backwards and now looked at the ceiling. He'd pretty much taken in the full dimensions of his office.

"Well in that case I don't think I'll be providing you with any information about the company you just mentioned."

"Fair enough, but I think you should know a few things before you decide to stay clammed up. Sherbrooke Industries recently sold a property, the old Bradford Soap Works to be precise, to a partnership of Wainwright and Ganetti. Wainwright, as you probably know, is the Republican County Chairman who recently turned up dead in what the *Journal* is describing as an execution style murder. On the other hand, the Ganetti in question is the son of one of Rhode Island's most notorious crime bosses. In my recent perusal of the deed transfer of the Soap Works, I find that your name is on it as the seller of record. I also discovered that Sherbrooke Industries isn't really a going concern, say like Champlain Lumber. Rather it's a business in name only. All of this added together seems to put you in a tight spot - a spot I might be able to help you get out of."

Champlain stared at Doherty but wasn't going to give up much, at least not at this time. "I'm afraid I'm not in a position to take you up on your offer, Mr. Doherty, though it's much appreciated. I can't do anything before I talk to some of the other members of our investment group."

"That's fine. You have my card with the phone number on it. My office is right up the street, on Brookside above Harry's Barber Shop."

They shook hands like gentlemen, but Doherty knew he'd rattled Champlain's cage. The lumberman also had unwittingly dropped the news that he wasn't in these deals on his own.

The Canuck bar was relatively quiet for a Friday evening. The men that were left on the afternoon mill shift at the Warwick would be in a few minutes. Then the cash register would be ringing all night as they emptied out their pay envelopes. Doherty assumed one of these men would be Gerald Broyard. This time the bartender didn't treat him like the invisible man. Once served Doherty nursed his Jameson with a 'Gansett back while he waited for his old schoolmate. Just past six Broyard and a couple of other burly young men pushed through the door of Tetrault's and assumed standing positions at the bar. The tender worked the taps for them without having to ask each man what he wanted.

They were boisterous, as would be expected on a Friday payday, though not in a good-hearted way. Doherty knew that by nine there would be trouble and he planned to be long gone before any fights broke out. For his part Gerald Broyard would probably be in the middle of them. When Broyard caught Doherty looking down the bar at him and his buddies he raised his beer glass and tipped it in his direction. A few minutes later his old acquaintance made his way over to where Doherty was sitting.

"Hey Hughie, you're becomin' a regular regular here. What's that about?"

"Oh, nothing. I just came by for a neighborly drink like the rest of the locals."

"Locals, my ass. What're you doin' down this way again - slummin'?"

Doherty tossed back the rest of his Jameson and followed it with a gulp of beer. "I came to thank you for the tip on Packy's. I got myself a nice '55 Chevy Bel Air on loan, and if I make a few more bucks this month I might even be able to buy it."

Broyard signaled the barman to replenish their rounds. He then turned sideways and studied his old pal. "What do you need this time, Doherty? You ain't here for the social life 'cause this ain't exactly your kind of tap room."

"I need another favor."

Broyard smiled knowingly. "I thought so. Whatever it is, it'll cost you."

"More than these two rounds?"

"Depends on what you need," Broyard said, a big smile enveloping his face.

"I need somebody to search out something for me up in Quebec. Do you know anybody who still has connections up there?"

Broyard laughed. "Well there's your friend Guy. You know, the little fella you was drinkin' with last time you was in here. But he don't know nobody up there 'cept old people and drunks on the dole."

"That won't do. I need somebody who's got some brains."

Broyard raised his beer glass and pointed down the bar. "See the guy over there drinkin' a whiskey. The one with the nice clothes on. Name's Jean-Claude somethin' or other. He came down here to work as a supervisor at the Warwick little over a year ago. Turns out most of his work was pink slippin' people. Poor bastard was laid off himself just last week. Now he spends most of his time in here gettin' shitfaced. At first we was pissed off seein' him in our place; then we heard he got axed too so we kinda felt sorry for him. Hey, it's only a matter of time before the rest of us join him."

"Will you introduce me?"

"I'll try, but he don't like me too much. Thinks I'm just a dumb meathead. What he don't know is that I saved his ass two times from gettin' the shit kicked outta him by some of the mill guys. C'mon, we'll give it a try. Maybe he'll like you 'cause you talk better than the rest of the bums in here."

The two men walked to the corner of the bar where the guy named Jean-Claude sat nursing his drink. Doherty took the seat beside him while Broyard stood behind it.

"What're you drinking there pal?" Doherty said leaning in. Jean-Claude had a large head with oiled hair that rode back on his scalp in a series of waves. He sat slumped forward on his stool smelling of Brylcreem and tobacco. Some dandruff flakes had taken up residence on the shoulders of his dark sport coat. He looked back at Doherty and said, "I prefer to drink alone." There was a distinct French accent to his speech.

"Hey Jean-Claude," Broyard said stepping forward and resting one of his large hands on the older man's shoulder. "Don't be such a hard-on. My friend here wants to buy you a drink. I think you should accept." Gerald's tone indicated that Jean-Claude would be wise not to reject Doherty's offer.

"Canadian Club, on the rocks," he said reluctantly. Broyard called the bartender over and a new round was set up for all three of them.

"Gerald here tells me you're from Quebec; is that right?"

Jean-Claude took a sip of his CC; his hand was shaking a little. Broyard must've rattled him. "I am. I came down here last year to work for the Warwick Company. They promised me a big salary. Turns out all they wanted me to do was draw up plans for contracting their operation. By that they meant laying off workers. They thought if they brought in an outsider to do their dirty work it would be easier for them. Once I'd done what they asked me to they reduced me out of my job too, the bastards." Doherty was right about the French accent.

Broyard laughed. "Looks like you're kinda fucked from both sides, eh mon ami. The mill boys don't like you 'cause you pink slipped them and now the company's got no use for you neither. If I was you, I'd go back up to Canada."

Jean-Claude sipped more of his drink. "I can't. I got an ex-wife up there suing me for alimony. Only way I can avoid paying her is to stay down here in the States."

"Maybe we can help you out a little. My friend Doherty here's got a proposition for you. He'll pay good money. You tell 'im, Hughie," Broyard then elbowed Doherty harder in his upper arm than he needed to.

For the first time Jean-Claude turned his head to look at Doherty. He was still not committing to anything yet. "Let's hear your offer."

Doherty cleared his throat. "I need some information on a company that operates out of Sherbrooke. You know the place?"

Jean-Claude nodded his head. "Sure, I know it well. It's one of the biggest cities in Quebec. I been there dozens of times. What do you need?"

"I need to know about a company based there named Sherbrooke Industries. You know, like who owns it, or if it's a corporation, who sits on the board of directors. Stuff like that. Can you get that information for me?"

Jean-Claude nodded. "I could try if I felt like it. I'd have to make some calls. I can get you what you want depending on how much you're willing to pay."

Doherty looked at Broyard and then back at Jean-Claude. "How about a double sawbuck?"

"That's a start. Keep going."

"Forty."

"Make it an even fifty; twenty now and the rest if I get the information you want." Doherty reluctantly pulled a twenty out of his billfold and handed it to Jean-Claude.

"I'll need to send something to my people up in Canada as well."

Broyard again put a strong hand on the man's shoulder and said, "That comes out of your end, right Hughie?" Doherty had no choice but to agree. He handed Jean-Claude one of his new business cards. Broyard immediately grabbed it out of the man's hand and read it slowly. He whistled and handed it back to Jean-Claude.

"Damn, Hughie, you're like an official investigator, ain't you."

Ignoring Broyard's comment Doherty asked Jean-Claude, "When can I expect to hear from you?"

The man waved the bartender over and ordered another CC on the rocks. "Meet me here early next week, around this time. If I don't get what you want, I'll give you back the twenty, less what it cost me in long distance calls."

Satisfied, Doherty paid their tab and turned to leave. Broyard grabbed his arm before he hit the door. "What about a little taste for me. I mean I did introduce you to the guy, right?" Doherty slipped Broyard a fin and now was officially tapped out going into the weekend.

When he woke up Saturday morning he was hungry and a little hung over. He didn't have much more in the house than some coffee, a few eggs and a half a loaf of stale bread. He fixed a pot of coffee and drank three cups while eating fried eggs and buttered toast. He then made an egg sandwich and poured the rest of the coffee into a thermos. Once that was done Doherty headed uptown to the office, mainly because he was broke and didn't know what else to do with himself.

Walking away from his apartment he failed to notice the two toned, blue Buick with three men in it parked diagonally across Main in front of Cadaret's Hardware store. As he approached Arctic he flirted briefly with the notion of stopping in to see Millie St. Jean at Francine's, then thought better of it. In light of recent events he couldn't promise her that it was any safer to be around him than it was when the attack occurred at his apartment. Still he held out some hope that their relationship could be salvaged once his investigation into Spencer Wainwright's murder was over.

Doherty was so engrossed in his thoughts about Millie that he didn't see the Buick now parked against the curb a block down from his office. Agnes had not been in so the place looked like he'd left it the previous day. He sat down behind his desk, poured a cup of coffee from the thermos and lit a Camel. He'd just leaned back and put his heels in their usual place on the desk when the office door burst open. The two guys who had jacked him up at the Arcade came through, with a third man who immediately caught Doherty's attention.

Once inside the big man named Angelo positioned himself against the office door to insure they wouldn't be disturbed. This left Doherty no means of escape. Today Angelo wore a dark brown turtleneck sweater under a black sport coat. He had on the same fedora he'd worn the other day. The little guy stepped toward the desk. He was wearing a too loud yellow Perry Como sweater over a dark gray shirt. Doherty could see the bulge at his hip where his piece was barely concealed.

The third man followed behind them. He was aged somewhere between the other two, but wasn't dressed like them. Instead, he wore an expensive suit covered by a tan topcoat. His black hair was well oiled and combed over his forehead in Ivy League style. When he slid his hands forward, Doherty noticed expensive links fastening the cuffs of his white shirt. He completed the picture with the kind of striped tie favored by bankers and politicians.

Doherty continued to smoke as casually as he could under the circumstances, carefully taking in the three men as he did.

"Gentlemen," he said slowly. "To what do I owe the honor of this visit?"

The weasel tried to speak, but the guy in the camel hair coat raised his hand to silence him. He came forward and said, "We haven't met; my name is Frank Ganetti, Mr. Doherty, and I'm here to talk business with you." His speech was precise and he sounded educated, unlike the two gumbas with him. He took a seat without being offered it. Ganetti was clearly the kind of man who did as he pleased.

"Shoot," Doherty said immediately wishing he'd used another word. The two goons looked at one another and laughed. Ganetti didn't nor did he take his piercing brown eyes off Doherty either.

"As you know, my friend and business partner Spencer Wainwright was tragically murdered the other night. A sad, and unfortunate occurrence for me – both personally and professionally."

"For Spencer Wainwright as well," Doherty said. "What exactly is, or was, your professional involvement with the deceased?"

Ganetti took his time before responding. In the meantime he studied the bare essentials of Doherty's office. The eye trip lasted about ten seconds.

"Spencer and I had a number of irons in the fire and well, it will be very difficult for me to bring some of those plans to fruition now that he's no longer with us." *Fruition.* When did gangsters start using words like fruition Doherty wondered?

"That's funny. It was my understanding that you were using Wainwright and his real estate connections to launder money for the Manton Avenue gang," Doherty said, walking out on a tight rope.

"Hey," Bobby said sitting up straighter in his chair.

"Please Bobby, let Mr. Doherty have his say. I believe he was hired to find Spencer Wainwright and is now feeling somewhat, shall we say guilty, that he was unable to locate him before his untimely death. Now go on, Mr. Doherty. Tell us what else you've discovered in your investigation."

Doherty took in the three men once again, not sure if what he was about to say would buy him a ticket to the cemetery.

"I was hired to find Wainwright by a girl he was seeing outside of his marriage, simple as that. However, when I stumbled across the information that your joint plan to redevelop the Soap Works had hit a snag, my initial conclusion was that you, or someone in your organization, had him murdered because of the $30,000 that was lost."

"A logical conclusion," Ganetti said in a soft voice. "But fortunately for you, *and me*, not an accurate one. You see Spencer and I had quite a few plans in the works. I would supply the funds and he would supply the real estate know-how. Don't get me wrong; our part of the thirty Gs is not something we can easily write off. Yet my interests with Wainwright were a little more wide ranging than that."

"What about the people whose money was put up in the deal? They can't be too happy about losing that kind of dough."

"You're absolutely right about that. Which was why I decided to go underground after Spencer was killed while Bobby and Angelo here tried to find out if I too was in danger."

"And are you?"

Ganetti smiled and said in a silken voice, "That's really none of your concern."

There was an uncomfortable pause in the conversation. Finally Doherty asked, "So where do I fit into all this?"

"That's a good question," Ganetti said. He then reached inside his coat pocket and pulled out a gold cigarette case and offered Doherty a smoke. The cigarettes inside it were filtered so Doherty shook him off and instead knocked a Camel out of his own pack. Ganetti did not offer a cigarette to either Angelo or Bobby. He lit Doherty's and his own with a fancy gold lighter.

"There are things going on in my father's organization that we have to attend to," he said taking in Bobby and Angelo as the *we*. "These are things that *you* don't need to know about. But so far as we can tell they aren't directly related to Wainwright's death. As for my own safety, I'd like to think that the people involved in these investments have no desire to kill the goose that lays the golden eggs. That message, I know, has come down from on high. However, there are other people in our business who are not so enlightened. Some of the old mustache Petes don't understand these new initiatives. So they may have to be made to see the light."

"What do you want from me?"

Ganetti nodded in Angelo's direction and the big man stepped forward and reached inside his sport coat. For a second Doherty froze. Angelo handed Ganetti an envelope, which he in turn tossed on the desk in front of Doherty.

"Go ahead, open it."

Doherty gingerly picked up the white envelope and looked inside. Five portraits of America's first inventor Benjamin Franklin stared back at him.

"What did I do to deserve this?" Doherty asked holding the envelope between them a few inches off the desk.

"Nothing yet. I'm hiring you to find out who killed Spencer Wainwright and why. You get me that information and there's another five-hundred in it for you."

"A thousand bucks just to find out who killed your business partner?"

"Yes, a thousand dollars. I'm willing to pay that much because such an investigation could turn out to be dangerous for you." Ganetti then turned to the younger of the two henchmen and said, "Bobby." The smaller man pulled a thirty-eight out from the small of his back and placed it on the desk.

"It's fully loaded and registered to a man named Mike Morello, who is a good friend of yours if anyone asks. Here's Morello's address and phone number," Ganetti said as he handed Doherty a slip of paper. "He's been briefed so he'll cover for you if anything were to happen that puts you in trouble with the law."

Bobby then handed Doherty an extra box of shells just in case. Doherty picked up the .38 and studied it for a few seconds. It was in much better condition than the gun Gus had given him. He slipped the piece and the extra bullets into the top drawer of his desk.

"Look, Mr. Ganetti, I got to be honest with you, I'm not sure I really want this job."

Ganetti nodded in sympathy. "I'm afraid that's not an option. From your previous efforts it turns out you may know more about Spencer Wainwright's dealings than anyone. That's why I'm hiring you. Let me assure you, if Spencer's death had anything to do with dynamics of what's going on inside my father's organization, we will take care of that before anyone besides us knows you even exist. This I promise." Doherty wasn't sure such a pledge could be kept; he also knew he was in no position to refuse Ganetti's employment.

"So, Mr. Doherty, do you have any questions?"

Doherty pulled hard on his Camel. "A few hundred, but none that are jumping out right now."

Ganetti smiled and handed Doherty his business card. "Call me when you find out something, or if you need my help. My secretary will have instructions to put you through directly to me."

"I do have one question, Mr. Ganetti."

"Please call me Frank. Just don't call me Junior, right Angelo," he said turning toward the big man.

"That's right boss."

"How did you get hooked up with Wainwright in the first place?"

"Why, he contacted me."

"Out of the blue?"

"Yes. He said he heard I had some serious money I wished to invest in real estate."

"And you never asked him how he got your name?"

"Not really. I assumed he knew me by reputation. I was rather enthralled with the projects he was pitching my way. They all sounded like great opportunities. And when I had Wainwright checked out he came up A-1 right across the boards. Everyone I talked to said he was one of the sharpest real estate men in the state. And, of course, he had a great pedigree as well being a rich WASP and a big deal in the Republican Party to boot. Spencer Wainwright fit our needs perfectly."

Ganetti stood and shook Doherty's hand. The three visitors slowly exited the office. The young one, Bobby, gave him a wry smile as he left.

Doherty sat silently looking at the five hundred dollars Ganetti had given him. First he'd taken $500 from Martin DeCenza, the Democrats' major political boss, and now he'd taken another $500 from the son of one of Rhode Island's most notorious gangsters. In the past two weeks Doherty's little security agency had suddenly gone big time. It made him consider whether he'd gotten himself into the right line of work after all. Still, he had to eat and pay rents on his office and apartment. At least this five hundred would allow him to chew on something better than a fried egg sandwich.

On Sunday Doherty called Agnes and told her it was okay to come back to work on Tuesday. He wasn't completely sure the coast was clear, yet he was ready for his life to get back to normal. He banked three of Ganetti's five hundred Monday morning and turned the other two into lesser bills. No business in town would be willing to change a hundred dollar bill for lunch or a few drinks without becoming suspicious. He went to Tetrault's Monday night and sat for an hour keeping company with two glasses of Jamesons without catching sight of either Jean-Claude or Gerald Broyard. Monday was usually a slow drinking night for the mill workers as most of them had already shot their wads over the weekend.

In the morning he tried calling Annette Patrullo at her cousin's without getting an answer. He tried four more times during the day without success. When Agnes returned to work later in the day she was polite enough not to ask any questions about the previous week's scare. He told her he had a new client and that this job would be strictly off the books. She wasn't happy with such an arrangement. The extra thirty bucks he slipped her at the end of the day, however, eased any concerns she was harboring.

Doherty found Jean-Claude sitting in his usual spot at Tetrault's that night, wearing the same basic outfit as he had at their previous meeting. He slid onto the stool beside the Canadian and didn't say anything until the bartender brought him a Jameson and a beer without being asked. He made a mental note not to become a regular at Tetrault's.

"How'd you make out with what I asked you to get me from Quebec?" he asked out of the side of his mouth.

Jean-Claude slowly sipped his Canadian Club on the rocks. He didn't reply right away. Doherty lit a smoke and waited patiently. Finally the Canadian spoke. "Turns out Sherbrooke Industries aren't really industries at all. As you suspected, they exist solely as a company on paper. They're a group of investors who buy up other companies – mostly ones that are failing or have declared bankruptcy. They don't make anything or employ anybody except lawyers and accountants."

"I'm not sure I follow."

Jean-Claude smiled. "They're an investment group, nothing more. They make money on the failures and miseries of others. They buy companies for a song, dump the workers and sell off the assets for a profit. Simple as that."

"Were you able to find out who the partners were in this so-called enterprise?"

"Yeah, I got a list for you. One of the things you'll be surprised to learn is that a few of the men on it are from here."

"Here meaning?"

"Rhode Island. Even a couple from West Warwick." Just then Gerald Broyard burst into the bar and immediately spotted Doherty and Jean-Claude. He slid into a seat next to Jean-Claude and ordered a shot and beer for himself.

"So," he said loudly, "has my man here been any help to you, Hughie?" He threw an unwanted arm over Jean-Claude's shoulder as he spoke.

"Gerald, I think you need to give me and our friend some time alone," Doherty said firmly. Broyard looked offended, then smiled and moved a few stools down the bar. Once he was out of earshot, Doherty pulled out two twenties and a ten and placed them on the bar in front of Jean-Claude. Feeling flush from the cash he'd gotten from Ganetti he decided to add an extra twenty to Jean-Claude's fee if the info he'd gotten was satisfactory.

"This is for you if what you got proves to be useful." Jean-Claude reached into his jacket pocket and placed a piece of folded lined paper on the bar between them. Doherty turned so that Broyard couldn't see him look at the sheet. Jean-Claude had indeed gotten the names and addresses of the main partners in Sherbrooke Industries. Most were Canadians, though a few local names jumped off the page. Doherty slipped the paper into his pants pocket before Broyard saw him. He didn't want Gerald involved in this business beyond his initial introduction of Jean-Claude. He nodded and the Quebecer palmed the bills and quickly put them in his wallet.

Doherty shook Jean-Claude's hand and got up to leave, quietly thanking him as he did. Broyard watched him move toward the exit. He looked offended but didn't say anything. Once outside Doherty lit a Camel and tried to figure out how he would use this new information about Sherbrooke Industries. He was so lost in thought that he failed to see the three men who came up and surrounded him as he turned to walk up Main.

"Out drinkin' with the Frenchies, eh?" the big man said. Doherty hadn't seen Rene Desjardins since the night he worked him over with his Louisville Slugger. The other two were too deep in the shadows for Doherty to get a good look at them. He drew on his smoke hoping to buy some time to assess his situation.

"You don't seem so brave without your ball bat, Doherty."

"And you're not so tough unless you got some other punks by your side. I hope for your sake these two are tougher than Charboneau was."

"Eh, sometimes the odds just ain't in your favor smart guy." Before he knew what was happening one of Desjardins backups had pinned Doherty's arms to his side and the big Canuck hit him square in the jaw. He hadn't broken anything yet, but Doherty knew this wasn't going to turn out too good for him. As he tried to free himself from the guy behind him the third one stepped forward to help. Doherty figured his chances were about even with Desjardins alone, and less than nothing against the three of them. Just as he was about to lower himself into a more defensive posture another body unexpectedly entered the fray.

"What's goin' on out here," the voice said. Doherty happily recognized it as belonging to Gerald Broyard.

"This ain't none of your business, mill boy," Desjardins said.

"Three on one don't look so fair to me. Maybe I should even things up." With that Broyard grabbed the head of the third guy and smashed it against his own forehead breaking the man's nose in one thrust. Doherty could hear the distinct crack as the two heads collided. The one who'd been holding Doherty's arms quickly let go and started running up Main as fast as his legs would carry him. The other was on his knees whimpering and trying to hold what remained of his nose together.

As Desjardins was checking out the situation, Doherty wheeled on him and hit him as hard as he could in the stomach, where he knew the big guy was soft. When the Canuck slumped over, Doherty kneed him in the jaw and heard the crunch of teeth as he did so. Broyard laughed and then walked over to the one who was leaning on his knees and punched him on the side of the head with such force that the guy flipped over and landed flat on his back.

"Just like back in the old schoolyard, eh, Hughie. Who're these bums anyways?"

Breathlessly Doherty said, "The big one does heavy lifting for Judge DeCenza. I don't know who the other two are. I've never seen them before."

"I come out to see why you dint say nothin' to me before you left," Broyard said sounding offended. "Good thing I did, huh?"

"I've got to say, I was never so glad to see you, Gerry," Doherty replied.

"We better get outta here," Broyard said. "Tetrault don't like fightin' outside his place. Says it brings the cops down on him."

The two men shook hands and headed in opposite directions. Once home in the apartment Doherty applied some ice to his jaw and his fist, both of which now hurt more than they had at the time of the fight. At least nothing was broken and none of his teeth were loose.

Chapter Twelve

BOBBY CARNAVALLE

Doherty kept an ice pack against his jaw all morning and didn't go into the office until noon. It was Agnes' day off so there was no one there to question him about the swelling on the left side of his face. He tried calling Annette twice more and still got no answer. Restless and bored he got the Chevy out of the garage and drove up to the East Side of Providence. It took him a few missed turns before he located the street where he'd dropped Annette at her cousin's.

When he found what he thought was the right house he was relieved to see no cars in the driveway. Maybe Annette had taken his advice after all and beaten it out of town. Doherty parked in front and rang the doorbell. He waited and then rang it again. When no one responded he knocked loudly. After a few minutes he safely concluded that no one was home. He tried the door but it was locked. Unlike in West Warwick, people in Providence now regularly locked their doors when they went out. He walked down the driveway and peered into the garage. Despite the thin film of dirt that encrusted the windows Doherty was able to make out Annette's green and white Metro parked inside. If she'd left town, which he now doubted, it wasn't in her car.

A narrow porch spanned the back of the house. He tried the back door; it too was locked. He moved further along the porch and put his face up against one of the windows. It looked in on the kitchen. There were three chairs and a baby's high chair surrounding a red, Formica topped table. Plates with crusted food on them were piled in the sink. He noticed that one of the windows was unlocked though it had a screen in front of it. Doherty took out his pocketknife and slit around the edge of the screen. He pulled it away and lifted the window so he could gain entry into the kitchen. After taking a good look around to make sure none of the neighbors could see him, he slid through the open window. Once inside he quickly shut it.

The room smelled of trash and uneaten breakfast. Doherty stealthily moved through the house. The downstairs consisted of a living room off one side of a small front hall and a den off the other. Aside from the kitchen that was all there was to the first floor. A staircase ascended a few paces across from the front door. As he trod up the carpeted steps he stopped briefly to make sure there weren't any sounds upstairs that he hadn't accounted for. Straight ahead at the top was a small bathroom. It was decorated with pink and black tiling. The wallpaper was also pink as were the toilet, sink and tub. The towels hanging on the rack were pink as well.

There were bedrooms on either side down a short hall that ran in front of the bathroom. The one to the right was the master bedroom. Doherty gave it a cursory once over. There was a large bed with a matching bureau and chest. A crib was parked in the middle of the room. Its presence didn't seem right for a room of that size. He thought it might've been rolled in on a temporary basis.

There were two beds in the other room. One was covered with a collection of stuffed animals in various stages of deterioration. The other had a kid's quilt on it but no other childlike accessories. Across the room was a toy chest bursting with plastic playthings. Some markings on the carpet indicated that the crib had been parked in this room before being rolled into the other bedroom. A woman's overnight bag was sitting on the floor between the two beds with a pair of dark nylons hanging out of it. Doherty lifted the bag and placed it on the bed. Inside were women's underpants, a couple of extra bras, one black, one white, and two blouses, one of which Annette Patrullo had been wearing the day he dropped her off here.

He reached deeper into the bag and came out with an address book. It was red with a batik design on the cover. He flipped through the pages. Under W there were three different numbers with the initials S.W. scratched beside them. No doubt they once belonged to Spencer Wainwright. He found two numbers for Ben Cooper; one was the same as one of the S.W. numbers.

Doherty assumed it was the main number for the real estate office. The other was a Warwick exchange that was probably Cooper's home phone.

As Doherty continued to flip through the book he came across a few other numbers that caught his eye. One was simply for Sal, while another was Doherty's office number; a third was for somebody named Bobby Carnavalle. It was a Providence exchange. He wondered if this was for the same Bobby he'd recently encountered at the Arcade and then at his office in the company of Frank Ganetti, Jr. He took out his pad and wrote down the number along with several others from the address book. He then carefully replaced the book in the overnight bag.

He was about to return the bag to its place on the floor when he noticed that something didn't feel right. The weight of the bag seemed heavier than it should've been given its flimsy content. He picked it up again and reached down to the bottom. That's when he noticed that the floor of the main compartment did not match the bottom of the bag itself. Doherty dug down into it and found the bottom seam. He carefully ran his fingers along it and pried up the bottom layer of the bag. When he reached beneath it his hand found something that felt like a handful of bills. He extracted them from their hiding place and dropped them on the bed.

The pile of bills was made up of twenties and tens. He gave it a quick count. It came to over a thousand dollars. What was Annette doing with that much money squirreled away in the fake compartment of her overnight bag? Maybe she was about to hit the road and this was her getaway cash. Doherty plucked five twenties from the pile, which he estimated was what she owed him for his troubles, and returned the rest of the cash to its hiding place. He then dropped the bag on the floor where he'd found it.

Just as Doherty was descending the stairs the front door opened and a woman was standing there holding a grocery bag in one arm and a small child in the other. Behind her was a tall skinny guy with greasy hair and sideburns like Elvis Presley. He was likewise holding grocery bags. Neither of them saw Doherty until he was right in front of them.

"What the hell," the side-burned guy shouted. Doherty held his hands in front of him trying to indicate that he didn't mean them any harm. The woman was so startled she dropped the grocery bag; fortunately she held onto the child.

"What are you doin' in my house?" she shrieked.

"Please calm down. It's okay. I'm not a thief. I was just looking for Annette."

The husband put down his bags and rushed past Doherty into the kitchen. When he returned he was brandishing a large carving knife. "Call the cops, Lorraine. And don't you move an inch," he said to Doherty.

Doherty reached into his pocket and pulled out the snubnose. He pointed it in the husband's direction though he purposely did not stick it in his face. He stepped forward and closed the front door, careful not to take his eyes off the guy with the knife. The woman was still holding the child; she hadn't moved at all.

"Put the knife down and no one'll get hurt." The baby began to cry and the mother commenced shaking it. The cousin and her husband looked scared and uncertain as to what to do next.

"I said put the knife down, NOW!' Doherty spoke with more authority this time. The husband let the blade drop to the floor and Doherty kicked it into the den.

"Now let's all sit down and have a nice talk, okay?" Annette's cousin and her husband both nodded. The baby was still fussing though no longer crying. They trooped into the living room where the couple took seats next to each other on a green upholstered couch while Doherty sat in a matching easy chair across from them. The wife propped the baby up on her shoulder keeping her attention on the intruder the whole time. Doherty rested the gun in his lap but did not take his hand off it.

The husband was wearing a black jacket over a white striped shirt. He looked to be in his early thirties, wiry but not threatening. The wife was pretty yet going to fat. Her hair was dark and thick and she wore too much make-up for someone out grocery shopping. There was a slight resemblance to Annette Patrullo, though not one anybody would remark upon unless the two women were standing side by side. After squeezing out two kids, the cousin would never again have a body like Annette's - if she ever did.

"My name is Doherty. I'm a private investigator and I was hired by your cousin to find a guy who was missing." He tried to modulate his voice so as not to scare the two of them. He didn't want them to do anything rash that might force him to use the gun. "The guy she hired me to find turned up dead, shot in the head at close range. I drove Annette up here the other day because I was afraid for her safety. I suggested she get out of town, but apparently she hasn't taken my advice. Now, what can you two tell me about her whereabouts?"

The cousin and the husband looked at each other but didn't say anything. Doherty waited patiently.

"Why should we tell you anythin'?" the husband said defiantly,

"How about because I got a gun in my hand and you don't. That should count for something. Now, could you please tell me where she is?"

"She ain't here," the husband said with a sneer. He was trying to sound tough though wasn't very convincing.

"No kidding. I can see that for myself."

This time the wife spoke first. "She left. Day before yesterday. For good I hope."

"Really. For good, huh. Then how come she didn't take her car or her clothes with her?"

They each began to fidget. Doherty moved the gun from one thigh to the other just as a reminder to the couple that it was still there between them.

"I have reason to believe that Annette may be in some serious trouble, and it's not from me. I'm the one who told her to leave town and she obviously didn't take my advice. I don't know what else to say. And if you don't want to cooperate then there's nothing more I can do to protect her."

"She went with him."

"Shut up, Lorraine," the husband snapped.

"Went with who?"

"With that punk Bobby. She went with him even though I told her not to. I told her he was nothin' but trouble, but she wouldn't listen to me."

"Did she go willingly?"

"Yeah, she went willin'ly," the husband snapped. "One look at Bobby and I could tell she was mixed up with a bad actor - and I told her so. She didn't pay no attention to either of us. She comes here and tells Lorraine she has to stay for a few days 'cause she's got some kind of man trouble. Now you're tellin' me that by bein' here she put us and our kids in danger. Then she and Bobby breeze off like nothin' ever happened."

"And by Bobby, do you mean Bobby Carnavalle?"

"I think that's his name," the wife said.

"Is he a skinny guy with black hair; got yellow teeth, looks a little like a weasel?"

"Yeah, yeah, that's the one," the husband answered. "Drives a big two-toned blue Buick. I didn't like his looks the first time he came here. I could tell he was carryin' a gun from the bulge under his jacket. Didn't even try to hide it. He's gonna get her into trouble, ain't he?"

"I don't know for sure. But if she's with who I think she's with, she's already in trouble. Can you tell me how she knows this guy?"

"She told me he was one of the neighborhood boys she used to hang out with when she was younger. I guess they once had a thing for each other. Then she moved down to Warwick and started workin' in real estate. I hadn't seen her since then till she showed up here the other day," the cousin said. "Is she in the kinda trouble you can help her with?"

"I can try," Doherty said. He then stood and peeled a sawbuck out of his money clip. "Here's ten bucks for the screen I cut open on your back porch. And here's my business card," he said fishing one out of his jacket pocket. "If she shows up tell her I've been here and she should get in touch. If you want my help you've got to promise not to tell anybody but Annette I was here. And whatever you do, don't say anything about me to that Bobby. Got that?"

Annette's cousin Lorraine and her husband nodded their heads in unison. Doherty left, still not sure what this all added up to or who he could trust anymore.

When he came into work the next day there were two suits waiting for him. Agnes was at her desk and she gave him an eye flick in the direction of the two men.

The older of the two looked at his watch and said, "Your secretary told us you'd be in by ten; it's now going on ten-twenty." Doherty was going to apologize then changed his mind. The man stepped forward. "I'm Lieutenant Halloran of the Providence PD. This is my partner Sgt. Sqillante."

Doherty shook hands with the two cops and invited them into his office. He took the seat behind his desk and Halloran sat in the chair across from him. The younger cop, Squillante, chose to stand, roughly where Ganetti's thug Angelo had stood the other day. Doherty took out his Camels and offered one to Halloran, who waved him off. Squillante pulled out his own pack of Luckies and Doherty reached out with his Zippo to light his cig. Squillante took notice of the logo of Doherty's old outfit on the lighter but made no comment.

Each of the men was wearing a cheap suit and brown shoes, standard plain clothes cop outfits. Halloran had a thin topcoat on, which he shrugged off and let fall over the back of his chair. The lieutenant was somewhere in his late forties, had a square head, and a thatch of Irish red hair with patches of gray around the temples. The broken capillaries in his nose signaled that he had some familiarity with hard liquor. Squillante was younger, wore a flashy tie, and had dark hair combed into a pompadour. He was thin, and leaned against the wall in what Doherty and his pals used to call the "street corner slouch."

Halloran began, "We understand you recently worked a case involving a guy named Spencer Wainwright."

"That's right. He'd gone missing. Unfortunately before I could find him he ended up dead."

Halloran coughed as a way to prepare himself for the next question. "Do you mind if we ask who hired you to find this guy?"

"In most circumstances I would say 'yes, I do mind', but in this case since he turned up dead and the client never paid me in full I can tell you. It was his secretary, a girl named Annette Patrullo."

Halloran looked at Squillante. His partner shook his head indicating that the name didn't ring a bell. Doherty thought if he gave the cops Annette's name they might be able to pick her up, which would put her in a safer company than with Bobby Carnavalle.

"Why did she want you to find Wainwright?"

"I'm not sure exactly. I think she was sweet on the guy and thought he'd run off with another girl. Or worse, gone back to his wife."

"Any reason she might've wanted him dead?" Halloran asked.

Doherty considered the question carefully. "Aside from jealousy, I don't think so. In any case, she couldn't've killed him if what I read in the papers is true. No way she would've put a bullet in his head and dragged his body some distance to throw it in the river. She's built, but not in that way." The two cops chuckled at this last remark.

"Any idea how to get in touch with this broad?" Squillante asked still leaning on the wall.

"I got her file here. It has her address and phone number on it. You could also try the real estate office where she worked with Wainwright. That's the best I can do. I never saw her anywhere else but here and at her office," Doherty lied. He reached into his file, pulled out Annette's contract and slid it in Halloran's direction. The lieutenant signaled his partner to come over to the desk and take some notes on Annette.

"What about the wife?" Halloran asked. "You meet her?"

"Briefly. I went by the house thinking he might've gone home after he left the girl. Apparently that was his pattern."

"Pattern?"

"According to the missus Wainwright fancied himself as something of a playboy. He'd shack up with some dolly for a while, get tired of her, or she with him, and then head back home to the wife."

"Jeez," Squillante said.

"What was your take on her?" Halloran asked.

Doherty shrugged, "Rich. Spoiled. Bitter. What you'd expect from a woman married to a guy who played around like Wainwright did."

"Do you think she could've killed him? I mean she does stand to inherit a fair amount of money with him bein' dead," Halloran speculated.

"Kill him? I doubt it. She wouldn't want to mess up her nails. As far as money is concerned, it sounded like Wainwright had most of his cash sunk into various development projects."

"How do you know that?"

"Because when I first met him he told me he was crazy about the Patrullo girl. I asked him why he didn't get a divorce and he said he couldn't afford the alimony what with his money all tied up in investments."

"Hmm," Halloran said nodding his head. "So you met Wainwright before his ... his demise?"

"Yeah, I did. Somebody else hired me to find him a little over a week before he went missing the second time."

"Wait a minute," Squillante busted in. "You were hired twice to find the same guy?"

Doherty was pleased that the cops were finding his story confusing. "The first time I was hired I found him shacked up with the Patrullo girl down at his beach house. That time I was able to convince him to go back home."

"Who hired you to find him then?" Halloran asked.

Doherty could have honored his confidentiality agreement with Judge DeCenza since no crime had been committed during that job. On the other hand he couldn't think of a good reason to protect the Judge any longer.

"Martin DeCenza."

"Judge Martin DeCenza?" Halloran said with evident surprise.

"The one and the same."

Halloran indicated to his partner that he should start taking some new notes. The younger cop pulled out his pad again. Doherty handed him one of Willy Legere's newly sharpened pencils.

"Why did DeCenza hire you to find Wainwright?"

"He said it was because of the election. You see DeCenza kind of runs things in this town. He's also the Democratic boss of Kent County. Wainwright was the chairman of the Republican Committee. DeCenza told me he was afraid that if Wainwright disappeared a month before the election and it got out to the public, he and his people might be blamed."

"And that's why he hired you to find Wainwright and bring him back?"

"So he said. Told me he wanted Wainwright returned to his *senses*, at least until the election was over. I found him all right and got him to go back home. I didn't even have to threaten him or anything. Wainwright went back to Warwick on his own."

"The first time you found him down at his beach house on Great Island making whoopie with this secretary?"

"Yeah, more or less. Apparently it was no big deal. He'd only been gone for a couple of days and the wife hadn't called the cops yet. She told me he did stuff like that all the time."

"Then why did DeCenza want him back so bad?"

"Like I said, he told me it was because of the election."

"So then why didn't he hire you the second time the guy disappeared?" Halloran asked, suspicion now worming its way into his voice.

"The Judge and I had a kind of falling out after the first job. Plus, I don't think DeCenza knew Wainwright had gone missing again."

"But the secretary did?"

"Course she did. She was the one sleeping with him. When he didn't show up at her place or at work she got worried."

"Do you have any idea who might've killed him?" Doherty thought about throwing Frank Ganetti, Jr. in their direction. Instead he decided to keep Ganetti to himself for the time being.

"None whatsoever. But you never know. A guy who played around with a lot of women like Wainwright did is going to piss somebody off along the way. If not a jilted lover then maybe a jealous husband or boyfriend."

"What about you?" Halloran asked.

"Are you asking if I killed Wainwright?"

"Just checkin' all possibilities," Halloran said in perfect cop speak.

"I had no reason to kill the guy. I kind of liked him. And to be honest with you, I was making good money off of him being missing."

"And you don't know where this Patrullo broad is?" Squillante asked.

"Not a clue. I'd say it's your business to find her now not mine. But if you do, tell her she still owes me some money for the job." The two cops looked at Doherty scornfully before leaving. It was the kind of lasting impression he wanted to leave them with Early the next morning Doherty prepared another thermos of coffee and picked up a couple of donuts at the Donut Kettle before heading over to Warwick. Getting there early allowed him to find the perfect spot to check out what was happening at Cooper and Wainwright without being detected. He even brought along a pair of high-powered binoculars he'd bought while working at Quonset.

Just after nine Ben Cooper pulled up in his late model Lincoln. He parked in front of the building and got out of the car holding a thick briefcase. As he rounded the hood he reached into his pocket and pulled out a handkerchief, which he used to buff up a spot on one of the fenders of his vehicle.

About twenty minutes later the older office girl, Margaret Whitemore, appeared. She bustled quickly inside like she was late for work. Doherty was now on his third cup of coffee and hoped that his bladder would hold. He'd brought along an empty Maxwell House coffee can just in case it didn't. Cooper sequestered himself in his office looking at documents, while Margaret moved about the place, watering plants, opening blinds and putting up an electric coffee urn. It was a typical day at Cooper and Wainwright minus the sexy secretary and the dead partner.

Growing bored, Doherty flipped on the radio and listened to the Godfrey Show for a while, being careful not to drain too much juice out of the car's battery. He ate both donuts, leaving a small pile of powdered sugar on his lap. Just before ten-thirty the dark Ford he'd been expecting pulled up and parked in front. The two men in suits got out and walked slowly inside. They were intercepted by Margaret, who then showed them the way to Cooper's office. Because a half glass partition separated Cooper's office from the rest of the agency, Doherty could watch the goings on inside quite easily through his binoculars.

Once again Halloran sat and Squillante stood. It must be a routine they'd worked out in advance. The younger cop was about to light up one of his Luckies when Cooper raised his arm and pointed in the cop's direction. No doubt telling him about his asthma and his aversion to smoke in his office. This transaction prompted Doherty to light up another smoke of his own. He lowered the glasses knowing exactly how the scene in Cooper's office would play out. After twenty minutes or so Halloran and Cooper stood, handshakes were offered all around, and the two Providence cops got back into the dark Ford and pulled out onto Warwick Ave. Doherty did likewise, but not before watching Cooper make a nervous phone call just seconds after the cops drove away.

Doherty stopped at the Arctic News on his way into town and ate a ham and cheese on wheat. Willy Legere was nowhere to be seen. That was just as well since there were no sports to talk about at this time of year. The newspapers were mostly filled with stories about the election that was barely a week away. The smart guys at the *Journal* were already giving the governorship to the Republican Del Sesto. Not surprising since the *Providence Journal-Bulletin* was the last bastion of Yankee Republicanism in a state now run almost entirely by Irish and Italian Democrats. Hell, even the Republican candidate for governor was Italian this time out. Del Sesto had jumped from the Dems a few years before just so he could run against them.

When Doherty got to the office Agnes, as usual, was on the phone with one of her girlfriends. She held her hand over the receiver and said, "You had a visitor this morning. I didn't know what to tell him cause you didn't say when you'd be in."

"Who was it?"

"The Judge's man, Tuohy."

"What did he want?"

Agnes still with her hand over the receiver, "He didn't say. All he told me was that he'd come back around one o'clock to 'get you'." Doherty went into his office to wait for Angel Tuohy. Just after one the big man lumbered in, huffing and puffing from climbing the stairs. Tuohy was getting fat; the good life working for the Judge was obviously spoiling him.

"Doherty."

"Angel. Don't tell me - the Judge wants to see me." Tuohy just smiled. Doherty put on his suit jacket and the two men hoofed it down Brookside to the office in the Plaza Hotel.

Once upstairs at Democratic headquarters above the flophouse, Tuohy ushered Doherty into the Judge's office. This time he left them alone, even closing the door behind him. Rene Desjardins was nowhere in sight.

DeCenza was standing on the far side of his oversized desk. Doherty took the liberty of parking himself in a chair in front of it and watched as the Judge paced back and forth on the other side.

Finally he swung in Doherty's direction. "Can I ask why you thought it was a good idea to send two Providence policeman up here to interrogate me about Spencer Wainwright's murder?" Doherty didn't answer. "I don't need that kind of distraction a week before the election."

"They were curious about Wainwright's recent disappearances."

"But you told me Wainwright went home. That everything was jake and that he was back on the straight and narrow."

"I don't know anything about 'straight and narrow,' but he did go home."

"So what happened?"

"He went home, then he took off again. Only the second time he didn't go home - and now he never will."

"I'm sorry, Mr. Doherty, but I'm a little confused here. After all I'm only a former judge with a college degree and a license to practice law. So could you please explain for me what the hell happened?"

Doherty lit a cigarette without asking permission. "Somebody shot Spencer Wainwright in the head."

Exasperated, DeCenza said, "I know that. It's been all over the news for days now. It's practically pushed the election off the front page. I simply asked you to find the Republican Chairman for this county, telling you how important it was to us that he be in his place come November 4th and the next thing I know he's been shot dead. Damnit, boy, this is not good for my peace of mind."

"Probably not too good for Mrs. Wainwright's either. I don't suppose you thought of that?"

Crimson was starting to seep up into the Judge's face. He pointed his finger at Doherty and said, "I thought when I contracted you I was promised confidentiality? That should have protected me from a police interrogation."

"Actually you never did sign a contract. It was your wish to keep all of our dealings off the books, remember? Plus that was before you sent Rene Desjardins and his sidekicks to rattle my cage. Far as I'm concerned I don't owe you a damn thing anymore, your honor."

"Listen to me, Doherty, I warned you about stirring things up in this town and now you've knocked over a whole hornet's nest of trouble. I don't need a couple of city cops coming down here nosing around in my business. Do I make myself clear?"

Doherty stood up but did not advance on the Judge. He didn't want to do anything that would cause Angel Tuohy to come back in. "By your business, Judge, are you referring to the Democratic Party or to Sherbrooke Industries?"

Doherty saw the Judge's head twitch at the mention of this last entity.

"Sherbrooke Industries? I don't think I've ever heard of them."

"Oh really, that's kind of strange, considering you're one of their named partners." Doherty took out the list Jean-Claude had given him, unfolded it and tossed it on the Judge's desk. DeCenza stared at it for a few seconds and then picked it up and gazed at it more carefully.

"Where did you get this?"

"Maybe you should ask 'how'."

"Okay, how did you get this?"

"I can't tell you that. I have to protect my client's right of confidentiality."

"You sonofabitch!"

"Why your honor. I thought bad language was prohibited in these offices where the *people's* business is conducted."

DeCenza continued to stare at the list. "You and Champlain were the only two locals I recognize. The third Rhode Island man, Gaudreau, I don't know," Doherty said.

"This doesn't mean anything," DeCenza replied throwing the list back in Doherty's direction.

"You're right. It only means that you and a couple of other big shots in this state are involved with a Canadian company that's buying up a bunch of abandoned mill properties for next to nothing. A percentage of back taxes as far as I can tell. Hey, if you script this right, you could make yourselves out to be local heroes trying to revitalize a dying mill town."

DeCenza smiled though his eyes told Doherty he was waiting for the next shoe to drop.

"Except that Spencer Wainwright was the stooge in all this. You played him for a sucker - a greedy one, but a sucker nevertheless. You sold him the Soap Works knowing full well that the water table was contaminated and that the plant would be useless for the kind of development he envisioned."

"That makes the fault entirely Wainwright's, not ours," the Judge said, a smug look crossing his face. "We dealt with him in good faith. He was the one who didn't take the necessary precautions to insure that his plan could be put into operation. Me thinks his greed got the better of him."

"I'm sure that in a court of law the liability would be on Wainwright; all of which is moot now that he's dead. Unless, of course, his widow chooses to pursue some kind of action against you. But then you and your pals down at the courthouse would just tie her up in legal knots until she was old and broke."

Once again the Judge's mouth smiled but not his eyes.

"But there is one fly in the ointment you didn't bargain on, Judge. Turns out Wainwright had some silent partners in this deal."

"Partners? What partners? All of our dealings were strictly with Spencer Wainwright."

"Yes, I know. But you see just as who owns Sherbrooke Industries is shrouded in mystery, so were Wainwright's backers. And unlike your group, his partners are not exactly pillars of the community. In fact, they are the kind of men who usually operate on the other side of the law."

"I don't follow."

"Oh, I think you do, Judge. You see Spencer was engaged in a number of plans with people who were using his real estate expertise to put together developments as a way for them to launder money acquired through various illegal means. For example, they now stand to lose a good part of $30,000 on the Soap Works deal alone. He was also setting up other development projects with them. Without him they've lost their main connection to the commercial real estate market. And I have a feeling they're not too happy about it."

"But I didn't kill Wainwright!" The Judge said indignantly. "Why in the world would I want him dead?"

"No, you didn't kill him. It wouldn't have served any purpose for you to have him dead. But you used me. You wanted Wainwright back in Warwick so that nothing would queer the Soap Works deal. Me finding him didn't have anything to do with the election, did it?"

The Judge stood firm and offered no immediate response. Finally he said, "You were well compensated for your efforts. Why do you care what my motives were?"

"Maybe I don't operate by the same twisted moral code as you do. Maybe that's why I left the cops. So I wouldn't be beholden to men like you."

"Ah, but as it turns out, Mr. Doherty, you are beholden to me."

"Don't be so sure. Looks to me like you got a much bigger problem on your hands right now. You see the men who were backing Wainwright don't always see things as logically as you and I. They can get very emotional sometimes, especially where their money is concerned."

"Are you trying to shake me down? Because if you are I…"

Doherty put up his hands. "Hold your horses, Judge. I don't give a shit about their part of the $30,000. For all I know those guys made that money selling heroin and running whores on the streets of Providence. What I want from you has nothing to do with money. I'll do my best to keep your name completely out of this for a few favors in return. Small favors I might add. You do them for me and nobody'll ever know that Sherbrooke Industries is just a front for some local hot shots out to make an easy score."

The Judge sat back down behind his desk, the red now drained from his face. He was back in his element. Talking turkey was what he did best. "So tell me what it is you need, Mr. Doherty."

"First of all, I would like you to stay the hell out of my business, both private and public."

The Judge patted his palm on his desk and said, "I can agree to that."

"And that includes Rene Desjardins. I don't want him slipping up on me in the dark anymore. The next time could end up being the last time."

"I will speak with Rene, but I can only guarantee his cooperation as long as he's in my employment."

"Fair enough."

"Is there anything else you desire?"

"Yeah, I'd like to be able to hang out at Harry's Barbershop whenever I want and for however long I want."

The Judge nodded. "Consider it done. I will speak with the landlord and Harry myself."

"And one final thing. You know the blind sailor, Willy Legere?"

"The boy who sits on a chair and sells pencils outside of the Arctic News?"

"Yeah that's the one. He isn't a boy. He's a young man, who lost his sight fighting for his country. He's a smart kid; reads Braille and is a wonder with numbers. I want you to give him a job. It doesn't have to pay a lot, but it's got to be a real job, not some made up job where he sits on his ass all day and collects a salary for doing nothing."

DeCenza stood again. "Why, Mr. Doherty, I didn't know you had such a soft heart."

"It has nothing to do with my heart. It's about doing the right thing by somebody."

"And in return for all this you promise what?"

"For starters I promise not to tell these mob guys that you chiseled them out of their share of the thirty grand. And if anybody asks, I'll tell them you had nothing to do with Spencer Wainwright's murder. I also think we can continue to keep Sherbrooke Industries a mysterious entity. But if I was you, Judge, the next time that company tries to sell off any other mill properties, you might want to be more honest in your dealings. You never know who the prospective buyers might be. I understand the people I mentioned are looking to spread a lot more money around the state buying up real estate."

He and Judge DeCenza shook hands on their deal. On the way out Doherty told himself to wash his hands as soon as possible.

Once back in the office Doherty rang up Frank Ganetti's number. The pixie answered the phone and said she would see if Mr. Ganetti was in. Of course, she knew if he was in or not. What she was really saying was that she'd find out if Ganetti would take his call. The next voice Doherty heard was that of Frank Ganetti, Jr.

"Mr. Doherty, nice to hear from you."

"Likewise I'm sure. We need to talk."

"I don't want to talk about anything on the phone. You never know who might be on this *party line*. Can you come up to my office tomorrow morning?" Doherty was well aware that the cops tapped the phones of guys who they thought were mobbed up. Often eavesdropping was the only way they could get information about men who otherwise took vows of silence on pain of death.

"I'll try to get there by nine. Is that okay?"

"Nine will be fine. See you then." Ganetti hung up without a good-bye. Doherty suspected the cops would eventually find out that Frank Junior was in business with Spencer Wainwright, and given the nature of Wainwright's death, would like Ganetti or one of his underlings for the murder.

Doherty arrived downtown shortly before nine and took a quick walk around the block before climbing the stairs to Ganetti's office. The secretary was at her desk, wearing a dark green corduroy jumper with a white turtleneck underneath. For some reason her outfit reminded Doherty of Robin Hood and his merry men, or women in this case. She smiled at Doherty and picked up the phone to tell her boss he was there. She then signaled for him go in.

Ganetti sat behind his desk in a crisp white shirt set off by a low-key banker's necktie. Every one of his hairs was immaculately in place. This time neither Angelo nor Bobby was present. However, another character sat in a chair off to the side. He was heavyset with a neck about the same width as his head. Ganetti signaled to the man who he introduced to Doherty as Gio.

The big guy had some trouble getting out his chair. Once on his feet he was surprisingly agile as he gave Doherty a thorough frisk. Gio was obviously well versed in this routine. When he was done Ganetti asked the fat man to leave the room.

"Didn't bring the thirty-eight with you?"

"Thought I'd leave it in the car as a sign of good faith. I'm not wearing a wire either," he added.

"I appreciate that. Now Mr. Doherty, do you have any idea where the Providence police are going with the Spencer Wainwright investigation?"

Doherty had to backtrack to recall who knew Wainwright was in business with Ganetti. Obviously Annette Patrullo knew and no doubt Ben Cooper, and now Judge DeCenza - and of course, Doherty himself. The cops had talked with Cooper, DeCenza and Doherty and as far as he knew Annette was still in the wind. Unless one of them tipped off Halloran or Squillante, the only way they could tie Ganetti to Wainwright was if they dug up the same documents Annette and Doherty had. They couldn't have done that unless they knew what they were looking for. Doherty was not about to give the Providence cops that much credit. He knew in time they'd make the connection, but only in time.

"I don't know. I can tell you right off that the only red meat I gave them to chew on was Martin DeCenza. That was the least I could do for the good judge."

"Do you think DeCenza had anything to do with Spencer's death?"

Doherty shook his head. "I doubt it. I'm inclined to believe just the opposite. It wouldn't look good for his political machine if Wainwright was dead. The Judge can be a vengeful bastard, but he's no killer. He has too many other ways of hurting people."

"Do you think the cops will attach me or any of my father's people to Spencer's murder?"

"They might because of the way he was killed. From what I was told it sounded like a professional job. Not something a guy would do who didn't have practice in that sort of thing."

"But as far as you can tell they haven't linked me to any of Spencer's business projects yet, is that correct?"

"That's right, but if they're good cops they eventually will. It took me some digging, but I knew what I was looking for. Right now I'm the only one with the original documents. From the questions they asked me I could tell they hadn't put you two together yet." Doherty knew that for the time being possession of the documents Annette had given him was his ace in the hole.

"I'm afraid if they find out about our dealings, it won't be long before they try to put a frame around me," Ganetti said. At this point he took out his gold cigarette case and offered it to Doherty. Doherty surprised himself by taking one of the filtered cigarettes, though he did use his Zippo to ignite their smokes. He noticed Ganetti admiring the engraving on the lighter.

"What about you, Doherty? Did you have any reason to want Spencer dead?"

Doherty laughed. "Me? Hell no. Tracking down Wainwright was the most profitable job I've had this year. I'm kind of sorry he's dead; it'll cut into my business as much as yours."

"Very sympathetic of you. I'm sure Wainwright's widow would appreciate your compassion." Doherty briefly thought about Wainwright's bitch of a wife then dismissed her just as quickly.

"Let's say we get down to business. What was it you wanted to speak to me about?" Ganetti asked.

Doherty took a couple of hits off the filtered cigarette. Although he drew deeply it didn't quite do the job like his Camels did. "You know how I told you I was hired by Wainwright's girlfriend to find him when he was missing the second time."

"You mean the one he was screwing on the side?"

"Yeah. Anyway I was convinced she didn't have anything to do with his death on account of her being sweet on him."

"Has something happened to change your mind about this mystery woman?"

Doherty explained how he helped her hide out at her cousin's, then later got suspicious and broke into the cousin's house and found Bobby Carnavalle's number in the woman's address book. "Yesterday when I asked the cousin and her husband where she was, they told me she'd taken off with Bobby. By their description of him and his car I've got to believe he's the same Bobby who works for you."

Ganetti leaned back and swiveled his chair. He rubbed his chin. "Technically he works for my father; and yes, it sounds like the same Bobby whose acquaintance you recently made." Doherty was impressed with how Frank Junior moved so easily from college speak to mob speak and back again. He also noticed how Ganetti's reserve dropped the minute he mentioned Carnavalle's name.

"What're you thinking here, Doherty?"

Doherty waited a few beats. "I'm thinking that it was this girl that put Wainwright in touch with you. She must've somehow found out through Bobby that you were looking to clean a lot of cash in legitimate investments. Meanwhile she also knew this real estate guy she was working for had ambitions to make some big scores. It's got to be your boy, I mean your father's boy, Carnavalle, who was the connection."

"And what else?"

"I'll try to say this as nicely as I can. If you didn't have something to do with Spencer getting murdered then maybe Bobby did."

Ganetti exhaled loudly and looked at the wall beyond Doherty. He was engulfed in some deep thoughts. When he turned back to Doherty he said, "Will you now tell me who this young lady is?"

"I will on one condition."

"And what's that?"

"That nothing bad happens to her. If one of my clients gets knocked off on account of me, that's not good for business."

"I'm afraid that's a tall order, and a promise I'm not sure I can make given these new circumstances."

"Then I won't give her up." Doherty stood and added, "I know, I know, you got ways to persuade me, and maybe that's what you'll have to do in the end. But for now, her name stays out of this."

"I must say, Doherty, I admire your integrity, if not your foresight." Once again Ganetti was the college boy gangster tossing out ten-dollar words.

On the drive back to town Doherty was convinced of one thing. He had to find Annette Patrullo before Ganetti and his men did and warn her about the danger she was in traipsing around with Bobby Carnavalle.

It was already dark when Doherty put the Chevy into Belanger's garage and started walking to his apartment. He hadn't gone more than ten paces when the Buick pulled up beside him and Angelo stepped out of the passenger side and blocked his path. Doherty looked in and saw that Carnavalle was behind the wheel. He might've made a run for it, except that he knew a guy like Angelo could easily gun him down before he got very far.

"Get in the car," the big guy said. It was not a request.

"If this is about Frank Junior, I just talked with him this afternoon and..."

Angelo did not let Doherty finish. "Shut the fuck up and get in the car." Doherty reluctantly did what he was told seeing no alternative.

He sat in the back with Angelo beside him. To make his point Ganetti's enforcer poked a gun into Doherty's ribs. Bobby sped away from the curb and took a number of side streets so as to avoid going through the center of Arctic. Stopping at a red light might give Doherty a chance to do something bold, or foolish. They drove down through Clyde and then bent left through the village of Phenix. Doherty watched the signs pass by and saw that they were headed north toward Cranston.

"Where're we going?" Doherty asked, hoping that conversation might give him a chance to play an angle.

"We're gonna take a nice little ride into the country if that's okay with you?" Bobby said with a snicker.

"Shut up and drive," Angelo barked. They drove on and no one spoke for a long while.

Bobby finally broke the silence. "So, Ang. Whattdya say? I got these two whois we can bang up with later if you want. This one, Maureen she'll do anythin' you ask her to. Last week this broad blew Tommy Marsello and me at the same time."

"Why doncha shut up?" Angelo said, obviously in no mood for conversation.

"What about Annette, Bobby? Aren't you suppose to be with her tonight?" Doherty piped in.

Bobby checked him out in the rearview. "What the fuck you talkin' about. I don't know no Annette." He could hear a slight crack in Bobby's voice.

"Course you do, Bobby. She's the one you used to set up Wainwright. Or was it the other way around? Did she use you to set him up?"

"Angelo, make this chump shut his yap," Bobby whined.

"Yeah, Angelo make me shut up. You don't want to hear about how Bobby killed your boss' business partner on account of this girl. What would Frank Junior say if he knew about that?"

Angelo stuck his piece deeper into Doherty's side. "Why don't botha yous shut the fuck up?" Once again Doherty detected a trace of the old country in Angelo's voice. Doherty was desperate even though he might be misreading the situation. It could be that Bobby and Angelo were taking Doherty for the long ride precisely *because* Bobby and Angelo had killed Wainwright. For all he knew both of these guys were in on it. He also had to remind himself that they were Frank Senior's men, not Frank Junior's. Maybe the old man hadn't bought into Junior's new ideas about the family's business future.

They were now in a part of West Cranston Doherty'd never been to before. It was all woods and open farm fields. Lights from houses were few and far between. As far as he was concerned, they were in the middle of nowhere. Bobby tried to raise the issue about the 'whois' again but Angelo was having none of it. Frankly, Doherty couldn't imagine Angelo with a woman. He couldn't even imagine the big guy taking his hat off.

They'd driven through wooded country for about fifteen minutes when Angelo told Bobby to take a sharp turn off the paved road onto a dirt path that looked like it might be a fire road or somebody's driveway. It was so narrow they could hear branches brushing the side of the car.

"Hey, Ang, them bushes are gonna scratch the paint offa my car," Bobby whined. The big man did not respond.

About a hundred yards in they reached a clearing where Angelo instructed Bobby to stop the car and cut the ignition and lights. Suddenly everything was starkly quiet. The big man prodded Doherty with his pistol and told him to get out of the car. Bobby stayed inside. He was singing lightly to himself and tapping a rhythm on the steering wheel.

Doherty had the unpleasant thought that the image of this greaseball bouncing his fingers on the steering wheel might be the last thing he'd see in this world. He tried to summon up some prayer he'd said back with the sisters at St. James but nothing would come. He remembered how when they were under bombardment in Italy, the guys next to him in the foxhole would be saying a novena or some other kind of prayer. Yet, even then, Doherty could never get anything going. His faith, or the memory of it, had been lost somewhere along the way.

Angelo told him to step behind the car. Doherty promised himself that he wouldn't die like a dog. Whatever he did, he wouldn't let this palooka shoot him in the back nor would he beg for mercy or wet his pants.

"Now turn around," Angelo said. Doherty didn't move; he just stood facing the big man and his revolver. There was no moon and out here in the country there were thousands of stars, more than Doherty'd ever seen before. For some reason he thought of Millie St. Jean and how embarrassed she'd been getting undressed, even in the dark. Doherty took a deep breath. As he did Angelo pointed the gun inside the car and blew a hole in Bobby Carnavalle's head. The sound of the discharge was unbelievably loud, though here in the sticks probably no one but the three of them heard it.

"Stay right der and don't move," Angelo said. "I ain't gonna hurt ya." The shooter took a handkerchief out of his coat pocket and started wiping down the back of the car. When he was done he wiped down the outside door handles. It was only then that Doherty noticed that Angelo was wearing a thin pair of gloves.

"Now start walkin' back the way we come," he said. Doherty obeyed, still trying to dope out what had just occurred, and why. It took ten minutes for them to get back to the paved road on foot. All the while Doherty studied the starry firmament above. When they got there, Angelo put his arm out to hold Doherty back from stepping onto the asphalt.

"We'll wait here," he said, as they stood hidden from sight by a stand of trees. They waited in silence for almost half an hour. Only one car went by during that time and as it approached Angelo stepped back deeper into the brush pushing Doherty behind him as he did. Finally a car drove up slowly and stopped a few yards before the dirt road. The fat guy Gio got out from behind the wheel leaving the car idling on the shoulder. When he came near the two of them he nodded at Angelo who then walked back to the car while Gio stood with Doherty.

"Nice stars," Doherty said for no reason.

Gio looked up and let out a small laugh. "A good night to buy the ranch, huh?" was the fat man's reply.

Doherty watched as Angelo leaned in the rear window of the idling car and spoke to someone in the backseat. Finally he came back to Doherty and Gio and said, "Let's go."

Angelo opened the back door of the black Cadillac for Doherty. Then he and Gio got into the front. As soon as they were inside a button was flipped that automatically locked all the doors.

"A special feature offered only on this Cadillac model," Frank Ganetti, Jr. said as he leaned in Doherty's direction.

"What the hell just happened, Frank?" Doherty asked.

"Here, have some of this," Ganetti replied as he handed Doherty a silver flask. Doherty took a healthy swig of what tasted like expensive scotch.

"Go ahead, have some more. I'm sure this has been a rather traumatic night for you," he added softly.

"Why Bobby? Why'd Angelo shoot Bobby and not me?" The two men in the front looked at one another and the one named Gio let out a small snicker.

"Killing you was never in the plans. We were just using you to lure Bobby out here to the country."

"Then why Bobby?"

"Well, you see Doherty, once you told me about Bobby and the girl a few other things started to fall into place. Remember how I explained to you that some changes were going on inside my father's organization. Apparently certain individuals figured that with my father in prison now would be a good time to make a move on his operations. Our late friend Bobby made the mistake of choosing the wrong side."

"What does that have to do with Spencer Wainwright getting killed?"

"I'm not entirely sure yet. I suspect there are people in our business who have no appreciation for what I was trying to accomplish in my collaborations with Wainwright. It could be that killing Spencer was meant to send a message to me."

"And that's why the poor bastard had to die."

Frank shook his head. "I am truly sorry about that. I was very fond of Spencer. He was a dreamer, and there are so few of them around nowadays. But as I'm sure you learned in the war, sometimes people die for the oddest reasons and in the strangest of circumstances."

Doherty pulled out a smoke and nervously lit it with a shaking hand.

"Excuse me, Frank, but that's not good enough. Spencer was killed because of *your* plans?"

"Grow up, Doherty. Spencer knew what he was involving himself in when he contacted me. He knew exactly how the people I work with make their money and precisely who he was getting into bed with. So please, don't play the bleeding heart sap for me."

"That's the second time this week somebody's called me a bleeding heart."

Ganetti patted Doherty knee and said in a much softer voice, "Sometimes the shoe fits."

They drove on in the direction of the old mill town. Doherty smoked and nothing more was said for while.

Doherty broke the silence by asking, "Why did Bobby shoot Spencer in the knee before he killed him? If they just wanted him dead, why would he have tortured him too?"

"You'll have to ask the girl that."

"The girl?"

"I'm thinking Bobby had a thing for this girl. That he was more than will-ing to kill Wainwright because in addition to wanting him out of the way for business reasons, he was jealous of Wainwright sleeping with her."

Doherty had to take a minute to digest this last suggestion.

"Now there's one other thing I need from you, Doherty. Think of it as reci-procity for my sparing your life."

"What's that?"

"Who's Annette?"

"Annette?"

"Don't play the fool with me; it doesn't suit you. Angelo said you asked Bobby why he wasn't with Annette tonight. I'm thinking she's the girl that hired you to find Wainwright, and is also the one who's been running around with Bobby Carnavalle. So why don't you save us all a lot of time and energy and just give me her whole name, and where I can find her."

"Then what?"

"Then it's none of your fucking business." This was the first time Doherty'd heard the refined Ganetti use a curse word. It almost sounded unseemly. Doherty clammed up.

"I know you're going to say we can do whatever we want to you, and if we kill you then we'll never find out who she is. I've seen all those movies too. But think about this: sooner or later we'll find out who and where she is, whether you tell us or not. On the other hand, why do you owe this girl anything? If what you've told me is true, she's complicit in Spencer death."

"*She* as opposed to one of your associates?"

"Stop acting like a child. What good would it do you if this piece of snatch gets you killed?"

"Patrullo," Doherty blurted out. "Annette Patrullo."

Gio looked in the rearview mirror and said, "Ain't that Sal Patrullo's kid?"

"Who?" Doherty asked.

"Shut up, Gio," Frank said, all pleasantness now absent from his voice. He moved his head up and down as if all the pieces were clicking into place. He turned to Doherty and said, "Everything makes sense now. Sal Patrullo is one of my father's most trusted lieutenants. It appears that your girl Annette was in on this from the beginning."

"Does that mean she was never crazy about Spencer like she claimed?"

"Not only that, Doherty, but it also appears that she was using you when she hired you to find him after he supposedly disappeared. For all you know Spencer saw what was coming and tried to hide out. He wasn't playing around with some other woman like you thought. I'm thinking this Patrullo girl was afraid he would split before Bobby could get to him."

Doherty slowly finished the thought, "And poor Wainwright still believed she was in love with him like she claimed. He trusted her and told her where he was – the poor bastard. She then hires me to find him at the very same time she's setting him up. She must have known where he was the whole time. She was using me to provide her with an alibi."

Ganetti broke in, "Okay, so now that we know who she is, can you tell me where she is?"

"I'm not sure. She was staying with some cousin up in Providence. When I spoke to the cousin two days ago, she told me Annette had left with Bobby and hadn't been seen since. Bobby knew where she was, but he can't help you now." Doherty decided he would get even with Annette Patrullo on his own terms. And he wasn't about to sic Ganetti and his goons on Annette's cousin and her family.

The Caddy pulled up at the corner of Main and Crossen and Ganetti motioned for Doherty to get out. It had been one hell of a night.

He didn't sleep well despite downing a half bottle of Jameson before hitting the sack. In the middle of the night Doherty had a dream he was being chased through the jungle by a bull elephant. It was a scene he'd once seen on the *Ramar of the Jungle* TV show. He awoke with a start. He tried reading for a while and even though he recognized the words, they weren't making any sense. When it finally turned light outside, he put up a pot of coffee and began to plan his next moves.

Just after nine he pulled the Chevy out of the garage and headed north toward the city. This time he remembered the way to the cousin's house perfectly. When he arrived there was no car in the driveway and he didn't bother to look to see if Annette's Metro was still in the garage. He rang the bell twice but no one answered. He then pounded on the door and saw the curtain beside it pull back an inch. The cousin opened the door as far as the safety chain would allow and asked Doherty what he wanted.

"I need to speak with Annette; it's urgent."

"She's not here." Doherty could see the cousin lightly bouncing her baby girl on her hip.

"Can I come in? We have to talk." The cousin was reluctant, so they stared each other down for nearly half a minute before she finally loosened the chain and opened the door. She offered him a cup of coffee and he accepted. They sat in the living room in the same configuration as his previous visit, except this time the husband wasn't part of the conversation.

"Tony's at work. He won't be home until after five. You're not gonna hurt us are you?" Doherty wondered why the cousin let him in the first place if she was afraid he would hurt her or her baby.

"No, I'm not going to hurt you. I need to tell you something and you have to listen very carefully, okay?"

The cousin nodded her head even though she still looked scared.

"When was the last time you saw Annette?"

"Like I told you yesterday, it was three days ago. She went off with that Bobby and I ain't seen her since. Is she in trouble?"

"Yeah, she's in big trouble, with some very dangerous people."

"What about Bobby? Can't he help her?"

"Bobby's dead."

"Jesus, Joseph and Mary! He's dead? What happened?" The woman was so upset she began to visibly shake. Doherty thought of comforting her, but he didn't have any comfort left in him.

"He was shot, last night. I saw it myself. It probably won't be in the papers for a couple of days. That's why I've got to find Annette before the people who killed Bobby do."

The cousin was now quivering and her eyes were watering up. "Are we in trouble? Me and Tony and the kids?"

"I don't think so," Doherty said, though he wasn't sure. "They're looking for Annette. I didn't tell them about you but these men have ways of finding things out. If they come here that could mean trouble for you and your family."

"Oh my God, oh my God! How did this happen?"

"You got an uncle named Sal?"

"Is he what this is all about? My Uncle Salvatore and his goombas?"

"Sort of. I haven't put it all together yet. If anything happens, call me right away, especially if Annette shows up." Once again Doherty handed Lorraine one of his business cards.

"What're you gonna do with her if you find her?"

Doherty thought about this question for a few seconds. "Probably turn her over to the police."

"The police! Is Annette in trouble with the law?"

"It looks like she helped get somebody killed. In any case, she'll be better off with the cops than with the men who killed Bobby. I think they'll kill Annette if they find her before I do."

The cousin stood, now vigorously shaking the baby at her hip. "Jesus Christ. How could she be so damn stupid?"

Doherty shook his head. "I can't answer that. I guess she thought she was being the smart one until she ran into some people who were smarter - and meaner." When Doherty left, the cousin triple locked the front door. He didn't think it would be enough to keep Ganetti's men at bay once they figured out who Annette's cousin was.

He was awoken that night by a ringing phone. He looked at the clock; it was just after 3:30. A frantic voice on the other end said, "She was here. Just now."

It took Doherty a minute to gain full consciousness. "Who is this?"

"It's Lorraine, Annette's cousin." Doherty could hear the husband Tony ranting in the background.

"Slow down. You woke me up." He swung his legs over the side of the bed and shook his head to clear it. He grabbed his Camels and sparked one. "Tell me exactly what happened."

"She came in maybe a half hour ago. She looked terrible, like she hadn't slept in days. She was hysterical. Tony tried to calm her down, but all she wanted was her stuff and some money. She said she needed a lot of money to get away."

"What did she say about Bobby?"

"She knew he was dead like you said. She kept sayin' that the people who killed Bobby were gonna kill her too if she didn't get outta town."

"Did you give her money?"

"We didn't have none. Tony gave her forty dollars, which was all that was here in the house. The rest of our money is down at the Old Stone Bank. He told her we could get her more in the mornin', but she was in too big of a hurry to wait."

"Did you tell her I came by?"

"Yeah, but she said you couldn't help her now."

"Did you call the police?" There was silence on the other end.

"I wasn't gonna call the cops just 'cause you said to. She's my cousin. I can't rat on her to the police."

"I understand. Did she say where she was going?"

"Not really. All she said was she knew somebody who'd give her money. Somebody who 'owed her big time', was how she put it. That's all. Then she jumped into that little car of her's and took off. Tony said he'd try to follow her, but I made him swear on the life of our children that he would stay right here. I'm still scared for her, though part of me is sayin' good riddance."

"Thanks Lorraine, thanks a lot. It was good of you to call me. Whatever happens, you keep that husband of yours at home."

Chapter Thirteen

BEN COOPER

Once again Doherty put up a thermos of hot coffee and grabbed his binoculars. He hadn't slept more than five hours over the previous two nights so he was going to need a lot of fuel to keep himself going. By the time he got to Hoxie Four Corners it was nearly 5 a.m. It was still dark with the only light coming from the airport, which set the horizon aglow. Like before he backed his car into the alley across from Cooper and Wainwright to get a good view of the now darkened office. Except for the sporadic traffic on Warwick Ave there were no signs of life anywhere. He slunk down in the seat, not wanting to be rousted by any local cops prowling the area.

Doherty slurped coffee out of the thermos top while he fought to stay awake. It was not an easy battle. Just as he was dozing off a car pulled up in front of the building across the street. It was Cooper's Lincoln. The old man got out and hurried to the door. He was not wearing his signature seersucker suit today. Rather he was dressed informally with his shirttail hanging out. Moving his eyes up enough to see above the dashboard, Doherty watched carefully as Cooper fumbled with his keys. He finally got the door open and went directly to his office in the back without turning on any lights. Doherty noticed that Cooper hadn't bothered to lock the front door behind him. Once in his cubicle he flipped on the desk lamp that provided only a dim aura.

Resting the binoculars on the dash, Doherty was able to get a good look at Cooper's movements as long as he stayed above the half glass partition. Unfortunately, at one point Cooper squatted down out of sight for a minute.

When he stood back up he reached to the top of one of his filing cabinets and took down a large manila envelope. He then shoveled something from his desktop into it and fixed the clasp. After that he sat down at his desk and rested his head between his hands. He looked like he was in pain. Doherty poured himself another cup of joe and waited.

It wasn't long before the little green and white Metropolitan pulled up and parked next to Cooper's larger vehicle. Annette Patrullo got out and quickly made her way to the door, or as quickly as her black high heels would allow her. Cooper looked up when she passed through the front door yet remained seated in his office. Doherty refocused the glasses and carefully watched the ensuing scene. Annette did indeed look disheveled, as her cousin had said. Her hair was no longer fixed up in its perfect beehive. It hung down on one side and in the front, where she kept nervously brushing it out of her eyes. Cooper stood behind his desk and the two of them were soon engaged in a heated conversation.

Doherty slid out of his Chevy, carefully keeping his finger on the button inside the door so that the interior light wouldn't go on. He then trotted across the street and marched into Cooper and Wainwright. Both Annette and the older man were startled when he casually walked into Ben Cooper's office.

All Cooper could get out was "What the?" Doherty told him to sit down and shut up. When Annette tried to slink her way out Doherty grabbed her roughly by the wrist and pushed her into one of the other chairs.

"You bastard," she spit out, as she rubbed her raw skin.

Doherty pointed at the girl and said, "Save your anger for later, sweetheart. Right now you two are going to tell me what the hell's going on here."

The pair of them looked at each other but neither said a word. Doherty noticed the manila envelope on Cooper's desk and went to pick it up. The old guy made a grab for it but Doherty was too fast for him. He looked inside. There was a sizable wad of bills held together with an elastic band.

"How much, Ben? How much you giving this chippy?"

It took the old man a while to answer. "Three thousand," Cooper finally mumbled.

"That's a lot of severance pay, isn't it?"

Cooper looked sheepish. He knew the jig was up. Annette, on the other hand, was hoping she had one more trick up her sleeve.

"What's all this to you anyway, Doherty?" she said. "You still pissed off 'cause I didn't pay you enough for not finding Spencer?" She casually took a hand mirror out of her purse and began fixing up her hair. When that was done she applied some new lipstick to her sensuous mouth. Annette Patrullo was going to play the tough girl right to the end.

Doherty lit a Camel despite Cooper's protests.

"I didn't find Spencer because he was dead, remember. And I think you and Mr. Cooper had something to do with that. I know the truth is right here in this room – maybe even in this envelope with the three thousand clams," Doherty said pulling on his smoke. "And by the way, I did get paid. I took a hundred bucks from the cash you hid in the false bottom of your overnight bag. That should cover my expenses."

Annette lit a cigarette of her own. "I guess I underestimated you as a private dick, and a money grubber."

"And I overestimated you as a lady," Doherty replied. They had a long stare down while Cooper rummaged through his desk.

Doherty turned in his direction, "Whatever you do, Ben, don't come out of that desk with a pistol in your hand 'cause you don't strike me as the killing type."

He then turned quickly and snatched up Annette's purse before she knew what was happening. He reached inside and drew out a small revolver.

He smiled at her and said, "You, on the other hand, sweetheart, would use something like this." Doherty slid the gun into his jacket pocket.

"Well kids, it looks like it's show and tell time. Why don't we start with you, Mr. Cooper? How did you get mixed up with Mata Hari here?" Annette looked confused, apparently too young to know who Mata Hari was. Maybe he should've called her The Dragon Lady. At least that would've given her credit for reading the funny pages.

"I never wanted to hire her, but Spencer insisted. He'd hire any cute little bundle in a tight skirt that came through the door. But you see I had my suspicions about Miss Patrullo right from the beginning."

"What kind of suspicions?"

Cooper eyed Annette with a look that could've killed. "She said she wanted to learn the real estate business. Gave us some sob story about how she was out on her own and didn't want to be just a secretary. She told us she wanted to become an agent. Asked Spencer if he'd teach her the business. Of course, he fell for it hook, line and sinker. But I knew all my partner was really interested in was getting into her undies – which I assume he eventually did."

"Why Ben, you dirty old bastard," Annette said with the trace of a smile on her face. Doherty watched her as she nonchalantly smoked her cigarette. As usual she left lipstick traces on the filter.

"What was the real reason you came to work here?" Doherty asked Annette.

"I don't have to tell you anything," she said defiantly.

"No you don't. But if I put a call in to Frank Ganetti, letting him know where you are, you're as good as dead."

Cooper blanched at the threat. Annette just smiled at Doherty and said, "You wouldn't do that. You're one of those noble types, like in the movies."

"I wouldn't be so sure of that. Somebody has to pay for Spencer's murder."

"I didn't kill Spencer, Bobby Carnavalle did. And now he's dead too. So we're even."

"But you set him up. You gave Spencer Frank Ganetti's number. You knew Ganetti was looking to get into the legitimate real estate business and once you got hired here you figured you could use your feminine wiles to get Spencer to do whatever you wanted."

"My feminine what?"

"Never mind. But why did Spencer have to get killed? Ganetti had no use for him if he was dead. Was there some other reason you wanted him out of the way? Was he that bad in bed?"

"It wasn't just me; he wanted him out too," Annette said pointing her cigarette at Cooper.

Cooper slammed his hands down on his desk. "Why you little strumpet. I never said I wanted Spencer killed. That was not part of the plan. You said that once he learned who he was getting involved with, he'd change his mind and stop doing business with their kind. The fool was sinking all of our assets into projects he thought would make us rich. But I knew in the end he would ruin us; ruin a business I've spent my whole life building. He was a vain and foolish man, but he didn't deserve to die for it." Again Cooper sat back and rested his head in his hands.

Doherty looked at the girl, "So why did he die?"

It was now Annette's turn to let her guard down. "I didn't realize when I first came to work here what it was all about. I liked Spencer. Hell, I slept with the chump, didn't I? My father told me the family wanted to invest in some legitimate businesses and Cooper and Wainwright were the kind of respectable real estate people nobody'd suspect them of being in cahoots with. He said this place would be the perfect front for cleaning a lot of their cash. It was his idea for me to have Spencer contact Frank Junior."

"How did Bobby play into this?"

Annette shook her head. "Bobby was a mug. I knew him from the neighborhood from when we were kids. He was a bad boy and I used to like the bad boys. Then I started working here and seeing Spencer. He was the first decent guy I'd ever been with. But I couldn't get rid of Bobby. He always had this thing for me. Told me he was jealous of me going out with Spencer. You know what they say, once you lie down with dogs it's hard not to come up with fleas."

"Bobby worked for Ganetti, didn't he?"

"Don't be so thick, Doherty. Think for a minute how this played out. Bobby didn't work for Ganetti, he worked for my father. Pop thought he'd come out on top if he got rid of Frank Junior while his old man was in the joint. He didn't think Junior had the balls to handle his father's operation. That's where you came in. You might've even helped since you were already digging into Spencer's projects, thanks to me. Once you figured out Spencer was in business with Junior, it wouldn't be long before the cops did too. Like you said, it's bad for business if the guy you're looking for ends up dead – and because you're a good investigator, you just had to find out why he was killed. I knew you wouldn't leave it alone. I figured in the end you'd lead the cops right to Frank Junior. My father's plan was that after Spencer was killed, they'd put two and two together and hang the murder on Junior because of the thirty grand Spencer lost on the Soap Works deal."

"What about this money?" Doherty asked holding up the manila envelope. "What's this for?"

Annette nodded at Cooper, who now seemed even smaller than ever sitting behind his big desk. "That's my 'go to hell' money. He was gonna give me money to get out of town, right Ben? Look at the poor bastard. He thought if he paid me, I'd keep my mouth shut about his role in this whole thing. Then he could go back to selling his little two-bedroom Capes and collecting his five percent commissions and nobody'd be the wiser. He'd be rid of me *and* Spencer and his over-the-moon schemes. At least Spencer had ambitions, Ben. He wanted to be somebody."

Cooper looked up and for the first time anger flashed across his face. "Yes, he was ambitious all right, and look what it got him. A fling with a cheap hussy who was using him the whole time, and a bullet through his head."

It was quiet in the small office as the shadow of Spencer Wainwright's death engulfed them all.

"So what happens now, Doherty?" Annette asked.

He thought about his answer but didn't speak right away. "I call the Providence police. Have them come down and arrest the two of you."

"Arrest us for what? You got no proof we did anything wrong. All you know is what we just told you. Once the cops get here, we'll tell 'em something different. Then it'll just be your word against ours. Right Ben?"

Cooper sat stoically behind his desk.

"How long do you think it'll take before they sweat the whole thing out of him?" Doherty said pointing at the old man. Annette moved toward the door. Doherty grabbed her arm. "Where do you think you're going?"

"I'm not sticking around to talk to the cops."

"You'll be better off with them than out there with Frank Junior's boys looking for you."

Annette stuck out her chest. "I'll take my chances," she said as she pulled away from Doherty's grasp. "Now what about that money?" she asked in reference to the three grand in the envelope.

"That stays here with Cooper. After all, it's his dough isn't it? You'll have to get by on the money left in your bag. But I still don't think you should take off."

"What are you gonna do if I try, Doherty, shoot me?"

With that Annette Patrullo turned toward the door. But Ben Cooper had other plans; he came out of his desk with a pistol in his hand. "You greasy little slut!" he shouted. Doherty saw him just in time and smashed down on his forearm hard enough for the pistol to discharge a bullet before it dropped to the floor. The only thing injured was one of the seascape prints that hung on the far wall. Annette looked shaken, though not enough to hang around any longer. She quickly walked out of Cooper and Wainwright, no doubt hoping it was for the last time. Doherty didn't move to stop her.

After she left Cooper sat sullenly at his desk while Doherty dialed the Providence Police Department. He left a message for Lieutenant Halloran to meet him at the office of Cooper and Wainwright, telling the desk clerk on the other end that it was in reference to the Wainwright murder.

Doherty then handed the manila envelope with the three thousand bucks back to Cooper. "Keep your money, Ben. You're going to need it for a good lawyer."

The old man knelt down and returned the cash to his safe.

Chapter Fourteen

LIEUTENANT BRIAN HALLORAN

Halloran and Squillante arrived an hour later. The lieutenant escorted Doherty to the outer office where they took seats on either side of Annette Patrullo's desk while Squillante questioned Cooper in his cubicle. Halloran looked as tired as Doherty felt. Still the interrogation went on for a good hour. Doherty began by giving Halloran a bare bones outline of the story, scrupulously leaving out the names of Frank Ganetti, Jr. and his men. He told the police lieutenant that Annette had more or less confessed to colluding in Spencer Wainwright's death with a greaseball from Providence named Bobby Carnavalle. The mention of the shooter immediately got Halloran's attention.

"Where is this Patrullo broad now?" Halloran asked.

"She took off after she and Cooper spilled the beans to me."

"Why didn't you stop her?"

"I'm a private detective, not a professional wrestler. If she wanted to leave what could I do to stop her. I told her she'd be better off talking to you, but I guess she had other plans."

"Any idea where she might've gone?"

"Beats me. She didn't leave a forwarding address."

"Well, if you give me a description of her and her car, I'll put out an APB. If she's still in the state, we'll find her." Doherty gave the cop as many details about Annette as he could. Halloran then excused himself and went out to his car to phone in the information on the girl and her Nash Metropolitan. While he was gone Doherty monkeyed around with the office's coffee urn and finally got the thing filled and perking. He figured they could all use some java.

When Halloran came back Doherty was sparking up a Camel. He offered one to the cop and he took it. "Given the kinda car she's drivin', it shouldn't be too hard to find this broad. You got any idea what their motive was for bumpin' off Wainwright? Do you think there was some kinda jealousy thing goin' on involvin' this Carnavalle character?"

"I don't know. She said something to that effect, though she might've just been blowing smoke to take the glare off herself," Doherty said evasively.

Halloran leaned across the desk. His big square face was covered in stubble, no time to shave this early in the day. "You see what makes this all very interestin' is that this Carnavalle chump you just mentioned had his brains blown all over his nice new Buick a coupla nights ago. Happened out in the middle of nowhere in West Cranston. She didn't say anythin' to you about that did she?"

Doherty feigned ignorance. "No, not really. Carnavalle's name only came up in connection with the Wainwright shooting."

Halloran offered up a non-committal grunt. "So let me get this straight, the only connection you had with any of this is that the broad hired you to find Wainwright, who unfortunately ended up dead before you could locate him. And like Carnavalle, he too took a bullet in the head. Since he was already dead I gotta wonder what exactly brought you over here in the middle of the night?"

"Like I told you before, I had a hunch right from the beginning that Wainwright's partner was somehow mixed up in this. I'd been up to visit the girl's cousin where she was hiding out after she found out Spencer was dead. The cousin told me she'd taken off with Carnavalle so I left my card there. Last night the cousin called me when Annette came back. She told me Annette was hysterical and there was no sign of Carnavalle. According to the cousin, she was fit to be tied. She split when the cousin and her husband couldn't give her any money. Before she left she told the cousin she knew where she could get the money she needed. I couldn't think of anybody else with that kind of dough who might be mixed up in this except Cooper."

"You think she was hysterical 'cause she found out Carnavalle'd been killed? Like maybe she felt she was next on somebody's hit list?"

"Could be. That's all a little beyond me. What I can tell you is when I got here she was trying to shake down Cooper for money so she could blow town. And no matter what I said she was in no mood to stick around until you guys got here."

Halloran looked over at Cooper's office where the old man was sitting at his desk while Squillante, still standing, was giving him the third degree. Halloran took down as much information about Annette's cousin as Doherty was willing to give him. He knew it wouldn't be a bad idea for the cousin and her family to be on the cops' radar just in case Ganetti's men showed up at her house.

"Somethin' doesn't seem right," Halloran mumbled, more to himself than to Doherty. "Cooper doesn't strike me as the murderin' type."

"He told me he never wanted Wainwright dead. He just wanted him scared off from doing business with people he thought would ruin his nice little set-up here. He kept talking about how he was afraid Wainwright's big plans would destroy everything he'd built up. But he must've been involved in some kind of cover-up. Why else would he be willing to give the girl three thousand bucks to keep him out of it?"

Halloran considered the question for a moment. "I don't see any three grand, do you? You told me you snatched the money up before the girl could get at it. So where is it now?"

"Like I said, I gave it back to Cooper and he put it in his safe."

Halloran looked skeptical. He got up and went to the coffee urn and poured himself a cup. He threw in three spoonfuls of sugar. There wasn't any cream around. Doherty followed and helped himself to a cup of black. While he did, Halloran went into Cooper's office and told the other two men that there was fresh coffee. Then he and Doherty sat back down and started their dance all over again.

"There's something else Miss Patrullo said that might have some bearing on this case."

"Yeah, what's that?"

Doherty would have to be careful here. He wanted to keep Frank Ganetti, Jr. out of the conversation if he could. "She said she took this job in the first place because of her father. That it was his idea."

"So?"

"His name is Sal Patrullo. Does that mean anything to you?"

This caused Halloran to bolt upright. "'Sal the Snake' Patrullo?"

"I guess. Whoever that is."

"Don't you ever read the papers, Doherty?"

"You know everybody keeps asking me that. As a rule I try to keep my reading to the sports pages and the comics."

Halloran laughed mirthlessly. "For your information Sal Patrullo is an underboss in Frank Ganetti's crew. Familiar with that name?"

"Ganetti? No, not really."

"Jesus, what kinda private eye are you?"

"Small time. Most of my business is finding people who are lost - usually husbands who run off with women not their wives. That plus industrial undercover pretty much covers my territory. Wainwright was my first murder."

Halloran leaned back in the swivel chair and drank some more of his coffee. He was trying to figure out how this last bit of information about Annette Patrullo fit into a bigger picture.

He brought his chair forward. "Sounds like your client, this Patrullo broad, may've been actin' as a go-between for her father and Wainwright. But what I don't understand is why."

Doherty assumed it wouldn't take long before Halloran figured out that Wainwright's real estate connections were being used as a means to launder money. The only question remaining was when Frank Ganetti, Jr's. name would surface.

At that moment Squillante came out of Cooper's office while the old man stayed put behind his desk.

Halloran turned to his partner and said, "Whaddya got, Jeru?"

"Nothin' really. The old guy said the girl called him in the middle of the night and told him to meet her down here, that it was urgent. When he got here she tried to shake him down for some money. Accordin' to Cooper, she told him he'd get what Wainwright got if he didn't pony up at least five Gs."

Doherty jumped in, "That's not true. She told me the money was for her to keep her mouth shut about Cooper's role in Wainwright's murder."

Squillante looked at Doherty disdainfully. "Sorry, pal, but that ain't what the old man's sayin'."

"Well he's lying. I bet if you take him downtown and sweat him a little, he'll fess up."

Squillante shook his head. "Too late for that. He already called his lawyer and filled him in on everythin'. Sorry boss, but I don't see any reason to run him in. He said he refused to give the girl any dough so she split. Far as I can see we got nothin' on him till we catch up with her."

"Oh, we got somethin' all right," Halloran said. "We got two murders, this one and the Carnavalle one, that're somehow connected. On top of that, it turns out the broad is the daughter of Sal the Snake."

"Sal Patrullo?'

"That's the one."

"What about this mamaluke?" Squillante asked referring to Doherty.

Halloran considered the question. "I think he knows more than he's lettin' on, but we've been around the block six different ways and he's not givin' up any more than he already has. We could take him downtown though we'd have nothin' to hold him on; it'd just be a waste of time and paper work. For now I think we gotta let him go."

"I assume we'll be able to find you over in West Warwick if we need you again, right?" Halloran asked Doherty.

Doherty nodded and handed Halloran one of his business cards. He got up to leave.

"I probably don't need to say this, Doherty, but if I was you I wouldn't leave the state."

Doherty chuckled. "After the last few weeks I might never leave West Warwick again."

"And if for some reason this Patrullo broad gets in touch with you, I suggest you give us a call right away." Doherty agreed, though he wasn't sure if he would or not.

On Monday morning he casually walked into Harry's Barbershop and took a seat in Bill Fiore's chair. Doherty felt vindicated now that the Judge had lifted his ban. Nevertheless, he still got a much-needed trim and a shave. Fiore was as effusive as ever, talking politics and women, though not necessarily in equal doses. Bill was a little disappointed when Doherty told him that he and Millie St. Jean had agreed to cool it for a while since he'd taken credit for getting them together in the first place. Mostly though he'd miss being able to gossip with Doherty about his personal life. It was as if all those girls in the caricature of Fiore near his chair had gone to his head.

After the shave and haircut, Doherty loitered just long enough to get under Harry's skin. He then got a quick shine and headed uptown. He ducked into Francine's where, as the only man in the shop, he easily got Millie St. Jean's attention. Her boss, Mr. Mendelson, was nowhere to be seen. Millie smiled at Doherty as she approached.

"Hello, Millie, how have you been?" he asked.

She seemed nervous and consciously kept enough distance between them that he'd have to lean in awkwardly to touch her. "Oh I've been fine," she said hazily, careful not to add anything more.

"I'd like to talk with you sometime."

Millie looked around the shop. It wasn't very busy, but she was on the clock so this was not a good time for conversation. "Why don't you stop by when I get off at six? We can talk then." Doherty said he'd see her at six and turned to leave.

"By the way, Doherty," she said to his back, "I was sorry to hear about your friend Mr. Wainwright. I hope you're not in any danger."

"He wasn't a friend, he was somebody a client hired me to find," Doherty said more harshly than he needed to. "And I'm fine. All in one piece: no cuts, no bruises, no broken bones."

Doherty stopped for his usual lunch before heading to work. The chill he felt from Millie left him in a sour mood. He didn't joke with the gals at the News and they quickly sensed his bad humor, as did Agnes when he finally got to the office.

"Aren't we Mr. Grumpy today, " Agnes said after Doherty growled at her. "I wasn't sure you were even coming in today, boss."

"What's the matter, Agnes, can't talk to your girlfriends on the phone unless I'm here. You could do your nails if you really want to get under my skin," he said bringing up his secretary's two favorite activities when she should've been working.

Agnes uttered a "sheesh," and Doherty plodded into the back room on tired legs. Lack of sleep and not knowing how the Wainwright case was going to shake out coupled with Millie keeping him at arm's length put Doherty in a dark frame of mind. He hoisted his feet up on his desk, lit a Camel and stared at the four walls. He thought maybe he should put some pictures up one of these days, though he wasn't sure of what. He had no family photographs or photographs of himself with famous people to adorn them with. Maybe he should get some seascapes like the one Ben Cooper put a bullet through in his office.

About an hour later Agnes knocked softly and tentatively stuck her head in, not sure if Doherty would bite it off again. This time he didn't even nibble. "There's a man here to see you. A big, scary looking man."

"Great. Show him in." Just what Doherty needed today - a big, scary looking man. Ganetti's gunman Angelo walked in and looked around the office. Doherty wondered if Angelo was noticing the same blank walls he'd been studying earlier. The big man was wearing a black turtleneck, his usual fedora and the sport coat he'd worn on the night he shot Bobby Carnavalle. Doherty looked closely at his jacket for signs of blood splatter.

"Frank Junior wanted me to give you this," he said flatly as he tossed an envelope on Doherty's desk. Doherty peeked inside; it contained five more Uncle Bens.

"What's this for?"

"I just deliver the mail. I don't ask what's in it or what it's for."

"Is this for me to keep my mouth shut about Bobby?"

"Bobby who?" Angelo said in the same unfeeling tone. Doherty slipped the envelope into his desk and told Angelo to thank his boss for him. The big, scary man left without saying another word.

When he was gone Doherty took out the envelope and looked inside again. Clipped to the money was one of Frank Ganetti, Jr.'s business cards. Doherty fingered it for a while and then tossed it into the wastebasket.

He called Agnes in. She entered the office with her head down, not knowing if her boss was about to hurl another insult her way. Doherty pulled one of the hundreds out of the envelope and handed it to her.

"Here, go buy yourself a dress."

She handled the bill like it was the Hope Diamond. She even held it up to the light.

"Don't worry, it's real enough."

"Jeez, boss. I've never seen one of these before."

"I suggest you go to the bank and break it down into smaller bills. I don't know if any of the shops in Arctic'll cash a C-note."

"Thanks, boss. Thanks a million."

"Only a hundred, Agnes. Only a hundred."

"There is one thing I gotta ask you. Are you gonna need me tomorrow?"

"Why what's tomorrow?"

"It's Election Day. Everything'll be closed here in town."

"Everything except the bars."

Agnes ignored this last remark. "It's my mother. I told her I'd take her down to vote. She doesn't get around too good on her own anymore."

"Sure, Agnes, you can take the day off. And be sure to vote. As we say here in West Warwick, vote early and often."

Doherty was standing outside of Francine's cuffing the last of his cigarette when Millie came out. She was hastily buttoning up her pink cloth coat. The weather had turned chilly all of a sudden as if autumn finally remembered to show up. He smiled at her though he noticed that Millie was keeping the same safe distance from him as she had earlier in the shop. At that moment Doherty realized how much he missed her. They stood nervously eyeing one another.

"I was thinking maybe we could go to the pictures together again if you'd like. There's a Tony Curtis chain gang movie playing at the Palace. I heard it was pretty good. You like Tony Curtis, don't you?" Millie didn't respond right away so Doherty felt the need to add a kick line. "All that bad business that was going on before, it's over now," he said as if he were trying to convince himself as much as her.

Millie stepped forward and placed her hand on Doherty's forearm. "I'm sorry, Hugh, but I can't do this anymore."

"Look, Millie," he began to say but she quickly interrupted him.

"I've been seeing someone else, Doherty. A boy, I mean a man I met at church. To be honest with you, he's somebody my father in-law introduced me to. His name is Gene and he works for Kemper Insurance," she said nervously.

"But I thought … I thought we were having a good time together."

With her hand still on his arm, Millie smiled at Doherty. "We were. It was more than good. And if I didn't have my boys to think about maybe things could go on. But you live in a different world than me - one that's exciting, but also dangerous. I can't afford that, not in my situation. In time I think my mother-in-law might even accept me seeing someone like Gene. I'm afraid she wouldn't have ever abided by the likes of you and what you do for a living."

"Didn't our," Doherty was at a loss for the appropriate word. "Our love-making mean anything to you?"

Millie looked away, embarrassed that Doherty would put words to what they had done. "Of course it did," she said now gripping Doherty's arm more tightly though still not looking at his face. "It meant everything to me. A girl like me doesn't give herself to just anybody. Who knows, in time I might've even fallen in love with you, but that's not going to happen. Not now, not ever. We have separate lives and it would always be that way. I'm a mother with two children who lives with her husband's rather traditional parents. I can't change that and neither can you."

Doherty could feel Millie St. Jean slipping away from him. He didn't know what else he could say to change her mind. "Well, I suppose I'll see you around town then," he said trying to sound casual and not succeeding.

Millie reached out and hugged him and gave him a little kiss on the cheek. "I guess we'll never see those pyramids together, will we?"

"Nor the marketplace in old Algiers."

"Wherever that is," Millie said finishing the line for him.

Doherty walked slowly home, sorry that he wouldn't be seeing the new Tony Curtis movie at the Palace with Millie St. Jean. Once inside his apartment he dropped into his favorite chair and spread the four remaining hundred dollar bills out on his coffee table. He used one as a coaster for the bottle of Jameson that helped him get to sleep that night.

Tuesday, November 4th, was Election Day. Just as Agnes had said everything was closed in the mill town except of course the bars. Even the mills had shut down for the day shift, though there wasn't much work in them these days anyway. Several had been completely shuttered, while the ones still operating had drawn down to just one or two shifts. The textile industry was moving to the South where people were happy to work for minimum wage and unions were all but non-existent. The mills were leaving West Warwick and they weren't ever coming back.

The town's taprooms served an important function on Election Day. That was where the precinct captains went to drag out drunken men to vote. They were also where straw men were found that the captains would give 'walking around money' to and send out to vote for dead people or people who no longer lived in town but whose names were still on the voting rolls.

Not only would money be doled out at the drinking holes, it was circulated at the actual voting stations as well. The machine's men would stand outside the polls holding signs and shaking hands with prospective voters. With each handshake a palm card would be passed on to voters telling them to vote the straight Democratic ticket. These cards suggested that it was much easier to pull the main party lever than to read through the entire ballot and choose candidates for each office. If a voter looked uncertain or a bit shaky, often a dollar bill would be exchanged along with the palm card. It wasn't much though it would buy a few beers or a couple of shots of cheap whiskey.

By four in the afternoon the bars would be bursting at the seams and half the men in town would be soused. That's when the captains would make their second round of the day looking for anyone who hadn't voted yet. And pity the poor voter who'd been too busy drinking to bother to cast his ballot. Not only would his alcohol intake be shut off, he might even catch a beating from one of DeCenza's thugs for not exercising his right of franchise.

Doherty wandered up to his polling station at the old Odeon Theater on Eddy Street just outside of Arctic. The Odeon had once been a movie theater and before that a vaudeville house. Now it was used exclusively for live events and public meetings. As a kid Doherty and his sister had gone there for Halloween parties and live kid shows. The only one he remembered well was the one where a guy performed acrobatic tricks while slinging a yo-yo.

He hadn't decided whom he was going to vote for yet except in the governor's race where he'd hold his nose and vote for the Republican Del Sesto. Like a lot of staunch Democrats, he couldn't justify rewarding Governor Roberts after he'd stolen the election two years earlier. Besides, Del Sesto was Italian, a former Democrat and protégé of old man Green back when the senior Senator was governor himself. Hopefully, if elected, Del Sesto wouldn't sell out the working stiffs to the blue bloods who still ran the Republican Party in Rhode Island.

Doherty was surprised when he entered the hall to see Willy Legere sitting at a table off to the side next to one of the elderly ladies who crossed off voters' names before they voted. These were the lists that the machine's poll watchers would track all day to determine who hadn't voted yet. Willy obviously couldn't see Doherty nor detect the smell of his familiar aftershave in the dank hall. He watched as the blind man tapped out keys on an adding machine while the woman next to him fed him information.

"Hey, Willy, how's the boy?" Doherty said finally.

"Mr. D. What're you doin' here?"

"What do you think I'm doing? I'm here to vote like a good American." Willy laughed as if Doherty was putting him on. "A better question is what are you doing here?"

"Who me? I'm workin' the polls like Mr. Tuohy asked me to. Look at this Mr. D.," Willy said as he swung the adding machine around so Doherty could get a better look at it. "It's a Braille addin' machine. Mr. Tuohy bought it 'specially for me."

Willy showed him how every time he hit one of the Braille keys, the paper printout came out with regular numbers on it.

"That's pretty slick, Willy. Are you working for Angel Tuohy now?"

Willy smiled with pride. "Yeah, but not just here. I got a regular job down at the Water Department too. Workin' full time."

"How'd that happen?"

"Don't know really. Mr. Tuohy came by my stand in front of the News one day and asked me if I wanted a job. Said he heard I was good with numbers. The fella who had the job before me kept showin' up drunk so they fired him. Next time you get your water bill, Mr. D., it'll be comin' from me."

Doherty patted Willy on the shoulder. "That's great, Willy. Just great. But how're we going to shoot the breeze about baseball with you not being at the News anymore?"

"Ah, don't worry about that. Just come down to the Water Department office anytime; we'll have coffee and chew the fat just like we always done."

"Won't your boss get mad?"

"That won't be a problem. Mr. Tuohy is the water commissioner and he's hardly ever in the office. He's mostly out in town doin' inspections."

"I'll bet he is," Doherty mumbled. Out doing grunt work for Judge DeCenza is more like it. He then turned to the woman and gave her his address. It took her a while to find his name despite the fact that the list showed only a few voters resided on Crossen Street. As Doherty turned to enter one of the alcoves in front of a voting machine, Willy said loudly, "Make sure you vote for the right people, Mr. D."

"I always do, Willy."

Once he'd pulled the curtain Doherty perused the ballot carefully, though he knew full well that his vote wouldn't matter much in a town where Martin DeCenza's chosen candidates always won. He did vote for Del Sesto and then for most of the Democrats running for statewide offices. As far as the county and town contests were concerned, he only voted for the men he knew for sure weren't stooges for the machine. As a result he left three quarters of his ballot blank. So what. At least he'd feel cleaner when he went to bed tonight.

As expected, by three in the afternoon most of the bars in town were doing a roadhouse business. Doherty dropped in at Duffy's to have a shot and a beer and to listen to the scuttlebutt about how the election was going to turn out. One drunk was offering a ten spot that Roberts would win again. He kept insisting that the party would find a way to steal the election, especially with Roberts having a brother on the state Supreme Court. Doherty was sure that the incumbent wouldn't be able to pull the same scam with the absentee ballots as he had two years ago. He took the guy's bet even though he didn't know who the windbag was. In order to insure that things would be fair, they both gave their sawbucks to the bartender. The winner could collect once the results were in.

As the smart guys had predicted, Del Sesto won the governorship by a little over 6,000 votes. There was no attempt by the Roberts camp to invalidate the absentee ballots this time, especially since the state Supreme Court had already ruled on their admissibility months before. Even if all of the 5,000 absentees had voted for Roberts, it wouldn't have made up the difference. As it turned out, the absentee votes split about evenly between the two candidates. The Republican owned *Providence Journal-Bulletin* crowed about the GOP win, despite the fact that the Democrats swept all of the other statewide offices as well as retaining the two U.S. House seats.

The state legislature stayed firmly in Democratic hands as well. In the end, the Del Sesto win was an anomaly among the results, more a vote against Denny Roberts than a vote for his opponent. Most of DeCenza's candidates kept their offices meaning the Judge could continue to dole out patronage in West Warwick and other parts of the county. As expected, Del Sesto's margin of victory was in Kent County, despite the fact that the Republican county chairman was lying in a cemetery with a bullet through his head.

For days after the election the papers were still picking through the detritus of the gubernatorial results. The speculation was that the newly elected Democratic Lieutenant-Governor, John Notte, would challenge Del Sesto in 1960. Since Rhode Island ran its statewide elections every two years, it wasn't long after one was over that the next one started up. The *Journal* pointed out that Notte had garnered nearly 12,000 more votes in his contest than Del Sesto did in his. It should have been mentioned, however, that Del Sesto was running against a sitting governor while no one would even remember who Notte's opponent was a month from now. Meanwhile Roberts was already making rumblings about running for Green's senate seat when Theodore Francis stepped down in two years. Fat chance given that he'd just been turned out as governor in the most heavily Democratic state in America.

A week after the election Doherty was eating lunch at the downstairs counter of the Arctic News skimming the sports pages for some interesting stories when a large body sat down heavily on the stool beside him. It was Lt. Halloran, come to pay the small town a visit.

"Your secretary said I'd find you here," Halloran muttered as a greeting.

"I'm fine, thanks. How are you?"

"Whaddya recommend?"

"I like the ham and cheese; they do a good egg salad too. And you can never go wrong with the grilled cheese and soup combo."

Wendy, the new young waitress, set down some silver and a coffee cup in front of the Providence cop. Halloran ordered a cup of tomato soup and a grilled cheese sandwich.

"Smart choice," Doherty said. "Always a good idea to go with something simple when you're in a place you never ate at before." Halloran picked up a section of the *Journal* and gave it a glance.

"You hear the latest from Providence?"

"You mean about Roberts wanting to run for Green's seat?"

Halloran laughed derisively. "No, I mean about the crackdown on Frank Ganetti's gang."

"Sorry, I've just been so consumed by the election I haven't had time to…"

"Cut the crap, Doherty. Whaddya know about these arrests?"

"What do I know? Gee, Halloran, last time I checked you were the cop, not me. What I know is what you just told me."

Halloran's soup arrived and he purposely waited until the young waitress left before he spoke again. He crunched up some crackers and dropped them into the tomato broth.

"A federal task force swooped in two days ago and arrested three higher-ups in Ganetti's crew. One was 'Sal the Snake' Patrullo, the father of your missin' girlfriend."

"I don't like you referring to her as my girlfriend. It makes me look bad."

'To who?" Halloran said as he looked around the small lunch counter. Then he loudly slurped up some of his soup.

"Don't tell me, the feds did all this without letting you and your little friend Squillante in on the deal. Am I right?"

Halloran wiped some soup off his chin. The big cop had already dribbled on his tie. "That ain't all of it. We pulled two more bodies outta the Providence River day before yesterday. Both of them were small time players in the Ganetti family."

"His real family?" Doherty asked thinking immediately of Frank Junior.

"Naw. What we like to call his *crime* family. At least those murders fall within our jurisdiction, and not the feds'."

"I bet that tuned you boys up pretty good. So what do you make of it all?" Doherty asked trying not to sound too interested.

"I dunno. Somethin's going on in the wise guy world, but we can't figure out what it is. Could be that the big boss is tryin' to make a grab for Ganetti's action while the old man is in the can, or…"

"Or what?"

"Or it's an internal struggle, and somebody inside Ganetti's organization has decided to take out the garbage. I don't suppose you'd know anythin' about that."

"Me? Why would I know anything about that kind of stuff? I'm just a small town investigator."

"I was thinkin' maybe Patrullo's daughter spilled somethin' to you before she blew town."

"All I know was what I told you over at Cooper's. The girl was scared after Wainwright's death. She thought she might be the next in line. That's why she wanted money from Cooper. She said she wanted to go somewhere safe and set herself up in a new life. Personally I thought she'd be better off in protective custody with you guys."

The waitress dropped Halloran's sandwich in front of him and refilled Doherty's coffee. They ate in silence for a while.

Finally Doherty asked, "Any idea how the feds were able to close the deal on Patrullo and his *associates*?"

"The only thing I heard is that they had a stoolie inside the organization. Otherwise they're keepin' things pretty tightly wrapped. I'm thinkin' they kept us out of it 'cause they suspect they're some dirty cops inside the department."

"In Providence? Jeez, what a surprise that would be. Still, squealing on guys like that's got to be dangerous business."

"Yeah. Especially since the word is that Ganetti is still runnin' things from his cell at the ACI. If he is then we got a whole new ball game."

"How so?"

"Well for one, with Patrullo and his mugs gone, there'll be some new faces controllin' that crew on the outside. Possibly people we don't know nothin' about."

Halloran finished his sandwich and stood up. He wiped some crumbs off the front of his suit coat and threw two singles on the counter. "Lunch is on me."

"What's the occasion?"

"I'm celebratin'. I voted for Del Sesto. You hear from that Patrullo broad, you give me a ring, okay."

"Sure. Whatever you say."

Agnes was working over her nails with an emery board when Doherty got back to the office.

"Anything new?" he asked fully expecting that there wasn't. Agnes didn't even look up from her nail work, just shook her head. Doherty turned toward his office.

"The mail's on your desk," she said as an afterthought.

Doherty hung up his coat and lit a Camel before he sat down and shuffled through the mail. There were two advertisements trying to sell him office equipment he didn't need and a copy of the latest *Sporting News*. On the cover of the sports paper were colored photos of Ernie Banks and Jackie Jensen, voted by the publication as Players of the Year in their respective leagues. It was odd to think of any Red Sox besides Ted Williams winning an award. Guess it was time for Sox fans to start uttering, "Wait till next year."

Doherty pried open the *News* and as he did a post card slid out from inside. It must've gotten stuck in there. On the front was a scene from Miami Beach. A couple of palm trees framed a nighttime shot of the Miami skyline lit by the moon. Above them were scripted the words "Moon over Miami." On the back was a message addressed to Doherty and Associates. It read, "Be seein' ya, sucker – Love A."

Doherty looked at the postmark; it was from a week ago. All the postcard told him was that Annette Patrullo was still alive last week when she sent it from the city of palm trees and sunny skies. Doherty stared at the piece of cardboard for a good five minutes. Then he flicked his Zippo and torched the edge of the card. He held it until the flame neared his fingers and then dropped it into the large ashtray that sat at the edge of the desk. It smoldered there until it turned to ash.

Some time later Agnes came to the door. "There's a man here to see you. Looks like a potential client." Doherty instructed her to send him in.

The man was in his thirties, of medium height with a round pink face. He was a little heavy in the middle and wore a pork pie hat and a baseball jacket with leather sleeves. He seemed nervous.

"You Doherty?" he asked.

"That's me. How can I help you, Mr...?"

The man reached out his hand and shook with Doherty. His palm was unpleasantly moist. "George Stravato. I hear you're good at findin' people."

"That's my specialty," Doherty said, trying not to sound like he was bragging. "Who's missing?" The man took off his hat and fingered it nervously.

"It's my wife Tina. I think she's run off with my best friend Jimmy. Can you get her to come back?"

Doherty stayed standing and stared at the man for a few seconds. "I can find her, but I can't guarantee she'll come home unless she wants to."

The man was breathing heavily. "How much do you charge?"

"My standard fee is fifty dollars plus expenses. If I find her and she doesn't want come home I'll knock a little off the charges."

Doherty reached into his file cabinet, took out one of his standard forms and handed it to his new client. Stravato sat down and began to read it. His lips moved as he did. Doherty sat as well, put his hands behind his head and smiled. He was back where he belonged.

THE END

PERSONAL NOTES

I grew up in West Warwick in the 1950s. My father was a merchant who owned a paint store on the outskirts of Arctic for seven years until he moved his business and our family to Cranston. During the years I lived in Rhode Island I was always fascinated by the large mills that were scattered throughout the many villages that made up West Warwick. Many of them were already closed by the time we lived there, though their hulking skeletons were still very much a part of the town's landscape. As far as I know, the Bradford Soap Works, which continues to occupy the Valley Queen Mill building, remains in the business of manufacturing bar soap and soap bases to this day.

In doing research for this book I made a number of trips back to West Warwick in an effort to recall what it looked and felt like at the time the story is set. The commercial center of Arctic is now a pale imitation of the thriving downtown that I remember from my youth. The West Warwick I have tried to recapture in this novel is one of a bygone era. I have used many real places from then while making up others for convenience or dramatic purposes. Most of the characters in this story are entirely fictitious, though a few are based on real persons from that time. My narratives of the gubernatorial elections of 1956 and 1958 are as accurate as my research allowed me to make them.

ACKNOWLEDGEMENTS

I am deeply beholden to Cecilia St. Jean (no relation to Millie – purely co-incidental) of the Pawtuxet Valley Preservation and Historical Society for answering my many questions about West Warwick in the 1950s. She also sent me a copy of a small booklet called "The Villages of the Town of West Warwick: A Self-Guided Tour," with an accompanying CD. In the process of writing this book I took all or part of this guided tour several times. In addition I would like to thank another longtime West Warwick resident, Denis Roch, for sending me two articles I found very useful. One was called "The Square," which, in his words, was "a stroll down memory lane" that entailed a walk through Arctic in 1950. The other article was about the Jewish merchants of West Warwick, a subject Mr. Roch has done a great deal of research on. In this article I was surprised to find my father being quoted. In it he explained that many of West Warwick's original Jewish inhabitants left the town because they saw no future there for their children.

Another great aid was Raymond A. Wolf's entry into the Arcadia Publications History Books series called *Images of America: West Warwick*. His collection of historic West Warwick photographs was invaluable in bringing back many scenes of the town as I remembered them in the 1950s. Of particular interest was a photo of Belanger's Market on page 51 that stood a stone's throw from where my family (and Doherty) lived. I would also like to thank the old timers who sit in the park where the Majestic Building used to stand. The conversation my brother and I engaged in with them likewise brought back many old memories.

I am deeply indebted to my wife and best friend, Jeanne Berkman, who did a thorough reading and editing job on *The Mill Town*, and to my brother,

Don Kafrissen, who suggested the idea for the novel after reading a short story I had written for our writers group called "Harry's Barbershop." Finally I owe a debt of gratitude to my parents, Fred and Silvia Kafrissen, now deceased, and their many friends who settled in West Warwick after World War Two and made the town such a vivid place for me in my formative years.

39789881R00146

Made in the USA
Middletown, DE
25 January 2017